AWAKEN MY FIRE

JENNIFER HORSMAN

An Avon Romantic Treasure

AVON BOOKS ◆ NEW YORK

AWAKEN MY FIRE is an original publication of Avon Books. This
work has never before appeared in book form. This work is a novel.
Any similarity to actual persons or events is purely coincidental.

AVON BOOKS
A division of
The Hearst Corporation
1350 Avenue of the Americas
New York, New York 10019

Copyright © 1992 by Jennifer Horsman
Excerpt from *Fire at Midnight* copyright © 1992 by Barbara Dawson Smith
Published by arrangement with the author
Library of Congress Catalog Card Number: 91-92442
ISBN: 0-380-76701-5

First Avon Books Printing: July 1992

AVON TRADEMARK REG. U.S. PAT. OFF. AND IN OTHER COUNTRIES, MARCA
REGISTRADA, HECHO EN U.S.A.

Printed in the U.S.A.

RA   10 9 8 7 6 5 4 3 2 1

AWAKEN MY FIRE

The intimate brush of his gaze made her painfully aware of her nakedness beneath the thin cotton gown. Roshelle closed her eyes, trying to steel her thoughts away from it, from him, Vincent, the Duke of Suffolk.

"You little fool." He leaned over, his voice a warm whisper brushing her ear. "Your rebellion is over. Did you ever doubt there could be any other ending to this ill-begotten insurrection?"

"Aye," she said passionately as she turned to meet the steely intensity of those dark eyes. "I dared to imagine a country free of the most virulent pestilence ever to shadow the land. The English! Your people have taught me well to hate!"

"'Tis your own wretched countrymen who rape and pillage. The whole world knows Frenchmen as barbarians."

A protest sprang to her lips, one he immediately silenced by gently putting his finger on her mouth. His lips hovered a scant half-inch from her face. Her cheeks grew hot as her emotions swelled. A chill ran through her . . .

AWAKEN MY FIRE

Prologue

"'Tis Lady Roshelle!"
            "That be the famous mare Charles just gave her—"
    "Saints alive! Look! She means to jump the hedge!"
    "She'll break her neck!"
    "Mon Dieu—"
    The surprised members of the Duke of Orleans' hunting party held their collective breath, their gazes wide, riveted to the fast-moving streak made of the blue gossamer of the young lady's gown over the reddish brown of the mare's coat. Tension seized the men as the girl leaned forward, clinging tightly as the horse flew toward them like the wind. Four mercilessly short paces from the waist-high hedge, the magnificent creature leaped high into the air. For a long magical moment horse and rider appeared gloriously suspended in space. Hooves crashed to the ground amidst the cheers and wild applause of the men.
    "No other girl in Christendom can ride like that!"
    "Precious few knights as well!"
    "And it 'twill no doubt get her buried—"
    Roshelle Marie slowed the creature's speed, tightening the bit as she turned her in fast pretty circles before the group. She was in no mood to banter with the lords and barons of her guardian's court. Not now. For unmasked fury shimmered in her blue eyes, the emotion seemingly incongruent with the delicate lines that drew her deceptively angelic beauty—deceptive, for the great passions that

1

ruled her were anything but angelic; no wilder creature lived in all of France. Presently her blue eyes sought and found her guardian amongst his men. She came right to the point.

"I will not marry that beast!"

Louis Valois, the Duke of Orleans, just stared. For a long moment he said nothing as he stared at the girl he loved, as if only now realizing what he had done. *Mon Dieu*, it hurt to look at her. Sitting atop that half-wild horse against the backdrop of woods and beneath the bright blue sky, Roshelle Marie Saint Lille, the Countess of Lyons and Bourges, looked incredibly beautiful.

Roshelle Marie was but ten and three, tall and as slim as a boy, her slender figure just beginning to blossom with the promise of womanhood. A pretty blue beret crowned the untamed cascade of her rich auburn hair, tousled and wild-looking from her ride. The color of her hair matched perfectly the color of her horse. (It had taken Charles, the Dauphin, ten servants and three months to find a match in both spirit and color.) And while usually she took pains to hide the white streak in her hair, not so now. Against the auburn color, the white streak proclaimed her wholly unique position in his court like a banner.

Louis needed no reminder of the fact. With the exception of Papillion and perhaps young Charles himself, no one loved the girl more than he did. Giving her up would be the single hardest thing he had ever done. "Roshelle Marie," he began but stopped, changed his mind and motioned to the handlers to quiet the dogs. "Who told you of this?"

"Then it is true! You do think to marry me to Philip the Bad, the Lord of Normandy!"

Shocked gasps sounded from the interested, now silent audience. Only a few knew the awful news, for Louis had wanted desperately to keep it a secret as long as possible. Roshelle held her breath, too, part of her unable to believe this was happening, that he wasn't denying it. She had been so certain Papillion's court spies had been wrong.

The duke handed over his bow to his ever-obsequious squire before removing a lace mouchoir from the pocket of his elaborately brocaded hunting jacket. This he pressed to his forehead, and on the heels of a long pause, he admitted, "I did not mean for you to find out now—"

"This I am quite certain of! You no doubt meant to sugarcoat this bit of news with presents and sweet talk. Let me save you the expense of those precious presents— I will not marry that beast! Not for all the jewels in heaven!"

"For shame!" Pol de Sain stepped forward. He was one of Louis's chancellors and one of the few men immune to Roshelle Marie's charms. "How dare you speak to his Grace with an insolent tongue! How dare you—"

The dogs' renewed barking interrupted him, though not for long. Nothing could stop the old man once he gasped enough wind for one of his meandering speeches. This particular speech somehow made the queer connection between rebellious young ladies—meaning Lady Roshelle— and their love of horses, two grievances that would inevitably escalate into a scathing indictment on declining faith, sinking morals and the failure of the Crusades. "This"— he turned to the others, his craggy voice rising above the dogs—"be what ye get for elevating the girl's mind with books and the irreligious and all these, these horses—"

"Hush now!"

Roshelle's sharp rebuke silenced everyone, all the men, Louis and especially Pol de Sain. Not even the girl could speak to a lord that way with impunity. Yet the dogs quieted, too, dropping to lowered haunches, their show of obedience suggesting she had rebuked them, not Pol de Sain.

Red-faced anger replaced Lord Pol de Sain's confusion, but he had to ask, "Young lady, were you speaking to me or the dogs with that tone?"

"Milord de Sain!" Roshelle appeared quite shocked at the suggestion. "Can you even imagine that I would address you in the same tone I restrict for the noise made by barking dogs?''

Pol de Sain stared up at the girl's less-than-innocent gaze, still shimmering with fury, and thereby missed the smiles and laughter of the men behind him, which were hidden in sudden coughing fits and the abrupt activity of the grooms, falconers, lords and barons alike. He started to shake an angry finger, but Louis caught his hand, stopping him. ''Please, leave us now,'' Louis said, dismissing Lord Pol de Sain with the rest of the hunting party before Roshelle Marie made the old man look even more foolish.

Within minutes, lords, squires, grooms, falconers, dogs and horses all dispersed to the open field some hundred or so paces ahead, and Roshelle was alone with her guardian. It seemed suddenly quiet. The hunting party sounded distant and far away. Nesting robins sang overhead, a peaceful sound that was at odds with her strained emotions.

''You do not know the stakes being wagered here, Roshelle Marie,'' Louis cautioned in a tone both solemn and foreboding. ''At last Papillion's prophecy hath come to pass. I kept thinking it would not, that Papillion was wrong, that there was nothing that would ever make me give you up. Rodez, though—God, I curse the day he was born!—wants only you. I offered every possible concession to my hateful brother's voracious appetites for lands and power, but all he wanted, the only thing he would take in exchange for his wretched army, is you, in this ill-fated marriage to his demon 'copain,' Philip the Bad. I assume, because Lord Philip is so old—'' He paused uncomfortably with the thought. ''And since most of Philip's lands fall under Rodez's duchy, Rodez is content to wait until the wretch dies.''

''Aye! And Rodez knows I would not bear Philip any children, so he hath only to wait for his death. Then Rodez will inherit not just the Normandy lands but my guardianship as well! The prophecy come true!''

''I know, but I must carry out this exchange with my

brother! Do not you see, 'twill save all of France, the country, all of the people you love—you will save them!''

She raised her face to the heavens, offering a frantic prayer to slow her mounting desperation long enough to think. Papillion had always warned that Rodez would have his revenge where it hurt the most: "He will strike you, Roshelle . . ."

"Why, Papillion? Why me?"

"Because you mean the most to me in this life. Just as Angelique meant the most to him. He will bring your life despair and you will be cursed. I see it now . . ."

She remembered the panic, the terror of his words. Rodez was now a man ruled by hatred, all because he had once known love. He had fallen in love with a poor baroness named Angelique Von Elliote, and had abnegated on a marriage contract in order to marry her, losing a fortune in the process. Roshelle was one of the few people alive who knew the awful truth of how Rodez had lost Angelique to the church, and why he blamed Papillion for the heartbreaking loss.

"Do you mean . . . Papillion, am I to die before my time?"

"No, no, sweetling." He had shaken his head, and she'd felt a moment's relief, but just a moment's, for then he had asked her: "What are the most powerful of all things on earth?"

"Love and God."

"Aye. Love and God, two of the same. And what is the most painful and sorrowful of all things on earth?"

Her blue eyes had searched his. "I think, the loss of that love." She had gasped. "Like Rodez . . ."

"Aye, like Rodez." Then Papillion had stared off at a distance where he could see her future. She followed his gaze to the place where the blue sky sat on the earth, and a distinct line made the horizon. Then she caught the reflection of the last rays of the sun on Papillion's gold ring.

Papillion claimed that one night as he slept he was given the vision of this gold ring, that it would come with the gift of prophecy. He was shown a forest glen he knew from his travels where he would find the ring. The next morning he set off for the glen, a two-day trip from the forest house. When he finally reached this place, he found a wounded hawk lying under a tree. The creature's leg was bleeding, entangled in an old fishing line, and on this fishing line was the gold ring.

Of course, this unlikely story was probably the result of an old man's imagination and a young girl's love of a tale. Still, sometimes, like now when she looked at it just so, the intricate latticework seemed to move, as if it were alive, full of mystery and magic . . .

And he had said: "The curse will protect you, like an invisible veil over your life. It will keep you safe—"

"But if it be a curse!"

"Aye, a curse because it will keep you safe, but not, I fear, with impunity. Oh, no . . . I see someone is coming to teach you that to know love, however briefly, is to never regret. Her name is—"A warm smile changed his face. "Aye, her name be Joan . . ."

She had been so frightened by the words, especially after the rain-washed night when she met Joan, that with Louis's permission she had spent her fortune on making a new order of Saint Catherine in Orleans: an order of sisters dedicated to ministering to the poor and downtrodden. Fifty thousand livres to build the small convent and chapel, five thousand more just to pay the only masons in France who could cut and erect the stone for its bell tower, ten thousand livres more to keep the sisters there and, *mon Dieu*, she had thought she had escaped this curse and despair . . .

Roshelle's thoughts returned to the present. "There must be another way, there must! We can stop it! I know we can stop it. I will not be sacrificed to a man I loathe! I will not!"

The petulant tone of her voice made her seem as young as she was. Ten and three. Louis tried to keep in mind the vulnerability of her youth, and was even more determined to do so when he noticed the slight tremble in her hands on the reins. Roshelle's blue eyes followed his and she gasped slightly, startled by just how desperate she felt.

Roshelle dropped the reins and slid from her horse, rushing at him. "My Grace!" She fell to her knees on the forest floor, lifting her clasped hands in prayerful supplication to him. "My Grace, you know, you must know, I would march verily unto death for Charles, for you, for France, and that of course I am not so silly or foolish a creature as to ever dream of love in my marriage, but you cannot sacrifice me to a man who is responsible for the deaths of half the people I loved—including my uncle and my last two cousins! Why, his very name says all: Philip the Bad! He is said to have once punished a servant by killing the poor wretch's child! He is a mad, bloodthirsty beast and but a sniveling pawn of the House of Burgundy. How can you think to have me marry him? How can you think to let him have his revenge? 'Tis as if you are making Papillion's awful prophecy come true. Stop it! Stop it now and set me free—"

"Listen to me, Roshelle!" He grabbed her thin arms in order to command her attention. "As we speak, Henry of England is amassing his army on the Dover shore. My spies report an army numbering four thousand this time. Four thousand warring knights! We have no chance this time. None—unless I swallow my hate and pride and join forces with my brother. We must join armies! And you, Roshelle, know this—"

"Aye! I know full well the threat that shadows our land. I know we must have all the knights of France to fight Henry, but—"

"And you will get me this! Your marriage in exchange for my brother's army, and while Papillion warned us both about my dear brother, about sacrificing you at the altar, he also has left me no choice. 'Tis a bargain made in hell, but the only one Rodez will make!"

A tremor of fear passed through Roshelle and she closed her eyes, the images of that dark night flashing dizzily through her mind: Papillion's throat and the blood streaming from the jeweled dagger and Rodez's desperate demand, "I must have it! Give it to me!" and the sudden manifestation of the diabolical parchment in Papillion's hand and as Rodez seized it, as his fingers touched it, the burst of fire . . .

"That night he threatened this! To use me for revenge! To teach Papillion, he said he would use me to enact revenge. You know this!"

The words were said like a warning. Louis nodded. "Aye, Roshelle, and what's just as bad is he gets to squeeze my heart in the bargain. 'Tis just like Rodez to make me squirm and suffer, to pick the one thing that would be hardest for me to give up." Then he added in a tone of utter defeat, "The jewel of my court . . . married to that wretched old man—"

"Tell him you changed your mind, that you cannot agree to such a marriage! Your brother will concede, he has to! After all, he stands to lose as much to the English. He needs us as much as we need him—"

"Does he? My spies bring me reports of Rodez's correspondence with Henry."

"What?" She stared in disbelief. "Nay! This cannot be—"

Yet the gravity on Louis's face as he nodded said it was true. The shocking news rocked her back on her heels, and her eyes widened with incredulity as she tried in vain to imagine even Rodez Valois sinking so low as to negotiate with the archenemy of all France, Henry, the King of England. "Be that the reason you agreed to my ill-fated marriage?" With dawning understanding and defeat, she whispered, "You are afraid Rodez will turn traitor and join with Henry against you, and, dear Lord, did not Papillion say 'twould be a thing you had to do . . ."

He nodded slowly, watching her closely now. He did not have to say the rest. He knew well how quickly her mind worked.

The news changed everything and nothing. At least she

understood why she was to be sacrificed, and aye, 'twas a
goodly reason for sure. Yet still she did not understand
how he could do this to her. Papillion would stop him, he
always said he would stop him . . . yet Papillion was in
Paris, then Basel for two, maybe three more fortnights. A
tremor of fear shot up her spine. *"Mon Dieu!"* She slowly
shook her head in denial. "Milord, oh, *Dieu,* you have
put a date on this ill-fated marriage?"

"Aye." He nodded again as his kindly brown eyes filled
with the pain of it. "The Sunday after next. My brother
and your newly betrothed have already embarked for Orleans. Their parties should be here by week's end."

Roshelle's blue eyes widened with the shock of it. Papillion had taught her the infallibility of math, a subject not
usually considered ambiguous, but one she found different
now: her fastest messenger riding Charles's fastest horse
could arrive in Paris in two days if all went well, an uncertain proposition in these dark days of brigands and ban-
dits. 'Twould then take another day, maybe two and maybe
longer, to find Papillion. He would be lecturing at the
Sorbonne if the quality of students pleased him, but if not,
he would have already left for Basel where philosophers
and their students congregated, and if so, 'twould take
another two days to reach Basel from Paris—

Dear Lord! A trembling hand went to her forehead.
Papillion would not likely make it back in time! Dread
filled her chest; she went weak with it.

"Roshelle, child," Louis said as he reached to hold her
up, "I did not want to tell you. Not like this. Come to
me, *petite,* and let us get ye to your women, where I can
spend the rest of my miserable life begging your forgiveness—"

"My forgiveness?" she repeated, startled by this as her
own pain and anger met the fear in his eyes. "You need
not bother begging my forgiveness! I am but your vassal
after all, a pretty pawn you must sacrifice in this deadly
game of chess played with your awful brother. You think
Henry be thine enemy and aye, he and his unholy ambi-

tions cast a dark shadow over France indeed. But the true threat to Charles and a united France sits upon a throne in Burgundy, and he hath the deadly combination of France's royal blood, Papillion's teachings and a leaden heart. Rodez is our enemy!''

Louis clenched his fists and mouth as he demanded, "Would you rather I give Henry the French crown?''

Roshelle stared for a long minute, the fateful question singing in her mind. She turned away at last and marched back to her waiting horse. She grabbed the fallen reins, lifted the bell-laden ropes over her mare's fine high head, then agilely vaulted the strong back. Before she kicked heels to the creature's side, she said, "Papillion did warn you, my Grace. When you sacrifice me, you will be full of goodly reasons and holy cause. So it hath come. My destruction is writ in stone.''

Roshelle Marie Saint Lille knelt at the altar before the Bishop of Orleans, a prayer turning over and over, faster and faster, as the bishop's soft-spoken Latin mass resounded off the towering stone walls of the Cathedral of Orleans. The four most powerful bishops of the Avignon papacy stood to the right, their bright crimson vestments contrasting sharply with the cold gray stone of the church and the darker, somber colors worn by the priests who surrounded them in two long neat rows of twelve. An even more impressive array of color and personages stood to the left of the altar: gathered there among various barons and counts of the Valois court stood the two most powerful grand dukes in France: Rodez Valois, the Duke of Burgundy, and his older brother, Louis Valois, the Duke of Orleans.

The young and frail Dauphin, Charles VII of Valois, the boy who would be king, stood between his two powerful uncles. Though he had always lived under the protection of his older uncle, Louis, for the first time in his life he stood as an equal next to his uncle Rodez.

The mere pretense of equality with his frail, doomed

nephew filled Rodez Valois's dark gaze with sardonic pleasure, somewhat less of a pleasure than that which he received from staring at the famous young girl at the altar. She was his now, and for nothing more than a promise, the elaborate charade of standing alongside his nephew for all the world to see.

A long pale hand reached to the black rose that hung at his neck, and his eyes lit with the passion of his victory. Roshelle is mine, Papillion, mine! With Roshelle comes the third of your loves and the triangle is complete; the lowest apex points to hell. For I shall hold your precious rose beneath a slow-burning fire until the white petals darken unto ash and the fear of God is burned from your soul . . .

As you burned it from mine, for mine . . .

"I saw your fate in a dream, Rodez!" Papillion had interrupted a long-ago sword fight, and with a pointing finger he announced to all: "You are doomed, doomed—torn asunder from God Almighty! The girl's unanswered love be only a mask for your relentless thirst for this power. Dear God, you will be separated for eternity . . ."

Papillion's words echoed louder than the monotonous drone of the bishop's Latin, and he remembered the occasion as the very last time he had known fear. The very last time. No more Papillion, for it was done. He was separated . . .

Thinking of it at this moment of triumph, Rodez felt a strange energy begin to radiate from his tall, princely form, a power surpassing that which could be brought to bear by his unparalleled status, surpassing the simple lift of his hand that sent legions of servants scurrying like rats in fire to escape his wrath; or his signature, which mobilized and moved whole armies across France. An energy he used to become the invincible and legendary swordsman, reputed to be the best in all the Continent and probably England as well. One had only to draw close to feel the occult power of his presence, and while his dark gaze usually revealed only a supreme indifference to the world, to solicit his interest, as many unsuspecting servants had learned, was to feel an awful mesmerizing effect alight every strained nerve of one's body.

Standing at Rodez's side, Louis felt it as a precursor of doom, his very own, but he had felt it since the day of his brother's birth and every day since. He felt it in force now, and just as he felt Rodez's strange aura of energy, he also felt the presence of Papillion's ire as he watched Roshelle at the altar of sacrifice. *Mon Dieu!* He glanced up, cursed the archbishop for his slow musical incantation of each sacred word, then his younger brother for his hatred, then Roshelle herself for looking so . . . so beautiful. As if she had maliciously wanted to make it even more difficult for him to see her taken away.

She looked more beautiful than words. The elite personages of her audience saw only the long trail of the girl's famous, rich auburn hair cascading over the pale rose silk of her long-sleeved, loosely fitting gown. A crown of early-spring white roses—her namesake—cleverly concealed the white streak that marked her hair and her life, and though many tried to see it, none could. Her lowered lids were like a curtain on her heart, concealing the sheer desperation of the emotions plain in her large, widely spaced eyes, a desperation increasing each moment Papillion failed to appear to save her.

Through sorrowful brown eyes, Charles watched helplessly as his dearest childhood friend listened to her betrothed echo the words that would bind them before God and all of Christendom unto death. Unto death. Tears welled in his eyes; he felt certain he could feel the fear pounding in Roshelle's heart as her wonderful blue eyes darted frantically to and from the old man at her side, a man only forty-seven years older than her ten and three. Roshelle, the jewel of the Valois court, joined to a beast unto death. Unto death, dear Lord; why did Charles expect the man to be struck down dead as he said his vows?

Because of Papillion, the old man of the forest. Most people, and especially the learned, felt Papillion was all

sage and saint, the disseminator of the combined knowledge of five countries and three dead languages, healer of
the wounded and sick, God's greatest gift to the Valois
court. Others thought he was made of the elements and
their magic, of the secrets of the alchemist, secrets that
drew upon darkness as often as upon light. Still others—
a certain political faction within the church, jealous as it
was of the man's miracles—believed that he was nothing
more than a clever deceiver, a purveyor of magical tricks,
tricks that relied on the susceptibility of foolish old women,
hysterical young ones and the pervasive ignorance of common folks. Yet no matter what one believed, no one had
any doubt that, unlike most other mortal beings, Papillion
owned the awesome power to make his will manifest in
reality.

The bishop's voice broke through Roshelle's frantic rev-
erie and she heard the awful last words that bound her to
the man at her side unto death. The sudden silence came
as a great shock; her eyes flew open as a weathered hand
came beneath hers to assist her to stand. The room held
its collective breath as the Duke of Normandy kissed his
young bride. The first unchaste kiss of her life, and the
cold, demanding mouth on hers brought the terrible reality
of the near future crashing down on her, a sick dread rising like bile in her throat; and as he broke the kiss and
encountered her obvious distress, he replied with a smile
at once condescending and maddening.

"You look so surprised," he whispered as he beheld
his third and by far most beautiful bride. "Did you, too,
truly believe that poor trickster could save you from your
destiny as my wife?"

Her antipathy for her husband shimmered in Roshelle's
eyes as she drew herself up to squarely meet his gaze.
They were nearly of a height. Graying dark hair framed
his face: his small dark eyes and pinched mouth; and as
if time and its dispensation were the clever hand of a
sculptor, cruelty had etched hard, deep lines there. Papillion had taught her the intuitive art of physiognomy, and

what his face said scared her to the depth of her soul: his blackened heart was indeed merciless enough to kill an innocent child in order to punish a helpless parent.

An impertinent reply trembled on her lips, but she knew to stop herself; the last thing she wanted was a demonstration of her new husband's hostilities on this of all nights. She would have his lifetime to express her animosity. She bit her lip and lowered her eyes as, chuckling, indeed hardly able to contain himself, he took her elbow to escort her down the rose-petal-strewn aisle to the cathedral doors.

As if as he, too, were the groom, Rodez stepped to her other side, against protocol. Her blue eyes shot to him, his tall, slender and awfully graceful form, lifting to view the thin and very pale face set against the raven black of his long curly hair and the oddity of his pointed goatee, a meticulously trimmed point that made his long face seem even longer. Always his hand rested on the pommel of his sword. Reputed to be the greatest swordsman in all of France, and she believed this, as he exercised darkly occult powers Papillion had so vehemently denied her. A chill raced down her spine as Rodez's wide, dark gaze came to her, as if sensing hers. She could feel it, as if he claimed her by his gaze alone!

Fear and dread filled her, like a great weight on her chest; she could hardly breathe. She just couldn't believe this was happening, that it had happened to her. 'Twas a nightmare she desperately needed to wake from—

She found no comfort as Charles and Louis followed them; her handmaid, Cisely, her other women and the multitudes of churchmen fell into step behind them; but as if in answer to her prayers, as she stepped outside beneath the dark clouds to the frantic clanging of the heavy church bells, a curious numbness swept over her from head to toe. She felt suddenly as if she watched the proceeding from a safe distance far above, as if she were not the sad, doomed and abandoned creature being escorted across the courtyard . . .

The people of Orleans gathered behind the thick iron bars of the castle gate at the far end of the grassy courtyard, their faces solemn and hostile and disbelieving as they watched the wedding parade proceed to the great hall. To lose Lady Roshelle Marie Saint Lille to Philip, the Duke of Normandy, felt like a knife put to heart, for the girl belonged, if to anyone, to the people of Orleans, who loved her.

The young lady might be wild, but she also owned God's greatest grace in an abundance that many felt would make her a saint—marked as she was by the white streak and Papillion's teachings. The young lady herself was often seen at the nunnery she had founded dispensing the wealth of Papillion's medicinal knowledge and skill, just as she appeared on the doorsteps of the unfortunates in Orleans—women and children whose husbands had abandoned them, the sick or the infirm—with a basket in hand, her highborn women in tow, and often with some miraculous means to alleviate their suffering. The people loved her, this unlikely young girl who crossed the long high bridge that separated the nobility from the masses as if it weren't there at all; they would always love Roshelle Marie. And while the weddings of the highborn normally brought cheers and festivities throughout the land, this did not happen now. As the people watched their young champion walk to the great hall on the arm of Philip the Bad, murmured disapproval rippled through the crowd, disapproval growing with a chant:

> *"Wedding day rain*
> *Be God's angry curse*
> *The groom will get pain*
> *And then he gets worse!"*

Distant thunder rolled over the mountains and a few fat drops fell, spotting Roshelle's lovely gown. The people pulled mantles and shawls over their heads as it began to rain heavily. They chanted more loudly now, but Roshelle still neither heard nor noticed them. She felt the moisture seep through her silk slippers, the cold numbness through her fingers. Fingertips felt hot to the touch and Philip abruptly withdrew his hand as the wedding party quickly passed through the tall, tapestry-lined walls of the wide, grand entrance hall, down the corridor and into the great hall itself.

A long white-clothed table was set on the dais above the main floor. Four other long tables stood in four neat rows below the high table, separated by a center aisle for serving. Elaborate tapestries hung on the walls and each depicted a scene of Orleans' history. The finest musicians in Orleans serenaded the bride—still dazed and seemingly lost in a soul-saving trance—and groom as they took their seats at the long table on the dais.

The lords and ladies of the court quickly filed in, everyone wanting to witness the historic setting as the Dauphin took his rightful seat, beneath the bright orange-and-white canopy, and between his two warring uncles for the first time since his birth. Poor Charles! Sneezing into his mouchoir, his hand trembling as he signaled the others to sit, his mistrustful eyes darting to and fro, as if to spot a would-be assassin. How frail he looked, how nervous and overwhelmed!

The pantler, head of the pantry, rushed forward with the bread rolls wrapped in lovely gold-embroidered napkins and placed his trenchers near the large ceremonial covered saltcellars before servants hurried to do the same for the lesser tables. The cup bearers began filling goblets with expensive wine. Before the courses began, as he always did, Charles conceded the right of first toast to Louis, who stood for the honor. Roshelle barely heard the speech about how the marriage joined the two houses of France to unite the country against the invasion of the English king. More toasts followed, Rodez hardly appeasing the court's worries when his toast barely mentioned the joint effort against England and centered instead on the lovely young lady at his side: her beauty and charms, her gifts and how the loss of the Orleans court "is now the treasure of all Flanders and my lands beyond."

The words felt like salt in their wounds, the collective sentiment revealed in the silence that followed. Louis, desperate to maintain the promise of his younger brother's army and monies, nervously started the applause, and only then did the people follow, noticeably without enthusiasm. More toasts followed, an endless song comprised of toasts as the servants brought out the first course of gooseneck soup served in beautiful hand-carved ash-wood bowls, stewed peas, dates and almonds and roasted sturgeon and frogs' legs. Cup bearers rushed to keep wine in the heavy silver goblets.

Roshelle abruptly woke to feel Rodez's gaze again, as if she were a painting on a wall and he a patron of the arts who was weighing her aesthetic value. She felt the hard, unnatural pounding of her heart as she abruptly realized they talked of her as if she weren't there, and with a vulgarity that shocked.

"There is an art to the proper use of a virgin."

"As an appreciative connoisseur of youth"—her husband's weathered hand went to her hair, a finger toyed with the rose-laden rope of the white streak—"I am well acquainted with many different methods. Though as of this moment, I haven't yet decided which will best mold her for my use."

"Multiple uses, and because of that, I have a suggestion . . ."

Then amidst whispered laughter she heard a discussion no girl should ever hear, about the fine line between fear and excitement and how best to trespass it. She blanched, alarmed to realize just how frightened she felt, a fear far exceeding any thirteen-year-old virgin's fears on her wedding night. She would not survive. Papillion! Did you know I would not survive?

"You will need her obedience." Rodez dipped a succulent frog's leg in the soup bowl, lifting it to his mouth.

"Of course, commanding a woman's obedience is usually easier than a hound's or a mastiff's, but not so Roshelle. Papillion's influence again. I shall have to be clever about it. Which reminds me: Roshelle, child, have you noticed the rain outside?"

The idea of rain put in mind Joan and her fear of it.

Roshelle's blue eyes riveted on Rodez.

"The other day as I was riding through Clisson, I happened upon a fascinating ecclesiastic trial," Rodez said. "It seems the townsfolk got it in mind that the devil was speaking through a village idiot's gibberish, and naturally the church, with its wealth of wisdom, decided the simple man should be tormented unto death—to rid his soul of its host." He laughed as he watched the girl's eyes. "And the simple fool was smiling up until the very moment he felt . . ."

The room started spinning; she stopped breathing. From far away she saw a rush of movement. Signaled by an alarmed Cisely, and seated in various positions at the tables below, her women rose to go to her. There was a sudden blur of colors made from their gowns as they rushed to where she sat. Roshelle felt the merciful comfort of Cisely's arm about her before Nel, another favorite, knocked over a goblet onto Philip's lap.

Philip's curses filled the hall, the music came to an abrupt halt and a startled silence came over the room as heads turned. A young page rushed forward, cloth in hand to wipe the wine from the rich velvet of the duke's elaborate doublet. The incident distracted the crowd just long enough to get Roshelle out before she was subjected to the traditional shouts and jeers of any maid, highborn or otherwise, off to her wedding bed.

The strange silence in the hall lingered and stretched, inexplicable and for no reason anyone knew or could guess until, one by one, gazes turned, to behold the man who stood at the open doors of the hall. He looked at once magnificent and grand, every bit as legendary as his reputation. He wore plain gray robes—austerely decorated with vestments of red and black and white—cloth that contrasted and yet was similar to the somber black of a priest's robes. Like Moses before Pharaoh, he held in his hand a staff as tall as his own impressive height. His hair was short and sage-white, like his beard, accenting the rich golden color of his unlined skin. Yet all anyone noticed about Papillion was his eyes. Thick raven-black brows arched dramatically over large blue eyes, eyes filled with magic, mischief, wisdom—it was said that Papillion's gaze could mesmerize a man across a crowded room, dropping his victim where he stood.·

A trick Rodez knew well . . .

"My dear Louis!" Rodez turned in a pretense of addressing his alarmed brother, though his eyes remained firmly fixed on the old man. "You neglected to inform me of the treat! You invited Papillion, the famous court magician of Orleans!" The words and tone made a mockery of all Papillion was and all he had once meant to the duke. "Why, Louis," he continued, smiling generously, a hand toying with the sharp point of his goatee, "I am thrilled. I anticipated only the banalities of the traditional minstrel or two, a juggler or an acrobat. How welcome a clever trick or an amusing ruse will be!"

Philip chuckled, but he was the only one; not even the handful of lords and barons brought from Flanders and Normandy dared to mock the famous sage. No one drew a breath as each person turned to watch the effect of the insult on Papillion. Yet there was none. Papillion did not heed the challenge; he did not have to. There was only one reason he had appeared, and that was to save the girl he loved more than life.

Suddenly four gray doves flew into the hall, appearing, it seemed, from hidden folds in Papillion's robe. Whispered amazement raced through the crowd as heads lifted to watch the four gray birds fly about the room, circling and circling until at last they lit upon the four distinct goblets of the three dukes and the Dauphin at the table raised on the dais.

Sergio, Papillion's servant, stepped back, thrilled with his success. Everything depended upon the doves, he knew. The whole thing . . .

Scattered applause followed the neat trick, but so did confusion, for everyone knew Papillion had not attended the ill-begotten ceremony to provide such lowly entertainment. Yet as the tall, impressive figure moved down the center aisle between the tables, magic spilled into the room.

A woman cried out in fright, then laughed as she withdrew a tiny kitten from the gold bodice of her cream-colored gown. The audience broke out in applause. Another lady felt a stirring up her sleeve and pulled out a miniature white puppy. "Oh, so petite!" The roomful of people laughed with delight. Viscount Gian Valentine laughed as he discovered a gold coin in the sugar-coated candy in his mouth. Three colorful balls rolled from unseen places onto the two center tabletops. A woman holding a napkin found herself holding a bouquet of fresh roses. A page watched in no small horror as the wine pitcher bubbled up and began spilling onto the floor, a similar situation occurring in nearly all of the soup bowls. Another lady shrieked the second she saw a tiny white mouse running up her arm, then fainted dead away when she noticed the little monsters everywhere on her black velvet gown.

Quite suddenly everything changed.

Anticipating a treat, people reached greedy hands for the balls. The slightest touch broke what was a mercilessly fragile membrane and from one ball poured out dozens of tiny black spiders, from another came lizards, still another produced strange, tiny slithering creatures—too small for snakes but too large for worms. Laughter turned to screams. The thorns on the bouquet of roses pricked its recipient's hands and burned with an acid poison. Lord Valentine started choking on the wretched taste of the coin. People jumped up to escape the little beasties crawling from those balls, knocking over the benches as they did.

Wine and soup still spurted unnaturally from their containers, yet now appeared as a most foul-smelling cesspool. The little dog abruptly urinated in the fright of screams, then worse, causing the lady a start of horror that scared her neighbor's kitten and made the tiny creature bare claws on her face.

A high-ranking bishop, Sal de Boviar, stood up, and as a soldier grabs his sword, he clutched his rosary and with scathing fury shouted, "In the name of God Almighty, I command thy demons . . . There once be a lady named Eva! Who came to the hall as Godiva, but a change in the lights showed a tear in her tights, and a low fellow present yelled Beaver!"

Hearing this, witnessing the devil's own possession, the other men of the cloth jumped up to flee in horror. The endless stream of wine covered the floor, foul-smelling soup over that, and one of them slipped; the other bent to pick him up but slipped too. Chaos fueled the entire hall: shouts and screams, fallen benches, spilled wine and wild, frantic creatures.

Philip watched the scene with plain fascination, that was all, though seeing the stumbling priests nearly made him lose the mouthful of wine in his goblet and he swallowed it whole before bursting out with a great roar of laughter. And more as the bishop continued the stream of asinine verse: ". . . love is the fart of every heart, of mine and yours and all the worlds . . ." Charles scarcely breathed, let alone moved, while Louis, too, only stared helplessly at this grotesque parody of a court magician's tricks, a show of power and not, he knew, of Papillion's.

Papillion kept his back to the chaos, as if it were not happening, and stared only at Rodez, meeting the amusement in that man's gaze dispassionately. No one overheard the warning as he said to Rodez, "I will stop you, Rodez." His hand came across his heart, the torchlight caught and reflected the gold band on his finger and he said, "The third apex of the triangle that sits upon my heart points to the stars and the heavens beyond. The next time thine eyes behold the ring, you will be pierced by the just sword of a pure heart.''

Rodez's eyes blazed with scorn and mockery and, most of all, disbelief. A fool's trick! An absurdly simple fool's trick; the mere suggestion to the mind makes it come true: prophesy a painful calamity to a man and he will trip over the first stone in his path. One of the very first lessons Papillion had taught him. ''A child's ploy, Papillion. A child's ploy . . .''

Papillion watched as Rodez opened his hand and revealed a beautiful gold-and-blue butterfly, the frantic flutter of its wings demanding freedom, and Papillion knew his cruel trick. For many years ago, when he had still tried to believe in Rodez, he had found a black velvet box in Rodez's trunk, not even hidden, and full of dead and decaying butterflies . . .

Rodez reached for the candle. Yet something slippery touched his fingers and his hand jerked instinctively. The butterfly flew free into space. Hot wax spilled over his hand. With fury, he looked back at Papillion.

''But a child's ploy, Rodez . . .''

Louis abruptly stood and, desperate to save himself, he ordered, ''Enough, Papillion! Enough!''

As if his wish were a command, and far quicker than it took to make, Papillion raised his hand, that was all. The chaos abruptly vanished, replaced by a sudden silence. Only the physical traces of a wicked hand remained: the toppled benches, the spilled wine and soup, all but a few of the little animals and the rapid breaths of the lords and ladies as they turned at Louis's voice.

Rodez alone understood the power in play here.

''I had to do it,'' Louis cried out, desperate to redeem himself. ''I had to! For France!''

Papillion still only stared at Rodez but answered, ''And though I could never stop this thing you did, I will not let Roshelle be sacrificed.''

''Yet 'tis done, Papillion, 'tis done! 'Tis too late to save her now!''

Chapter 1

T he tall, dark man leaped out from the shadows in front of her and Roshelle's gasp came in a startled cry as her hands flew to her heart.

"Madonna!" The gaze of Edward de la Eresman, the Lord of Suffolk, lit with pleasure as his long arms came on either side of her to rest against the stone wall behind her. "You are alone!" The hall's torchlight cast his face in darkness, hiding the devilish excitement playing in an amused grin. "Bless my sweet luck!"

Roshelle's eyes widened dramatically to encompass the shape towering over her, cornering her against the wall, before she looked frantically down the long, empty hall. Empty. Curse it! The torches shed light in the hall, but no one moved there. All her women, maids and guards were asleep, and not having wanted to rouse them for such a trifling errand, certain the English, too, would be asleep at the late hour, she had left the safety of the solar alone. Only to be accosted by none other than him, the high-and-mighty himself. "Loose me! Just—"

She stopped with another muted cry as a strong hand snaked tightly around her arm while the other covered her mouth. As if scorched by the heat of his body, the terrifying scent of spiced wine—he was quite drunk!—she pressed her backside hard against the cold stone wall, her eyes wide and furious as she glared up at him.

She had never stood so close to him, having always taken great pains to keep her distance. He stood a half

25

foot taller than most men, able and strong too, a knightly warrior in his prime. Curly light brown hair framed the handsome bearded face, its extremely regular features marred by a wide red scar across his cheek—as if his cheek had been cut by a jagged knife. The moment she saw where his gaze dropped, she tore his hand from her mouth. "Loose me! Loose me or I'll—"

"Or you'll what? Scream? Call a guard?" Humor lit the handsome commander's pale blue eyes. "One of these fearless French knights of yours?"

Roshelle understood the insult only too well. The past tumultuous years had changed the very light in her eyes. For she had lived through the nightmarish sweep of history, a nightmare without end. The French knights were well known for their fearlessness, a fool's courage that had seen them massacred in the infamous battle of Agincourt, where one thousand English soldiers had fought and soundly beaten nearly ten thousand French, virtually wiping French nobility from the face of the earth. Including her second husband, Count Millicent de la Nevers. Of course she knew Louis's excuses; indeed, she had heard them hundreds of times, but the fact remained—French knights were no match for the English warriors, and the English pigs never for a moment let them forget it.

Like the Lord of Suffolk now. Last year, over half the French kingdom had joined the Burgundians under the duchy of Burgundy in an unholy alliance with the English. Louis had been captured at Agincourt and imprisoned in the Tower of London, leaving Charles without his guidance and strength, alone among the wolves of his court. All of northern France and Brittany had fallen to the English, leaving only the southern part of France under the banner of the duchy of Orleans as the domain of poor Charles.

Reales had been Millicent's land, but because of his death and his fealty to Rodez, the Duke of Burgundy, Roshelle was forced to house the English garrison here, at Castle Reales. Her castle and her prison. This wretched garrison was commanded by him—Lord Edward de la Eresman of Suffolk, younger brother to the famed Vincent de la Eresman, the Duke of Suffolk. His French name owed itself to the time in history when the French and the English aristocracy were fond of marrying each other, but this distant French blood did nothing to mitigate his utterly English tyranny. She could imagine no more brutal a feudal lord than this man before her, and no one had ever accused her of owning a limited vision.

The arrogance of the House of Suffolk shone in Edward's pale, cold eyes as he mocked her apparent helplessness, a potentially fatal mistake, but of course he knew that. So what was it he wanted?

"What is it you want?"

A soft chuckle sounded briefly before Edward bit his lip as if to restrain his amusement. "What is it I want? Oh, milady, I have waited to find you alone for some two long months now."

"Yes? Why?"

The question came as a demand, impatient at that. She was not daft; in fact, most considered her wise far beyond her ten and seven years. Nor was she in any way ignorant of the effect her beauty—the worst part of her curse—had on men. True, she had the lowest opinion of Englishmen, all of them, convinced the entire people were crude, hopelessly uncivilized, the lowest kind of bloodthirsty barbarians, that like a legion of demons, words could not adequately describe just how horrid they were. She knew every detail of their waves of violence against the poor people of Brittany and she knew the result, a poverty that left the simple folk on the brink of starvation—the slowest and most painful of all deaths.

Lord Edward was responsible for much of it. Highborn though he be, he was a vile creature indeed: tyrannical, greedy and as full of vice as the desert serpent. Yet as low as this opinion was of Edward, she never suspected he was, well, stupid. Not until he answered her question with the heat of his gaze as he pressed his body against her.

Shocked blue eyes shot to his face. Was he mad? He couldn't mean to, he just couldn't! He would die, to act on the desire her wretched beauty inspired landed a death blow, everyone knew that! Did he imagine he was immune to it?

"Milord! Your thoughts are mercilessly transparent—I, I confess my surprise. Are you not afraid of the curse?"

Edward chuckled with bravado, which wavered ever so briefly as his gaze found the startling white streak woven into the beautiful hair that loosely framed her face before falling in a long, neat pile down her back, past her narrow waist. "Ah, your curse. Well, you see, the other day as my men and I watched you ride out on that wild steed of yours, we got to discussing your 'curse.' Suppose, we wondered, the most beautiful maid in Brittany was un-married, widowed twice, and suppose this beautiful maid had developed—no doubt by her dead husband's clumsy hands—a distaste for the marriage bed? And suppose this lady dreamed up an amusing charade that not only saved her from another disastrous marriage but also afforded her absolute protection from every red-blooded male in two kingdoms—"

"You are a fool! A fool—"

"Rodez said the curse was a lie."

Her blue eyes widened. "He wants you dead!"

"He is my friend—"

"That beast is friend to no man—"

"You lie to save yourself."

"No, no—" She frantically shook her head. "Rodez tricked my second husband in the same way. He told Mil-licent my curse was a trick, a ruse, but really all he wanted was Millicent's lands, which he got when Millicent died. I tried to warn Millicent, I did, but it didn't matter. Even though he never forced his matrimonial rights to my bed, he still died one week after our vows. He died of sudden apoplexy on the way to Flanders—"

She stopped with a gasp as Edward's fingers strayed to the long line of her neck and his voice dropped to a whisper. "I do not believe this wild tale of fancy. I have a wager with my men, a wager that says I live to see the light of day after I lie with you, that this whole fabrication is little more than a precious key to an imaginary chastity belt—"

"Nay, 'tis not! I have two dead husbands to prove it!"

The humor in Edward's gaze told her he only toyed with her. So! The fool merely found a little fun in frightening her! Like a well-fed cat toying with a mouse, he found great amusement in frightening her with this pretense.

Her fists clenched, indicating the rise of her temper, well known to be at least as menacing as the very curse itself. "Milord," she began in a deceptively angelic voice, "while I am well aware of the rumors that lords of the House of Suffolk are godless whoresons, made of equal parts deprivation and savagery, all the while maintaining pretensions to finer, higher things, until this moment I had not believed it. I had been thinking you simply lacked the common graces given to pigs—"

A strong hand came over her mouth. To say that Lord Edward of Suffolk was unaccustomed to hearing a litany of insults from a woman he meant to seduce was an understatement; he had in fact never heard a disparaging word against his noble family, especially his famous brother. Not even his ill-mannered wife would dare that. No one had until now. Until Lady Roshelle.

"You are as reckless and wild with your tongue as you are on that horse. My men think its sting, like that of a honeybee, protects a sweet wealth within—"

That did it! Roshelle ripped his hand from her mouth. "Mercy! Spare me your poor metaphors and even worse poetry—I have no wish to hear either. Now let me pass in peace—"

He laughed. "Oh, my lovely lady, I have far more than poor metaphors for you. I have waited long for a chance to win your favor."

"My favor? My favor is a deadly poison!"

Roshelle started forward, but he held her firmly. She

still did not quite believe this was happening, that he truly
meant to harm her. Nor had she assessed quite how drunk
the man was until he said, "Come, come, my lovely lady,
confess: you've been waiting for the man bold enough to
challenge the lie told about you; you want me as much as
I want to—"

"You are mad!"

She pushed with all her strength. Edward laughed and
grabbed her hands, suppressing her brief struggle before
bringing her hands up sharply behind her back.

"Loose me! Loose—"

"Why should I?" Then, not at all wanting a raping and
certain this was but the pretense of a reluctant maid, he
changed the tone of his voice, like a shift of a breeze.
"Roshelle, Roshelle," he whispered in a lover's voice,
and as he kept her hands behind her back, he let his gaze
drink in the scope and power of her beauty, a beauty
cursed, yet sung across Brittany, he knew. A loosened
mass of auburn hair framing the delicately sculpted face,
the high color rising on her cheeks, the small, pert nose
raised with indignation and the thin dark brows that arched
like wings over those lovely blue eyes, eyes sparkling with
the light of her fury. Fury he'd melt with but a touch of
his mouth.

His pale blue gaze dropped to the ample curves of her
breasts. Dear Lord. The combined assault on his senses
of her nearness left him dazed and weak with desire,
though her breath came hard and fast and he'd have to be
blind not to see the wild fear in her eyes. A wild thing for
sure; he knew well her impertinence and rebellious nature, the way she took pains to avoid him, indeed all of
his men; and with an effort he tried to harness the hot
blood coursing through him to show her an easier way. He
released her hand, but only to bring her fingertips to his
lips for a kiss.

Which merely confused her. She suffered a moment's
misunderstanding by his changed tack, grasping the hope
that he'd let her pass in peace until he whispered, "Easy,

my lovely lady.'' His curled fingers fell to the long lines of her neck. "I will not hurt you, Roshelle. Never that. Lend me half a chance for your heart. I could give you things . . ."

"Give me things? Give me—" She suffered an incredulous moment of disbelief, at once forgetting the curse and the whole disastrous situation as her entire fury greeted the idea that he thought her a simple maid willing to spread her thighs for a trinket or a coin!

With an open hand, she raised her arm to land a well-aimed slap to his face. He caught her hand midway but she twisted free, her strength catching him by surprise, and with this surprising strength she landed a hard blow to his face. His gaze went glassy; he suffered a brief moment's dizziness before he realized he was staring at the satisfied smirk brought by a job well done. "Why, you little vixen—"

He recaptured her arms, then her hands. Pain made her cry out as he forced them high against her back, suppressing her struggle with the weight of his body. Then, to her horror, he laughed.

Sweet Madonna, how she made his blood race!

"I've seen your claws, milady, now let me hear a purr."

"Purr! You are an arse! Purr! Methinks I shall be ill before too long—" She stopped as he laughed and, ignoring her words, held her with one hand.

She cried out, squirming violently as his free hand brushed the full circle of her breast beneath the worn green gown, then cupped its soft weight in his hand. Through the voluptuous flesh he felt the frantic pounding of her heart, but pleasure made him weak. He reached behind her to grasp a handful of hair. He tugged once, bringing her head up for his kiss. "One taste of these lips, Roshelle, one—"

Lips pressed lightly over her mouth, muting her frantic "Nooo—"

Her entire being recoiled from the kiss as fear and fury surged. She opened her mouth, and just as he thought no woman was ever more ripe for seduction, he felt the sharp, merciless bite of her small white teeth on his tongue. He leaped back, clasping his hand over his mouth. "Blood! I am bleeding!"

She took in the result of her violence and with a regal tilt of her head, she said slowly, and with venom, "I, as all my people, have endured unspeakable brutality at the hands of our English oppressors, and until we rid our land of the English pestilence, I shall no doubt have to suffer more. Be forewarned, though." Her blue eyes narrowed dangerously. "A raping shall not be one of them! 'Twould bring your death, I say!"

With a lift of her skirts, she turned to flee. Red-faced with fury and humiliation, desire turned to a blinding rage that transformed the handsome features of his face into something dangerous and deadly, he stumbled once before righting himself and giving chase. Roshelle glanced around just in time to see this. She screamed for her guards and, stumbling forward, reached under her skirts for the anlace gartered at her thigh. A small hand clasped the dagger. Unmindful of the obscenities Edward shouted after her as he chased her, she fled down the hall. For a drunken man, he was quick, and before she reached the corner, his strong hands snaked around her waist. She screamed as he lifted her off the ground. "Why, you little tangemon! I'll teach you a measure of French humility! A raping you loathe and a raping you shall get!"

Roshelle screamed again as he tossed her like so much baggage over his shoulder. With dagger clasped firmly in hand, she raised her arm and struck his flesh with surprising force. Edward cried out with shock more than with pain, dropping her to the ground. She fell bottom-first, her backside hitting the cold stone floor.

Edward never understood the rage she put into his blood. No woman in his life had dared, and, cursed or no, she would pay for this. Seeing his fury, she ignored the jarring pain shooting through her backside to scramble to all fours just as she heard his terrifying chuckle. "Now you have had it, my lovely little princess.'' Reaching behind him, he pulled the dagger from the hard muscle of his buttock, then tossed it unceremoniously against the wall. ''Judgment Day has arrived and I, milady, am your judge.''

Looking up from her position on all fours, Roshelle slowly shook her head in absolute denial of the devil's own amusement in his eyes. He could not be doing this, he just couldn't! Dear Mother in Heaven, 'twas suicide!

Roshelle wasted no time in jumping up to run, only to scream again as his arms came around her, and once again he threw her over his shoulder. Her fists pummeled against his back and she kicked for all she was worth, but he was an unusually strong man, a knight hardened to the lances and halberts of war, hardly deterred by a woman's weight, much less by her fists on his back.

But she would not stop. Fueled by a mounting terror, she furiously hit his back while twisting off his shoulder with a frantic denial of ''NOOO!'' He dropped her with another vicious curse. She fell again on her backside. Before she could jump to her feet, his arms swooped under her and, tightly clasping her hands beneath her, he lifted her up and continued quickly down the dark hall.

She tried desperately to twist free. ''Loose me! Loose me! You do not understand! You will never get away with this! Never!''

Yet he was. Fear choked her and she panicked, unmindful of the devastating consequences of what was happening. ''Potiers, Potiers!'' She screamed her faithful servant's name, begging for help. Help that would cost so much, since her men would die defending her. Edward carried her swiftly down the halls to the spiral staircase that led to the floor below, where his chambers lay. He took the stairs two at a time, reaching the second landing before the guards answered her screams. A group of armed men rushed up the staircase, each wearing the hated English colors, blue and white. Edward's guards.

''Milord!'' The captain held his arm back to move the men against the wall, allowing Edward passage as if he were a grand king in his very own palace, and he was. Dear God, he was. A grin spread across the harsh features of the captain, Sir Miles Hartman, as he accurately guessed the situation and mocked, "Well, if 'tisn't the heralded Lady Roshelle! Out for a little midnight splaying, milady?"

The men laughed. "Aye!" Edward answered as he started past. " 'Tis about time I lay to rest this curse and taste this precious piece, think ye not, Miles?"

He nodded, smiling, until she, more desperate to stop this than anyone could know, spat at his face.

"Why, you little hellcat!" Edward dropped her legs but held her arms, forcing her slender back into a near painful arch. "Apologize!"

"Apologize! You are mad, you are all stark raving mad! Why would I apologize to the wretched beasts who stand there mocking my terror and condoning unholy abuse! Apologize? I rather curse the bastards and you to the devil! I half hope you do just so I can watch your death!"

"I have had enough of this! You are mine, girl! Mine! You are little more than the as-yet-untouched spoils of a war hard fought and won. This ill-conceived curse of yours will no longer save you!" His pale eyes blazed with emotion as he stared down at the girl, and for all her talk of terror, only fury brightened her blue eyes. With a harsh hand he turned her to face the interested stares of the men, while his other strong hand slipped down the bodice of her gown.

Roshelle squeezed her eyes shut against the humiliation of it.

"I can do what I want with you. Anything, milady," he whispered in her ear, "anything. Now would you like an audience or the privacy of my chambers for this lesson in French subjugation?"

There was no choice to make. Both options revolted her. With tightly shut eyes and feeling more desperate than a man could know, she shook her head fiercely before she felt a sudden heat as if a bolt from the heavens had struck her. Edward felt only a sudden blinding dizziness. Ro-

for the parade of women who passed through the doors to his solar chambers. The reflection showed a strangely compelling face, but one few people found handsome; his dark features were rather too prominent for that word. Thick dark brows arched over dark, widely spaced and intelligent eyes, eyes often filled with an amused cynicism at the sheer folly of his fellow beings. Like the beak of a bird of prey, his nose appeared hooked and far too large, as if it had met too many fists—though thankfully by the time he reached eighteen, few fists ever landed anymore. Women loved best his mouth—the way, despite his sophistication and strong, decisive voice, he could not stop the curve of an endearing, boyish kind of grin when greeting anything that pleased him. Yet this was countered by a smooth, clean-shaven skin covering his square chin, marked by a perfect cleft.

He had just brushed and tied his long dark hair neatly at the nape of his neck when a soft knock sounded at the door. "Aye," bade his husky whisper as he picked up a richly embroidered cloth and dipped it in the fresh dressing water to bathe.

Bogo le Wyse, the Abbot of Suffolk and the duke's steward, opened the door and stepped inside the spacious wealth of his lord's chambers. The older man looked to the enormous feather bed, where a lovely woman slept wearing naught but a she-cat's smile, one he had seen on a hundred or more women sleeping in that bed. Saints alive, but the duke's bedroom agility was becoming as famous as the wield of his sword. Ever since the death of his second wife in childbirth, these very doors seemed open to an endless stream of women. Bogo half expected to see a line outside his master's solar every time he approached.

"Shh," Vincent said, motioning to where the woman slept. "The lady is still asleep."

"Lady?" Bogo questioned, incredulous. "Where does milord see a lady? Is that harlot not Elsbeth MacClenan, the one and only?"

Vincent looked up to see the small man's finger pointed at the bed and he sighed, having long since resigned himself to Bogo's impertinence, trying as it was. "Bogo, did you come to offer comment on the sorry state of my personal affairs, or do you have something of import to say?"

"Indeed. His Majesty's courtier, Sir Gilgood, awaits you in the hall. He says 'tis a matter of the utmost importance."

Vincent's gaze shot to Bogo's face to ascertain the truth of it, his expression darkening instantly. "Curse my good king to hell, I will not send more knights to his wretched war!" The exclamation caused the sleeping lady to sink into the rich velvet quilt as if for protection, but neither man noticed now. "He has my worthless excuse of a brother and one hundred of my men of arms, and that is enough. I will give him not one more man for this vain and foolish quest of a French title—"

"And I, milord, am not asking for any. However—"

"Bogo, go off and prepare him for my descent." Vincent dismissed his steward as he pulled a gold velvet doublet over his broad shoulders, belting it with a thick black belt, as was his habit. "I shall attend him in the hour."

Knowing when to exit, Bogo shut the door behind him. Vincent pushed his large feet into knee-high black boots before standing to his full height. His back was ramrod-straight, a lingering remnant of an otherwise forgotten boyhood tutor, and this impressive posture pronounced an already unconventional height. A formidable presence, at least formidable enough to give the king's courtier a piece of his anger with his absolute refusal to participate a single man or coin more in Henry's little game of war.

The Duke of Suffolk maintained an adversarial friendship with his king, the only lord of the realm with that claim. Adversarial because he often disagreed with King Henry's policies with emphatic, if not violent, eloquence that more than once had disastrous effects on Henry's solicitation for support from his lords for this foreign war for the French throne. While he was a ferocious debater, merciless when he wanted to be, the Duke of Suffolk presented well-reasoned arguments, which everyone, including the king, found himself listening to, if not agreeing with—except, of course, on the dominant issue of France.

Unlike other lords, particularly Henry himself, Vincent did not care a whit about his French neighbor's troubles: its inept and often disastrously insane succession of dauphins or its covetous, power-hungry dukes, its famines or its religious schisms. He cared nothing for these catastrophes except as they affected his land and his people, which only happened when Henry wanted something from him. He alone among the lords seemed to understand what the startling English battle victories meant. Unlike everyone else, King Henry especially, he did not think the victories supported the idea that God Himself was arbitrating for Henry's claim to the French throne. The French losses only reflected the dismal state of French knights and their pathetic leadership.

Yet Henry loved no one of his lords better. He had even given Vincent the duchy and made him a duke, done in a generous sweep of an enormous land grant that joined the two separate properties of Vincent's family. This had made Vincent one of the most land-rich dukes in England. The generous gift was a reward, not for Vincent's unsurpassed battle skills or for his past support in three of Henry's war efforts, or for his far-less-frequently-sung "domestic" policies, farming and taxing policies that created the wealthiest holdings in the realm and, more important, the most content populace anywhere—no peasant revolt ever brewed in Suffolk. Rather, Henry rewarded Vincent with the duchy because Vincent gave him the one thing no one else could—a friendship of equals. Not only did Henry depend on Vincent's mercilessly frank counsel, which was stripped of flattery, lies and deceptions, but Henry enjoyed Vincent's company the most for what little private life he managed as king: weekend hunts, long precious nights of nothing more than drunken revelries, embarrassingly frantic wenching and well-matched games of competition, games of wrestling, archery, sword fights and, of course, chess.

It started years ago when a courtier unwittingly mentioned to Henry that the young, eighteen-year-old Vincent de la Eresman, the Lord of Suffolk, could not be beaten in the game of chess. Since Henry owned the title in his realm, he immediately demanded that the young man be brought to him for a match. Presented at court, Vincent received his first instructions.

These instructions were simple: "Let the king win."

"I beg your pardon?"

"You must let Henry win. The king does not like to lose."

"What a coincidence! Neither do I!"

The courtier only smiled and mumbled something about kings and their God-given rights, before presenting Vincent to Henry. After an hour of pomp and fanfare, Vincent soon sat opposite his young king, the chessboard between them. Soon after that, Henry heard two words he had never heard from another's lips. "Check and mate."

The king, along with two dozen courtiers, stared at the jeweled ivory pieces on the checkerboard with great shock. "No one hath ever beaten me before!"

"Indeed?" Vincent's dark brow rose, an amused light filling the darkly intelligent eyes. "If one did not know better, one might suspect there was an unspoken conspiracy afoot to grace your Majesty with the unearned title of chess master. Imagine treating you like a spoiled child, as if you, Henry, king of all England and Wales, were not strong enough to accept a fair loss!" He shook his head, appearing to scoff at the preposterous idea. "Of course that cannot be true. Your loss is no doubt a reflection of my own unnatural luck."

All gazes flew to the king's face to await his reaction— many a man had died for less. Vincent alone appeared utterly unalarmed by the silence, which stretched taut like the strings of a deadly bow. Then tauter still, until the moment filled with the fine, deep sound of Henry's laughter. "Only a shallow man believes in luck. The strong man believes in cause and effect."

"Aye." Vincent grinned. "The power of luck is confessed to only by the miserable; the happy impute success to merit."

"And you?" the king inquired.

"Happy, milord. Very."

Everyone laughed at that, Henry most of all. "So, young Vincent de la Eresman, I am also told you cannot be beaten with the sword or lance either?"

"Is this an inquiry, your Highness?"

"Indeed."

"Does your Majesty demand modesty, which I must say feels as unnatural as priestly vows, or shall I confess? It is true—I've yet to be beaten."

The king's audience laughed nervously at the young man's boldness, but Henry just stared at Vincent: for here at last was a refreshing change from the tiresome obsequiousness he had endured his whole life. The thinly veiled challenge did not go unanswered. Henry was young and strong and just as proud of his athletic achievements—their friendship had begun.

Presently, Vincent was of a mind to end it.

Two long-robed bishops accompanied the king's messenger, Sir Gilgood of Manchester. The duke entered the hall without formality, fully prepared to blast the silver-tongued Gilgood and his puppet bishops back to Westminster at the first mention of his fealty to King Henry, the subsequent demand for more knights from Suffolk. This was it.

Gilgood jumped up from the cushioned bench, bending his corpulent frame in deference. "Milord, Duke of Suffolk, and most noble signature to—"

A scowl on his face, Vincent waved his hand impatiently as he came to stand before the table where they had been waiting. "Dispense with the formalities, and get ye to the point. And God save you if Henry wants more of my knights. I say enough—"

"Nay, milord, please. 'Tis tragic news we bear all the way from Reales."

"Reales? Now what has my brother done?"

"The French hath seized the castle back. A rebellion is spreading, one I fear has been brought on by the tragic death of Edward, your dearly beloved brother, the Lord of Suffolk and overlord of Reales."

Gilgood paused to let this sink in, watching Vincent's dark eyes search the terrible truth from the solemn faces of the three men Henry had sent to tell him.

"Edward? No." A simple matter. It could not be Edward, his only sibling and half at that, the younger Lord of Suffolk. Not now. Not after he'd lost his second sweet wife in childbirth, a tragedy that had left him no heir. Vincent hadn't been bothered much by this situation until Edward announced he had married Lady Terese of Flanders.

Married Rodez Valois's famous whore. He still could hardly believe it. He had watched Edward grow from a whining, quarrelsome and resentful lad given to violent tantrums to a man of worse vices and greater vanities: greed, drunkenness and cruelty among them. As low as his opinion was of Edward, he had never considered him stupid. Until this marriage. Only the most dim-witted idiot would be blind to the obvious ploy to transfer the Suffolk duchy into Rodez Valois's hands! And Edward had said he thought himself in love with the harlot, a woman already famous—well known throughout all of Burgundy, Vincent's agents had reported!—for marrying well, and as luck or evil would have it, finding herself happily widowed months later. And Edward had married her without his permission or even his knowledge. Without Henry's permission or knowledge. And now Edward was dead.

Vincent went to the mantel, leaning on it for support, his mind rushing over the magnitude of this disaster. "Curse you, Henry! I told you Edward was a no-good lecher, best sent on a faraway Crusade or a mission to a godforsaken place of disease and warring mongrels. I told you!''

The fool! Against his righteous pleas, Henry had insisted on giving Edward the lordship of Reales, certain as Henry was that Edward's problems were simply the result of living a life overshadowed at every turn by his famous older brother. ''Huh!'' Vincent had scoffed. ''Even if that is true, in a world full of sorrows, that is a slight one indeed.'' Henry had refused to hear Vincent's long list of grievances, insisting that all the ''boy'' needed to show his colors and find his manhood was the care and responsibility of faraway Reales.

At first Henry had been so pleased with Edward's performance, waving letter after letter from his stewards in Reales in Vincent's face, letters that described all the good things Edward was doing for those people: building a new mill, tilling twice as many crops, increasing the livestock and so on. Vincent had remained quietly skeptical. For each letter also had ended with a request for more monies, which Henry had sent and sent until the very day word arrived of Edward's marriage.

Henry had been furious for not having been asked permission, more furious because, ''Dear God, I do indeed know that woman! A claim true for every red-blooded male on the Continent—that hussy is like a great welcoming choir for every landed staff in France. We need to pray your new sister-in-law is barren. We cannot have your lands passed on to her whoreson, her French whoreson. I need to find you an innocent gentlewoman to marry quickly and get with your sons . . .''

Like a mushrooming cloud of doom, it had got worse still. Word had soon arrived that both of Henry's stewards had died suspiciously in a flux at Reales. Vincent had immediately sent his own man, Saladyn, to Reales to investigate just as word had come that Terese had given birth to a son seven short months after her marriage, a son christened with Rodez's hateful name and a boy even Edward had known was not his. And now Edward was dead

and the only thing standing between Rodez Valois and
Vincent's duchy was his next breath. The idea that Edward
had been assassinated led to the important question:
"How?"

Gilgood's eyes narrowed as he said the startling words,
"I am afraid to say Edward, the Lord of Suffolk, hath been
murdered."

A surge of dread filled Vincent's chest. From somewhere far away he heard himself demand, "Murdered?"

"Aye, milord. Countess Roshelle de la Nevers hath
murdered your dearly beloved brother most cruelly before
going on to lead a rebellion that Henry fears might grow
and spread across all of the kingdom of Brittany. And this,
your Grace, is our problem . . ."

The river Reales etched its way through the center of
the tree-lined valley where the shadows of the castle's towers fell over the English camp. Tents stretched on the
southern side as far as the eye could see. The fields surrounding Reales were just being prepared for planting.
First the wheat fields—the bulk of its yield to go to the
estate and the church—then finally the fields of barley and
oats, peas and beans. All able-bodied men labored ardu-
ously behind the plows—since all the oxen had many years
ago been sold off or killed in these depressed times.

Little food remained in the peasants' cottages by spring-
time. All grains, fruits and vegetables had long ago been
consumed; water had replaced ale, and even the wild berries, roots and nuts—the wild supplements on which many
of the people were forced to subsist—had long since been
eaten. The peasants' spring labor was done with bodies
weak from hunger.

So occasionally when a farmer stopped to wipe his brow
and catch his breath, he looked across the hard-worked
soil to where the Englishmen of the army wasted their
time, idling away their afternoon hours on full stomachs—
full stomachs bought by *their* ceaseless labor. When he

returned to his labor, it was with a resentment nearly as consuming as his hatred.

A slight breeze rippled the grass-covered hills rising behind the castle, as well as the black-and-orange colors flying from the towers. A small group of guards stood at the base of the castle and, having little to do, they used the flag for target practice. The English were famous for their skill with the bow, and bets were placed on how many shots would be fired before a strike. To the wild cheers of the men, an older veteran soon hit the flag, ripping a good-size hole in its center before the arrow fell with an audible clang somewhere inside. More guards joined in the game, a vent for their frustration at the two long months spent looking at nothing but the closed walls of the impenetrable fortress.

A messenger rode at a gallop into the camp outside Castle Reales, reining his horse in at the front of the English captain's tent. A servant heralded the arrival with loud shouts that brought the commanding knights running, as well as a host of foot soldiers, grooms and pages. Hearing the call, the captain, John of Suffolk, pushed away his plate of venison, stewed peas and potatoes, and after a swallow of his wine—the only blessed good in the entire wretched country was its wine, sweeter than a whore, he oft thought—the swarthy, stout knight rushed into the late afternoon sunshine to get the long-awaited news.

The rider handed down the scrolled message. "From Rodez Valois, the Duke of Burgundy, in the court of Flanders, sir."

The captain snatched the scrolled paper from the Frenchman's hands and growled, "Better be good this time, or I'm liable to mount my horse and ride to Burgundy to oust the bastard from his velvet-lined seat meself!"

He tore the ridiculous ribbon off the scrolled roll and, neither knowing nor caring a whit how to read, handed the message to the young lieutenant at his side. As a num-

ber of men gathered around, the younger man commenced
reading the carefully scripted paper:

" 'To John of Suffolk, the good and noble captain of
guards of his most exalted and majestic—' ''

"Damn ye," the captain said, more vexed than angry,
"I do not have till sunset! Skip the man's groveling and
get ye on with it."

"Aye, aye." The anxious young man scanned the
lengthy address to get to the text of the letter:

" 'My good Captain, I sleep easy knowing you are in
full control of the most regrettable situation at my Castle
Reales. Lo to my incorrigible young dependent! What
madness hath struck Lady Roshelle I cannot hope to understand—the workings of a woman's mind stray forever
from a man's grasp. Tell the lady to stop her folly and
desist at once! I command thus! Tell her to open those
gates to our English friends today, the very moment she
hears these carefully penned words from her faithful
guardian and lord. Knowing Lady Roshelle rather well, I
have little doubt concerning her compliance.'

" 'I hasten to assure you, my good Captain, should
these rumors regarding my dearest dependent be true—
that her small, slight hand struck Lord Edward a death
blow—you can believe that I fully intend to deal her a most
harsh and just punishment when I at last lay eyes upon
her. So I ask you, my fine and noble friend, to provide
Lady Roshelle with four of the most capable and worthy
knights to escort her at once to Burgundy, where she shall
see a severe punishment for this fabulous farce of hers. I
ask that you provide these four good and noble men with
the livery and colors of Reales, including the necessary
provisions for overnight stays at the inns of Rouen,
Alençon, Angers. The four knights need not be put up in
rooms, though provisions should be extended for their
meals and—' ''

"Stop!" At this point the captain's face appeared beet
red as he clenched his fist and stamped his booted foot,
brimming with fury. "Doth the bastard think me daft?

Doth he think this be some child's game we play here? Good God!'' he cursed, his hand splaying on his forehead as he fought for some control. ''Dispense with his nonsense about the lady's travel plans—does he tell me where these damn passageways are?''

The nervous young man scanned the long paragraphs made of travel ideas, these a slap in their face, as after a two-month-long siege it was abundantly clear the lady had no intention of responding to her guardian's directives— the captain's messages to the Duke of Burgundy at the Flanders court had emphasized this the first week of the siege. Three weeks later, one full month into the siege, the captain had abandoned all hope that the Duke of Burgundy would arrive to end the siege, and why should he when messages like this made it perfectly clear the Burgundian court viewed the Reales siege with bountiful amusement? No doubt the bastards laughed themselves silly over the fools Lady Roshelle was making of the English garrison.

The rebellion spread throughout Brittany as well. Skirmishes sprang up in nearly all the townships flying King Henry's colors, the peasants and common folk gaining courage from the lady's bold, unprecedented move. So far the English managed to suppress these small though significant rebellions, but with each passing day the situation became more volatile. Now the common folk began to express the belief that Lady Roshelle—marked by the famed white streak and cursed to chastity—was aided by God, that He sent an army of angels to further her cause, that the necessary foodstuffs to maintain all fifty or so people inside the castle walls miraculously appeared in the courtyard each sunrise—much like Christ and the wine and bread. Even some of the levelheaded English had begun to believe supernatural powers aided the lady's cause, though not by the powers from above. All the captain knew was that somehow, some way, the lady managed to sneak foodstuffs inside. Of course, Castle Reales had once been wealthy in food substances and grain storage, but Edward had long since dispensed these reserves to his army. So the pressing question was, How did the girl get these provisions inside those wretched walls?

"Ah, here 'tis, Captain. I read as follows: 'I really do not know how they eat at Castle Reales these days. Unlike most other castles built at the turn of the century, this one does not have any secret passageways in or out of the walls—these were cemented and boarded by the Count de la Nevers's maternal grandfather, Count Basil de Reales, some many years past, under the wise premise that if one could get out, then one's enemies could get in. At least this is my understanding. I knew Roshelle was a clever girl the day I married her to her poor late husband, but she must be very clever indeed to fool the entire English garrison, think you not?'

" 'One more note before I sign off, Captain. We at the grand court of Burgundy have heard it said the eminent and legendary, exalted King Henry is most displeased with the whole unfortunate affair at Reales, the famous Duke of Suffolk even more so. We have further heard the goodly knights of Suffolk shall soon be seeing that exalted personage in the flesh at Reales soon—' "

"What be that?" The captain interrupted to demand in a subdued voice, afraid he had heard wrong. "Did he say the duke . . . coming . . . to Reales?"

The young man read the words again, a grin spreading over his face as the glad news brought a loud and long cheer from the men gathered around them. Tension left the captain's face upon confirmation of those words: for the captain's last correspondence with the House of Suffolk had been with Bogo le Wyse, the duke's steward, who simply reported the news had been a blow of incalculable magnitude to the duke, that arrangements were being made to remedy the situation posthaste. Justice, the letter said, would soon be done. The captain never dared to hope that the duke himself would condescend to appear in this wretched hellhole, though God knew, in truth, 'twas a dangerous situation. Henry stood to lose everything if the rebellion kept spreading.

The duke was coming, thank the blessed powers that be! Let those far worthier shoulders carry the growing burden of Reales; he had traveled far, far past his wit's end. At last the wild, rebellious young lady of Castle Reales would meet her demise. No doubt 'twould be painful indeed.

He slapped the young lieutenant on the back and laughed. "Huh! Fifty guldens say the duke fells the castle inside of a fortnight!"

The wager was not popular, for all those who had fought with the duke in earlier campaigns knew it would not take Vincent de la Eresman half that long.

Chapter 2

T he full moon shone brightly behind an arch of smooth gray clouds, providing enough light to toss shadows of old ash and oak trees along the side of the road where two riders rode at a gallop. A terrifying scene emerged vividly in the younger rider's mind: arrows lit aflame, flying through the night to ignite the humble cottages of the country folk, the frantic occupants rushing outdoors, confused, screaming for mercy as they clutched their modest belongings tightly against their hearts. But mercy the English never gave as they viciously murdered, raped and pillaged. This was a scene so common in Brittany as to make it the devil's very playground, a living hell on earth.

"Dear God, let the people be saved!" the rider prayed, spurring the horse to even greater speed.

An old church bell tolled in the far distance, warning the sleepy village of Greve of the riders' fast approach. One by one, men cautiously emerged from their cottages, their pounding hearts chasing any last remnant of sleep from their faces. A number of men ran down from the cottages built against the hillside to join their fellows against this potential threat. Callused, work-torn hands gripped sickles, hammers and butcher knifes, any weapon they could grab as they watched the riders swiftly approach the edge of the village. Scrawny dogs barked wildly. Roosters awoke with crows. Hushing the children, women cautiously poked their heads out from the doorways.

"She be touched by God for sure, destined to saint-
hood—"

"Is Reales still under siege?"

"Aye," the knight said as he fought his mount for the
bit and explained. "The castle is still under siege, but we
have escaped to warn the poor and good people of Brittany. Henry wants revenge. He will see the lady burned
as a heretic, a murderess or a traitor!" He added with
feeling, "That is, if he can catch her. Henry has sent none
other than the infamous Vincent de la Eresman, the Duke
of Suffolk, to reclaim the castle. And this man hath landed
on the shores of Brittany with knights numbering two hundred. The godless barbarians shall ride through Greve on
their way to Reales to subdue the rebellion."

Fearful whisperings expressed the apprehension and
dread this news brought to the simple peasants of Greve.
They shifted nervously on their feet, their minds greeting
this worst of all possibilities. "God have mercy on me
weary soul!"

"The fields—"

"At least the crops have not sprung yet—all the Goddamns can burn is the soil—"

"And my roof! 'Twill take a month to raise up the
cottages, and with no oxen in the next seven villages to
help—"

"Get ye the goats—'tis the only thing keeping the wee
ones from starvation through the famine—that and roots
and berries—"

The knight's eyes narrowed with a wealth of antipathy
as he interrupted. "Aye! Do what ye must! The English
beasts will be mad with a thirst for revenge against the
people. Hide thy womenfolk and children and beasts—
what little they haven't already burned or sacked or pillaged. Let their thirst for French blood go unquenched.
And pray ye for God Almighty's judgment to send them
to much-deserved deaths!"

Potiers' voice—so strangely deep and forceful in the still
night air—inspired a growing fear. All reason dissipated,

swallowed up in the darkness. Two overwrought women ran to the group, crying, "'Tis the Armageddon! Henry be the true Antichrist!"

"The Duke of Suffolk be his disciple! The judgment of the faithful is upon us!"

"Aye! The Antichrist!" An old, withered man suddenly shouted, "It hath been said that when the time hath come, a foreign king shall rise in the west: this king shall be a lord of deceits and killer of men, an esteemer of gold and enemy of the faithful! He hath come! He is Henry of England!"

Shivers raced up spines and tension seized the men as they began exchanging the many signs of the impending Armageddon in a rush of heated words:

"Bands of brigands sacking cities and countryside!"

"Four rainbows arched across the sky less than a fortnight ago! Remember?"

"Two popes in one world, that be the worst sign. If God is not a-shudder at that folly—"

"Hush, good people of Greve!"

All looked up to the young boy.

"Fear ye not God's judgment—the faithful shall be brought into the bosom of heaven! Are ye not the faithful? Are ye not the very souls for whom Christ suffered?" The melodic voice, even more than the reasoned words, quieted the people's fears, and unlike their priests, this young knight promised heaven rather than hell. "Besides, who can say when Armageddon shall be upon us? God alone knows this. And though there be few more wicked men on earth, Henry cannot be the Antichrist. Simply because Henry shall be defeated by the force of good on earth. By us! By the people of France! And his time has come. Let the rebellion spread, let it consume our hearts and minds! The people shall not be subjugated to a false king!"

These words sent a loud and long cheer up, louder as the young knight added, "Long live Charles! And may God soon see him to his rightful crown!"

Like a sudden shift in the wind, the mood of the people

changed, becoming hopeful. When the last cheers died, a call rose from the crowd for the young rider's name.

"What be thy name, young sir?"

"What saint hath warned us, and thereby saved our wives and daughters, and spared what frail beasts we have left—"

"Aye," another cried out, "whose praise shall we sing?"

The rider had turned the stallion toward the road, yet looked back to answer. As the reins were kept checked in one hand, the other thin hand lowered the hood. The men gasped at the sight of a maid, her hair lifted into a crown of braids, each as thick as a man's fist. A maid more fair than a hundred others, they would tell their wives, a maid who looked like an angel and rode like a demon.

"You know my name—I am Roshelle of Reales!"

The cheers died beneath the thunder of hooves as Roshelle and Potiers gave their mounts free rein, racing back to the road. Grinning from ear to ear, Potiers raced after her. Two more villages were left. They would easily make it back before daylight and, with a little luck, slip into the passageway without being seen before the captain woke from his drunken stupor. Four barrels of wine had miraculously appeared on the edge of the army camp—Roshelle's idea, of course—and all the captain would find of their night's adventure would be two mysteriously spent horses.

The wind swept up the sound of Potiers' laughter as they raced along. Within minutes they reached the crossroad, where they split in two different directions. Only two more villages left. And the night was still young.

"Like all of your sex—you are a beast!"

The disparaging words sounded loud in the quiet night as Roshelle sat atop the roan-colored stallion waiting at the crossroad for the rendezvous with Potiers. Knights only rode stallions, which had provided her with a fine choice of mares all her life. She had never before ridden a stallion. The foolish English guards had been so drunk, she and Potiers had decided to steal these right from the heart of the camp, thereby saving themselves the walk to Reales, where their horses were kept hidden. No wonder all knights had spurs! After she'd ridden fast for at least four long hours through the countryside, shouting warnings to every château, cottage and village, and after she'd battled the spirited stallion for control the entire way, the feisty beast still had some fight left in him.

She had only sore bones, tired arms and a keen, new appreciation for knightly spurs that she had never found necessary to use. Seeming to agree, the horse tossed his fine head back, and danced round a circle. Roshelle used her last strength to pull him up again. "Easy, easy, my pet," she whispered as she stroked his sleek neck. "Just a few more minutes, and I'll turn you toward home, hmm?"

This had been the last stop they dared—the army should be just behind. Less than six hours of darkness left to get home again, and through the secret door before the camp began waking.

Potiers, where are you?

As if the question produced the reality, the sound of pounding horse's hooves came from the north. She pulled the stallion up hard and held perfectly still as the dark shape came ever closer into view.

"Potiers!" She led the horse out to the road.

"Milady! Sorry it took so long, but the village Sanmone fell to hysterics. Like before. Ye know how badly they got it when Edward came through—wasn't a woman there who didn't take to running. I sent a boy to warn the people at the château, and then I had to help the menfolk gather the animals. Seems they built some kind of special corral to hide them in—"

"Likewise at Chinon," she said as she reined the horse around. Animals were essential to the peasants' survival. Manure made the difference between a poor crop and a bountiful one, which made it more valuable than gold.

Besides, when foodstuffs were at the lowest point during early spring, a single cow's or goat's milk often kept a family from starvation. "This time we have saved them. The Duke of Suffolk will have no revenge from the poor people of Brittany."

Potiers nodded as they turned their horses east toward Reales, though the simple statement struck at the heart of the matter. Somehow Roshelle Marie felt the responsibility for the people's welfare belonged on her shoulders and she must sacrifice her happiness for them. As Papillion had always warned, she would find her peace and transcend her despair through charity . . .

Papillion's fate . . .

Shortly after Roshelle's first wedding, Rodez generously pledged two hundred livres to Cardinal Cecile de Grair for his ambitious plans to build the largest cathedral in France. Within a week the cardinal announced that Papillion was wanted to stand trial for the sorcery, witchcraft and Satanic domination so diabolically displayed at Lady Roshelle Marie's first wedding.

For many months it was a jest that entertained the entire Orleans court, keeping them all in stitches as Papillion played cat and mouse with the cardinal and his bumbling bands of soldiers, duping them time and time again. No one believed the cardinal would do anything anyway, for everyone, all the world, knew and loved the old sage of the forest house. Papillion had more friends than a honeybee in a summer garden. Why, half the church owed their lives to his medicines! So everyone laughed uproariously as the bishop's men would rush to the guilds or the marketplace, only to discover that Papillion had left long ago or minutes ago or that he had not been there for days or that in fact he was at that exact moment lecturing on the very steps of the cardinal's house . . .

Then one fateful day Papillion's faithful servant Sergio lay on his deathbed, apparently a victim of poisoning. Without a thought of the consequences, Papillion attended him, easing the terrible pain of his last hours. The Christian soldiers appeared and took him away. Within hours they had tortured him and tried him as a heretic of the Christian world. The nightmarish scene emerged in Potiers' mind: Roshelle behind the Orleans guards who forced a way for their passage, so that Roshelle burst into the hall to see Papillion moments before his death. Papillion stood naked and in chains before the inquisition, his body wrecked by torture.

Potiers spotted Rodez immediately as he came up behind Roshelle. He would never live long enough to forget the shock in her eyes as she beheld Rodez's revenge as the cardinal's sentence echoed in the eerie silence of the hall. ". . . condemned unto death to live in darkness and without light, so that your soul shall discover the remorse of living out its eternity in the absence of the God Almighty you have so wickedly shunned—"

Rodez's smile vanished as Roshelle cried, "You have killed him! Oh, God, in the name of revenge you have killed him! God's vengeance shall shine in the memory of her eyes! 'Tis my vengeance as well! Angelique's eyes reveal your doom! Forevermore you are doomed!"

Potiers never knew what happened after that, no one did. For Papillion suddenly cried out, a loud and mournful moan that Roshelle swore formed the words "Beware the ring, Rodez . . ." And then he was dead. Roshelle screamed in a faint, and as Potiers caught the girl in his arms he watched Rodez rush to the body. To get the ring? Did he get the ring? Or had it been gone already? Or was he just making certain Papillion was dead?

That was the beginning of these past torturous years that had at last led to this sorrowful time. The light in the girl's eyes had died with Papillion; she was thrown into the chaos and poverty and destitution that was France as well as her own sad fate. The older man sighed, and hopelessly tossed his gaze to the dark surroundings, trying to distract himself from the unpleasant future.

The air felt moist, fresh and unusually mild for spring. Oak trees lined the road and created a dark canopy over-

head, blocking out the light of the moon riding high across
the cloud-filled sky. The only sound came as the steady
rhythm of the horses' hooves picking their way home. Ha-
zel trees and field maple shrubs dotted the gently rolling
hills and appeared only slightly darker than the night sky.

How she longed for the peace of prayers! The peace that
let her escape from the endless circle of her tired thoughts:
thoughts of the people and their trials and suffering, of the
endless war thrust upon her land, of the dark shadow the
Duke of Burgundy cast over Joan's life. She felt the yearning, the terrible yearning, to find a measure of peace, and
with it, freedom . . .

There was no peace to be found now, and even less
chance for freedom. The thought led her to the encroaching woods and she said, "The forests always return with
the English laying claim to the hard-worked tilled fields.
For one hundred years the history of France is told by the
encroaching forests of beech and oaks and ash. Innocent
timber tells of murder, raping and death brought by the
hands of godless island beasts!"

"Aye," he said, wanting to ease her burden and turn
her thoughts. "Someday it shall be farmland again, milady. I've no doubt you will see to it single-handedly. Are
ye hungry, milady?"

"Hungry? I've a notion of solving both my problems
by getting off this horse and roasting him!"

Potiers laughed, for the lady's appetite was almost as
famous as her gifts. Which was a problem with the poor
foodstuffs of the castle and villages. They kept the horses
at a walk as Potiers handed her an apple and a piece of
cheese wrapped in bread, which she hungrily devoured.
"A maid gave me these, saying 'twas the least she could
do as her thanks."

"Aye," Roshelle said. "In all my years I've never seen
such gratitude as tonight—"

She stopped in mid-sentence and reined the horse to a
stop, turning him around. Instantly Potiers checked his
mount as well, abruptly cautioned by the sound of riders

coming up fast behind them. "Curse the heavens! A scouting party of the duke, I wager!" He withdrew his sword. "Quick, into the trees."

With heels to her horse, Roshelle went quickly through the trees. Tossing his head back for control, the startled horse raced up the hillside at a gallop, Potiers at her side. Too late.

"Halt, ye trespassers! Halt! In the name of the glorious and grand Duke of Suffolk!"

Neither Potiers nor Roshelle heard the ribald laughter that followed the command. All Potiers knew was that his horse was long spent; he'd never beat a chase. He brought his horse up sharp. Seeing this, not understanding, Roshelle, too, pulled on her reins with all her strength. The stallion neighed furiously, raising himself high in the air. Roshelle screamed as she flew through the air, landing hard on her back, the wind knocked out of her. Her hip hit a hard rock. Pain shot through her side, but she ignored it, scrambling up quickly. Potiers jumped off his horse, careful to keep his reins in hand as he came to her aid. "Get on my horse. Quick."

"Nay! You are outnumbered—"

"Get ye on my horse! I've seen worse odds in my day, but I have no chance if I have to defend ye as well! Now—" Five riders broke through the trees. With one hand holding the reins and his sword, Potiers reached down to lift her to her feet, throwing her over the horse and slapping it hard. "Go, milady, go!"

The horse leaped into a gallop.

"Catch the bastard! To the chase!" An anguished cry of distress sounded mute against the wind of her flight as she heard the furious clang of steel. She stole a glance back to see Potiers fighting two men while one circled the fight on horseback, laughing menacingly as he cost Potiers a safe retreat. Two men raced toward her, scaring her nervous horse senseless. The tired mount gave the chase his last legs, but in the wrong direction, the creature so frightened that he no longer responded to the bit in his mouth.

Roshelle cried out as the horse carried her west at wind speed—directly toward the full regiment of the Duke of Suffolk.

She didn't think, couldn't think how to save herself. Darkness sped past her, the wind whipped her face and tears raced down her cheeks. The spooked creature raced past the forked road where she had just waited for Potiers. She clung tightly to the wild beast's side, more afraid of falling off or treacherous rocks and gullies hidden in the dark landscape than she was of the quickly approaching riders. Breathing dangerously hard and fast, and lathered white, the horse suddenly broke into a fast trot.

A small cluster of four or five farmhouses appeared off the road ahead. Roshelle did not hesitate. She flew off the horse as it slowed more, her feet running before they touched the ground. She raced off the road, turning to see the riders speed past on the road. She ran up to the first small cottage, and practically into the door, pounding furiously to wake the occupants.

"Mercy! Mercy! In the name of God and by all that is holy, open the door!"

Several seconds passed before a kindling stick struck a tallow candle, then another. The door opened. With sinking dismay Roshelle viewed the man she would ask to save her. "Wits, Roshelle, wits," Papillion once told her. "You have no strength, but wits pitted against strength wins time and again . . ." As she watched the shadows dance behind the scared old man on crutches, she tried to find some small hope in the fact that Papillion was rarely wrong.

The fastest rider came up at a gallop to the now abandoned horse. Tattooed with the French word for "prince," his strong hand reached out and grabbed the reins even as he turned back around. "The little bastard must have sought shelter from those farmhouses back there!"

Spurs set to mounts, the two riders raced back, stopping again when they met up with their two comrades who had fought that fool with the delusions of grandeur and the heroics of knights. Prince, the leader of the band, eyed

Fort, who held the reins of the finest stallion he had seen inside of a year. "A fine piece of horseflesh."

"Worth his weight in gold, Prince, but lust not. He be mine!"

The dark-haired giant laughed. "Is he, now?" He dropped the reins of the other horse. A sword manifested in his hand and proferred a sudden, vicious strike. Fort cried out and grabbed his stomach. Blood quickly covered his arms as he fell unceremoniously to a heap on the ground, and the others only laughed as Prince grabbed the stallion's reins. "Now let's go get that little bastard and see what he has that's worth dying for. I mean besides his stallion."

"Hide thy hair!"

Deft fingers tied the string laces of an old woman's cotton patchwork gown—the kindly man's long-dead wife's peasant rag. The gown dropped to her knees—the length that separated the laboring class from merchant and noble. A strange light appeared briefly in the kindly old man's eyes as he viewed Roshelle in the painfully familiar rag, and he said, "Somehow I could not bear to part with her things."

Roshelle nodded her understanding, glad for the sentiment that might just save her yet, for the knights would be looking for a boy. No time to contemplate human feeling now, though, as with her heart hammering wildly, not daring to think of Potiers and his fate, she hurriedly unlaced her boots. Peasants were inevitably barefooted and she was now a peasant. She took the scarf to hide the white streak in her hair. The discovery of her identity would be the worst possible fate—they would no doubt use her to force her men to surrender. The man hid the boots with the rest of her clothes in back of a small cupboard in the buttery. He watched the lady dash up the ladder to the straw-covered loft where he used to sleep, before slowly making his way to his modest cot. With an effort, he sat down.

It was Lady Roshelle Marie St. Lille in his humble dwelling, and he still could hardly believe it. He wouldn't believe it if not for that white streak woven into her hair. He had seen her once before at her wedding-day parade, but 'twas from afar and in vastly different circumstances. The idea that Lady Roshelle would be dressed as a boy riding through the countryside to warn of the army's advance fit what he knew of her perfectly; after two months in which the English had been held off at Reales, there wasn't a person in the whole of France who did not herald the name of Lady Roshelle.

Lady Roshelle sat up in his loft, his, the loft of humble Gilles of Brittany, and she depended on his aid to get her through the night alive, needing him to defend her person; he could hardly believe it. His gaze fell to his outstretched broken leg and he cursed it. He had just been making repairs on the roof when—

It did not matter. He would aid the lady or die in the trying. He might not be made of knightly stuff, but he was loyal to the French colors, to the noble lady and to the French cause, and he'd fight—

"Here they come, milady!"

Roshelle threw her head down in a pretense of sleep. Blood pounded furiously in her ears. If the duke's men had but an ounce of decency, they would inquire if there was a boy there, perhaps search the small place, then leave. Please to God keep the good old man safe; she murmured this prayer over and over until—

The sound of horses' hooves thundered up the road. Ribald laughter, curses and shouts came from outside. She held perfectly still, her fingers clutching the dagger, not daring a breath as boots came up to the door.

They did not knock.

The door fell with a solid kick and a loud clamor as it hit the floor. The sudden scent of perspiration, hot, unwashed bodies and foul wine rose from below. She blanched, her gaze flying wildly about the small space. Oh, God, oh, God—

"Where is the little bastard?"

She heard Gilles's pretense of outrage as he struggled up to meet the intruders, his broken leg sliding over the rush-covered earthen floor. "What goes here? In the name of God—"

A hard *thawk* sounded. Gilles's voice stopped in mid-sentence as he fell in a heap over the fallen door. Pale hands flew to her mouth to stop her scream just as drunken laughter sounded below.

"Strike a torch—I need to see."

Did they kill him, dear God, did they murder for no cause? What had she been expecting? A pleasant chat to inquire if the good man of the house might not be hiding any outlaws?

The logs in the tiny hearth crackled with flame and a torch was struck from that—one that would surely bring the whole house down in flames. Then she heard, "Now find me the little wretch."

The demand came with the loud slap of boots on the hard wood ladder and grunts. Her blue eyes darted about the small space, riveting on the bucket left in the corner. She scrambled over and picked it up just as a bearded, ungainly face appeared at the top of the ladder. He took one look at her. "Mercy Madonna—"

Roshelle tossed the bucket with all her might. Luck made her hit his head, and hard. With a brief howl he fell down the four steps into a dizzy heap on the floor. Her knife in hand, she edged quickly to the side of the ladder.

"A goddamn little wildcat up there—"

Yet he was laughing as he grabbed his head, the laughter more frightening than the curses. Another man started up and just as he reached the top, Roshelle thrust the dagger into his arm. He howled, grabbed his arm. Desperately, she tried to pull the dagger out. Flesh ripped viciously as the man fell back and Roshelle screamed. He landed five paces to the floor on his back, the dagger thrust into the thick, ripped muscle of his arm.

The nightmare began.

Roshelle's gaze flew frantically about the tiny space. Nothing left but a thin layer of straw over the hard wood! Her hands went clammy; she panicked some more. Quick as a wink, she scrambled to the far dark corner, but a mercilessly strong hand caught and held her bare foot and she screamed again. A hand wrapped tightly around the other foot, twisting it until she cried from the pain; then, with laughter, he pulled her toward him. Arms wrapped around her waist, squeezing. For a moment she couldn't breathe and desperately she tried to pry his arm loose as he jumped to the ground.

She went wild. Nails raked his bearded face, drawing three neat, thin lines of blood, returning again as her feet pounded and thrashed against the hard muscles of his legs for all she was worth. The frightful giant laughed at this, her struggle putting fire in his loins. "Look at her! Ah, I like my wenches hot!" Abruptly the hands left her person. She stumbled two steps, drew a gasping breath, her heart hammering like a savage drum. She suffered the briefest moment's confusion before she leaped toward the door. Only to be caught by another, his laughter the devil's own as he threw her back to the giant named Prince.

The room spun with dark colors and shapes and shadows and nightmarish faces. Hot, sweaty hands grabbed at her, pinched and hurt her amidst a noise made of howls and hoots, obscene words and laughter, the terrified screams of a young girl as they tossed her back and forth around a circle.

Her screams became a long, ceaseless cry. The hands, the terrible hands, the foul smell of stale wine and sweat and raunch, and the hands, get thine hands off me, make it stop, please to God make it stop . . .

Sick terror formed a desperate, loud and long NO in her mind. The bloodied arm pushed her back to the man Prince. His hands were like spiders crawling over her skin; she had to get them off her, to stop it, to make them stop. A knee lifted into a groin. An unnatural animallike cry sounded above the laughter. An open hand landed hard on her face. She was jolted against the wall, pain shooting from her neck and cheek. "Nooo" sounded weakly as more hands came to her person, lifting her up and holding her with an arm against the hot, foul flesh of a body.

The spinning stopped. Terror seized her heart, she couldn't breathe, as her eyes beheld shadows dancing across the leering faces of four men. Prince caught her flailing arms, bringing them high on her shoulders until she threw her head back and arched in pain. Pale thin legs thrashed like a doomed and hung man. Pain in her arms shot through her body. She didn't know she still screamed until abruptly the sound stopped.

Stopped because the man rose, the one with the knife wound in his arm. Breathing hard and fast, she slowly shook her head as he wiped his mouth with his sleeve, stepping to stand in front of her. The bloody weapon was put to her face. "You like to play with knives, little girl?"

The men laughed at the stark terror in her blue eyes, mounting, growing as the man, unmindful of the grotesque ripped flesh of his arm, ran the dagger lightly across a cheek, then her throat. She closed her eyes tight, bracing to feel the sting of the sharp blade, yet hearing uproarious laughter instead.

"Never seen such a fine, ripe piece! Like a picture, she is!" The words sounded with curious surprise, as if a small miracle stood before them, and in a way she was. "The maid's too pretty by far to ruin with a knife!"

"Cut her open, Beggar!"

The blue eyes flew open as the knife was put to her chest. She tried to scream, but terror made her choke. A bare foot kicked the bloody man in the groin, and he doubled over and fell back. Abruptly she was released. She stumbled forward with a small, weak cry, only to receive another well-aimed blow across her face. She dropped to the floor, washed in a wave of blackness, returning only to feel a mind-numbing pain pounding through her head.

"I'm gonna stick it to you till your innards spill out!"

She was crying, then screaming as his hands came

around her waist and he lifted her up. A knife ripped open her dress. She was thrown down with her backside to the ground. Hands came over hers, pinning them to the floor, then her legs, as the men began placing bets on how many rods the slender figure would take before she died . . .

Wearing the colors of the House of Suffolk, the knights rode east at a lope on the river road. Word that a small band of outlaws using the Duke of Suffolk's name to spread terror to the country folk had reached Vincent just after landing. The illegitimate use of his name was a capital offense; he immediately organized a patrol of his personal knights, demanding they be caught this night. The patrol rode at a fast sprint, knowing the outlaws were somewhere ahead.

Just as they approached yet another split in the roadway, Wilhelm called out, "Halt!"

Vincent tugged once on Gascon's reins and the stallion halted. A lift of his hand, that was all, and the twelve knights behind him brought their stallions up. The dust settled, and the well-trained horses kept still.

"I swear I heard something," Wilhelm, the red-haired knight, said.

The men listened to the pleasant hum of crickets, the nearby rushing river, the soft rustle of a breeze through the trees, all sounding with the shuffle and snorts of their mounts—

There it was, a scream sounded in the far distance, barely audible but enough for Wilhelm to cry out, "From ahead, Vince! Those cottages up ahead!"

Spurs hit the beasts' sides, and twelve mounted knights leaped into an abrupt charge. A cloud of dirt grew behind the riders as they quickly reached the narrow road leading to the cottages. They did not have to wonder which of the four humble dwellings the scream had issued from, for the nearest one had no door. In the darkness they saw the peasants running into the hills behind the house, frightened that they would be next. A child cried out in the night; soft, weakened cries came from the house, too weak to be heard above the chaos and noise of twelve mounted knights rushing up to the house. Sword drawn, Vincent leaped agilely from his horse before Gascon had stopped.

Prince dropped his leggings and Roshelle cried weakly, twisting violently as he went to his knees before her, far too shocked to even know how badly she wanted to die before this thing happened—

Like the charge of Apollo, Vincent burst through the door, and before his gaze had absorbed the scene in front of him, in a burst of inhuman strength and even greater speed, his sword flew. Suddenly the small room filled with colors, bright rich colors of green and blue, swirling, moving colors. For a moment Roshelle thought God had spared her from a moment more of the choking horror; then the colors changed to red. Bright red blood spreading across the naked chest and groin of the man kneeling before her. A weak scream sounded, lost in the sudden chaos of movement. Her arms and legs were released as men jostled in a rush of shouts to reach their swords, but the man's inhuman speed slew another before the scream had even stopped. Four other knights rushed inside. Men were dying with agonized last calls to a God they did not deserve.

The eye could not absorb the speed of his movement or that of his knights. It was over before she even knew it had begun. She felt a sudden warmth draw close to her bare skin, like a gift from heaven, a great blanket of warmth enveloping her as strong arms slipped under her person and brought her body against the great comfort of a man's unnatural strength. More men rushed in to remove the bodies. The clear, decisive, aristocratic voice sounded far away as the man called questions and orders to his men.

"Is the wretch dead? Yes? And that one?"

"Nay, milord—"

"Save him, then—I want him hung at morning light as an example to all outlaws who would dare. Do not ease his pain, though; he deserves every blessed second of it. Look at this child. Dear God, she is in shock. I need a blanket here posthaste!''

Vincent's dark eyes fell on the man beside the door. ''Who is that man? Not one of them?''

''Nay, milord. Methinks the girl's father or husband.''

''Be he dead?''

''Nay, milord. Looks like only a blow to the head.''

''Attend him at once. If he wakes, assure him the girl was saved.''

The girl had buried her face in the velvet doublet across his chest, and her long, scarf-covered auburn hair fell in two braids over his arm. Such long hair, each plait as thick as his fist and the color of red fox pelts. His dark gaze fell to the small pale hand clutching at the hard muscles of his arm as he spoke, a desperate gesture as if to keep him there. The extreme vulnerability and fragility of that small hand tugged at the strings of his heart, and without real awareness as he orchestrated the activities of his men, he reached his hand to hers. She clasped his thumb tightly, as if it were a lifeline, and then like two pieces of a puzzle, his hand covered hers.

Wilhelm handed him a blanket. As Vincent attempted to wrap her cold and naked form, he came to discover his mistake. This was no child. A single brow rose as his dark eyes beheld her slender arms and shoulders, the round, full mounds of her breasts tipped with prominent pink buds—a tease he felt particularly vulnerable to—the mercilessly tiny waist and rounded flare of her hips, before traveling over impossibly long, slender legs. Desire in flesh . . .

Violent shivers shook the small form, reminding him of what she had just survived. The blanket came quickly over her nakedness.

Roshelle drew huge, gasping gulps of air, her consciousness fragmented, and still many minutes behind on the horror she would never live long enough to forget. Hers was a violent time, made up of all manner of death and terrors: wars, pestilence, and brutal slayings, and yet for all of it, little of the violence reached her eyes, far less her person. Her status protected her, like a great glass-enclosed palace; she rarely dwelled in the world gone mad. And though Potiers had taught her defensive measures—how to toss an anlace and wield a saber—though she often rode through the dark dead of night on her secret missions, she had never experienced violence. With the noted exception of Lord Edward, no one had ever touched her with ill will.

The power of the curse shocked her. Nearly three years had passed since she last lay her weary gaze on the old man she loved more than life, but only now did she grasp its power, her first husband and maybe her second, Edward and now these men. The curse had sent this man to slay her evil assailants, so she might survive the fate worse than death. It hardly mattered that he was not just English but an underlord of the Duke of Suffolk, no doubt one of the commanders in the army that marched to Reales to subdue her rebellion. All that mattered was that the curse had stopped the raping that surely would have brought her death. The curse had saved her once again.

The understanding felt heavy, not yet crystallized in her dazed and shocked mind, yielding to the more immediate understanding that it was over, she was safe. Frantically mobilized to fight, her body had yet to respond to the changed circumstances: her heart and pulse still raced, she drew breath first fast, then too slow, then several seconds deprived, in great gasps. She felt hot and cold and shaky all at once. The man spoke the common English with barely a hint of the aristocratic French accent—French was spoken almost exclusively among the English nobility and court. Like Papillion, too. One could never tell from Papillion's accent where he was from: a person was likely to guess an Italian state, a northern German or Arabic one, or that emerald island of the English, though Papillion preferred to speak English and so she had, too. Now even

Cisely, much to Cisely's horror, often found herself speaking the peasants' language . . .

Roshelle tried to gather the fragments of her thoughts to concentrate on the words in the room, but it all sounded distant and vague, like the echoes of a dream. As if he knew, he began whispering soft words of comfort. "'Tis over now . . . 'Tis all over . . . You are safe now . . . you are safe."

He sat upon the straw pallet, careful to keep her in his arms. A gentle hand brought the long ropes of her hair from under his arm, then tucked the edge of the blanket more securely around her. "Let me see your face now, sweetling. I need to see that you are unharmed."

Sweetling. Papillion had called her that . . .

Her blue eyes lifted hesitantly to his face to view him through a hot sting. Blurred pieces of an image formed in her mind: dark hair tied straight back, thick dark brows over widely spaced dark eyes, intelligent eyes searching hers, a brow lifting with curiosity or concern as he did so.

The beauty of her face struck his ability to speak, and for a long moment he could only stare at the lovely blue eyes, so large and translucent as to seem painted by oil colors, then at the delicately sculpted nose and the full, wide lips. A bruise quickly formed on one side and he cursed the idea that the man who did it had but one death. Her skin seemed unnaturally pale but exquisite, nearly flawless save for a small, faint mark of a childhood bout with the pox on her chin. What in heaven's name was such a beauty doing in a peasant hovel?

His gaze took in the humble dwelling, then returned to her face as if he were trying to reconcile the two. She hid again in his chest. A peasant's days filled with little more than arduous toils, labors that took a toll on faces and hands. Hands—

He lifted her small hand for a close examination. Yet another contradiction. Smooth, pale skin covered a lady's delicate hand on one side, yet small calluses showed on the other. A gentle thumb traced over a small callus, one got from . . . reins.

She did not belong to that elderly man of the cottage by either marriage or blood, that much seemed sure. Few peasants could afford even an ox, let alone a horse, to aid in tilling the fields; none could afford a beast to mount. Besides, her beauty would no doubt draw out the purses of every man who viewed her. Here was something else—

"Milord, the man has come to. He says the girl is not his. She and her man were traveling at night when the outlaws overtook them and she ran to his house for help—"

A violent shiver shook her, and she reached for his hand. "Please help my servant. He was attacked in the field just to the north of here. I fear the worst—"

He watched anxiety and pain fill her blue eyes. "Wilhelm—"

"Aye, at once."

"Dear God, he will be needing me." She started up, but his arms gently restrained her. "I must go to him—"

"Nay, not yet. You are too weak, trembling still. My men will attend him. If he be wounded, they will bring him to you."

She turned her face against his tunic, the entire force of her being centered on a prayer for Potiers' safety. Potiers was her most faithful servant and friend. She did not want to think of what her life would be like without his companionship and aid and strength.

"The man is someone you care about?"

She nodded. "He has served me nearly all my days and there are few alive I love more, methinks, and if he is wounded or . . . oh, *Dieu!* No, make him live—please, if he be wounded, I need, I need to be ready. My clothes—"

Vincent set her easily onto the pallet, stood up and looked about the room for the discarded remnants of her gown. "I do not think—"

"No, not those." She shook her head, trying hard to concentrate. She felt so strangely numb, her heart pounding first fast, then slow, then fast again. She could not stop shaking. "I . . . I wore the good man's deceased wife's clothes to trick them, knowing they were looking for a boy. The good man hid my clothes behind the cupboard in the buttery there."

Maids dressing as boys to disguise their sex was a common enough practice to have the church declare it a venial sin, and while Vincent offered no comment, his eyes alone managed to express what he thought of the practice. Or perhaps what he thought of a world where such tactics were necessary.

He found her clothes and handed them to her, staring at her as he did so. Her blue eyes met his as if seeing him for the first time, and she was. The fire danced in the small hearth and shadows played over the uncommon strength revealed in the arresting features of his face: the thick, neatly combed hair, the remarkable eyes—lit with an unmistakable restlessness and impatience—and thick brows, the fine, large nose and mouth, a square-cut, cleanly shaven chin with, *mon Dieu,* the mark of a perfect cleft! "Beware the perfect cleft, a mark of the most powerful, a man whose unnatural luck and fortune is nothing compared to the force of his will," Papillion had once told her. She had plenty of reason to believe it now, for she abruptly grasped that here was a lord of King Henry's realm.

His clothes were an austere expression of his status. The coat of arms of the House of Suffolk—two crossed swords over a torch lit with flames—stood out in blue-and-gold velvet stitched against the thick dark green gambeson, fastened by a metal-studded, thick black belt. Brass-metal breastplates were sewn into the chest, and the shoulders were lined with thick black leather that perfectly matched suede breeches. He wore no other armor, not even chain mail. His height and the width of his shoulders spoke of a well-exercised and uncommon strength, while his ease and presence spoke of barely restrained power.

"Your name?" he asked in a deep whisper that hinted

at an uncanny suspicion. "I would know your Christian name."

The hairs lifted slowly on the back of her neck. Her name was absolutely the last thing he'd ever hear spoken from her lips. Footsteps sounded and she hurriedly pulled the long doublet over her head, pulling it down before letting the blanket fall. Leggings followed. She reached to her boots.

In four strides, the great red giant appeared at the door, bending so as not to hit his head. Between the two knights, the room shrank. Flaming red hair brushed his broad shoulders, and firelight danced in his sharp brown eyes. Every maid's worst nightmare, like his master, the tall, red-haired lion looked made of muscle and ready to fight, clad in a dark brown, ermine-lined doublet, suede breeches and tall black boots. A long sword hung from his thick black belt. Before she understood what it meant, the unusual compassion on the man's face struck her like a blow, at first because the plain emotion seemed ill-suited for his face and appearance, then because she realized the emotion was meant for her.

"The man. He be badly wounded."

"*No.*" The word came as a plea as she jumped up and ran two paces before the room of wooded colors and firelight and shadows swirled into a melting gray that stole her breath. She stumbled, tried to catch herself. Those strong arms swept under her, she heard a curse before, with sheer force of will, she attempted to pull herself up from the darkness that threatened. "Please . . . I can walk, I—"

"Apparently not without fainting. I will take you to his side."

He carried her out into the night air. His knights had lit the area with torches. Peasants gathered on the side, solemn and still shaken, though no longer frightened, due to the aid and assurances of the knights. Potiers lay on a litter. The sight gave her strength, and with a desperate twist of her legs, she touched the ground and ran to his side. "Potiers! Potiers! *Mon Dieu.*" She stared upon his ripped and bloodied jerkin. Blood oozed from a huge, jagged chest wound. Another wound bled at his thigh. Either wound alone was enough to lay a far younger man to the ground. Still, no one on earth could manage to call up more hope than the girl at his side. "I need torchlight here," she said as she hurriedly pulled off his boot. "Shears and boiling water and cloth for bandages. Use the ripped dress in the cottage. Hurry. *S'il vous plaît*—hurry."

The men exchanged confused glances, certain the wounded man needed only a priest. Vincent motioned with his head, that was all, and two men rushed to do her bidding. She pulled off his other boot. With an effort she ripped open a legging, then the other side. These she wrapped quickly around her hands, which she then pressed to Potiers' chest to stop the bleeding. With a grimace he woke up, took one look and managed to smile. "Blessed saints, ye are well!"

With all her strength she forced away her tears and graced him with a smile. "Aye! And little thanks to you! I had to be rescued by the English!"

"Ye gawds, a fate worse than death. I shall never hear the end of it."

"And why, just look at yourself," she scolded, desperate to keep him to her as she felt the precious lifeblood soak over her hands. "Not just one wound, but two. Two of them. You will probably be wanting a month of free days for your recovery, and what am I supposed to do without you, I wonder—"

A woman rushed up with a pair of shears just as a man returned with the dress, torn into strips. "The water is heating as I speak."

She quickly discarded the soaked bandages and wrapped her hands in the other two, returning them at once to the wound. She felt the dull throb of his wound, slowing. His face blurred; she caught her lip as someone knelt beside her. A gentle hand came to her eyes, wiping the tears so that she might see, Vincent moved beyond words by the depth of the young girl's love for her servant.

Potiers stared up at her. "Milady, milady," he said in a whisper, "there is something I must tell you now . . ."

Tears washed her eyes and she leaned closer so that no one might overhear. "Papillion wanted me to tell you when the time came, when you at last found peace, but I cannot wait—"

"Tell me what?"

"Your mother, Roshelle. Papillion loved your mother. You are his daughter . . ."

Shocked disbelief changed her eyes, but just for a moment. For as her mind greeted the revelation, it was only to see it was not really a revelation at all. As if she had always known it, and she supposed she had. For to look into Papillion's eyes was to see her own, and Papillion had always been her father in heart. And she knew the Count of Lyons and Bourges could not have been her father, except in name . . .

"You . . . you are not surprised?"

She shook her head.

"Milady"—he forced a smile—"keep Joan safe from the rain."

"Aye. Always . . ."

"I love you, milady . . . I have always loved you. May God keep you forever safe . . ."

"Potiers." She placed her trembling lips over his, but the slow beat of his pulse stopped. He went very still. She shook her head. "No . . . no, Potiers." But it was too late. The bandages came off and she grabbed his still warm hand, burying her face against it. Vincent let her stay that way as long as he could before he reached down to pull her away, motioning to his men to cover the servant's body. "No." She tried to escape, but with a sage's wisdom, Vincent held her firm until she collapsed with the acceptance.

A dark cloud settled over her dazed and weary mind, and she was hardly aware of what happened next as her mind repeated the denial over and over again. She vaguely understood the man's orders to one of his knights to return to camp and have the army prepare for the march to Reales at morning light, that they would join them when they reached that spot. All this was said as he took her back inside the cottage. Just outside the door she heard the Frenchman's gushing words of inexpressible gratitude for something, some compensation given him, yet this, too, was but a haze in her mind. Holding her in his arms on the small pallet, the man wrapped his strong arms around her while her slender frame shook softly with tears.

Gradually the denial began to fade, like the distant echo of a nightmare too terrible to be real. Consciousness became a haze as her senses filled with their surroundings: a clean masculine scent of hard-worked leather and sea-washed skin. She heard the quiet crackle of the fire in the hearth against the swift, steady beat of his heart as she succumbed to the utterly intoxicating warmth of his arms. An unknowing finger traced a feather-light line over the prominent muscle of his forearm, unaware of the effect of this. No man had ever held her such. Yet she did not wonder at this strange comfort. Too tired and dazed to think, she yielded to the compelling warmth and security got by the press of his body against hers until . . .

Long dark lashes fluttered over the mesmerizing blue eyes, and he released his first easy breath, his entire body rigid and hot with previously unknown desire, his body maddeningly unconcerned with the horror and tragedy the young lady had just survived.

Not since he was thirteen!

He stared for a long moment at her still and sleeping form bathed in firelight. That she was beautiful was an understatement, but beauty alone rarely dictated the race of his blood. Not to this extent. Nay, there was something else here, the heroic proportions of her struggle and fight, a certain vulnerability and innocence, all of which sat alongside her love for her servant. "I love you . . . I have always loved you . . .'' He understood how she had in-spired such devotion. The girl was a rare and beautiful creature indeed.

Soft breaths came from her slightly parted lips and he gently traced a line across the edge of the scarf that hid her hair. He wanted to see that hair—

"A little warm for ye in here, Vincent?"

He looked over to see Wilhelm bending in the doorway. "Warm? Nay, more like drawn alongside a raging fire. Her beauty is like a delicate—"

"Delicate? You should have a look at the wound her dagger put in one of them, this girl who looks as fragile as a porcelain vase but who rides a half-wild stallion bare-back across a war-torn countryside in the dark middle of the night dressed as a boy. Delicate? Methinks not."

Vincent conceded the point with a grin. "I need to know her name," he began as he stepped outside with Wilhelm, but stopped when he discovered the sea of peasants' faces gathered in this night outside the small house. The men held shovels.

The Duke of Suffolk commanded a frightening pres-ence. He stood to his full height, hands on hips. The light of the cottage fire shone behind him, outlining his im-pressive form. His intelligent eyes searched the back-ground where his men had already collected the necessary logs and twigs for the funeral pyre in anticipation of his wishes.

"Milord." Gilles, the older man, stepped nervously forward. A hand went to his bandaged head as he looked behind him for support before turning back to the Duke of Suffolk. "They be godless beasts in this life for sure, but their souls belong to God for the judgment. 'Tis a sin and heresy not to bury them proper."

Standing off to the side, the knights of Suffolk smiled, familiar as they were with Vincent's iconoclastic views of the church, the one in question being that the church's insistence on burial had nothing to do with God and everything to do with the church's burial fee. "Huh." He scowled, irritated but kind enough to answer the peasants' concern within the limits of their own understanding. "Think you God needs a boxed body to make a judgment? More to the point, think these wretches are deserving of your hard labor and sweat, old man? And do we have any doubt of where their pitiful souls are headed?" He shook his head. "Disease is known to fester on rotting flesh, and God knows this wretched land has seen enough disease. Nay—my will be done. I say they burn into ashes. The wind and air can bury their sorry souls."

The peasants exchanged confused glances. A woman took Gilles's sleeve in hand and, too timid to pose the question to the duke, she forced Gilles to do it. For they both knew who the lady was and therefore what her servant deserved. "Milord, the lady's servant. Surely he is deserving of a Christian burial?"

A surprised brow lifted. "Lady? I knew she belonged in the clerical class, but a lady?" Actually, he had been thinking some lord's by-blow, but— "Know you her name?"

The surprise question and the frightened silence brought the men of Suffolk to abrupt attention, the group of peasants receiving their interested gazes. The sudden tension among the peasant folk filled with fear, and a great fear it was as anxious eyes searched their neighbors' faces. "Nay." An older woman found her courage, a courage shadowed by a faint tremble in her voice. " 'Twas but a slight, milord. We do not know the girl or her name."

Their fear increased tenfold each second Vincent's steely gaze held them to his will. So the girl, whoever she was, was known around the countryside and able to solicit the uncommon courage and protection of the peasantry. Only one person he knew of could do that.

Something dark and dangerous came into his eyes as he answered his own question. "So 'tis a knight of Reales whom you ask me to bury, and for a lady who belongs in the court of Countess Roshelle of Reales. Perhaps even one of the countess's women?''

Not quite, but predictably, no one thought to correct his error. Intrigues made many things better left unsaid. Roshelle's name and title were two of them.

Chapter 3

A gainst the sound of obscene laughter, vicious hands came to her person, grabbing, squeezing, pushing—
"No!" Roshelle bolted up, a hand came to her mouth to stop her scream and terrified eyes opened to see—

"Gilles! Oh, God." Her stomach somersaulted twice, then once again. She grabbed her chest as the whole terrible world came back at her in a rush. "Oh, dear God, 'tis you—"

"Shh." A weathered finger on his lips, he glanced at the door. "Milady, he hath discovered, not yet your name, but that you be from the court of Reales. He be plannin' to use you as a hostage, he is! He be thinkin' the sight of you will open the castle gates to his army. 'Twould work only too well! You must escape!"

She took this in as she searched his face. "Where is he now?"

"Down by the road. In the company of his knights. He has sent orders for the army to march. Hurry—'twill be now or never."

Roshelle swung her feet to the ground and rose, cautiously approaching the door to peer out. As if waiting for the moment her consciousness returned, tears immediately formed in her eyes, threatening to overwhelm her once again. Potiers was dead, dead, and she would be without his strength and support for the rest of her days and how, dear God, how could she carry on without him? After

81

Louis and Papillion? When she realized she couldn't, emotions swirled, bursting through her—

Nay, not now! Not now!

Roshelle drew a deep breath. With all the force of her will, she pushed the emotions back. She had to get out of here. Now, before 'twas too late! That lord's kindness depended wholly on his ignorance of her name. "He placed me at court?"

"Aye. He thinks that you must be one of your women. They are for the moment distracted, their backs to the house. See them down by the road?"

"Aye." She nodded as she stared at the horses, tied at the fence post. The sound of a rooster spoke of the imminence of dawn's light. The quiet whispers of men conversing came from far away. A horse neighed, a horse—

She needed a horse.

As if she had survived a holocaust—and she had—weakness racked her each and every limb. She clasped her hands together to stop the trembles that shook through her. Chilled and the worst kind, from the inside out.

"Do ye think ye can slip past them?"

"Aye, I am well trained in such. I must take a horse, too. Stay quiet inside until I am gone, then slip back outside so as not to be blamed." Her blue eyes filled with unspoken gratitude, she took his hands and held them tightly. "One day I shall return to give you proper thanks." She kissed his forehead. "God be with you."

"May God keep ye safe, milady."

She forced herself up and to the door, the slight movement causing a wild thumping of her heart. The gray light of dawn spread over the landscape. It was quiet; not a breeze stirred. The rooster crowed again. From the distance she heard the quiet whispers of men conversing. Her gaze swept the darkened landscape, stopping at an old cart, where the knights were gathered round. She made out his tall shape and that of his man Wilhelm; both their backs were to her.

Papillion had taught her how to disguise her scent with

clover and then move in the near perfect silence of the night, forcing her to practice over and over until, like a cat stalking prey, she could approach almost any creature in the utter quiet of the dark without rousing its keen senses. She exercised the hard-learned lesson now. Her feet made not a crack or a creep, her breathing sounded low and still and only she could hear the steady pounding of her overworked heart as she crept alongside the house, then passed swiftly out from its side before coming to the half circle of horses tied to a tree post.

There he was, the stallion she had ridden. Through the gray light she saw his dark eyes watch her with interest. He tossed his head back as if in greeting, and in the way that Papillion had taught her to commune with the creatures, she closed her eyes, focused her consciousness and tossed it to the horse, a trick that required, among other things, a leap of faith undreamed of by the most pious theologians—a leap few rational mortals could make. In the wink of an eye, the familiar queer numbness overcame her body, as she became only a consciousness that focused entirely on the creature. Focused with the express demand of his cooperation and calmness as she untied the reins.

The beast did not move. Indeed, he seemed to have stopped even his breath as she brought him out from between two others, then silently led him over the rocky terrain behind the house. At the top of the hillside and out of sight, she pulled the reins over his head, leaped onto his back, and in that moment she and the creature became the wind.

Not much later Wilhelm stepped inside to check on the lady. A soft, vicious curse sounded as he shouted, "Vincent, the lady hath fled!"

The Duke of Suffolk's gaze shot to the horses, where he saw the missing stallion. Nothing would have frightened Roshelle more than the impressive sound of his amusement, laughter that said he was hardly surprised and certainly not alarmed. For the Duke of Suffolk had absolutely no doubt he would be laying eyes upon the girl again, and soon. Only too soon.

The sun had not yet reached the meridian when Roshelle dismounted a safe distance from the army camp. She slapped the beast's back. Hooves lifted into the air and the spirited animal galloped off toward the camp. She quickly disappeared into the forest, heading through the thick brush and the cover of the trees toward the passageway.

Anxious blue eyes peered through the bushes at the bustling camp activity as the men prepared for the imminent arrival of the duke and his army. Three men carried fresh water to the troughs, four others cleaned the corral, a handful of others raked the ground in preparation of erecting new tents. Another large group went through the paces of a drill. No one looked her way, and while usually she and Potiers would never dare to slip down the hatch in broad daylight, she had no choice now. She must return at any cost.

Careful not to displace too much dirt, she lifted the wood door and, as quiet as a mouse, her lithe body disappeared. The latch shut the light out. She threw the bolt. A complete darkness surrounded her and its security made her knees weak. Suede boots touched the cold, wet stones of the ground as she oriented herself. No light ever shone here. The dank passageways had been boarded up for decades, but it had been a simple matter of two weeks' work to open them up again. The English had never found them.

With one hand on the wall like a blind person, she ran along the tall and narrow corridor for several minutes, tripping when she at last came to the short flight of stairs going down beneath the moat. The tiny patter of rodents' feet and the steady drip of water sounded in the wet and narrow passageway, louder than her labored breaths. A chill raced up her spine. She slowed her pace just a bit until at last the stairs went up again. The passageway widened beneath the great hall. She ran until she reached the long stairs.

* * *

Cisely stared in terror at the bright light streaming through the window and abruptly jumped to her feet from where she had been kneeling in prayer. "Merciful Mother, where is she? 'Tis almost noon! *Mon Dieu,* why has she not returned?"

Joan smiled. "Roshelle is coming."

Cisely's anxious gaze shot to Joan, sitting peacefully on the bed with that cat she loved so, smiling at her with neither a care nor a thought. Roshelle was right: God breathed His spirit into the simpleton's heart. All Joan ever knew was love and simple joys: the splash of sunshine on her face, a warm winter fire near her feet, the delicious scent of Roshelle's fresh-picked roses, a new colt or lamb in the stables, a slide leading to a cushioned pile of hay. Worse than a child, she was only ignorance and bliss.

"Oh, what do you know, Joan? Why is she not back yet? The sun is high and oh, *Dieu!*" She felt the unnatural pounding of her weak heart, and it frightened her. "What if she does not return to us?"

Joan stroked the cat's head. "Roshelle is coming."

Fear seized Cisely's pretty face, and ignoring Joan, she clasped her hands tightly together to stop their trembling. She was four years Roshelle's senior, and a distant second cousin by marriage on Roshelle' father's side. Cisely had known Roshelle since the day Roshelle was born and she was Roshelle's favorite; she had always been Roshelle's favorite. They had been raised in the Orleans court, and except for the time Roshelle had spent in the forest cottage with the old man, Papillion, the two young women had shared the same life: the same guardians and tutors, history and friends. With the exception of Roshelle's sojourns with Papillion to the university in Paris and to Basel, in all her life she had been separated from Roshelle only once, and it had taught her an important lesson.

Upon coming of age, Cisely had married her betrothed, Count de la Soissons, and moved to his household, a fine château in Limoges. Two short months later he died in the famous battle of Agincourt, along with nine-tenths of the nobility. Secretly, shamefully, she had been relieved by her husband's death—so much so that she had considerable trouble concealing a burst of joy upon receiving the news. Not just because her greatest fear was childbirth, or even because her relationship with her husband had been cold, distant and painfully formal—his mistress had actually lived in the château with them—but mostly because the two months she had lived in her husband's house were the most unhappy of her life.

For she had missed Roshelle with every breath.

Nothing had prepared Cisely for the contrast between life with Roshelle and life without her. Despite her ongoing complaints about the hair-raising anxieties and constant catastrophes of Roshelle's life, about Roshelle's relentless energies, her never-ending ministries and alms to the needy, the curse, the rebellions and battles against ills and the terrible effect all this had on Cisely's fragile health, despite all this and much to her surprise, life without Roshelle had been empty. As worthless and hollow as a house without walls. She still didn't quite understand it. All of Roshelle's love, she supposed—Papillion had always said love was as essential to human beings as food and drink and what if that were true, then she would die with Roshelle—

The thought made her panic. "She has died! I know she has died—''

"Roshelle is coming."

Joan's very pronouncement sounded as the slight creak of the latch opening brought Cisely's head around in the instant. Wide amber eyes flew to the spot and Cisely took one look before collapsing with her relief. "Roshelle! Oh, Roshelle. Merciful Mother in Heaven—''

The sight of Cisely's pale, pretty face surrounded by a halo of tight dark curls brought Roshelle a swift swell of emotion. She collapsed half in and half out of the trapdoor opening. Gathering her poor skirts, Cisely dropped to the floor and using all her strength, she pulled Roshelle through. Or tried to. Cisely's slight, reed-thin frame left her hopelessly weak of limb.

As dependable as the sun rising on darkness, Joan came quickly to help. She knelt beside the latch door, the neat plaits of her knee-length blond hair—like spun gold, it was—coiling beside her. Strong hands came under Roshelle's arms, lifting her into the room. "You have come." Seeing Joan's treasured smile brought another surge of emotion, as if Roshelle had been gone a year.

For Joan was Papillion's gift to her life.

The latch door fell with a thud.

Roshelle tried to catch her breath as Joan's loving hands went to smooth her tousled hair. Yet as Cisely took in the shock of Roshelle's appearance, her eyes widened. "Look at you, milady! You look terrible! Why, you are as, as filthy as a penned pig and, and, dear Lord, what, what in heaven's name are you doing wearing those, those awful . . . Achoo—"

Cisely sneezed, removing a mouchoir from her sleeve. Roshelle tried to catch her breath as her friend sneezed again. Horses made Cisely sneeze, and after the long ride, Roshelle had enough hair and sweat on her person to cause the same effect.

Daintily Cisely wiped her nose. But as soon as she saw the blood covering Roshelle's tattered clothes, her joy disappeared. Oh, dear God. Roshelle was wounded, Roshelle was bleeding—

Her delicate hands went clammy; her face drained of color. She tried to scream, but no sound issued from her throat as with some small wonder she abruptly realized she had stopped breathing . . .

"Cisely! Cisely—no, do not faint—"

Too late. Like a sheet dropped to the ground, the young lady folded into a neat pile on the floor. Joan stared at the spectacle with mild interest. "Cisely is not well."

Dismay and, perhaps unkindly, irritation lifted in Roshelle's grief-stricken face. That girl dropped at the sight of blood with the same regularity that a rooster crowed! "No,

she is not well,'' Roshelle said breathlessly, stumbled up,
with Joan's help. ''Thank the heavens for you, Joan.''

Thank heaven indeed. Papillion had sent Joan—the
third of his loves, he always said, after her mother and
herself—to ease the pain and anguish of these past long
years, not knowing how much more the sanctity of this
golden love would cost. How she cursed and blessed the
rain-washed night so long ago when Papillion had awakened her from a deep, dream-filled sleep. ''Up, up! Get
dressed, Roshelle. Hurry—''

''Dressed? What? Why? 'Tis raining. Nay, nay, pouring—''

''She is calling to you. She is awash in a sea of distress,
more frightened than we can know. Potiers and four other
knights will go with you—''

''Where? Who? Papillion, I do not—''

''Hurry, Roshelle. Outside. Somewhere—no, wait, she's
outside the cathedral in—oh, God, 'tis worse than I
thought. Hurry on!''

And so, with Potiers and four knights, she marched out
into the driving rain of a dark night. Rain pounded the
two-story-high stone houses that lined the street. Thinking
her quite mad, the good knights waited for her instructions
and she felt a good deal more than foolish as she pointed
to the cathedral. Yet she could not move; her boots had
sunk so far in the river of mud that Potiers had to literally
lift her out.

'Twas madness, or so she thought, remembering all the
many times Papillion had sent her on wild-goose chases
before confessing, ''I suppose I was wrong about that . . .
Ah, well . . .'' Yet as they rounded the corner of the far
cornice of the cathedral tower, she heard the whisper of a
voice: ''Helpmesavemehelpmesavemehelpmesaveme . . .''

A terrified young girl sat waist-high in mud beneath the
pounding rain, her arms and legs pinned in the locked
wood scaffold of the stocks. She had been forgotten. The
street cleaners had piled a small mountain of manure
mixed with hay nearby, and in the pounding rain the pile

drained in a river of mud higher. and higher against the scaffold. Abject confusion and fear mixed with the desperate whisper of her plea, a plea that echoed through her dreams even now, many years later: "Helpmesavemehelpmesaveme . . ."

"Potiers, your halbert! Quickly!"

"Milady," another man said as Potiers raised his halbert to free the girl, "interfering with the church's punishment could land a death sentence—"

"Just do it! Now. I will take the responsibility."

"Helpmesavemehelpmesaveme . . ."

"I will save you, I will help you . . ."

And no one ever discovered why the girl had been punished, a punishment that more often than not resulted in death. Afterward, when it became clear that Joan was not suffering from shock but was simple, Louis made the inquiries. Yet no one in the church seemed to remember the girl or her crime, or even, strangely, her condemnation. To know Joan, too, was to know 'twas absolutely impossible for her to have ever committed a crime, any crime . . .

For Joan's spirit was as sweet and pure as sunshine, more precious than any other. Which was why Rodez used Joan to command Roshelle's obedience. For Joan was the one person, the only person, whom she would always keep safe; forevermore she vowed to keep her from the fear of rain-washed nights . . .

Roshelle's hand came to Joan's lovely face. The girl was so beautiful! Unlike many other simpletons, she revealed nothing of this by her appearance. The girl's strength defied her average height and slim, comely figure. A flawless complexion added to her healthful good looks and, of course, the uncut hair—long gold hair that fell in neat plaits to her knees.

"You have come," Joan repeated.

"Aye, but Potiers, he hath been killed."

The deep brown eyes lowered with sadness before she

genuflected. "Potiers hath been killed," she repeated in her strange, even tone. "This is sad."

"Aye." Roshelle's eyes filled with fresh tears. "My heart is weak with grief. You must go tell the others. Tell them Potiers died after we warned the countryside of the advancing army." She closed her eyes, trying to collect her thoughts, but somehow she could only think of the hands ripping at her person. "I need, I very much need a bath. Tell the kitchen maids to heat the water. And"—she cast her gaze on her fallen friend—"ask Jean Luc to come here and put Cisely to her bed."

Joan nodded and set off at once.

Within minutes the bells had rung and the guards lowered the French colors on the battlements. Father Martin prepared for mass to be sung in Potiers' name. Jean Luc, one of Roshelle's personal guards, hurriedly arrived to lift Cisely to her bed. A hot bath was being prepared as three maidservants fussed over and comforted Roshelle.

Within an hour Roshelle's head lay on Joan's lap. Joan's gentle fingers soothed back Roshelle's wet hair while she listened to the large orange cat purr and Roshelle's last words: "I know now why Papillion gave the curse to me." Roshelle closed her eyes, shuddering visibly as she remembered the hands, the terrible hands grabbing, ripping, hurting, the threat of a fate worse than death. "To save me from a fate worse than death."

"The curse kills men. They are dead now." This apparently was all Joan had gathered from Roshelle's story, and she added as habit, knowing she should, "Mercy for their souls." After a moment she said, feeling she ought, "Bless the lord who saved you."

"The lord who saved me?" The erroneous idea gave Roshelle a sudden burst of energy and she sat halfway up. "He was a brute! Like all English lords!"

"Aye, brutes. All men are bad."

"Well, not all men," Roshelle said tiredly, feeling she should correct this idea. One never knew where Joan's ideas might lead, and though usually they led nowhere at all, she knew from experience to be careful in explaining things. "Think of Papillion. Was he bad?"

"Papillion cursed you."

"But that is my point. The curse saved me, Joan, it saved me."

"Bless the lord who saved you."

Roshelle sighed, seeing it was no use. Sometimes Joan seemed to understand almost everything, while at other times it was obvious the girl did not grasp the simplest statement. Although Joan could easily follow a series of ten orders given only once, she could never repeat one of them. Then out of the blue she might become confused, not knowing where she was or what she was doing. Papillion had believed her feeblemindedness was the result of a blow to the head that injured her reasoning faculties, damage that fluctuated according to unknown conditions.

As Joan gently eased Roshelle's head back onto her lap, a vivid memory sprang to mind to counter the passionate exclamation, a memory of his consuming warmth and great strength, the compelling light in those remarkable, darkly intelligent eyes. The unexpected memory made her thin dark brows go cross and she repeated harshly, "That English lord was but the means, no more. 'Twas my curse that saved me!"

"Aye, bless the lord."

Roshelle sighed. "I hope you mean the one in heaven and not the one destined for hell."

"We will see Potiers in heaven."

"Not soon, I hope," Roshelle replied distractedly as she thought of the future. "If we can just hold out against the duke's army for another month, maybe two, then Charles will be able to persuade those impotent old counselors of his to secure enough men of arms for another French army! And if that happens, then do you not see, Joan, Rodez will have to show his French colors! He'll have to! Surely the Duke of Suffolk is as pernicious and greedy as his brother and he will tire of paying his army to do no more than sit under the battlements." A deliciously wicked thought entered her mind. ''And perhaps, why, yes, I shall put a flux in their drinking water—Papillion gave me the recipe for one once. I believe it's listed on that worn parchment in the book.''

''Flux is bad. Edward is bad. Men are bad, but not him, not the lord that saved you.''

Roshelle no longer listened as Joan lovingly stroked her long wet hair. A good two feet of wet auburn hair lay across the bed; Roshelle's skin glowed pink from her womenfolk's scrubbing. Yet dark red rings circled her eyes from weariness, a bruise formed on one side of her face, more showed on her arms and her hands were raw from the relentless tug of leather reins. Just as sleep pulled her gently into darkness, the image of a handsome face, darkly intelligent eyes, wide, full lips and the perfect cleft chin emerged unbidden in her mind. She tried to banish it, but the image remained, spinning into her dreams . . .

The warm sun filled the afternoon sky, appearing as a heavenly sent light shining through enormous billowing white clouds. Into the quiet afternoon air, Reales' bells suddenly sang out, ringing in a quick succession of frantically clanging sounds. A fine, strong breeze rippled through the bright green grass edging the woods where a group of barefoot peasant girls gathered what they might to subdue the persistent roar of their stomachs—nuts, berries and an occasional root or two for the porridge pot. The ringing of the bells made them stop and look up.

'' 'Tis the English duke and his army! *Mon Dieu!*''

The girls burst into a dash down the hall. ''Mama said to find her before going to watch—''

Too late. Despite the word that this English army's approach had been peaceful and orderly with no raping, pillaging or even looting, the French had long ago grown wary of any advancing English army. And every child had heard the fanciful stories of coin-tossing into the crowds by certain members of the English aristocracy, and though the duke had reason to punish the entire township of Re-

ales, the idea of a coin in their hands and what it would
mean for their families, on top of the excitement of the
march, bade the girls, indeed all the people, to toss caution to the wind and race outdoors to see the famous man.

The townsfolk arrived first, gathering four-deep at the
roadside. What little business remained in Reales came to
a stop as the large Boulanger family—all eleven of them—
set down stoneware and cooled the ovens before stepping
outside. The smithy workers—also the armorer, the work-
less tailors, even Phillips, the township's poor, ailing
shoemaker—who everyone knew refused to stop work even
on the Sabbath—stepped outside his modest shop to watch.

Phillips tried to flex his three dead fingers as, gathering
his squashed courage, he forced his gaze down the road.
*God help us all if the Duke of Suffolk has even half of his
dead brother's brutality. God help Lady Roshelle . . .*

Stony-faced and silent, the people of Reales held their
breath as the first of the two hundred and four foot soldiers
appeared, marching straight and proud twelve abreast in
seventeen neatly formed rows. The people stared in wonder and awe, for none had seen such fine livery as the neat
blue-and-green uniforms on these men—even the foot soldiers wore the colors! Surely they would bring coins to the
township!

The banner of Suffolk came next. Ripples of wonder
raced through the crowd. The honor of carrying the banner
went to the Lord of Huntingdon, Joseph Eyes, and his
knights. The knights of the House of Suffolk followed.
Necks turned and gazes riveted to none other than the
Duke of Suffolk.

With his dark features, straight, proud back and broad
shoulders, Vincent de la Eresman, the Duke of Suffolk,
looked like a mythological being atop an enormous black
horse. The creature needed only wings to be transformed
into myth. The coat of arms of the House of Suffolk was
emblazoned beneath the richly carved metal plates on his
chest. Two swords and a dagger fell from his thick black
belt, his only weapons—that is, if one did not notice the

metal caps on his gloved hands. A red band circled his head, and he wore absolutely no jewels. And still he looked more prideful than Satan. Indeed, aristocratic arrogance marked the strong, strangely compelling features of his face, and plainest of all, it appeared in the noticeable narrowing of his remarkable gaze. A startling contradiction appeared there as well.

For unlike all others who were highborn, Vincent did not pretend to see through the people's very skin, as if they were invisible beings of absolutely no consequence, not worth even seeing. Instead each person there felt the intimate brush of his intelligent eyes. A startled hushed silence came over his victims. Without at first realizing it, they abruptly straightened and squared their shoulders, nervously smoothed down disheveled hair, adjusted breeches and smocks; mothers hurriedly wiped smudges from children's cheeks before raising their own chins. A few found themselves offering hesitant smiles before abruptly realizing this man was their sworn enemy, the one man who thought to bring Lady Roshelle to her knees.

Two men of his personal guard rode on either side of the duke, eight men behind, knights each, though noticeably without the cumbersome weight of armor. "Not seen a more arrogant face on a mere mortal in all my days," Thomson, the Reales sheriff, whispered, adding, "And that includes the day my eyes beheld King Henry himself on his march through the town of Go."

No one could say who started it; it would be argued for days, but as the duke rode through the town, a bold voice suddenly sang out Roshelle's name. Another took it up and another. A chorus of voices took up the chant made of Roshelle de la Nevers's name, and by the time the duke reached the end of town, the chant had become a chorus of scrutinized voices.

He raised a gloved hand, that was all. The one hundred and fifty-two knights behind him, their horses, the two hundred or so servants behind them, all the women who followed—of ill repute, hoping to live nicely off the wages of this fine army—the young boys and their dogs who chased after that, all these people came to an abrupt halt. The chant died an instant death. Silence filled the air. Each person became unnervingly aware of his escalating heartbeat, more symbolically aware of his limited mortality as Vincent turned his mount around. That strangely compelling gaze searched the sea of frightened faces; he selected a man at random and brought his stallion to dance in front of him. "My good man, your name?"

The crowd stared in horror. The great and mighty duke could slay the poor man in a half second and no one and nothing would move. Fully, terribly aware of this fact, the stout man dropped his jowls, his face blanching. Certain this was his end, his absolute end, he tried to swallow. "Saul, milord, the name is Saul."

"Indeed, Saul." Vincent smiled as if the name pleased him, a smile that did not reach his eyes until the man fell to his knees to beg his mercy.

"By thy witness, I did not mean to offend your Grace! No, *mon Dieu*, never that. A thousand and one pardons, your Grace. 'Tis just that, oh, God . . . well, Lady Roshelle. She owns our hearts, she does—the beautiful lady hath always owned the heart of the townspeople. Not that it means disobedience. I mean, our alliance is with . . . well, oh, God, you must see, I meant no disrespect—"

"Indeed," Vincent interrupted when the man had rambled long enough and appeared a hairbreadth from falling faint. "I am pleased to hear this good news. However . . . ah, Saul, is it? Yes? I only meant to inquire where in this charming town"—his gloved hand swept to the side and he leaned casually forward in his saddle—"might I get a new pair of boots made?"

The man stared with a dumbfounded stupor into a less-than-innocent dark gaze of the Duke of Suffolk. Wilhelm, mounted at Vincent's side, laughed first and perhaps longest. A near violent wave of relief swept the crowd; without so much as a drop of blood spilled, no one would ever mock the Duke of Suffolk with the lady's name again.

Only Phillips shrank back in terror, his mind racing between the idea of the duke's innocence and the idea that he knew full well what his brother had done to Reales' only shoemaker.

Many people pointed to Phillips' modest shop to save Saul the difficulty of answering with a mute tongue. With a plainly sardonic thanks, Vincent turned his mount back around and the march resumed. Yet now the famous English marching song replaced the chant of Roshelle de la Nevers's name.

John of Suffolk and the five carefully dressed officers behind him dropped to their knees as Vincent and his personal guard rode into the camp. "Ah, a good day to you, Captain and fellows. Please dispense with the formalities, since they are neither welcome nor necessary," Vincent said as he, Wilhelm and young Gregory dismounted. Reins were handed over to waiting grooms, the horses quickly led away.

"Wilhelm, see to the men. Suffolk guards may have a one-hour rest. All others are to assemble in that field, lances in hand."

"Aye, at once." Wilhelm left to do his bidding.

"Water, please," Vincent said to no one in particular, causing three nearby servants to jump. He began to remove his thick riding gloves as his gaze carefully swept the castle and surrounding landscape, its towers and battlements and its position near the river.

"A most welcome sight, milord!" The captain looked nervously about, feeling inexplicably slighted. "I trust all went well with your journey?"

"Relatively speaking. As with all things."

"Good, good." John of Suffolk could not be solicitous enough. "Please, your Grace, this way." He motioned to the large tent where supper and wine were being readied for serving. "Allow me the honor of hosting your first supper in Reales. I have the best wine and my chef is preparing—"

Vincent waved his hand in dismissal of the invitation; he had other plans. "I want this thing over. Tonight."

John looked nervously at his officers as if they might know what their Grace wanted, but only found blank faces reflecting his own confusion. He looked back at the duke. "What thing is that, your Grace?"

Gloves tucked into the thick black belt, hands on hips, Vincent looked surprised. "Why, the siege, my good Captain, the siege. I want to be inside that castle by nightfall."

The captain looked for a long moment stunned, then glanced again at his officers. He decided this was a jest. Grinning, he rocked back on his heels. "Ah, well—"

He stopped as Vincent continued to search the countryside as if looking for something. At last he turned back to the nervous captain, accepting the goblet as a servant poured the water. This was drained, then held out for more. "I need a table here. Get me all maps made of the castle and the area—I hope there are maps? Good. And this foul odor? The moat, I presume?"

"Aye. The moat—"

"Now the measures you've taken, Captain. I understand they've withstood two attacks, am I right? Yes? And that both times you led our archers to the moat to challenge the cross fire as men attempted to fill it in to get a belfry up to the wall. Where is that belfry?"

"Armory is kept there, behind the corral."

"Yes, very well. How many catapults?"

"Three, your Grace."

"I shall want to see these, though one look at those battlements and I can guess how this failed. The only thing made well at that castle is the battlements; I'd be surprised if you saw a single of the bowmen firing at you."

The captain looked at his officers, amazed at how quickly his Grace perceived the difficulties here. "Aye, the sky rained with their arrows—"

"And Greek fire?"

The reference was to arrows lit with flames fueled by a

poison, naphtha. ''Aye!'' The captain nodded. ''They took down the only thatched roof in the castle, leaving the animals stabled beneath the night sky as a roof.''

''One would hope the French were at least smart enough to prefer chilled stable animals to burned ones.'' He drank another gobletful of water, his gaze still searching his surroundings. ''What other defense measures have they, Captain?''

The question sounded rhetorical, and the captain hesitated as his mind raced to keep up with the duke's inhuman speed. ''Well, they have their archers and oil bins and, of course, the foul moat. The men complain bitterly of that moat—''

''Leaving you with the two choices: sacrifice your men's lives or starve the French out. You have chosen the latter, a wise choice if only it worked. Apparently the problem is no one in there is starving, am I right?''

''There you have it, milord, there you have it—''

''Indeed? Quite the contrary, Captain. I have nothing; my plan is to get it. Now, how many horses have you here, Captain?''

John of Suffolk stood for a long moment mute as his mind struggled to keep up with the rapid-fire questions.

''Captain?''

''Ah, over fifty.''

''Corralled over there, I see. Is that it?''

''Another corral on the west side, just behind those trees there.''

''Yes, I see.'' He started toward the corrals. ''See that those maps are arranged by my return. Captain, if you will.''

Abruptly realizing he was to follow, the captain leaped forward and rushed to fall in step behind the duke. He had of course seen the duke before but had never worked a campaign with him. Naturally, Vincent de la Eresman's reputation reached legendary proportions; everyone knew of his decisiveness, speed, the efficiency and effort he demanded from all those around him, especially in battle.

Characteristics presently reflected in the speed of his even gate; the captain found he had to practically run just to keep up with him.

Vincent inspected the horses. "Yes, there he is."

To the captain's utter amazement, the duke pointed to his very own prized stallion. His chest swelled with pride; now they were on a footing he understood. "Pardon my boldness, milord"—he smiled broadly—"but ye do have a fine eye for the beasts. He's my prize stallion, no finer horse lives in the whole of this wretched country—" He laughed. "You won't believe it, but I was hoping to present him to you—"

"You are aware the horse was stolen last night?"

"Stolen? What? Why, how could that be? The horses are kept under guard the whole night long—" He broke off as at last the darkly intelligent gaze came to his person, stopping his blood cold.

"Exactly the problem."

"Oh, God Almighty." The captain swallowed a sick dread rising from the pit of his stomach, worsening as he thought of the miraculous appearance of four barrels of wine. "I begin to believe the lady is bewitched."

"Aye, the lady is bewitched, and the power of her bewitchment lies in the unpleasant fact that a mere girl hath made fools of an entire English garrison!"

With that Vincent turned back and marched off to the captain's tent. There he found his officers gathered around the table, where the maps were spread out like a tablecloth. Vincent made a brief study of them. He kept looking up at the landscape, then returning to the map. "One hour of light left. Very well. We can safely eliminate the entire east side of the river—the ground is too soft and wet to support an underground tunnel. We might be equally assured of eliminating all open space here and here—I daresay they would have been spotted by now. Even with the vigilance of the captain's guards." The captain's face reddened with the implied criticism. "I eliminate this area for no other reason than my intuitive power—we will explore it last. My guess is that the tunnel's exit hatch lies somewhere in here.'' A long finger circled the wooded area near the corrals. ''I want six dozen men to surround the area in a circle, shoulder to shoulder, lances raised two hands to the front.''

Wilhelm shouted out the order. Within ten minutes over sixty men assembled in a perfect circle around the area. Vincent and Wilhelm rode mounted in a circle around them, the duke's clear voice sounding loud in the hour of twilight. ''We are looking for a trapdoor covered by brush. No man may step out of alignment; each must march with his fellows, lances pounding to the ground.'' And then revealing one of the many reasons he was so popular with his men, he added, ''Five pounds silver to the first man who finds it.''

A happy shout sounded well before the sun had sunk over the hills.

She was running for her life down an endless dark tunnel, desperate to find the ring. If only she had the ring, she would be safe. Where was it? Faces watched from the side as if her terror were an amusing show. Rats scurried unseen from her path; spiderwebs brushed her hot skin. She stopped suddenly, gasping and terrified, but the footsteps still chased after her. A wicked laugh sounded behind her. She swung around with a startled scream. Only darkness greeted her vision at first. Then she saw Rodez. He reached out to her. She backed up in horror, then pivoted around to go the other way. She hit a black wall, screaming as a dark shape emerged from the blackness, then another and another and the hands came upon her. She swung wildly, trying to fight them off—

Roshelle bolted up in bed. Her heart pounded and her pulse raced as her eyes darted about the unnaturally still and quiet room. A gentle breeze blew through the open window, ruffling the gold tassels hanging from the tapestry above the bed and flickering the light in the brass lantern on the hand-carved trunk. Her falcon, Greyman, slept soundly on his perch there. Two cats slept as well in the alcove.

'Twas a dream. The predictable night terrors brought by last night's horror. Oh, Potiers! Grief swelled in her chest, and for a moment she could hardly breathe. How could she go on without him? He had been at her side since she was twelve. She depended on him for everything; they all did. "Oh, Potiers!"

She drew a deep, even breath before tossing back the thick quilt covers and placing her bare feet on the cold stone floor. Dazed, she made her way to the chamber pot behind the partition, stepping over a half-finished puzzle of the great Cathedral of Chartres, a pack of cards from a game played and won by her maids the other night and a rolled-up tapestry they had been working on.

The solar chambers reflected the unfair competition between two competing forces: the wide scope of Roshelle's interests and her servants' somewhat limited energies, resulting in a wall-to-wall menagerie of finished and half-finished projects. Clarice, one of her maid's little girls, had a little wooden doll house and its three dozen pieces sitting in the corner, arranged to occupy the child as her mother and Roshelle worked to finish the tapestry neatly rolled up nearby—they needed yellow thread from Flanders, the only color Roshelle could not make. Three sewing boxes lay in the alcove, threads and cloth spilling from each, while one of her huge trunks opened to reveal a modest assortment of folded woolen gowns and night clothes. A caul lay discarded on the floor alongside the boy's clothes. Her saber—lighter than a sword, easier for her to wield—and her dagger leaned against the wall, her maids never knowing just where to set these weapons.

A long, carefully made wooden working table stood along one side of the far wall, and this area was scrupulously neat and clean. Here sat all manner of strange and wonderful things in glass jars: spices, fragrant herbs, plants, dozens of roots, flower petals, waxes, all kinds and various carefully marked mixes of things, all of it producing a fragrance so sweet and enticing as to have all the servants want to attend Roshelle in the privacy of her solar. This room alone escaped the foul air of the moat. Another trunk sat locked against the wall; the tools in there were worth far more than gold, while a wooden rack held over a dozen scrolls above Roshelle's small, fine writing desk. Five priceless, gold-trimmed, leather-bound books—all of these on the use of herbs—stood in a neat row there, while dozens of scrolled parchments sat on a bookshelf nearby, each a treasured gift from Papillion. Without exception, each and every thing in her room was a treasure to her, and so the only thing she feared more than an English king on the French throne was fire. Five buckets of water sat in a neat row outside her chamber doors at all times.

She returned to the bed. Her blue eyes fell on a tray Joan had left for her: an early green apple and a meager bowl of thin porridge, and a tall cup of goat's milk. She reached for the cup—

A strange sound came from beneath her bed.

The hairs at the nape of her neck lifted. She backed away slowly from the bed, her eyes flying wildly around the room, settling at once on her saber resting against the wall. She rushed to it, but before she could call out an alarm, before she had even grasped the nature of the threat, the bolt flew off and the trapdoor at the foot of the bed lifted.

Saber in hand, she cried out for help as she rushed to the spot. Two bare feet jumped firmly on the wooden square, smashing it back into place. "Cisely!" she shouted. "Joan! Help! Lo! Jean Luc!"

Several seconds passed while a strange tapping sound came from below, a sound she didn't hear as an enormous surge of panic rose through her, her entire being going into screams for help. Squawking with excitement, Greyman, her prized falcon, flew around the room, then apparently thinking it too dangerous, the traitor vanished out the open window.

With a sudden burst, the trapdoor opened. Like a child's precariously balanced tower of blocks, she crashed to the floor. Backside to the ground, Roshelle took one look and cried, "You! 'Tis you!"

Vincent wisely knew to get to his feet before discussing his unannounced presence. He started to move, but she scrambled to her hands and knees and that was it; his breath caught and he froze, for one too many seconds he froze as he took in the innocently seductive pose. Surprise was writ in her parted lips and rounded, large eyes, an expression that would live in his mind forever. Her thin arms braced against the stone floor. Long, thick, loosened hair fell on either side of her arms in a cascade of rich auburn color, curling on the stone floor. Yet for all of it, the exposed seduction of this pose, his gaze riveted on the thin cotton nightdress where it dropped from a view he could die for.

Only too true. By the time he had collected the fragments of his stunned wits, she was on her feet. The very next breath came with the sharp point of her saber at his neck. For a girl, she was quick.

"Oh, no . . . Oh, no," she said in a heated whisper. "Do not move . . . just do not move. Joan! Oh, God, where are you? Cisely!" She stepped back and forth in a frightened dance. What to do—

Get him back down!

"All right, all right," she said as she watched his gaze sweep the room, brows lifting with confusion before at last his gaze returned to her person. "I shall not kill you if you go back down. That's it, English. Back down!"

Vincent made no move to comply.

"Move or you will feel the sharp point of my saber pierce your flesh!"

An amused light appeared in his darkly intelligent eyes. "As you wish."

A gloved hand snaked around the sharp blade of her saber to keep it still just as his other arm straightened, and in a shocking feat of strength, he lifted his weight and leaped from the trapdoor. Before she had drawn a breath. She jumped safely back with a startled cry, impressing him again with her speed; she stood feet apart and arms raised to attack. "Oh, no—get back, just get back!"

"Get back? After I spent the last hour getting in? I do not think you understand. This is a siege. I am here to take the castle back by force! And though I'm often inclined to heed a maid's directives, considering the circumstances—"

That was as far as he got. Roshelle had started to listen to his words just long enough to realize he mocked her, then she swung hard. She caught him by surprise, but he managed to parry just in time. She swung again, and he leaped back so as to save himself from a neat slice across his waist. She stepped back, appraising her opponent, the strange light in his eyes as he measured her in turn.

Oh, God, she thought, taking in the size and scope of the man, remembering the speed with which he had slain the outlaws, and Papillion's warning, "Beware the perfect cleft . . ." She had little doubt she needed the full force of her guard. At least. Yet seeing the light in his eyes, she said, "You think this a jest?"

"A jest?" A brow rose, that strange light shining bright in his eyes. "Nay, I would not use that word with you—"

Roshelle never fought fair, and with malicious forethought, she struck without warning as he spoke. He neatly parried, his gaze moving over her as he studied the shape and form of his unlikely opponent. And studied. Bare feet apart in an attack stance, both hands gripping her raised weapon, the long auburn hair framing the pale, delicately boned face before falling in silken streams past the small of her waist. He tried to ignore the bruise there. An easy feat as he watched the maddening play of light and shadow beneath the thin cotton of her nightdress, sleeveless save for an inch of cloth meant for straps, a dress that only hinted at the startling proportions there, a tease that stole every last thought.

Roshelle swung, struck steel, swung again. The fight

was on. Desperate, knowing she could not beat this man single-handed as she swung and struck, she screamed a frantic list of names, then another, the musical lilt to her voice disappearing in the desperate call for her guards, and this spurred his decision to enlighten the wild young lady. Her mistress had obviously let her sleep through the day after all she had been through. She had yet to realize just how bad her situation was. "They are in the chapel for an evening mass—no doubt sung for your dead servant. They cannot hear you."

How did he know that? How? Oh, God—

Roshelle circled slowly, trying to think until she noticed the strange look in his eyes, that he had struck a pose so casual it might be used for a portrait setting: a gloved hand resting comfortably on the handle of his sword, its point to the ground as he continued to appraise her with a maddening, boyish kind of grin.

So maddening, she thought to cut it from his face! "You!" she hissed as she raised the saber. "You fiend! I shall die before I let you through here!"

His gaze lit with wild amusement as he assured her, "I am set to trembling." Then with feeling, he added, "I surrender, love, I surrender."

Fury livened her eyes as she swung. "I forfeit your surrender, you beast—" The saber sliced the air, strong and clean toward his chest. Vincent stepped cleanly away, while she stumbled with the force of her energies.

"You would dare laugh!"

"Nay, nay," he quickly tried to assure her as a hand went to his eye in the pretense. "There's something in my eye, 'tis all—"

She struck with surprising force, coming round with all her strength set in a quick, hard swing. With a speed that shocked, his sword raised again in a neat parry. Pain shot up her arms as her saber met the unyielding metal of his sword with a resounding clang.

Now he nearly doubled over with his laughter. "Oh, love, I did not mean to hurt you—"

He got no further. She swung to the side, her blade coming within a scant inch before he managed to respond to her strike. His sword met the saber once more, then twice and again in a quick succession of parries. Quick and lithe, she spun around in a circle, giving the next strike the force of her momentum and forcing him to jump back to save himself. Which she anticipated with a leaping strike.

A brow rose as he countered; he was a good deal more than impressed. He was fascinated. Again and again, she agilely wielded the weapon, and with surprising if not shocking skill. Someone—and he cursed the bastard to hell—had trained her to the weapon and trained her well.

With every fiber of his being, he tried to concentrate on restraining his strength as he countered her swift, clean strikes. No easy feat. Not as she danced around him, breathless and, dear God, so beautiful, determination set in her bright blue eyes and a hot flush spreading over her pale skin. He dropped his sword to the ground, countering her sudden swing at his legs just in time. She came up and swung down again. Too late to counter, he had to jump back. Two more swings and she had him cornered.

For small beads of perspiration lined her brow as a strap fell off her shoulder, and even worse, what made his breath catch—the light shining behind her now made the thin cloth no more than a transparent veil.

He had to sit down. "Sweet mercy—"

She abruptly dropped, jumping as she brought the saber down hard. He caught it just in time. The metal clanged loudly and she fell back out of reach, pausing for a moment to catch her breath.

She called out again and again, knowing only that she had to slay him and close that trapdoor or—less likely—convince him to return. "Joan, Ooowens! Mother in Heaven, where are you?"

"Tired, love? Shall we rest a moment?"

"Not yet, you nefarious, no-good villain of a whoreson!"

He caught his lip between his teeth to stop the laugh, his gaze dancing wildly at this. "Nefarious, no-good what—"

He stopped in mid-sentence as she swung with a breathless shout. "You heard me, you—" He countered but she swung again and again and again, pressing her advantage as he began to lose it, his responses slowing. Victory gave her strength and she attacked more fiercely, pushing him back and back until—

Until she stepped on one of little Clarice's small wooden jacks. A sharp shooting pain made her stumble with a cry. She fell to an undignified position on her hands and knees, took one look at his face and clutched tight the saber beneath her hand. Vincent bit his lip so hard he drew blood as he dropped his sword to help her up. Catching him completely off guard, she swung up as she leaped back to her feet. With his sword dropped, he could not parry. He bent back, and only the quickest reflexes she'd ever witnessed saved him from a neat slice across the chest as he raised his sword to counter her follow-up.

"The next time you're gelded!" she cried.

"Gelded? Oh, God—"

One more minute and he'd collapse. Quite desperate now, Vincent looked behind him to see the long worktable just as Roshelle pressed a hard strike to his legs. He managed to counter in time but, just as quick, she swung swiftly up, then down to cross at his knees again. He countered but just barely as he sat down, dropping his head as he collapsed in the nearly unbearable misery of his agony.

His agony mounted. More so as the warring beauty swung up, and only his unnerving instincts brought his sword up in time to prevent a painful slice to his neck; then even more as the high musical voice said in apparently mistaken triumph, "Forfeit your sword or meet your sorry end!"

Breathless and flushed, she stood poised, saber high, ready to land him a death blow when she abruptly froze, her hot gaze riveted on him. She suddenly saw he was struggling fiercely—struggling fiercely to stop from laughing out loud! Not fiercely enough, as the sound of his amusement abruptly burst out in the chambers; he could not for his life stop his laughter. Another sound of laughter came from behind, but she didn't hear, couldn't hear as her mind fastened on the horror of a sudden realization: not once had he swung his sword offensively.

Not once this whole time.

"You are not even fighting!"

Amusement shone as a bright light in his gaze, along with an unidentifiable something else she did not pause to contemplate. "Quite the contrary. I have never been more fiercely engaged; I am in fact fighting for my life."

She went wild. The saber came down with all her strength, hitting his sword with a resounding hard clang, echoing off the walls, and before it even stopped she swung again and again, striking his swift counters as if by doing so she could silence the very laughter on his lips.

With hands on hips and amusement bright in his eyes, Wilhelm watched this from the corner of the room. Seven of Vincent's best knights had slipped quietly in behind him while he carefully kept the girl's back to the trapdoor. Each knight now hid in a strategic place inside the castle, necessary in the unfortunate event Vincent's peaceful means of ending the siege failed, which seemed ever more likely if the man did not get a grip on his hot blood. Vincent's agony, as Wilhelm watched the girl try to geld him, would be a source of mirth the rest of their long days, no doubt; never had he enjoyed a show more. Until he noticed the girl's arms set to trembling with the exertion. "Enough, Vincent—"

Vincent saw it, too, his amusement dying at once as he cursed himself for not realizing sooner. "Aye." The very next strike of her saber hit an utterly unyielding force. It was the most shocking and maddening thing she had ever witnessed, the slight flick of his wrist, that was all. The saber flew from her hands across the room, hitting the wall and falling to the floor with a loud clamor that sounded with her scream. A scream that stopped as she spun around and saw Wilhelm.

Roshelle spun back around, staring in the utter horror of the name he had answered to. "Vincent . . ." she said on the heels of a frightened whisper as she shook her head. "Vincent de la Eresman! You are . . . you are the Duke of Suffolk!"

She did not think to wait for his acknowledgment; she bolted to the door. Not quickly enough. He caught her in three strides, his strong arms snaking around her thin ones as he pulled her against the hard length of his body. Fear seized the whole of her, overcoming her utter exhaustion, and she screamed, twisting and kicking for all she was worth and then some until—

Vincent tensed with the shock and feel of the small body against his, stiffening more as a lightning-like jolt passed through him, so powerful as to make him weak with the sudden rush of plain hot lust. "Good God, girl," he cursed beneath a warm chuckle. "Enough! You can believe, after the torment you put me through, this spirited struggle hardly helps to, ah, temper my response to you."

A shocking physical sensation gave sudden meaning to his words; she went limp in his arms. Only to hear another warm chuckle against her ear. Shivers rushed from the spot, her breath caught and she blushed hotly.

"Christ never had such temptation," he said in an amused whisper, his free hand brushing back a stray wisp of her hair. "And I assure you, I don't have his patience, much less his grace."

This she did not doubt. Her blue eyes shot to the open trapdoor, then to the giant watching from the side. Dear Lord, they were but two men. If she could just get through the door to sound the alarm—

"I need to know your name," he said, holding her slender figure with the gentlest of restraints. "I have waited to hear it long enough."

He did not know? "My . . . name?"

"Your name. What is it?"

"Ah . . . ah—"

"Are we slow-witted or merely preparing a lie?"

Fury brightened her eyes. "We are nothing if not sworn enemies! As for your wits, I can attest to their sorry inadequacies, as only the very slowest wit would ever bother maintaining the elaborate pretenses of knighthood when all the world knows he is a black-hearted, lecherous, loathsome bastard—"

A gentle hand came to her mouth to stop the enumeration of insults. "Not slow-witted, I see. So you would lie. Now the question is, why?"

Vincent's gaze traveled slowly around the room, noticing, among all the various things here, the open and shelved books, the tools and jars of a practicing alchemist or herbalist. His gaze went to her hair. He ran a hand through the long locks, pushing the stray wisps back until he saw it: the white streak that started at her temple and ran down the length of it.

Then he knew who he held in his arms.

"Roshelle of Reales—"

"Roshelle!"

All gazes flew to Cisely in the doorway.

"Run! Run, Cisely—"

With wide, terrified eyes, Cisely took one step back and started to turn. Too late. To the woman's utter surprise, five guards emerged behind her exactly as Roshelle felt a mercilessly sharp dagger at her throat. Cisely's hands went to her own throat in terror.

Vincent kept his eyes on Roshelle but addressed Cisely. "You are the countess's waiting woman?"

Cisely managed to nod.

"You will tell the French guard of Reales that the Duke of Suffolk now holds their mistress in her chambers by the point of a dagger at her throat. You are to instruct them to open the gates before assembling in the courtyard, weapons laid at their feet," he said as easily as if ordering supper, adding just as easily, "They are to do this within ten minutes or I shall hang her head from that window."

"No, Cisely! No—"

The arm around her shoulders lifted to cover her mouth, the dagger pointing to a place where her pulse pounded wildly. Cisely paled, but for once she fought back the feeling of fainting to scream out instead, "Oh, God, do not hurt her! Please, I beg of you—"

"Enough," he said in a deep, clear voice, adding as his darkly menacing gaze fell upon Roshelle, "Only after the castle has been surrendered will I entertain pleas to spare her life."

Chapter 4

Windows opened out to the courtyard below. Jean Luc of the French guard raced from corner to corner to light the torches. Vincent stood behind Roshelle in the alcove, his strong, large hand circling her upper arm, a small but meaningful act signifying extreme mistrust of his brother's murderess. Over forty of his best knights waited in the hall outside her chamber doors, ready in the event the Reales guards did not lay down their arms to save her life. Still he would not trust the girl.

He had reason aplenty to be suspicious.

He still had trouble believing she was Roshelle of Reales: a young woman who rode a half-wild stallion through the dark of night to warn peasants of his army's approach; who valiantly, though ridiculously, tried to fight that band of cutthroat brigands; a young lady who faced the terror of an enemy knight in her private chambers with incredible but foolish courage and determination, meeting a knight's strength and sword with a saber in the most memorable sword fight of his life; the same young lady who had—somehow!—murdered his brother before going on to fight back a goodly number of the finest knights in the world, capturing at last and holding this castle for some two long months now, single-handedly inspiring an entire war-torn land to rebellion. He had even more trouble believing all this foolhardy courage and bravery was packaged in the most alluring one hundred or so pounds it had ever been his misfortune to encounter.

Feeling the wild race of her pulse beneath his fingertips on her arm, he let his gaze fall to her breasts, hidden now by crossed arms, before it finally settled on the long white streak that started at her temple and disappeared along the length of her still tousled mass of hair cascading down her straight, slender back. He understood only too well now why the peasants, with droll minds colored by every conceivable superstition and irrationality, claimed the girl was bewitched; he half believed this himself.

She felt it! A shiver raced up her spine. The intimate brush of his gaze on her made her painfully aware of her nakedness beneath the thin cotton morning gown. She closed her eyes, trying to steel her thoughts away from it, from him, the entire force of her being battling furiously not to bolt. Every nerve and muscle in her body was afire with a strange awareness and fear of him. Like a tickle all over, she felt as if she stood on the precipice of a great high cliff, staring down in that single split second before the fall, only the second stretched, and with it the sensations—heightened senses, a somersaulting stomach and racing heart and pulse. She half expected her life to pass before her eyes—

Dear Lord, was she so afraid to die?

He would be killing her now, would he not?

Mickael, another of the Reales guards, appeared first, causing her a slight gasp as he dropped his sword and stepped back unarmed. Vincent cursed the bewilderment and mounting agony in her lovely blue eyes as, one by one, the Reales guards appeared in the center of the courtyard, dropping their swords in a pile before the gate until they numbered twenty-four. A loud cheer went up as his knights swarmed around them, Wilhelm himself giving the order to open the gate. Three men turned the great wheel to lower the drawbridge, while another five labored to open the gate.

Her rebellion was over now. He had smashed it as if it were no more than a fly on the wall. She would not cry, not now—

"You little fool." He leaned over, his voice a warm whisper brushing over her ear. "Were you expecting any other ending to this ill-begotten insurrection? Did you ever doubt there could be any other ending?"

His lips hovered a scant half inch from a spot above her ear, where a chill raced. Her cheeks grew hot. Emotions swelled through her and she closed her eyes in abject helplessness, the humiliation of being taunted so.

She had imagined a different outcome, and a thousand times, no less! All these past wondrous months she had lived on the hope of the dream of a free and united France, lived on that precious hope as a beggar lives on little more than the air and water of a harsh, unkind world. Only to have the hope crushed by his hand and her country beaten once again.

"Aye," she said in a passionate whisper as she turned to meet the steely intensity of those dark eyes, "I dared to imagine a different world. For these last months I dared to imagine my country free of the most virulent pestilence to ever shadow the land, any land, anywhere through all of human history. The English! Your people have taught me well to hate. My whole life long I have witnessed my country reduced time and again to poor, starving and frightened masses, the peasants who know no physical or emotional comfort, their every small possession ripped from their hands by you and your unholy armies as they march through the land raping and pillaging and setting the fields to flames! Yes, I dared to imagine a different world!"

The fury and passion of her temper trembled through her, more as her heartfelt words filled his dark gaze with naught but some small irritation mixed inexplicably with some much larger amusement. As if she were an amusing though bothersome child! How maddening he was! She wanted to slap it from his face—

"Are ye goin' to tolerate her outrageous lies and half-truths like that?"

They turned to see Wilhelm in the doorway, standing

with his hand on Cisely's arm much as Vincent still held hers. Frightened like a child, Cisely broke from the giant's grasp before rushing into Roshelle's arms. Watching Roshelle still, Vincent shrugged. "Believe, I would not condescend to answer the lies and delusions of France's greatest, and no doubt last, patriot. Is the castle secured?"

"Aye," Wilhelm said as Cisely, nodding to Roshelle's whispered words of comfort, and always mindful of appearances, rushed to Roshelle's trunk and returned with a walking robe to place over Roshelle's shoulders. Vincent's gaze remained, seeing the same love in the girl's woman as he had seen in her servant. No simple girl here, and while her words irritated him, her passion played a different tune entirely, becoming a crescendo when he briefly imagined harnessing it.

The extent of his lasciviousness for the girl felt increasingly alarming, for she was not just his bane—a hurricane on the open sea would be less trouble!—but here at last he beheld the unlikely form of his brother's murderess. Try as he might, he could not reconcile the two. As if searching for a clue, he cast his gaze to the strange menagerie and collection of oddities in her room.

Wilhelm came to stand in front of Roshelle, hands on hips, finger pointing like a school master, apparently intending to set her straight. "The lady hath accused you, my lord, of holding the unjust sword, therefore meself, by means of being your servant. The only truth in these words, milady, is that no one in all the world doubts this wretched hellhole called France is the most sorrowful and pitiful place on all earth—"

"Torn asunder by you, the English armies! Like Reales now. Just look," she said as she stared out at the swarm of Englishmen through the gates. "They have no right, no right—"

"No right? Why, all of Brittany, if not all of France, belongs to King Henry!"

"Never! France belongs to God, and the rightful heir to her throne is and always will be Charles of Valois!"

"The reason our armies are here has everything to do with this insane line of so-called 'dauphins' you and the Orleans duchy indulge. A poorer king could not be found—this last one is the worst. He is as weak and frightened as a titmouse in a moonlit field; I hear he needs knighted escorts for a trip to the guardlope, trembling and quaking as he goes! Huh!'' he said with clear masculine scorn. "This is the man you would have as king?"

She could hardly believe it. Charles was not just her king but a much-loved friend, and to hear this man's disparaging remarks challenging his very manhood renewed the bright red color in her cheeks. A finger pointed as she managed through clenched teeth, "How dare you slander the Dauphin with a dishonest tongue! Just because he is not as strong and sound of body as, as you—"

"An understatement, but damning enough. A king must be strong to get the respect and admiration of his men in battle, feared enough to own the absolute fealty of his lords—this so-called Dauphin has neither."

"He will, he will. He is a good and just and decent soul—"

"Decent?" Wilhelm actually laughed. "Only a woman could think decency could matter when ruling the world of men."

"Only an Englishman would think that it does not!"

"Ah." A wave of his hand dismissed this. "Take my word for it—decency will not rein the voracious appetites of the wolves at his throats, his own power-mad dukes of Burgundy and Berry. Now there's a fine crowd of Frenchmen for you. Which is another point." His brown eyes narrowed dangerously. "All this raping and pillaging you throw in his Grace's face. 'Tis your own wretched countrymen who rape and pillage. The whole world knows Frenchmen as barbarians—"

She stopped him with a pained cry. French barbarism?"

"Aye! All Frenchmen who are not starving and destitute, too weak to feed their families, let alone protect

Vincent laugh. "Your grasp of politics is limited indeed. If only that were half true."

"Has he not joined Henry against us?"

"Aye, he has sworn fealty to Henry, but I fear his oath lacks the necessary credibility of his actions. And speaking of actions, milady, the particular act of murder—"

"I did not kill your brother!"

"The common cry of murderers and, I suppose, murderesses, not that these last are very common, and thank God for that. Most of your sex have the good sense to keep home and hearth, minding children and underlings. And speaking of these things, madame, why the devil are you unmarried still? Leaving three sizable fiefdoms without a lordship."

The question first confused her. Why was she not married? All the world knew why she was not married. No man, be he highborn or low, would have her.

"Do you mean to taunt me with that question?"

"Taunt you?" His thick dark brows drew together with his own confusion at this response. For a long moment he was lost in the strange sadness that had sprung into her eyes. He could hardly explain the effect, just what it was and how it displayed itself. Perhaps a faint veil of tears changed the light in those bright pools, making a brief though haunting manifestation of some carefully suppressed grief. "How might my simple question mock you?"

Innocent blue eyes widened; she could hardly believe this. "You must know how! If you think these barbed comments pain me, think again." And she lied. "They do not! I am resigned to my dire fate."

"Your dire fate?" Vincent questioned, glancing at Wilhelm, who shrugged with the same confusion. All he knew was that the tangemont before him had been widowed twice and land-rich to start; she was one of the richest women on the Continent. By law she should be married. By title alone, her issue would stand to inherit a goodly portion of this wretched country.

Unless what she meant by her dire fate was that Henry wanted—nay, demanded—her head. Which was, of course, a problem. Rodez Valois's correspondence to the good captain of the garrison, John of Suffolk, had made it very clear that the entire Burgundian court thought it wildly amusing that a young girl held off an entire English garrison for two months, despite their forsworn fealty to Henry. What was far worse, those carefully penned words left little doubt that Rodez Valois would not intercede to save the girl's head from the sharp, exacting blade of the guillotine.

The question was why Rodez Valois wouldn't intercede for the girl. Moral obligations aside, if Roshelle de la Nevers died before she was married again, the church would gain her lands. Rodez would lose everything. And why hadn't the church forced Rodez to get her married again?

"Milady," Vincent began with a pretense of diplomacy, "I will ask again. All I want to know is why the Duke of Burgundy hasn't married you off."

Roshelle's blue eyes widened slightly, as if he had raised an angry hand to her face. As if he had insulted her.

Slowly, with mounting ire, she replied, "You would make me say it! Why? To amuse yourself at my expense? To make tired masculine jests about it? Do you not think I have not heard these poor jokesters all these years? And I daresay anyway"—she lowered her eyes—"the duke is content to collect his outrageous rents and tithes from my land, leaving me to God's will."

The words made little sense and he stared as if she were daft. Indeed, Wilhelm leaned toward him and whispered just out of the girl's hearing, "The lady makes as much sense as a drunken beggar at dawn . . ."

"Aye," Vincent agreed, then of Roshelle, he asked, "What be this God's will? Do we have a language problem?" The question was asked in French, as if she would make more sense in her own tongue. "Even if the duke is greedily raping your land, why does the church let him? I have never heard of the church contentedly watching such a dowry waste away like this."

"The church is as impotent as he is! My fate belongs to God, His will be done—"

Two guards entered without knocking, approaching Vincent to confer in whispers. Just like that, she was forgotten. A red-hot fury took hold of her; she had never felt violence as she did now. It was all so unfair! The sheer injustice of the situation seized the whole of her, worse with her utter damnable helplessness to change the reality of his presence: the very idea that he, the Duke of Suffolk, lord of the English realm, stood in her private chambers insulting her, then again with his maddening, capricious inattention!

"Tsk, tsk." Wilhelm leaned toward her, confiding intimately, "Mind thy manners, milady. You already have too much of his attention, and trust me, you want no more of it."

Her blue eyes flew to his face in outrage.

"Playing with the duke is not just playing with fire, but, well"—Wilhelm only laughed—" 'tis playing with fire when your own flesh is but made of straw."

The great big man chuckled heartily, and she half expected to feel the palm of his hand on her back, as if 'twas a fine jest indeed. For a moment she was speechless, utterly speechless. No mortal soul had ever spoken to her so . . . so familiarly—

She stared in disbelief as Moonshine, one of her favorite cats, curled around the duke's legs. The traitorous feline! The capricious, no-good traitor—she would string him up and hang him out her window!

Fascinated, Roshelle watched as Vincent bent down, picked the cat up and stood again, his fine, strong hands gently coaxing a loud purr from the fellow as he leveled a series of quick orders. He then dismissed the guards and at last turned back to Roshelle. He started to speak, but a small voice stopped him. His darkly intelligent eyes found Cisely, noticing her for the first time as she said, "Please, you must withdraw now so that milady may digest the sorrows of our day.''

He started to object, but Wilhelm's hand on his shoulder cautioned him, and Cisely was thankful for the intervention. All she knew was the way the duke stared at Roshelle scared her to the depth of her soul. As if he would devour Roshelle where she stood. All they needed now was two dead lords of Suffolk. Gathering all her courage, she added, ''Milady hath been through much. She needs to rest.''

Wilhelm looked at the slight, petite woman with new respect. Vincent considered her words and finally nodded. ''Very well. We shall save this, ah, less-than-enlightening conversation for later.'' He turned to Wilhelm, suddenly speaking in a strange tongue Roshelle had never heard. An animated conversation ensued. She still watched the cat in his arms, vaguely grasping Henry's name, and *mortis,* which meant death, but she could hardly pay the strange English patois a piece of her mind, the intensity of his stare so unnerved her, somehow fueling the fury she felt. Then with an equally maddening, boyish kind of grin, he remarked, ''Saints alive, look at the girl's eyes—like bright blue flames, they are! Ah, Wilhelm, I am in trouble this time.'' He chuckled. ''The fates have played me a cruel hand indeed.''

''I tried to warn the lass, but I might have saved my breath—Adam being the first man, though God knows not the last, to realize there's no talking sense to a woman.''

With chuckles and nods, they turned to leave. ''Ah.'' Vincent turned back with an afterthought. ''Until your noticeably negligent guardian can be summoned to appear at your trial to speak for you, you will be confined to these chambers.''

Every last semblance of decorum and indeed sense fled as her chest filled like a sail caught in the wind. Cisely, shaken to her bones, dropped to her knees in distress, missing the quick reach as Roshelle picked up the largest thing nearest her. A large, thick book hit Vincent square on the head. He swung back around, and before she managed to take aim with the large vase she clutched in both hands overhead, a booted foot flew through the air, knocking it against the open window. A crash sounded as it hit the ground.

Roshelle cried out in pain, ducking his arms. Too late. He had caught her back up against the overwhelming strength of his body, no consideration in the harsh hold. Until that moment she had not realized the extreme gentleness with which he had dealt with her; she noticed it now only because it was gone. "I hate you! I hate you! Your detestable English presence—I hate you—"

"Hate me all you want; I care little for the adolescent sentiments of a misbehaving young lady, but be forewarned: the very next time you raise a violent hand against me, I will let you feel the consequences of doing so." Then he thought to remind her. "Husband or no, guardian or no, only by my grace do you now draw breath. You, milady, would do well to remember it."

Shaking his head, Wilhelm followed Vincent down the hall. The situation seemed so much worse than Vincent's words. Received just that morning, Henry's message, full of sound and fury, commanded Vincent to set the girl on her knees beneath the blade of a guillotine. Henry cared not at all if her death made her a martyr, so long as it also suppressed any last idea of rebellion. That assurance was enough for him. No doubt Henry also sought to punish Rodez, the Duke of Burgundy—this for withholding the revenues and men that Henry claimed as King of England and Wales and now Brittany, Harcourt and Calais.

Henry wanted the girl's head.

The trouble was that Henry always got what he wanted.

"God Almighty!" Rob of Manchester cursed as he sat down at the white-clothed table on the dais in the great hall. "How can a man eat with this stench?"

"Only the wretched French could live with such a foul

odor—hell, it permeates their very skin from the day of birth—''

''I am hungry enough to ignore it,'' Thomas of Suffolk said, adding, ''For now.''

''Five pounds sterling 'tis the first thing his Grace sets right in the dung heap called Reales.''

The older man's hands trembled with rage and humiliation as he set goblets in front of these men, forced to serve the twelve men of the Duke of Suffolk's personal guard. Never had he heard of extending the privilege of sitting in a hall to one's personal guard: only the titled landed class reserved that right. At least in the civilized countries. The duke's order that put these men at the table upset his sensibilities to no end, more when no maid in all of Reales felt brave enough to serve them—''They are like giants! They look so mean and war-worn, as if they had never touched a soft thing in their life! I feel faint every time one casts his gaze my way!''

A common sentiment around Reales. Now he, Lance of Reales, ward of the kitchen, had to serve these savages, and he did so only for Lady Roshelle. Only for her. Roshelle had said to the people, ''We have been beaten but we have not lost. As long as we keep the courage to dream, we have not lost . . .'' He began pouring watered-down ale into the goblets, not bothering to hide his animosity. Why should he? When the duke kept Lady Roshelle prisoner in her rooms, preparing to try her for a crime she had not committed?

Bryce looked up to notice him. He sat tall and looked menacing, with his thick beard and long hair, unnaturally proud of the plaited tail it made halfway down his back. What Lance noticed were the battle scars on his arms, more battle scars than on the blessed Saint Sebastian himself. ''What goes here?'' Bryce wondered. ''Are there no women in Reales to serve our table?''

Tight-lipped, Lance managed, ''The women are engaged elsewhere.'' He moved on to the next, motioning to Peter, a weary young page, to place the rye bread out, wanting this over.

"A pity for sure, a sorrowful pity," Bryce replied, "France, this land of the dying and the damned, has only one redeeming issue, and that is the comeliness of the wenches. No finer-looking women in the world."

The great long table of men agreed heartily to the observation. "Aye," Thomas added, nodding. "Though their faces be plain and lead the eye to roam elsewhere, how the roaming is thus rewarded!"

The men laughed uproariously; Lance's face reddened as he listened to the increasingly ribald comments about Frenchwomen from these beastly men. "Though say," Thomas asked the group at large, "did you not see Lady Roshelle?"

"Ah, no finer painting have I ever seen of beauty. She is a sight to feast on. To hear Wilhelm tell of the famous sword fight, 'twas the closest Vince ever came to be gored—"

"Aye, so struck was he by what fate had put before him, Wilhelm said if he had not been standing there, he had no doubt Vince would have ended the girl's effort by landing her backside to the bed, slain for sure, though not by a cold metal but by equally hard flesh—" The men laughed until Thomas abruptly stopped to notice the stale bread set before them, just alongside the noticeably moldy cheese, all to be washed down by ale weaker than the most miserly fish mongers. "What manner of torment is this?"

Lance could take no more. "This," he said with trembling rage, "is your just deserts," and he poured the ale pitcher over the whole, tossed the pitcher on the table and headed through the doors.

Thomas let a jeweled dagger fly even as he stood. The knife struck the pole directly before Lance's eyes. An inch to the side and it would have been his skull. Sudden silence came over the room, and though it was well beneath the dignity of the duke's knights to challenge a servant, disciplining one was not.

" 'Twill be your back on a rack the next time you dare to insult a knight of the House of Suffolk. A house whose duke you should thank, as any other lord would surely have burned this dung pile, the servants with the guards. And keep in mind, man, the fire might still be made. Now," his fine, clear voice said, "you have before the next bell to set us a decent table."

Three other servants quickly arrived to set a decent table for the knights of the duke's personal guard, and one of them was Joan. She alone was not afraid of these men. Wearing her perfectly content smile, she held out the wrapped bread rolls, and immediately caught Bryce's eye.

"Ah, now here's a pretty lass indeed. What be your name?"

"Joan."

"Ah, Joan." He gently caught her hand, stopping her. A strange feeling tingled through her. Her heart pounded fast, as if she were running. In confusion, she stared at his large hand on hers. She saw his ring and smiled, beamed with the pleasure. "You do not look French."

She looked into dark blue pools, eyes like Roshelle's. She smiled.

"Are you from here?"

The question made little sense to her; she could hardly know the answer. She thought to nod. He smiled back before running his hand down one of the long ropes of her hair. "Gawd," he marveled, "like spun gold. And there be no end to it."

Pleasure brightening her cheeks, she hurried on to serve the others. She felt his eyes upon her. Eyes like Roshelle's. She kept smiling back.

Meanwhile, Lance anxiously repeated the story a dozen times, and it was repeated a dozen more times—the incident traveled from one mouth to the next like wildfire at the height of a summer drought, until finally straws were drawn and Fiona drew the short one. A plump hand went to her forehead in distress. Five other pairs of hands pushed her forward.

* * *

The image of her father's boots rose vividly in Roshelle's mind. Tall, worn brown leather, with mud-encased, thick gold spurs. She remembered wanting to wipe the mud from his spurs. Like her mother had always done. Her mother had carried a cloth in her sleeve, just so she might bend down and wipe the jeweled spurs when he entered the great hall. That cloth had been clasped in her mother's hands when she died, and Roshelle remembered wanting badly to take it from the cold, stiff fingers, but no, Father Constantine said she was not to touch her mother now . . .

The little girl hardly noticed the boots of the other knights, the men of her father's personal guard who always surrounded him. Yet she remembered their voices filled with awe and disbelief and something else she had not recognized as a young child. Fear. They were afraid. They were afraid of her.

For she had just ridden her father's war-horse.

"Dear God, the child be bewitched!"

"How is it possible?"

"Look at her! Just look! A goodly breeze could knock her over. As thin as a wisp, as slight as a reed—"

"By the fates, the child be enchanted!"

"Iberia be wild, untamed, a steed like no other. I would not dare a ride, yet—"

"How did she do it?"

"If I had not seen it with my own eyes, I would not believe it—"

Encouraged by their response, she tensed, anxiously awaiting her father's response. She dared not look up. Was he pleased? Was he very pleased with how strong she was, how very good? Did he realize it now?

Her father never noticed her. He never spoke a word to her, not even a "How fare thee?" As if she were invisible like angels, he did not even look at her. So she had mounted and ridden Iberia simply because she had heard him tell her two cousins it could not be done, that they would not be strong enough to mount his war-horse for many years. She thought to show him she was strong and good and worthy.

In the secret place of her heart she thought that if she could just show her father this, how very good she was, she might win his affection, and if he would only hold and kiss her like her mother had, it would not hurt so much. He might even remember the pony her mother had promised her.

Father Constantine stepped forward from the crowd of men, silencing the others. "Child," he said with anger in his voice, "did you bewitch the horse?"

Her long russet-colored plaits swung to and fro as she shook her head. Oh, no. Iberia was her friend. She always brought the great black horse carrots and apples from the kitchen, and though Franz, the stable master, refused to let her enter Iberia's stall or give him these treats, Franz took afternoon naps every day.

"How did you do it? Make the horse walk like that?"

"I am strong."

The men shifted uncomfortably, and the priest looked confused. "Why did you do it? Did you not know it was dangerous, that the beast might easily have killed you?"

She bit her lip, paused before suddenly blurting, "I . . . I wanted milord to . . . to smile at me."

A steely silence followed. In this silence a little girl held out her pain-filled heart for her father's blessing. A blessing he never gave her, for she heard then these awful words: "I cannot smile for thee. Do not expect it. Because to look at ye brings me a sharp prick of pain."

She thought she heard wrong. She forced herself to look up. Her father's gaze was on her. He was looking at her and in his eyes she saw his hate and fury.

Roshelle closed her eyes as her father's last spoken words to her echoed dizzily through her mind. "And what's more, daughter mine"—he spat the words viciously—"do not expect anything from me. 'Tis hard enough that ye have my name."

Hot tears filled her eyes, spilling over her cheeks as she stood there before him. Yet he turned away, pushing through his men, and with her back ramrod-straight, she withstood the harsh scrutiny of his men.

" 'Tis a shame. Her mother was so beautiful—"

"I still say the chit is bewitched—that hair of hers. She should be given over to the church before 'tis too late."

"Aye, 'twill be her only salvation."

"Aye, aye," they had all agreed, but she had barely heard, as she was running through the doors and into the bright sunshine of a spring day. She ran until her little legs collapsed. Hidden in the tall green grass and heather of the hillside, she cried and cried and cried until suddenly she felt a piercing gaze upon her. She looked up and wiped her face and swallowed. Then she blinked and blinked again. 'Twas his eyes, dark blue eyes filled with tenderness and something else, something dark and strange and wonderful.

She thought he was an angel. He said, "If ye cannot find what ye want in one place, ye must look elsewhere."

"Aye, monsieur, but where is elsewhere?"

He had laughed, a rich, warm sound full of mystery. Like afternoon rain on a window glass. "Look here, Roshelle Marie of Lyons and Bourges. Look here and then look yonder. Look yonder at the gift from your mother."

She had stared, first at him and then yonder, where a snow-white pony grazed in the sweet grass.

Papillion, dear Papillion, my father . . .

"What to do? What to do? What if they, they kill—"

Cisely clasped her pale hand over her mouth as if she were afraid to say the words, as if speaking of death brought it closer. "I am so afraid for you."

Roshelle turned from the open window to see Cisely's fearful amber eyes. She could not imagine her death; it seemed so far away. Heavy was her heart, though. Heavy with the mounting emotional toll of having lost Potiers and Reales by the sweep of that man's hand.

Vincent de la Eresman, the Duke of Suffolk . . .

His name echoed in her mind as she stepped over to her

trunk, reaching down to pull out a plain green work gown with elbow-length sleeves, embroidered there and in a straight line down the front with gold-and-yellow birds. This went over her head to fall longer than her feet by an inch in front and a whole pace in back. She pulled out her hair and began lacing the front. She picked up a long gold girdle to tie about her waist.

"The Burgundy court would not stand by and let the guillotine drop, Cisely. Nor would Louis or even Charles." Then she added with feeling, "I do not think even the Duke of Suffolk is so bold!"

"I have no faith in the Duke of Suffolk's temerity!" Cisely said in her own impassioned whisper. "He is a savage brute! I see the way he looks at you . . . and, well, all men look at you, your beauty, but he, he seems to devour you. Who can say what he would or would not do? And Louis, sweet Louis, stuck in that infernal English dungeon, and even dearest Charles himself, least of all Charles, how could they stop him? They have no men and even less money—they are helpless pawns in Henry's game—"

"Helplessness is a confession of defeat, and I will not make it—"

Outside, Fiona knocked urgently on the door, casting an anxious gaze at the guards posted at Roshelle's door. One sat on the ground, dozing, while the other man drew with charcoal on a piece of parchment pinned to a drawing board. Panic filled her. Trembling hands knocked again before the latch lifted and the door opened.

"Oh, Fiona! You frightened us. I thought 'twas him again—"

Roshelle's relief, while sweet, was also mercilessly short. Fiona shook her dark curls as her hands went to her round cheeks and she burst into tears, dropping to her knees. "The duke means to kill ye, milady! You and all the men, burned at the stake. The servants, too! Everyone! Meself! He will see us all hanged or . . . or burned—"

Cisely genuflected. "Oh, dear God—"

"Fiona, who told you this?" Roshelle asked. "It cannot be true—"

" 'Tis, 'tis! The knights told Lance as he served them. They said servants and guards will be burned at your side tomorrow—"

Roshelle's blue eyes widened with the terror of it. "No! Oh, no—" She never thought, only acted, rushing through the door and running down the hall.

"Milady! Where do ye go?" The guard knocked over his board and paper as he tried to stand, the other guard just waking. "Halt! Halt, I say—"

Yet Roshelle was gone. She raced to the stairway, flying down the treacherous steps two at a time, then down the second-story landing to Edward's old chamber, where the duke would reside.

Having sent the duke's sword and knife to armorers, Fossy went about arranging the neatly folded clothes in his Grace's trunk. The duke still slept. He had not slept this long since that time he and King Henry had disguised themselves as commoners and spent the whole weekend fighting, wenching and rabble-rousing in London's more notorious inns and holes. Admittedly he deserved this rest. He had not slept in nearly three days, since the ship—

The doors burst open. The older man looked up to see the most comely creature he had ever laid eyes on. In a split second he guessed who she must be, though it would take him five more years to guess why Roshelle of Reales stood at the doors to the duke's private chambers.

"Is he here? Is he in here?"

"His Grace? Why—"

With a sweep of her skirts, she rushed past him and slipped through the door before he could stop her. Fossy stared after her in shock. Either the rumors of the duke's bedroom agility had reached France well ahead of his actual appearance, or yet another calamity was about to visit the young and beautiful countess.

A fine morning for a long walk, he abruptly noticed.

* * *

She appeared in his dream . . .

Shrouded in a tousled mass of long auburn hair, the bright, wild eyes darkened with passion as he laid her to the ground, his own gaze drinking the pleasure of the naked beauty before him: her thin arms reaching out to him, her rounded breasts tapering to a small, thin waist, the impossibly long lines of her slender legs. He took the rosy tip of her breast into his mouth, drawing small circles there. A small cry of pleasure issued from her lips before he parted her thighs and mercifully sank his sex into the sweet moist—

"No! No! Oh, God, please, have mercy! Have mercy—"

A hand snaked around a dagger even as he woke with a start, bolting up to seize his assailant with a harsh hand. Instantly he pushed her backside to the bed and came partially on top of her, the sharp point of his dagger at her throat. Only to have his mind come fully awake to perceive the would-be attacker. For several long minutes he struggled to make sense of the situation, just what the girl was doing beneath him in his bed as he slept.

A sleep filled with lusty dreams, dreams made by a patently unwanted appetite for this very package somehow lying beneath him now, his entire body hot and hard with naked desire. His next breath greeted her very real presence with a potent jolt of it, a thing felt through every fiber of his being, worsening as his senses filled with that maddening, sweet scent of hers, the feel of her breasts pushing against his arm with each breath she drew, the spill of the long hair across the bedclothes. He tried to concentrate on her terror-filled eyes, but even that didn't come close to tempering the wild race of his pulse of blood. "An answer to a carnal dream or my next nightmare, which is it?" Then more to the point, he demanded, "What the devil are you doing here?"

She tried to swallow but could not. She felt fairly certain

he would be killing her now before she could plead for the others. The terror of a slit throat filled her eyes and seized her physically as her blue eyes took in the sheer size and shape of his naked body, then the strong, pronounced features of his face. His eyes were dark and menacing, filled with suspicion, animosity and something else she didn't understand. She studied his thick dark brows and fine large nose, the cruel curve that sat on his lips, not a smile, but not a frown either. A two days' growth of beard darkened the sun-washed skin, making him look even more threatening somehow.

Yet as menacing and dangerous as the handsome face appeared, the shocking heat of his body on her sensitive skin felt more so. A curious tingling rose in her chest from where his arm crossed her breasts, somehow causing the unnaturally slow thud of her heart. She could hardly breathe, her neck arched dramatically and she bit her lip, managing a desperate "Please."

Her blue eyes dropped from his face to the strong hand that still held the dagger to her throat. Vincent's gaze followed. He tossed the dagger to the floor, as if realizing he did not need a weapon in order to kill her. He made no move to ease his weight, and this confused her. Almost as much as the sight of his bare arms and the wide breadth of his chest and shoulders. He seemed nothing but muscles and more muscles, all tightly encased in taut bronze skin and marked with a curious map made of athletic veins and battle scars—

"Yes? I am waiting."

Breathlessly, not understanding what was happening, she said, "I can't speak like this." As if to add credibility to the complaint, she squirmed and twisted beneath his weight. Only to realize it was absolutely the worst thing to do. Her every nerve ignited with his heat and she gasped, suddenly aware of every place their bodies touched. He felt hot and hard and—

She felt it, him, the threat of his body through the mercilessly inadequate cloth of her gown and the thin cotton bed sheet. Her eyes flew to his face. Only to find a curious amusement there.

"A virgin's response," he observed. "Like the idea that you would interrupt a man's sleep to have a conversation. And these pleas of an innocent are uttered from a twice-married woman."

The criticism registered but vaguely on her dazed wits. Dazed by the queer serums heating up in her body and in the most unlikely places, the discomfort mounted and made her want to writhe and squirm. Yet the slightest movement, her every breath, seemed to shoot more of his heat beneath these serums; and desperate, frightened by it, she reached her small hands to his biceps to push him away. "I came only to beg you! 'Tis true I can hardly plead innocence—I will not try! Take me if you must—"

"Sweetling," he interrupted with a deep, husky chuckle, "innocent or no, you can dispense with the melodrama, though I do like my woman eager. I assure you, your very presence in my private chambers makes your, ah, desires all too clear."

A small bewildered cry escaped in a heated gasp as his bearded face brushed across her breasts, where he breathed deeply her tantalizing softness and scent. While her thoughts spun, her nerves leaped to greet him. "My God, you are so deceptively sweet," he whispered as his arm reached under her to pull her small body into a tight alignment against his hips. The slow bang of her heart dropped to her loins. A rush of heat shot between her legs and she gasped.

All confusion lifted in that instant.

"Oh, no. No." She shook her head, her small hands still braced against his arms, as if that might hold him back. "You cannot do this! You—"

"Indeed." A brow lifted over fine dark eyes, he might have laughed. "With each passing second I become ever more convinced I am capable of doing anything. Anything," he said with feeling. With that he gently took her

lower lip between his, kneading it softly until he heard her
release a small, pained gasp. She turned her head to escape with a frantic No, but his hand steadied her as his
tongue lightly brushed over her lips. Tingling shivers alit
there, and then, then he was kissing her.

His mouth took hers with violence, a barely restrained
force, a kiss given with as much pain as pleasure. Yet it
changed. Against his will, one taste of the incredibly delicious spice and softness of her mouth, and it changed.
Dear Lord, she tasted like late-summer strawberries,
sweeter than life itself, and he groaned, the sound dying
in their joined mouths as he brought her head back even
farther to drink deeper still.

The shock of it went through her like a lightning bolt
and she froze, her thoughts tumbling in a sudden panic.
Panic that exploded in a warm sea of hot, bright colors
and she was drowning, melting beneath his weight, the
hard press of his warm, firm lips. The sinking heat
turned to a pulsating warmth in the deepest part of herself.

He would die if he tried! Die—

The thought made her go wild, desperate to save herself. She pushed against his arms with all her small
strength and wrenched her mouth from his with a breathless, frightened "No!"

Vincent stopped the kiss and lifted partially up, staring
down at her lovely flushed face, his mind firmly fixed on
the taste of her mouth, the taunting press of her breasts
against his bare chest, the small body writhing beneath
him. "Oh, no," she said, more frightened than he could
know, for all she could think was that burning would be
the least merciful end to the slow death by torture demanded when his men found him dead. "You can't do
this. I—"

She could hardly breathe, let alone speak. He abruptly
perceived the unmasked fear and confusion in her eyes,
the extent of her struggle, revealed best in the desperate
clutch of her hands on his arms, the small, perfect nails

breaking skin. "A lie or an incredibly naive statement. I can, and you can believe I want to." He shifted his weight to catch her hands, pinning them to the bed as if to underline her helplessness.

The move scared her more and with all her strength she tried to twist free. She heard a husky groan as he stifled her struggle by letting her feel more of his weight. Instantly she stopped.

All she knew was that she had to stop him, she just had to! Two dead lords of Suffolk would bring King Henry himself to Reales. With this fear she cried, "Please to God, you cannot do this! No matter what, I don't deserve to be raped—"

"Raped?" The very light of his eyes changed with the accusation. "What manner of child's game is this? You would now cry rape? A young woman appearing in a man's bedchamber alone without escort, neither invited nor announced, to wake him from his sleep—"

"But I did not think of waking you! Even you must admit my impropriety pales against the news that you mean to punish my guards and servants by the unholy terror of the stake! I came to plead for their lives, to beg you: take me if you must, but please to God, let them go!"

His dark eyes stared intently as he absorbed her words. She thought he would be burning her guards and servants at the stake. Dear God—

"You, as the Duke of Suffolk"—she rushed on to seize this precious pause—"you must know that our servants and underlings are innocent in truth, raised from the day they were born to follow their master's every word, that absolute obedience is strictly demanded. They were but following my orders! I am responsible, only me—"

A finger came to her mouth, his expression darkening as he listened to her poor defense. "Aye," he said in a voice made frightening for the control placed on it, "they are innocent and you are responsible. You are responsible,'' he repeated to underline the sorry fact. "Another being's obedience comes at a heavy price, and damn you, girl, you should have thought of that responsibility before you exercised your will and forced those people into sedition, obeying your reckless, foolish whim. I have no intention, nor have I ever had any intention, of putting the people to death simply because they were idiotic enough to follow a young girl's ridiculous mission to save them from some imagined tyranny.''

Abruptly he released her.

Released her to keep her safe. For as guilty as she was—exercising the unprecedented conceit necessary to think that she could lead grown men, knighted warriors, no less, into battle, single-handedly causing enough trouble to pull two hundred men from home and country and landing a disaster on the poor people of Reales, and most damning of all, murdering in cold blood his brother—even she did not deserve a raping. And for the first time in his life he was catching a glimpse of the base kind of emotions that led to such violence.

He sat up and swung his legs over the side of the bed.

In a subdued voice she stated rather than asked, ''So you will not be punishing the people of Reales.'' Which led her to the obvious conclusion that he meant to kill only her. She had to escape, now, before it was too late—

She started off the bed. Only to discover he had risen and stood up to dress, utterly impervious to his nakedness. She had seen all manner of naked men—bathing and dressing; once, too, she had witnessed the curiosity of a coupling from afar, and even once on a long trip to the Sorbonne University in Paris, disguised as a boy prodigy of Papillion, she had witnessed the phenomenon of a dissection of a human corpse—but as worldly-wise as she was, she felt her eyes widen with the confrontation of the scope and size of the wonder of his unclad body in its present state. He turned to see this. She looked quickly away, color rising hot and fast to her cheeks.

Which only made him laugh, a mean-sounding chuckle edged with some small disgust or irritation. "Holy Mother in Heaven, I have seen everything now," he said as he pushed his legs into breeches. "The very girl who murders men and leads warriors to rebellion is set to trembles and blushes at the sight of a piece of a man's flesh! You missed your calling; you are a natural for the charades of the theater."

Roshelle's mind had stopped on the accusation and with feeling she declared, "I did not murder your brother!"

"So you say. I have spoken to the only other soul alive who witnessed it and he says differently. Considering all I know of you thus far, forgive me if I find your elaborate pretense a good deal less than convincing, to say nothing of growing ever more tiresome by the minute. Which leads me to wonder how the hell you got out of your chambers in the first place. More to the point, where the hell are those guards now?"

Fossy, who always exercised perfect timing, answered the question by opening the doors and announcing, "Two very distraught guards await in the outer room to escort the young lady back, your Grace." The older man stepped back to let the two men inside.

"Distraught," Vincent warned, "does not even begin to describe their predicament if she ever gets out again."

Not wanting to wait for his threats to turn to her again, Roshelle came quickly off the bed. She moved swiftly to the doors but then stopped. With her back to him, and not knowing exactly why it was so important but only that it was, she heard herself ask, "Did you love your brother very much?"

A long pause filled with the sudden intensity of his emotions. "I suppose our animosity toward each other is common knowledge. The answer, then, is no."

The surprise of this went through her with a small, audible gasp. She nodded slightly, then quickly exited, followed by two contrite guards who would never make the same mistake again. Fossy watched as Vincent grabbed a cloth towel from the chest of drawers and, still half naked, headed toward the doors. "And where is your Grace going dressed like that?"

"Into the cold spring waters of that river, Fossy."

Chapter 5

Torches lit the darkened cellar beneath the great hall where Vincent and Wilhelm, his chef and his assistants, stood examining the bare shelves of foodstuffs. Two bags of grain, a half-empty barrel of lard and moldy cheese, that was all that was left. No sugar or spices. Despite a lifelong familiarity with his younger brother's weaknesses and flaws, the implication of the starkness of these shelves was obscene and unbelievable.

Little wonder the girl had murdered him.

"Merciful Madonna," Wilhelm said in a whisper, as if frightened or awed, "what the devil was Edward doing? What could he have done with all the monies and supplies? There's not enough for a night, let alone the summer long—"

Vincent's aging chef, Mason, leaned hard on his cane as his gaze continued to sweep in wide circles over the bare shelves, certain he missed something. "What we have might last a fortnight, no more." He approached the lard barrel and with glass to his eye, he peered inside, looking for signs of rot or mold. "I fear ye'll have to send for supplies at once, your Grace."

"Aye." Vincent nodded, and feeling his temper building, wanting his servants dispensed before he exploded, he rushed with the orders. "Make a list, old man. Have James check it and send it out today with, ah—"

"Send it with Coitine," Wilhelm supplied. "He's quick as a hare, and with his wife just coming into her time—"

"Aye, and send out four or five patrols to scout supplies in the area. Offer up more than a fair market price for any livestock save chickens, maybe ten percent more. Hunting can keep us fed if it comes to that, but later. And put all men on their off hours out at that river with fishing poles—we'll need all the help we can get."

"Fish, a poor man's diet—"

"At once, your Grace."

Amidst clucks and shakes of heads, the men left Wilhelm and Vincent standing in the cold, barren room. Wilhelm waited patiently as, with thoughts racing, Vincent continued to stare at the empty shelves of what should have been a full cellar. Add to it the hesitant tales of the people's hardships under Edward's reign here, and Edward's legacy grew darker and darker.

"I had always thought Edward only a small-minded cockscomb." Wilhelm broke the silence, using the word normally reserved for those with the red caps, the men who made their profession being a fool. "But this—" His hand swept the naked shelves before them and he asked the question. "Do ye think he had the grit necessary to murder good Saladyn?"

A damning thought and Vincent said as much. "No one seems to know what happened to any of the men we sent, but may he be forever damned if he did." He shook his head, clenching his fist as if to contain the pressure of his fury at the thought. "Curse him to hell! My brother got even in the end—look at this cesspool of morass and terror he left for me!"

"Aye, and Reales and the young countess be hardly the worst of it, too."

"Aye. The worst of it is cradled two hundred miles north, the whoreson whose mother is no doubt celebrating the sudden fortune of Edward's death. No doubt it saved the harlot the trouble of murdering Edward herself. 'Twill take two years to clean up this mess—"

Both men turned as footsteps approached from the hall.

An anxious-looking guard rushed toward the cellar doors. "Your Grace! The lady, the lady—"

With hands on hips, Vincent asked: "Now what has she done?"

Breathing heavy and obviously alarmed or angered, the young man stopped before the two men and, forgoing the formality of a bow, motioning wildly with his hands, he hurriedly explained, "The lady was missing from her chambers at supper. Of course, since I was on guard with Mickael, we knew she could only have tried to escape again down through the tunnels. I know not why, as it was made clear to the lady since yesterday that the tunnels have been filled with rocks and mortar. Yet she was gone and that is the only way out. Her women would say nothing, refusing to answer any questions put to them, so I called forth four men from the yard and sent two of them down there to fetch her—"

"Yes?"

"Then nothing. They do not answer my calls, and it has been over ten minutes down—"

Vicious curses sang loud in the still night air. He was already running.

No light lit the space and the air smelled dank and of rot. Donned in Joan's tattered black mourning gown, Roshelle hid her face behind a black mouchoir. Her auburn hair fell in loosened waves down her back. Only the trembling white of her small hands showed, but they, too, disappeared behind her as she pressed herself against the cold stone wall, her eyes wide and luminous, her breathing fast and furious.

Cisely, Cisely, Cisely!

Oh, God 'twas not working! Cisely was supposed to call down when the hall was clear, if it got clear. Just as they feared, more guards must have been summoned to her chambers before these two went down into these dark tunnels. Yet how many now stood on guard? If only two, and

if those two decided to come after her in here, then
maybe—

Please saints in heaven make it so!

'Twas the only escape offered her! She had to try. The
duke meant to lay her head to the guillotine just as soon
as he fabricated her trial for his brother's death and treason, high treason. She had to escape! All of a sudden she
could only too easily imagine her death—and as she had
heard it reported four times now, the duke was oft heard
saying, "If I do any one thing here, 'twill be to see that
one hundred pounds of trouble hanging in the breeze."

Her hands went to her neck and she swallowed, closing
her eyes as she imagined Charles receiving the news of her
death. Aye, he would be weak with grief and mourn
her death, but she had to face squarely the fact that he
would not seek retribution against such a powerful adversary as the Duke of Suffolk. The duke not only could get
away with hanging her but no doubt would—

What was that?

The hairs on the nape of her neck slowly lifted. She
tensed, alerted. Slowly she knelt down and grabbed the
iron tongs—he had removed all her other weapons from
her chambers, of course, but no matter that. With all her
strength, she'd used the tongs to drop the guards where
they stood before they even had a chance to draw their
swords. Straining to see through the darkness, she watched
the tunnel. With a little more luck, this man would also
drop as easily. Then she would race down the tunnel and
through the door . . .

Gripping the tongs tightly in her hand, she raised it over
her head, forcing her breaths through her nose and wishing
she could silence the loud thud of her heart.

She needed only a one-second advantage . . .

A faint scraping sound came from ahead. Unseen rats
scurried toward her, the tiny pitter-patter of their feet the
only sign of their presence. Oh, mercy—

What was it?

Not rats. The sound drew closer and closer. The light

of a torch stretched around the turn. Someone moved slowly toward her! Hidden in the darkness, her knuckles turned white on the tongs. She held her breath, her eyes wide with anticipation.

A torch flew through the air. A surprised scream sounded. Blue eyes flew to the ball of light rolling at her feet. He leaped before her. 'Twas him! She swung the tongs down with sudden energy. Too late. Vincent ducked his head just in time, taking the blow on his shoulder.

Roshelle wasted no time in marveling at the force expelled from his lungs. The tongs swung again. He caught it in his hand and, with a vicious curse, twisted it from her grasp while simultaneously pinning her to the wall with his bare hand at her neck.

The tongs dropped with a soft thud to the dirt floor. Small white hands flew to his to stop him from killing her. She understood the metaphor "frozen with fear" as she never had before and she closed her eyes, waiting for him to squeeze the life from her.

Vincent shouted back to the men, "I have caught the little vixen. Rest easy."

Her blue eyes flew open, her stomach turning somersaults, settling like the uncertain wings of a bird as it landed. Every sensation felt strong and stinging. He would be killing her now for sure—

Torchlight lit his face, highlighting the anger in colors of gold and orange as his dark gaze bore into her. His long hair was pulled sharply back, accenting harsh lines that changed his eyes and crossed his forehead, as if he were considering something unpleasant indeed. She hated his height, the way it made her have to look up to him and, taken with his unmatched strength, a strength she felt even in the fingers that held her neck, made her feel so curiously weak and utterly, fatefully helpless.

She hated that most of all and she spat, "If you mean to kill me, be done with it!"

"Kill you? Nothing half so pleasant. Yet." Vincent felt her pulse fluttering wildly beneath his hands; her fear was palatable. He made absolutely no move to lessen it, for he believed she deserved at least the fear. "An escape attempt, I suppose?"

She saw no reason to lie and every reason to confess. She barely managed a nod beneath his grasp at her neck. "The guards? Where are they?"

Roshelle cast her gaze hesitantly behind him to the place where the two men sat tied and bound, still unconscious. Without releasing his grip, Vincent looked behind him. He could barely make out the shapes of the two men bent into balls on the ground.

"Two men in need of help down here—at once!"

Her gaze flew wildly around the dark space. Hope left her with her next breath and she bit her lip with a pained expression. He could not blame her for trying! She had to try to escape! 'Twas her very life!

There was only one chance left now. One chance that depended wholly on her circumstances changing after this feigned trial he insisted on—

Abruptly she saw how he stared at her.

A look magically connected to her still trembling stomach. She drew a sharp breath as his gaze brushed over her as if she stood naked before him, and it made her want to cover herself. Her heart hammered with warning when this was not necessary.

A strange light lit his eyes and why, yes—she could tell she amused him. "Milady," he asked with honeyed sarcasm, "are you frightened by something?"

Heat rose on her cheeks. She tried to look away, to collect the tumble of her thoughts, but his gaze held hers. More men rushed to this place at the end of the tunnels, filling the small space with torchlight, heated explanations and "Oh, my Gods." His fingers on her neck became light as a breath, teasing almost. Conscious of every movement, she swallowed, still lost in the depth of his eyes.

How did he do this to her?

Vincent pressed his weight against her slender form to

make room as his men cut the bindings and lifted the two
men to carry them out. The movement put the deep
warmth of his body on her. She inhaled the rich, clean
scent of him and breathed quickly, deeply, suddenly unable to get enough air, impossible as the muscles of his
thighs pressed against her hips over her loose and full
skirts. A quivering sensitivity made her thighs tingle. Like
two reeds in the wind, her knees went weak.

She swallowed once and closed her eyes. A mistake.
Every sensation grew in force. Her heart beat fast, signal-
ing an alert as the memory of the morning she had awakened him in bed darted quickly across her mind: how his
weight had pinned her to the bed, keeping her still and
trapped and frightened, and what that had done to her, the
touch of his lips to hers, the pinpricks of pleasure as his
arm crossed her breasts, like being sprinkled with fairy
dust, the way it had made a queer pulsating rhythm in her
most secret part, how all this appeared in embarrassingly
immodest dreams over and over as if, as if—

He had placed her under a spell.

She opened her eyes to see his, their slight narrowing,
the barest suggestion of amusement or mockery or both
as he seemed to guess her predicament.

Mortification made her lashes lower.

Which he understood only too well. He stifled the urge
to brush the stray wisps of hair from her face and to banish
the small smudge across one cheek. He tried to banish all
unwanted urges she inspired, of which there were many.
Far too many.

Such as the urge to take her lips in his and drink from
the sweetness of her mouth as he lifted her skirts and
stroked her sex—

"Anything else, milord?"

Vincent shook his head. Roshelle's eyes flew open in
alarm as she watched the last guard retreat. She found his
eyes instantly. His disastrous intentions seemed plain. She
started to shake her head. "Loose me—"

She pushed on his hands, still at her neck. Yet he made

no move to release her. "Not since Cleopatra has a woman given the world more trouble. I'm tired of your shenanigans—"

"Shenanigans?" she heard herself repeat in a question, her voice sounding strangely distant and far away. No doubt it was an unpleasant English word.

"Childish mischief," he supplied.

Fury shone with the torchlight in her eyes. How dare he think of her in terms used for children! How maddening his control and his power, his army, and most of all, his would-be king! "For all my trouble, you have not begun to see how much trouble I can be. I am a sharp thorn in your side, a pain that, I promise as I draw each new breath, will grow and grow, becoming so terrible and eternally lasting, you will begin to wish for God's own—"

His hand left her neck and covered her mouth, stifling the impertinent tongue and leaving only the bright eyes to convey these less-than-empty boasts. All she knew was that something dark and dangerous had returned when he said, "I see you need a lesson in manners and civility to your betters. Very well. You'll get it by exposure to the opposite." Abruptly he released her and turned away, "I leave you to your own devices, then."

Until that moment she had no idea how frightened she was of him. Her knees gave way and she dropped to the ground like a puppet without strings. Drawing quick, gasping breaths of relief, she confronted the mystery of her fear. It was not just his superiority to mere mortals, his awesome battle skills and sharper wit, the ease and confidence with which he commanded whole armies, the oh-so-curious attack his nearness made on her senses, but rather it was all of these things and more, much more. "God help me!" For the first time in her young life she felt like David meeting Goliath. She could but pray for David's God-given fortune, but now, with her last escape attempt thwarted by him—

Something brushed against her leg. She jumped up with a soft cry, staring at the dark space around her feet. Hot panic washed over her. She practically ran down the dark tunnel. No doubt she would have even more guards waiting outside her door now. And mercy, the only chance to escape was after the trial, when hopefully her circumstances would change—

Feeling the little beasties all around her, she leaped up the steps of the ladder. She pushed frantically on the latch to the trapdoor. "What?" She pounded her fist against it. "Open up! Open—"

After a full five minutes of furious pounding and shouting, all to no avail, she abruptly stopped. Terrified blue eyes slowly scanned the infinite dark space as she abruptly understood his last remark and fully faced how he would punish her.

"To Vincent de la Eresman, honored and revered Duke of Suffolk, defender of Champes and . . ." Vincent skipped the Duke of Burgundy's two paragraphs of formal address, all these honors and titles to read:

"What glad news the messengers bore of your successful end of the unfortunate siege of Castle Reales! I do hope my errant child, the good and fair noblewoman, Lady Roshelle de la Nevers, was solicitous and warm in her welcome of you and your noble army to our humble castle, as I know she, owing to her extremely solicitous and compliant temperament, is in practice of acting. I am sure my ever-obsequious dependent will provide you and your army with all she can to make your accommodations worthy of the finest army in our two most devout, revered and great Christian kingdoms.

"Just as I am equally certain there is a misunderstanding that has led you to entertain the ill-advised idea of bringing the said simple and meek child under the scrutiny of a trial. As I am equally assured the misunderstanding has been brought to light by the time you read these penned words and there is no longer a need for me to travel to Reales to mitigate for her. For my interests here forbid such a trip at this time.

"As for the court here, you will be glad to know your handsome young nephew is as 'bonny,' as you English like to say, and as healthy as they come. We know how much the young heir means to you—God's answer to your prayers—and rest assured, we will go to Herculean lengths to guarantee the boy's continued good health.

"Hence let us go on to our other, more important concerns: I beseech you to promptly forward the following rents from Roshelle Marie St. Lille's lands that are under my guardianship and tutelage. I have allowed modest increases in the amounts owed to me, increases frankly the result of what I'm sure will be your more thorough collection methods. The following list is bound to aid your tax collectors in this endeavor . . ."

Noises filled the warm afternoon air—the swing of axes, spikes and hammers, the rattle of wheels, the incessant neighing of the work horses amidst the shouts, songs and grunts of over a hundred laboring men—but Vincent heard none of it as he read the shocking words just brought by a messenger twice again. "Read this." He handed the letter to Bogo le Wyse. Bogo looked up from the scroll of gold-edged paper that he was studying and wiped the small beads of perspiration from his brow. His intense black eyes narrowed as he read beneath the bright afternoon sun. His long brow crinkled over his thin face, a striking face made of sharp angles and points, many leagues from handsome—though handsome mattered not at all when one worked with a mind as quick, thoughts as vivid, issues as pressing as his. He absently brushed a clump of his long gray hair back from his eyes, his thick gray brows forming a question mark as he read.

"Dear God," he muttered halfway through. "With a sweep of the quill, the depraved wretch abnegates his moral duty and holy vows!" He finished reading the letter, then read the relevant parts out loud for Wilhelm, who had just joined them from overseeing the nearby windmill construction. Like many other knights, Wilhelm did not read penned words well, having spent most hours of his early years practicing the warring arts.

"Huh!" Wilhelm said with plain masculine disgust. "He might easier have said: 'Take the girl, abuse her, hang her even—I do not care so long as you send me my rents!' "

"The situation worsens," Bogo said. "The duke's lack of familial concern will not mitigate Henry's cry for her head."

"Aye." Vincent took the letter back, crumpled it into a ball and tossed it into the foul waters of the moat beneath the platform where he, Wilhelm and Bogo stood. He looked up to shout at two men laboring to pull a wheel-barrow full of dirt up to the moat's edge, before he returned to his friends. "I can hardly believe it. I might be thanking the bastard for his gift if I only understood his motivation. Why would a man hand me a lovely young woman on a silver platter, one dripping with sarcasm and hatred both?"

"And to throw that bastard nephew in your face like that, the man has the brashness of a goose!"

The day had dawned warm and balmy. Dark clouds gathered on the mountaintop, though the sun warmed the air. Nature offered no respite from the foul odor rising off the moat, not even the wisp of a breeze—the branches of the trees hung still and lifeless; not a blade of grass stirred. Yet activity bustled all around them. Nearly fifty men labored to bring stones to the castle walls, the hardest and most arduous task, as the rocks were being dug from a hillside nearly half a mile away. Another fifty men labored to fill in the moat. Another twenty worked to begin dismantling the gatehouse. A group of men cut and cleared timber a mile away at the forest's edge. The land would be cleared, plowed and farmed, while the wood would be used in preparation of building a new mill. All other men sought food by hunting, fishing or scouting the depressed region for livestock to buy. Another large group worked to help till the fields for planting: plowing, gathering and spreading what little manure they had, hauling seed and whatnot.

The sun began to sink over the massive stone walls of the castle, drenching their crevices with blackened shadows. Instinctively the duke searched the lengthening shadows for still hidden details, needing to know everything and uncomfortably aware that he didn't.

What madness had inspired the abandonment of Rodez Valois's lawfully bound dependent to another man? A young woman who, aye, brought more trouble than a warring enemy army, but who was also more beautiful than a hundred others—nay a thousand!—a young woman more desirable than the light of the morning sun? Desire that was changing his sleep and intruding on his waking thoughts with a relentless urgency he had never felt before. "There is something about the young Lady Roshelle, a mystery—"

"The mystery," Bogo thought to explain, "is how such valor and courage became placed in that feminine package. All but the most devout must question God's own wisdom, assuming of course He is responsible . . ."

Bogo's voice faded in Vincent's mind as he closed his eyes, feeling the full oppressive weight of Reales in the tension gripping his neck and shoulders. Like a lead weight on his back. All this work he had orchestrated did little to detract from what these very ruins he stared at meant. He faced squarely the fact that his brother was responsible for the chaos and destruction of this land and her people. Little wonder the girl had murdered him! Despite all her ridiculous and misguided energies, including the conceit that let her play in a man's world, there was no doubt of the girl's great compassion for the people. Unlike the army of knights of France, that one maid had the courage to try to protect them.

The only person more guilty than his brother seemed to be the Duke of Burgundy. As far as he could tell, the duke sucked well over half of the revenues from this place.

More. That was the first thing he'd stop. The duke had grossly mistaken his prey this time. The mistake would cost much. He'd teach him a lesson that, like the one for the lovely Roshelle, would not soon be forgotten.

He had ordered the latch open this morning. Jackson, a guard, said the lady had emerged miraculously unaffected and unscathed from the ordeal, save for "spitting with fury and venom," then added, "Methinks your Grace should not like to hear the disparaging names the lady called ye. Suffice it to say 'twas a very long list."

"Having heard her shrewish tongue before," he had replied with a smile, "I can only thank you for your consideration."

"I feel half sorry for this grand duke," Bogo was saying as Vincent returned to trying to make sense of just how much board timber they needed and how long the boards.

"Aye," Wilhelm agreed. " 'Tisn't every fool stupid enough to make an enemy of you. At least 'twill be his last mistake."

"Indeed," Vincent agreed, but just that quickly his smile disappeared as he watched two men take axes to the stones on the gatehouse. The deep, rich sound of his voice sang in the warm afternoon air, reminding everyone of his ever-watchful gaze as he set off at once.

The sun continued its grand descent and only three hours of light remained when Roshelle rushed outside, followed by an army of guards—actually only four, but it might as well have been an army. Cisely had taken her up to the wall walk to view for herself this newest scourge sent by the Goddamns. With horror and disbelief, she had stared at the assembly of men busily laboring to bring down the castle's defenses like ants on a dead fly. Oh, God! So much activity and sweat and work for ill!

All she knew was she must make him stop.

With a lift of her skirts, Roshelle rushed onto the drawbridge, heading to the gatehouse before another stone could be cut. The guards came up behind her, an ever-anxious

Cisely clutching a mouchoir to her nose, and three servants behind them. Half the men stopped their backbreaking labor to look up and behold the beautiful girl standing before them, hands on hips and red-faced with either fury or disbelief.

"You there! Aye, you!" She pointed at a man who still swung an ax. "What do you think you are doing?"

"Why, we be taking down the gatehouse, milady."

"Desist at once, I say!" The order came in a high musical voice, but one quite accustomed to unquestioned authority. "And who ordered this destruction?"

The question brought grins and chuckles as, one by one, the men turned their gazes to a figure atop the gatehouse roof. Her blue eyes followed their path to perceive a man, or rather the shirtless, muscular back of a man. A four-inch-long ponytail of thick dark hair, tied with a piece of leather, fell over a powerful, sun-bronzed back. Battle scars over muscles and more muscles were carved into this back by the sweat of his labors—no doubt one of the duke's cretins. "You, sir! Stop at once to answer for your master."

The ax struck a board and the man straightened as he turned. She heard his chuckle before she saw his face. The shock of seeing the Duke of Suffolk himself, laboring like a common cotter, made a pretty circle of her mouth, "You! You!"

"Me, me," he repeated with a grin, removing a red kerchief to wipe perspiration from his brow. "Is something wrong with your normally verbose tongue, sweetling? Or have I finally left you mercifully speechless?"

She froze, struck silent, and not by the remarkable fact of having found him in labor. Her mind stopped on the endearment *sweetling*. He called her that again, the name Papillion had always used to call her . . .

A coincidence, one that meant nothing . . .

Vincent agilely leaped down from the roof and she gasped, taking a quick step back to avoid being knocked over. Yet he managed the ten-foot leap like a cat, bending gracefully before rising to his full height. A nearby man threw a wet towel down to him and he caught it, wiping the cool cloth over the skin of his muscular torso before swinging it around his neck, holding it with both hands at the ends as he stared.

And stared. Over a skin-tight undergarment of pale rose, whose long sleeves reached her knuckles, she wore a tight-fitting gown of pink and maroon. This had elbow-length sleeves and a low neckline. Too low, he realized as he stared too long at the fabric tightly drawn over her full breasts before noticing the pink belt tied snugly at her waist. The maroon color was striking against her pale skin and rich auburn hair, more than striking. A small gold cross hung from her neck, and like a cloistered nun, she clasped it tightly with one small hand. Her hair was braided and wrapped into two large round circles on either side of her head toward the back, not unlike a halo. A small wisp of red-brown hair escaped the delicate curve of her hairline, the russet color vivid and rich against the ivory of her skin. Her breaths came quick and shallow. Two red streaks spread, like the strokes of a careless painter, across her cheeks. She was hardly oblivious of his appraisal.

Desire struck him like a sharp shaft in his chest. He tried to banish it, but success proved as illusive as a dream upon waking. He settled for ignoring it.

"I see you've recovered from your ordeal." A wave of his hand dismissed her guards and servants. The four anxious men and her hesitant servants left. Cisely came to stand timidly behind Roshelle, her eyes widening as she took in the scope of the work being done all around her and the sheer force of the masculine presence surrounding them.

"No thanks to you. A lesser person would have floundered in there." Thanks to a devout upbringing, she knew how to put the full force of her mind into prayer—prayers, to her shame, that were interrupted only with maddeningly persistent thoughts of Vincent de la Eresman. Thanks to

Papillion, she knew how to keep unwanted creatures from trespassing too close—a relatively simple trick. Any other woman would have gone mad with terror.

The girl's frank arrogance made him smile. "No doubt true," he said, and in the same tone of voice: "Samson, fetch some water." A man shouted to another, and within the space of a minute, the cask appeared before him. He splashed some over his face, then set it to his lips and drained it. He seemed made of muscles upon muscles, all tightly encased in bronze, sunburned skin, and when he drew a deep breath—

Roshelle abruptly realized the idiocy of her stare. As if his every movement were a source of fascination! She looked away, gathering her tumultuous thoughts as she cleared her throat. "What do you mean by this?" Her hand swept the area in the way of an indictment.

"This? I assume you mean all this laboring, yes? I'm having the gatehouse taken down."

"What madness makes you do this? Has Reales not suffered enough destruction at English hands?"

To her surprise, the question seemed to anger him. "Indeed. And I am astonished by how much."

She was suddenly staring at the wide width of his back as he walked away. Confusion hit her hard. What did he mean by that? A confession?

The men returned to work. With a lift of her skirts, she rushed to catch up to him. Cisely nervously followed.

Roshelle practically had to run to keep pace. "You must stop! You must—"

As if her words were a command, he stopped and turned to face her again. She nearly ran into his towering frame.

"You must stop! The gatehouse is a perfectly sound structure and—"

He took her arm to move her from the path of a cart. " 'Twas a sound structure, but if you use your mind at all, milady"—he brushed her nose with his finger as if she were a young, ignorant child—"you can easily see it will be useless once the moat is filled in."

No sooner had the words been uttered than she caught sight of the men dumping dirt into the water. "The moat? Oh, not the moat, too! You cannot!" He had started walking again and she raced again to catch up. "We need the moat! 'Tis the primary defense at Reales! The first defense!"

He rejoined Bogo at the platform, immediately inundated with questions and news from the half-dozen men waiting for him there. Ignoring her cries for the moment, he alternately listened and issued orders. One by one, the men left, until only his small, hawkish steward, the man Bogo, Wilhelm—lending a hand and a smile to Cisely—Roshelle and he stood there. Roshelle noticed nothing and no one. All she knew was, "You cannot fill in the moat! Without it we shall be the unhappy victims of any army or brigands who pass through here—"

"Are you expecting an army, sweetling?"

The taunting reference to the deplorable lack of a viable force to fight him pressed her lips to a hard line. "You cannot do this to us!" She clenched her fists at her side, not even noticing until his amused gaze dropped there. "You cannot! The English"—she spat the very word—"shall not be here forever, and when you leave, we will need our defenses intact. You must see this!"

"Quite the contrary. I have no intention of leaving. Now or in the future. As to what I see"—his gaze brushed intimately over her figure again—"all I see is a young lady whose presence is disturbing, to say the least."

"As I find your presence more than disturbing!"

He laughed, and leaned over to whisper, "And believe me, I am fully aware of how much."

Her blue eyes shot to his face, trying to assess the exact meaning of his words, but he only chuckled again, while Wilhelm thought to try and distract Lady Cisely from Vince's brass ridicule. He pointed to the river, and though he knew very well, he asked the fair maid if she could tell him its source.

Roshelle did not understand how this man could taunt

her when all the world seemed to be crumbling at her feet. When his fist pounded the world to make it crumble. He was worse than his brother! Worse!

Then Vincent drew closer to explain, and his sudden nearness made her breath waver uncertainly, her gaze filled with the same. "And if it were just us, you and I, I do not think I would mind very much. However, it seems your presence has much the same effect on all men. Look."

Startled eyes lifted over their surroundings, where a number of men had stopped working, coalesced into small groups, nearly all of them smiling, chuckling, staring in her direction. Since the day she was born and her mother had held her over the castle tower for everyone to view, she had solicited the interested stares of people: it was a fact of life as common as drawing breath. That he thought it worthy of comment brought a surprised lift of her brow. "You would blame me for the sloth of your men?"

"Sloth?" He chuckled. "Sloth is not what you are inciting."

She ignored this comment as best she could. "We stray far from my point and purpose. I implore you to stop at once. The moat is our primary defense—"

"Ah, rest easy, milady." Wilhelm tore his gaze from a blushing Cisely and said in a more conciliatory tone, "We have more than enough men to defend this place, methinks, even in the worst of circumstances."

"This," Roshelle told them angrily, "is the worst of circumstances! These men cannot stay here forever, can they? Even you cannot hope to pay them for much longer."

"You demonstrate a surprising want of imagination," Bogo said, and with humor. "First, in possibly imagining this to be the worst of circumstances, and secondly, in assessing the limits to his Grace's fortune."

Her eyes locked with Vincent's as the others talked, and what she saw there caught her breath, holding her still and transfixed. Again. There were no limits to what her imagination saw in those darkly intelligent pools and what she saw as, peering thoughtfully over the rim of a goblet, he arrogantly brushed his gaze over her figure. Her face grew hot again. She covered her cheeks with her hands. He grinned at this, chuckling when she swung around in a transparent pretense of examining the work around her.

Wondering about that blush, Vincent motioned to a draftsman approaching with newly laid plans held reverently in his hands. "Bring these to me at supper. I will have a look." He turned behind him to call over to the place where the foundation for the new mill was dug. "Hanson, get two more dozen men there on the morrow. I want it finished in a fortnight." He pointed to where the foundation was being dug for the mill, turning back to find her staring at him, and came to the point. "I will not live with this foul odor a day more than I have to."

"Is that your reasoning? If you would give it but a week or so! That is all it takes before one learns to ignore it."

"Huh!" Wilhelm scoffed. "Look at Lady Cisely at your side, milady." All gazes turned to Cisely. "And how long has your very own sweet lady been here?"

Bogo and Vincent laughed as Cisely, blushing with embarrassment at having injured Roshelle's cause, slowly lowered the mouchoir she held at her nose.

"Well, well," Roshelle hastily tried to explain, "Cisely is, is, well, delicate! Very delicate. She always has been. I mean—"

"What a selfish brat!" Vincent said with a warm chuckle ending in an amused grin that caught her full attention with its boyish levity and ease. For a moment it held her transfixed, and in that space of a moment, there were no wars, countries, kings or blood between them. "Because you are the only one in all of Reales who has escaped the stench of this moat, you expect all others to suffer with it."

"Escaped? What can you mean?"

The words were said haltingly, the last one uttered with a small gasp, as he took her hand in his and brought it palm-up to his face so he could drink deeply of the sweet perfume of her skin.

"My senses fill with the proof, milady."

She forgot to breathe. He could not touch her with impunity. For a thousand tiny shivers raced up her arm, tingling down her spine. And the look on her face announced the sensations for all the world.

Bogo rolled his eyes and returned to the scroll, while Wilhelm chuckled. They had both witnessed Vincent's effect on the fairer sex too many times to be surprised, though it was still a source of endless amusement, and all the more because of Roshelle's endless profession of animosity for Vincent. Bogo often said he could hear women tremble with desire as Vincent passed, while Henry's comments were far more bawdy, and more to the point.

"Again we stray from the point," Roshelle said. "If 'tis just this odor, then I can fix you with sachets that will make the air in your chambers fine and sweet—"

"Do we have a hearing problem, sweetling? Even if you made the air sweeter than the heavens, that hell pit is still a breeding ground for disease. I will not—"

"What can you mean?" Her mind stopped on the issue of disease.

"Foul waters breed disease."

He might have just said the moon was made of sponge cake. "Water breeding diseases? I have never heard such a thing!" This was said as if proof of its existence depended on her knowledge of it. "Water breeding diseases? What lunacy! Diseases are bred by the unbalanced phlegms. All the world knows this."

"All the ignorant know it," Bogo corrected her, his mind leaping to the explanation as it always did; he didn't know yet that he had at last met his match in the unlikely form of Countess Roshelle de la Nevers. "The learned hath discovered that foul water breeds diseases. The theory was first postulated by none other than the great and controversial Venetian physician Raphael de Lago, of course, and now supported not just by all learned physicians but by all Venetians as well, anybody really who lives where waterways turn foul. For within a week after foul water is noticed, not only are insects many times multiplied, but so is the disease, both in types, severity and sheer numbers of those who succumb—''

''A spurious coincidence—no doubt the erroneous idea owes itself to the fact that the very factors that make water foul can also affect a body's balance of phlegms. And having studied with the wisest of all physicians, a mind far more knowledgeable of diseases and their ill effects than the next ten wisest physicians and surgeons in all the world, I can say with authority, 'tis simply not true.''

''Indeed! And who might this highly revered authority of disease be? The town's midwife, mayhap?''

With eyes full of spite and venom, Roshelle stared. 'Twas no use talking to these men. They would not listen to reason. Their purpose was to ruin the castle and the land it supported. They did not care a farthing for the people, her people, the good and simple folks of Reales.

''The name of my teacher was Papillion, and if you think I will let you slander—''

''Papillion?'' Shock changed Bogo's face. ''Why, I do know that famous name,'' he exclaimed, his voice changing from scorn to wonder with its sound, drawing Vincent's sudden attention, then answering it. ''I have personally heard a series of lectures by the famous man at the Sorbonne. I am even a correspondent with one of his followers. The man was once a Franciscan, a counselor to the Orleans court and, some said, a seer as well, though he himself dismissed that claim, standing against his own personal experience, which was one of his most widely discussed ontological points—''

''Oh, he stood for this and then for that,'' Roshelle said, dismissing this. Actually, she got few of Papillion's philosophical points straight, his philosophy always seemed so complicated and irrelevant, though it was the only part of his wisdom she dismissed.

''The man also dabbled in alchemy and, aye, he was

well known for his knowledge of medicine." Turning directly to Vincent, he said, "His lectures at the Sorrentino were famous, one of the best thinkers since Thomas Aquinas. I have given you some of them. Remember?"

"Yes." Vincent nodded, remembering a good deal more and suddenly curious. "Was he not also a heretic, chased and finally caught by the church?"

An amused smile lifted on Bogo's face. "Why, yes. Yet I never heard of his fate after that, though his secret writings still circulate—" He stopped and, suddenly curious himself, he demanded, "How is it you, Countess of Reales, came to be associated with that man Papillion?"

The question instantly subdued her temper but gave her pause. She exchanged glances with Cisely, an unspoken message passing between them.

"Among other things," Cisely shyly ventured, her voice but a whisper, "the countess was Papillion's student for many years."

"A female?" Bogo asked, as if drawing into question the very wisdom of such a thing. "And you are so young—!"

"Papillion always said Roshelle was the smartest girl he ever met."

"Aye, I can see that, but I'm curious," Vincent wondered out loud. "Did this man Papillion also comment on her penchant for trouble?"

"Oh, yes! He used to say—"

"Cisely!" Roshelle stopped her before she could impart Papillion's disparaging words about her penchant for trouble.

"Well—"

"What fate befell the famous man?" Bogo asked. "Is he still alive?"

Roshelle's blue eyes held Bogo for a long moment before their dark lashes closed; the thought of Papillion's fate, never far from mind, rocked her back on her heels. The answer was aye and nay. For she had watched his death, and yet when she knelt in prayer in the forest glen, she would suddenly feel Papillion's transcendence. A miracle, it was! His spirit, the very essence of his soul, came from the heavens, a place of light and love and peace, and she'd feel his love cascading over and around her, putting tears in her eyes and joy in her heart.

Then, like from a dream, she'd wake all of a sudden, greeted by the whispering, soft lyrics of the forest, and he was gone. It was all gone, as if it had never been. Had she imagined it? Was she so desperate to see Papillion that her mind conjured this wondrous vision of his transcendence? She did not know . . .

The poetry in her eyes transfixed Vincent for a long moment. There was something here, a mystery, and he wanted to know it. He wanted to ease the sadness in those eyes . . .

From the deep blue sky Greyman's cry sounded, bringing her blue eyes up. The magnificent creature circled overhead, spiraling lower and lower—the beast was ever cautious of his mistress's predicaments. Roshelle reached into her apron pocket, withdrawing the leather cloth that bore the many marks of his claws.

Seeing it, the falcon descended in a graceful swoop to her hand. Wings outstretched, he curled his claws around her hand before his small, keen eyes absorbed the surroundings and the foot-long feathers curved gracefully against a sleek brown body.

The men seemed to gawk; even Vincent appeared taken aback by the bird on her hand. None had ever known or heard of a woman falconer before. The sport of kings, the precious few trained falcons belonged to the wealthy nobles who could afford the magnificent bird warriors for sport hunting. "Ah, Gawd, he's a beaut, milady," Wilhelm said in awe. "He be yours?"

"In a manner of speaking," she said coldly. "As much as any creature can belong to another."

"Yet you do not have a falconer here, do ye?" Wilhelm questioned. The training of falcons was no easy task. One bird often required a year or even more of painstaking and patient training before it could be used in a hunt. Traditionally, the job was passed from father to son, but in recent years, owing to the ravages of the plague and war, then to a strange falcon's disease, the expertise necessary to train the birds had become increasingly hard to come by. Vince himself had searched for nearly a year, finally giving up the hope of ever finding a qualified falconer. Henry gave him two well-trained birds last year, but both had been struck by the falcon's disease, dying before the year's end.

"Nay. We do not. I trained Greyman myself. Or," she corrected herself, "I should say I tried to train Greyman myself. One of my best friends was the old man Gasper, the Falconer of Orleans, who taught me the necessary patience and tricks."

A brow rose and Vincent said, "I am impressed."

"What hunts does he work well?"

"None, that is, besides his own, of course. I do not countenance the hunt, so I did not train him to it."

Like all men, Wilhelm had oft heard these foolish notions from the gentle womenfolk. "A shame," he said with feeling. "He has the look of a strong, quick hunter."

Vincent removed a piece of dried beef from his pocket, a treat normally saved for the dogs. He brought this to Greyman's beak while gently reaching a long forefinger over the bird's belly. Greyman quickly saw he would have to perch upon the new hand in order to get the flesh. The greedy fellow did not hesitate overlong.

"Greyman." Roshelle hissed his name as a warning, displeased with his easy affection. Like the cat! The bird made no move to eat the treat. Roshelle did not allow him to take food from anyone else. "Give it back." The bird hopped from claw to claw. He wanted that meat. "You wicked fellow! You heard me!"

The bird dropped the morsel to the ground, then lifted with angry squawks and flapping wings. He dove toward Roshelle's head, making her duck before he rose with flight into the air. The men's laughter drowned out Roshelle's string of curses aimed at her feathered enemy. Even Cisely smiled for her embarrassment. Wilhelm slapped Vincent's back. "That's what ye get when ye put a woman out to do a man's job!"

The men's laughter pricked her temper. She saw she would have to force the duke's compliance. So be it. "Again we are diverted. I want you to stop your wretched hand of destruction. So I will warn you: I have a powerful potion. It brings a deadly flux to thine enemies." Her determined blue eyes did not waver as she added, "I am not adverse to using it."

The threat brought surprised, nay, she realized, shocked silence. She could see he had not expected this, that she would force his way. She had to! She would not let him—

His hand suddenly came around her arm, his hold gentle, not threatening until she tried to pull away. "Unhand me—"

Vincent ignored her request as he motioned to Wilhelm, who still was uncertain he had heard right. Uncertain simply because he could not believe a woman would dare. A dawning look of outrage on Bogo's stark face told him otherwise, while sweet Lady Cisely quickly lowered her gaze with horror and uncertainty, uncertainty not of Roshelle's meaning, but of the duke's retribution.

The red-haired giant gently slipped his arm around Cisely to lead her away. Frightened and uncertain, Cisely looked back, hesitating, but a tightness in Wilhelm's gentle hands left her no choice. Bogo abruptly decided to mind the armorers and oversee certain repairs that were in progress.

Then they stood alone.

He seemed suddenly a whole pace taller, that much more menacing as he stared down at her. She tried to step back but his hand still held her arm. "Loose me! You're hurting me—"

"Loose you! I've a mind to turn you over my knee. You know, Roshelle," he began calmly, "I have warned you. Henry even now wants your head after the pretense of a mock trial, and your guardian, the Duke of Burgundy, refuses to stand for you at this trial—''

"Nay!" She shook her head. "I do not believe you! Even he would not dare it! If I die he will lose all my lands to the church—''

"And he is inexplicably unconcerned about the prospect, no doubt imagining his rapacious band of merry lawyers could weasel out a goodly portion of them in the bargaining.''

"So! You will execute me!''

"This is the point, Roshelle; I might if I wanted to," he said in an intense whisper of a voice, and his free hand took hers, as if to emphasize the point. "What I will not suffer is these miserable manners of yours, far less these ridiculous threats.''

"The only way you will not suffer them is to leave—''

She stopped with a pained gasp as an exquisite pressure shot through her hand. Exercising miraculous control, he had gently pressed his thumb and forefinger over the pale extremity, and applied the lightest of pressures. Roshelle's eyes shot to her hand. Her free hand came over his to stop it. To no avail!

She gasped again, unable to stop and utterly unable to bear it. The pressure mounted until she suddenly cried out, not with pain but with the shock of an unbearable torment of sensation. Like being tickled past the point of tolerance, but worse.

Much worse. With a small, pained cry of surprise, she dropped to her knees before him.

"Better, milady," he addressed her supplication, utterly unmoved by her helplessness. "From this point on you shall be on your knees before me. As is my due. And just so you understand how I deal with threats, for every one man I lose to this, ah, flux of yours, any flux for that matter, I will personally slay two Frenchmen and I shall do so with the just sword.''

Roshelle gasped, whether in agony from his words or his hold, she didn't know. Tears sprang to her eyes, yet the unbearable pressure did not cease and she desperately began fighting not to cry out again, her free hand clawing feverishly to stop him.

"As for your manners, you shall henceforth address me only with the veneration and esteem due my title."

Her blue eyes shot up with furor and outrage.

"I will hear this now from thine honeyed lips."

Fury mixed with the unbearable agony, mounting, mounting, the former greater in force, and through clenched teeth, she spat, "Never! Never—you can kill me first—"

Yet he did not have to kill her. The pressure increased ever so slightly. "I will hear this now."

She could not bear the pressure a moment longer, and in desperation, she uttered, "Thy . . . thy Grace."

"Not good enough."

She spat in anguish, "Your . . . Grace."

"Not good enough still."

"Stop . . . please, I—"

"Say it."

"My . . . Grace!"

"Again."

"My Grace!"

He released her hand and, holding her arms, he brought her to her feet, only to realize he had to hold her up. Her knees shook like reeds in the wind, and her whole body trembled violently.

Yet not from pain. There was no pain. The sensations floated away from her hand as if they had never been there. Dissipating like magic, and yet she would have welcomed pain. She drew a shaky breath and fought back tears, absolutely the last thing she would let him see.

Yet it was through the veil of tear-washed eyes—eyes as tempestuous and dark as a storm-lashed sea—that she met the intensity of his stare. An unspoken message passed between them, emotions trembled through her, more as he whispered the surprising words, gentle words ushered with a strange intensity: "God, girl, you are wild and beautiful, more tempting than I ever knew a woman could be. I do not want to tame you. Do not make me.''

Then he released her and turned away. The weight of his words made her collapse all of a sudden, more frightened than she ever had been. *Mon Dieu,* she was in trouble!

She was hardly aware of Cisely running to her, dropping to her side, taking her in her arms. ''Roshelle, Roshelle, dear God, Wilhelm hath said, he just told me that the duke will see you tried on the morrow for his brother's death. That Henry makes him. And that Rodez Valois, the Duke of Burgundy, hath refused to stand for you—he is not coming—''

Roshelle nodded, but she was barely listening.

''He hath refused! Wilhelm says that Henry wants your head, and without your guardian to speak for you, he will force the duke to execute you. On the morrow. Wilhelm says the duke hath planned the means to satisfy Henry's thirst—''

Cisely could not say the words. She collapsed into tears and Roshelle took her against her breast, holding the girl tightly as Roshelle finished for her, ''Thirst to see me dead, to have his revenge . . . On the morrow . . .''

Yet death was not the worst possible fate she faced.

Chapter 6

"**A**re you sensing what I am?" Wilhelm asked Vincent with a toss of his red head toward the place where Miles Hartman sat uncomfortably on a hard wood bench before the dais in the great hall. Vincent, Bogo le Wyse and Wilhelm sat on the dais overlooking the great hall where the high court convened. They now waited for the appearance of Countess Roshelle Marie de la Nevers. There were no French people present. On two long benches on one side of the stone wall sat the twelve men of the duke's personal guard—to serve as legal counsel, a necessary formality. "About the last of Edward's guards there? Our witness?"

Vincent peered over the rim of his goblet as he swallowed the last of his water. "I'm not sure I am. What?"

Wilhelm tossed the roasted duckling to the plate before wiping his fingers on a napkin cloth. "He's as ripe as week-old pig rinds." He finished the watered-down ale before setting the goblet down with disgust. "Worst piss-ant ale I've ever tasted!"

Vincent ignored the oft-heard complaint and continued to stare at the man, knowing of course Wilhelm did not speak idly. The seemingly banal comment had import. "Wilhelm—"

"Ah, Vince, your mind's on other things. No doubt a wild young woman with sky-blue eyes. From the odor coming at me, I'd wager the man hath a fear of water."

A slow smile spread over Vincent's face.

Darkness filled the tall windows and torchlight cast dancing shadows on the bare and unadorned walls—apparently the tapestries here had been sold long ago. No modern features had been built within the stone walls either—no guardlope or hooded hearth or lamps or nearby buttery for a tired servant's ease in serving the hall. Torches lit the space from the walls, while in the dead center of the room sat a rounded hearth, its bright flames leaping up. "Like dancing gypsies," Wilhelm said, his grin the result of a long-ago memory of a particular gypsy maid. The duke had new tables and benches made after the old ones had collapsed the first time they felt the weight of his knights—the English were so much larger than the French—but the rush-covered stone floor overwhelmed the pleasant scent of freshly cut pine. The floor should have been swept out long ago, but as Wilhelm observed, "Even the servants here are depressed and lethargic."

Bogo le Wyse peered into the pages of a Bible, his eyes black and intense as, with more intellectual curiosity than religious fever, he pursued one of his and Vincent's entertaining competitions—finding contradictory passages in the Bible. Once he found a contradictory passage to a passage, he had to search for a verse that challenged Vincent in turn. Bogo pushed his thinning, shoulder-length gray hair back with a loud and pleased "Ah-huh!" He had found just the one. He thrust the book in front of Vincent, pointing an impatient finger at the passage.

Vincent stopped his conversation with Wilhelm, scanned the verse, and after a moment or two, quickly flipped the pages, found another verse and, with a triumphant grin, passed the book back to Bogo.

Bogo read the verse once, then twice again before he threw back his head with his laughter. Vincent's smile disappeared as he abruptly realized how long they had been made to wait. He interrupted Wilhelm in mid-sentence to demand, "What the devil is the delay? Where is she? You"—he motioned to a nearby servant—"fetch the lady at once—"

It was as if she had been waiting behind the closed doors for the exact moment in which to appear. For as the servant opened the door, Roshelle stepped into the gold light of the great hall. The silence alerted Vincent and he turned to see her there. For a long moment he stared, just stared, startled by the simplicity of her beauty.

Roshelle wore a modest gown of pale green cloth, spun on a spinner. Emerald-green- and gold-embroidered lines edged the square-cut bodice, the long flowing sleeves and the long skirt that fell from a vee at her hips. A handmade rope of green-and-gold woven thread belted her small waist, accenting the slender shape beneath. She wore no caul or overdress. A green band, like a halo, held her long hair back, which cascaded in its rich color past the small of her waist. Like an unadorned frame around a master-piece, all gazes were drawn to, then held by, the girl's beauty.

Wilhelm was staring at Cisely, admiring the firelight in her dark curls, wondering at the delicate and frail-looking creature who had captured his eye. Normally he liked large, bawdy women, the exact opposite of her, and—

With a regal tilt of her head that always spelled trouble, Roshelle thought to show Vincent she had recovered from his torment of yesterday. A pretense, she knew, for she might never truly recover from it. He frightened her sense-less, more now that this farce of justice would push her to her death.

"I appear here," she began, owning courage by the idea she would be escaping, never to lay eyes on him again, "not out of obedience to your summons or deference for this trial, but rather, I appear to provide a voice of dissent, representing all the good and poor people—"

Vincent cursed under his breath before he exploded. "Enough!"

The blue eyes shot to his face, half expecting him to find a comfortable spot before motioning her to proceed. Yet he only leaned back in his high chair, watching her with what appeared casual indifference, even boredom.

Save for those eyes. His eyes stared with intensity—she felt his gaze from the top of her head to the tips of her shoes. She felt it!

"Am I not allowed to address the court?"

He drained his refilled goblet and as he set it back on the table, still staring, he said: "No, you are not. I will warn you once: I've no mind to hear your tiresome litany of French invectives tonight. You will restrain your speech to only answering the questions put to you."

Color rushed to her cheeks and her fists clenched at her sides as the heated emotions—none of them pleasant—shimmered in her eyes. How dare he! Restrain her speech indeed! He would hear an earful before—

Before she escaped.

Roshelle cast her gaze back to Cisely, who glanced up at her quickly, offering sympathy and support. A barely perceptible nod passed between them before Cisely—who never could be trusted with any intrigue or secret—looked hesitantly toward the door as she actually genuflected.

Boldly meeting his gaze again, Roshelle tried to stifle her fury and indignation. She would show him! That is, if nothing went amiss, and she prayed this was so. For death itself awaited if she could not escape. As feudal lord, the duke would never let her appeal to Henry—not that Henry would ever condescend to hear her case, let alone rule any differently. The duke would personally set her upon the guillotine . . . and cut the rope—

Do not think of the guillotine, which is the common means of execution for the highborn. Not now. Not until the sting of its blade strikes my neck—

The thought made her gaze dance nervously around the room as Vincent motioned to Bogo to begin. She spotted a gloating Miles Hartman, her enemy, immediately. She barely graced him with a moment's consideration before passing on to the legion of the duke's knights. Not a kind face among them. Nor a French face either. She turned accusingly back to Vincent, the man responsible for this farce of justice, only to discover his gaze had not strayed from her.

Which somehow made her close her own eyes. How did he achieve it? This lifting sensation in her chest, the leap of her heart and the race of her pulse, the surge of response to him, a thing she had never felt before? After what he had done to her?

Roshelle glanced quickly up again, as if his appearance might provide a clue to the mystery. Vincent was so unusually tall. Seated, he was nearly the same height as his abbot, who was standing. Barbaric giants, the English. He wore a loose blue jerkin, and his dark hair was pulled straight back to reveal the harsh angles of his face, accenting the dark brows over his eyes.

After initial religious formalities, Bogo read from a sheet of golden parchment. "Here gathered is the high court of Reales, presided over by his Grace, Vincent de la Eresman, the Duke of Suffolk, and his honorable provosts, Wilhelm of Manchester, Sir Edwin of Salisbury, John of Huntingdon, Reginald of Essex, et cetera, et cetera . . ." He waved a hand, forgoing the rest of the titles to get to the point. "The court is convened to try the person of Roshelle de la Nevers, who stands before us accused of the murder of Lord Edward of Suffolk. Will the witness to this murder, the honorable and noble knight Sir Miles Hartman, stand and face the accused."

Roshelle stared for a long moment at the man before she retreated, closing her eyes for a moment only to conjure his leering grin as he'd watched Edward molest her with the intent of rape that night. When she reopened her eyes she found Sir Miles staring at her with unmasked hostility, no easy feat.

Bogo said, "Will you, Miles Hartman, tell us before God, the Father, and all gathered here what happened, exactly as it occurred, on the night Lord Edward was murdered."

One of the duke's knights, the man Bryce, abruptly stood up and, walking behind the dais, approached Vincent for a whispered conference. Vincent suddenly laughed. Bryce slapped him on the back and returned to his seat.

Roshelle stared with some small horror. How uncivil and ill-mannered! And how she'd give up a month of free days to know what had made him laugh. No doubt another disparaging remark, one whispered with laughter in the middle of her trial. She and her rebellion were little more than a colossal jest to these Englishmen. She tried to find comfort in the idea that David had had the last laugh against his persecutors, but somehow . . .

She glanced up. Bogo le Wyse read in silence from that great large book—he was too bored to listen, even!—and the duke and Wilhelm conferred in loud whispers as Miles Hartman began to speak with open hatred. ''There be not much to tell, as the tale of murder is as simple as a day be long. 'Tall starts with the lady herself. She be highborn, they say, but with the manners of the lowest French scum—''

Bogo's black eyes shot up from the book. ''French scum?'' The dark gaze alone was chastisement enough, though he only sighed with irritation. ''Henceforth refrain from slanderous nouns when addressing the accused, and I remind you, guilty or no, she is your better.''

Roshelle listened, staring with widening eyes and no small disbelief at these men. Neither Vincent nor his men, indeed least of all the abbot, paid any attention to the proceedings. Vincent bent over, now inspecting a pile of drafting sheets just brought him by his draftsman. The abbot still read and, even now, acted irritated with Miles's insult only because it interrupted him. The man Wilhelm, why, yes! He seemed to be leering at, at Cisely—

Roshelle's gaze shot to Cisely, only to find her blushing like a rose in spring! Indeed! She gave Cisely a disapproving glance. Cisely straightened, before lowering her eyes in apparent contrition.

Roshelle looked back at the redheaded giant. Smiling, he leaned his head back and seemed to doze. Four of the duke's knights played dice; another group conversed in not-too-quiet whispers. Here she was about to lose her life, and they acted as if listening to the proceedings was too taxing.

The idea brought anger, but inexplicable fear quickly followed. Why? Because killing her would be done with no heavy conscience or care! Just like that! She, as well as the people of France for whom she fought, meant nothing to them. Nothing . . .

"Well, she hates all things English, she does," Miles was saying. "We, all of us, knows 'tis her and her merry band of demons that go around spreading misery for us. Constant trouble." He snorted with disgust. "Like one time she put a foul-smellin' sticky substance in all our boots. Couldn't get rid of the odor for weeks. Those who could got new boots, and that's when we discovered she takes some of the profit from the town's bootmaker to give ta these lazy, no-good townsfolk around this hellhole!

"But Edward made her pay, 'e did," Miles continued, looking pleased. "He had the bootmaker put in public stocks for a week. The bastard learned 'is lesson well, 'e did, nearly lost 'is arm. To this day two fingers do not move." He laughed, wiping his mouth with his sleeve. "And then Edward forced the bootmaker to make the twenty of us new boots—for the charge of no coin, 'e did."

Like many others' in the hall, Vincent's wavering attention was caught by this last remark. He stopped talking and looked up. The words gave Bogo pause as well and he asked, "Was this bootmaker tried at hallmoot for this crime?"

Roshelle knew well the answer to the question. The hallmoot, the village court, was used for all matters of crime and punishment of common folks, save for the three high court matters of murder, rape and treason. Edward knew full well Phillips was unjustly accused, that he had nothing to do with the incident, but wanting free boots even more than he wanted to punish her, Edward decided the crime was petty treason, and therefore, the poor man deserved no trial by hallmoot.

" 'Twas considered a matter of petty treason, and so Lord Edward decided the matter himself.''

If Roshelle didn't know better, she would swear this upset the Duke of Suffolk. He exchanged glances with Wilhelm, whose own face appeared a studied expression of gravity. So this part concerned them! Why?

Confused by Vincent's expression, to say nothing of Bogo's, Miles Hartman hastily added, ''Any fool, even a woman, would have learned a lesson, but her? Oh, no.'' He shook his head, all but pointing a finger at her. ''The lady continued to harass Edward at every turn. A witch she be in truth. She made him lose 'is manhood for a spell—''

''What? Indeed!'' Vincent's tone was sarcastic, the surprising discourse holding his attention. ''And just how did the lady manage that trick?''

''No one knows how she did it. Only that she did. She maketh all these potions, ye see. One night she tricked the guards—fallen in their cups—to follow a merry dance into the foul-smelling moat, she did. Oh, the French folks had a hearty laugh at that one, they did. Then she sabotaged the wheelbarrows, so that every time a bloke used one, it broke down. I broke me toe with one! And she brought on the murrain that hath afflicted Edward's sheep here, and caused him a pretty price in profit, too, seeing how none of the townsfolk have hardly any sheep left and depended on his stock to provide some—''

''I take it''—Bogo's voice rose with unconcealed sarcasm, as he was now all attention—''you have no proof of these crimes either?''

The man looked both confused and alerted, as if he'd been asked a question in a foreign tongue and had to listen carefully to catch a phrase or two that he understood. ''Don't need proof,'' he decided to explain. ''We all knows she done it. Why, all the lady does is puff up the lazy, no-good townsfolk, bad-talkin' 'er betters and gettin' 'em as riled up as a hornet's nest on fire. And what for? For this rebellion she sprung on us, that's what—''

"The court will hear no more of these unsubstantiated claims against the accused," Bogo said with sudden impatience, if not exasperation. "Let us move on to the night in question. Restrict your speech to the specifics of that night."

"Aye, the night in question," Miles began. "That night meself and a half dozen of the men are walkin' up the staircase with 'is lordship. The windin' one right behind ye." He pointed. "Well! The lady was hiding in the shadows for us, and when we least expect it like, she springs forth and hits Lord Edward hard over the head—''

"Hits him over the head with what?" Bogo asked.

"Ah . . . with, with—''

"Yes? Did you not see the weapon?"

"Ah, well, methinks 'twas a rod iron or a cooking pan—''

"Which was it? A rod iron or a cooking pan?"

"Well, 'twas dark—''

"It was dark? How dark? Were there no torches on the stairway?"

"Oh, aye, but, well, it all happened so fast, ye see. And the point of the matter be she hit Lord Edward so hard, he fell to his death!" Lowering his gruff voice, he explained, "Suddenly all her guards appeared with swords drawn for the kill. The fight was on." His narrowed dark eyes turned from Roshelle to meet Vincent's. "A fight that, like yourself, your Grace, I lost me dear little brother in. Killed, slaughtered like a pig at Michaelmas. Because of her—the witch!''

The viciousness with which his last words were uttered shocked the crowded hall into a stunned silence. All gazes turned to Vincent as if for the guidance on how to respond. Vincent stared unkindly at the man for several long moments afterward, then at last turned his gaze to Roshelle. Not with the accusation, but rather with pity.

Had Roshelle seen this, she might have felt a moment

or two of hope, but as it was, the accusation of witchcraft—though rarely taken seriously by the church these days—could strike fear in the bravest of women. For in the not-too-distant past many an innocent girl had been burned for the offense. And with Papillion's training in alchemy and herbal medicine, she felt especially susceptible to accusation. The guillotine was frightening enough, but at least that was said to be quick and painless—though really, Roshelle oft wondered of late, who would know?—but few doubted that the stake was the slowest and most painful way to die.

Roshelle shivered from the heat of many gazes upon her. She kept her own on the plain tips of her worn slippers until she heard, "I would hear how the lady replies to the accusation."

"Yes," Bogo said, now quite interested, laying the large Bible on the table, "how does the lady reply to the accusation?"

She looked up to meet Bogo's gaze, sensing the unfaltering intelligence behind the man's misleading appearance, an intelligence that no doubt revealed the duke's perspicacity in choosing his people. Very well. Intelligence was a quality she was fully capable of answering.

In the span of a moment she had gathered her courage. "Which of this man's fallacious exaggerations and misleading accusations would you now have me answer?"

A gray brow rose. "Why, any that the lady feels is deserving of an answer."

"Very well," she said in her clear yet soft musical voice, knowing there was no doubt now that she had captured the full attention of these men. "I plead guilty to the accusation of ruining several of the English guards' boots, including the deceased Lord Edward's boots. I did so in retaliation for his raising the hearth tax as well as the mill fees by nearly half, which threw the already desperate townsfolk, villagers and farmers in Reales even further into debt. Few, if any, families will survive."

Roshelle tried desperately to state it as fact, without

emotion, but this was not possible. Somehow each word she uttered communicated her pain, her compassion, her anger.

Miles Hartman shouted, "If Frenchmen worked half as hard as an Englishman—"

"An oft-heard cry from the Goddamns!" Roshelle cut him off. "I ask you, though, why should a Frenchman work when he gets nothing for his labors but an aching back and sleepless nights listening to his children wake for want of food? Why should he?" She turned and without realizing it, she pleaded with Vincent for his understanding. "The number of freemen left among the farmers and villagers is but a handful after all of the duke's and your deceased brother's rents, taxes, fines. And furthermore, I took this form of protest only after my appeals to Lord Edward's sadly wanting sense of justice fell, as ever, on deaf ears. Yet Phillips, the goodly shoemaker of Reales, never had anything to do with my indiscretion—though, as you have just heard, he was made to suffer much for it." Before Vincent might have responded, she added quietly, "And as for the question of Edward's manhood, I did indeed fix a potion to make him impotent."

"I knew it!" Miles jumped to his feet, shaking an accusing finger at her. "We all knew she did it. That hair of hers and this curse business, why, she fools people with all 'er talk of starving children and all—"

"You what?" Vincent's aristocratic, incredulous voice cut straight through his inferior's speech. The outburst silenced Miles. Vincent stood up and, bracing his weight on his long, outstretched muscular arms, fastened his gaze on Roshelle. "Do you expect me to believe you made a potion that affected my brother's, ah, meandering?"

"Nay." She shook her head, her eyes wide and luminous, and fixed with a determination to make him see she'd had to do these things. "I do not expect you to believe anything I say. 'Tis nonetheless true. I had to. After my second maidservant came to me with stories of his raping, I thought it my only way of protecting my dependents—"

"She be lying through her teeth!" Miles Hartman pointed at her. "The witch be lying!"

Vincent just stared, his mind slowly absorbing the magnitude of her words. He strongly sensed her honesty and wondered if those blue eyes could hold a lie, any lie.

He did not think so.

"Remove him," Vincent said with quiet authority.

Guards rushed to the place where Miles Hartman stood. Hands came upon the burly man. He shoved them off and marched out furiously. "She be lying! She be bent on blinding ye with another spell—"

The great wide wood doors shut.

Roshelle studied the emotion the accusation had put in the duke's eyes before, as if penitent, he lowered them in a pause. The silence lengthened, confusing her. She might have accused the duke of the heinous deeds! The abbot, too, just stared, frozen, as if uncertain how to proceed all of a sudden. She didn't understand, understood even less as the great red giant placed his hand over Vincent's as if to try to calm or soothe him. Then Wilhelm asked quietly, "Do you swear that this be true? That Edward forcibly raped two of your maidservants?"

"Aye, 'tis true," Roshelle answered in a subdued tone. "One of the women was four months with child. She was bleeding when she came to me. The child was lost."

This was absorbed in another steely silence. The very same solemnity weighed on the faces of all who heard. These sober faces exchanged glances, shakes of heads and murmured disapproval. The exploited, half-starved people of Reales were only the beginning, it seemed. Bit by bit, ever more of Edward's abuses were coming to light, painting the picture of a small-minded and cruel despot—a man bad enough as a simple head of a family, a disaster as lord of the land.

The doors opened again. All heads turned to see a nervous servant rush into the hall, approaching Roshelle. The anxious maid curtsied before her lady and said in an audible whisper: "A thousand pardons, milady, but the woman Josephine, in Reales, asks ye to attend her immediately. 'Tis her time—''

"Oh, no! 'Tis weeks early! Oh, my—" Roshelle looked at Vincent. "I shall have to leave for the good woman Josephine. As you heard, she has just passed into her time—" She stopped, abruptly cautioned by how he stared. An expression of taxed amusement marked his handsome features, as if he had caught a child's sticky fingers in the sugar trough. Praying her intuition was wrong, knowing it wasn't, she quickly plunged ahead. "I, I must leave to attend a birth—"

She started forward.

"Well, well! A midwife among all these other unexpected talents! I don't know why I'm so surprised. And of course a village woman would come into her time in the middle of your trial!" The duke's smile was all condescension. "Of course you will not mind if, ah, Tyrone leaves ahead of you to confirm the, ah, exact nature of this emergency? So many women have false starts, do they not?"

With unmasked apprehension, Cisely and Roshelle exchanged glances. How, dear God, did he know? How? They had counted on the masculine tendency to defer to women on matters of childbirth. "This is hardly necessary!" Roshelle protested.

"I'm afraid it is."

"Would you jeopardize a newborn's life? An innocent woman? I cannot abide it—"

"Yet you have no choice, milady. Tyrone, follow this servant to the place in question and discover the exact nature of her need, if indeed there is even a need. The lady will await your return here."

"At once, milord."

Her bright blue eyes sparkling with heated antipathy and her heart hammering, Roshelle knew full well she was doomed now. "I suppose I should be shocked that an English lord has no mind or care for a Frenchwoman and an innocent child, but I confess I am not. 'Tis only yet another of your endless abuses reaped upon my people—''

"I believe I have instructed you to restrict your speech to those questions put to you. You have been twice warned. Enough now.'' He ignored the fury trembling visibly through the girl, and motioned to Bogo to proceed.

Wilhelm observed with a chuckle, "If looks could kill, Vince, ye would be down and buried.''

"Well, now.'' Bogo cleared his throat. "These particularly vicious crimes of Lord Edward's. Is that why you murdered him? You did murder him?''

Breathing heavily, she could hardly respond at first. For all her fury and violence, her mind began yielding to the threat of a guilty sentence and death. Fear, the close companion of death, began pounding in her breast. She could hardly listen, let alone think to save herself. "Well . . . I—'' She drew a deep breath, her pause filled with her struggle to compose her racing heart and pulse. "Aye,'' she said in a soft whisper, "in a manner of speaking, 'twas me who laid Edward to his grave, though not with malicious forethought—despite all the many reasons I had for doing so.''

"How did you?''

"Well . . . that eventide I was up late working on a particularly difficult medicine for one of the villagers. My servants and women were all asleep. I needed a smidgen of lard and, well, not wanting to wake anyone, I set off myself.

"I know not whether he lay in wait for me or if 'twas a terrible chance meeting—fatefully, I think, the latter. All I know is that Edward accosted me in the upper hall, jumping out from the shadows. He startled me. I asked him what he wanted. I could not believe my ears, but, but he meant to, to harm me—''

"You mean rape?'' Bogo made himself inquire.

She nodded, her gaze cast down to her hands, which tightened into fists as she remembered. "At first I thought 'twas a sick jest, that he teased me, but no. He truly meant it. He said he didn't believe in the curse, you see, that he had a wager with his men that he would live to see the sun rise the morning after he . . . he lay with me, that the whole curse had been fabricated by my guardian to protect me without affording me the proper number of guards.'' She looked up suddenly. ''Of course, I knew he would die if he tried! I tried to fight him off. I beat at him, I even tried to wound him with an anlace, but I had neither his strength nor his size. I could not deter him! I could not!''

Vincent tensed, confused by these words, though not by the emotions. She had uttered the last in some agony, as if it were somehow her fault she was no match for a knight bent on harming her. He did not want to hear more, because he felt alarmed by all the emotion her tale evoked in him. He was overwhelmed by violent feelings directed at an already dead man.

''He carried me down the stairs, meaning to take me to his chambers, when we met his guards coming up. I was calling—nay, screaming—for my own guards, even though I knew 'twould probably mean their death. I still tried to fight him off. He held me still and threatened to make his raping in front of others, and he molested me in view of his men. That's when, when the curse, oh, God, the curse . . .'' Her blue eyes swept the high ceiling, as if in appeal to the heavenly fate. ''I felt something strange and awful—like hot, charged air as it is struck by lightning—and it threw him down the stairs, he somersaulted over and over until, until that awful sound! His head hit the cold stones and, and the captain pronounced him dead before turning an accusing finger to me.''

The crowded hall was completely silent, and as the men took in the scope of her words, confusion lit on many of the faces, none the least Vincent's. His brow furrowed. While his brother's death rested with painful clarity in his mind, it occurred to him he didn't have a clue to what she was talking about.

''I do not understand this. What are you talking about?'' Vincent asked. ''What curse?''

"The curse!"

"Ah, the curse," Vincent said, as if that did in fact explain it. With feigned patience, he inquired, "And what curse is The Curse?"

What curse? What did he mean by asking that? She shot a confused glance at Cisely, who stared with the same confusion, before she asked in anger, "Would you jest about a matter of such gravity?"

"I would not."

Roshelle's face reddened in stages; her hands trembled slightly as she looked wildly about the crowded room. How could he not know? "Surely you have heard of my curse?"

"Nay, I have not."

"Yet, how, then, do you think your brother died?"

Vincent had known how to command people before he reached his sixth birthday, and by the time he reached twenty, his commanding voice had moved entire legions of warriors. Even King Henry found himself jumping inwardly at his commanding tone of voice. Roshelle did the same when Vincent said: "I will ask one last time: what curse do you speak of?"

"The curse that was placed on me forevermore, a curse that sentences any man who attempts to lie with me to a quick and certain death."

Vincent studied her, staring as he waited for some further explanation, a qualifying statement of this sudden lunacy or a simple dismissal of this poor jest. Yet none was forthcoming. Then his dark gaze shot to Wilhelm, as if to verify the reality of his senses. Wilhelm stared at the girl, his lip curving with the start of a grin. Like so many other men in the room.

"Holy Mother of mercy . . . ." One of Vincent's guards chuckled first before heated exclamations of disbelief and amazement sounded all at once, revealing the Englishmen's amusement at this grand evidence of the endless folly of Frenchmen. Wilhelm suddenly swore he would never be able to take a Frenchman seriously as long as he lived. Vincent too, like a number of his men, had in fact heard mention of Roshelle's curse or some strange affliction of hers, but at the time he had thought the person had been referring to the girl's endless temerity. And, of course, her hair. Or like Bryce, who was heard saying, "I did hear one of the old guard going on about some curse of the lady's. But I had thought he was talking about bleedings and woman problems and I told him I had no mind to hear such things . . ."

Vincent's large fingers now spanned his forehead, either to hide his own amusement or to ward off a sudden, gripping headache. Bogo had held his breath, he waited so long for an explanation, expelling it at last with, "What idiocy! In all my life—"

"No. Wait." Vincent held up a hand to stop him and he was smiling. "You can believe I want to hear this, despite how much control it will cost me. Milady," he addressed her, "are you saying you believe it was this, ah, curse that murdered my brother?"

"Aye! I saw it with my own eyes! If that man would tell the truth, he, too, would say it was so. One second Edward held me tight in his arms, the next came with a burst of energy that pushed Edward to his death."

"Ah-huh." Vincent nodded slightly, as if this were perfectly reasonable, an impression contradicted by an absolutely wicked light in his fine eyes. "So you believe my brother was struck by the heavens for attempting to lie with you?"

"Aye," she agreed, alarmed by this interrogation, or rather the dangerous light in his eyes, part mischief and part malice. She swallowed nervously, their unexpected responses making her as skittish as a newborn colt. How could they not have known? Dear Lord, all the world knew—

Vincent was biting his lip to keep from laughing. "Well, I'm fascinated," he told her, his statement verified by the expression in his eyes. "Truly. And tell me: just how is it your chastity came to be protected by the heavens?"

The men roared with laughter and ribald exclamations that brought even more color to Roshelle's cheeks. "A heavenly decreed chastity indeed!"

"No more preposterous than half the excuses I have heard from reluctant maids—"

"Not that you would know that, Vince," another shouted merrily. "You never hear those excuses—"

"Much less know a reluctant maid—"

"At least 'tis a more imaginative excuse than the nag's headache!"

"If slightly less believable," Vincent added with his own laughter. Roshelle abruptly bolted, a nervous Cisely quickly following in step behind her. "Stop, milady."

Roshelle froze; without looking up, she froze.

"I am not through with you yet. And now"—he chuckled—"I'm not sure when, if ever, I will be through with you. I still want to know how it is you came by this, ah, curse."

Stopped in the middle of the floor beneath the dais, Roshelle shut her eyes tight, wishing only that the earth would open to swallow her whole. Humiliation from these ribald taunts burned bright spots on her cheeks and she felt so strangely close to tears, which she would surely release just after she saw him in his much-deserved grave!

Never before had she needed to defend her curse. All the French world knew Papillion and his curse, and she, like the rest of the world, accepted it as fact. As much as the sun rising on the morrow, her chastity was forevermore. It had been challenged three times, and each time the promise of death had been inexplicably, inevitably fulfilled.

The people believed that, while Papillion had cursed her, God made the words a reality to keep her from earthly passions, leaving her strong and pure in the fight to free France. She did not know if this was true. 'Twas a grand conceit to think of oneself as chosen by God, but dare she believe it true? The events of her life did indeed point to the reality, and truly, was her God-given chastity any more or less preposterous than winged spirits in heaven, the perpetual, never-ending cycle of the sun moving around the earth or the winding that made a heart beat through a lifetime?

In a whisper she said: "You make it sound preposterous. Yet 'tis true! All the world knows that it is true! Papillion put the curse on me to protect me from harm on my wedding night—"

"You truly believe this!" Bogo stated it with pronounced disbelief. "And how is it, do you reason, that mere words can manifest a reality?"

"Papillion was not an ordinary man," she began, still unable to meet the light in Vincent's gaze as he listened. "Why, he could do many things others cannot. As you well know. I once saw him drop a man where he stood far across a crowded room, he has healed the wounded, made sense of the senseless, found sanity in madness. I do not know how the words manifest in reality—only that they do. Now I have had uttered the marriage vows twice, and both husbands have died soon after—"

"Did not Count Millicent de la Nevers die in the Agincourt battle?" Wilhelm asked.

"Not exactly."

"Well, how, then?"

"He died of apoplexy on his way to the battle, shortly after saying the marriage vows."

"A coincidence," Bogo said. "Surely!"

"Aye," Wilhelm said, ignoring the shake of her head. "And your first marriage. The old Duke of Normandy was thy first husband, and are ye suggesting the, ah, 'curse' killed him as well?"

"Aye," she said.

Every man there had heard many horror stories about the old duke. And while Roshelle's having been married to him sparked some large measure of sympathy for her from nearly all the men, including Vincent, Vincent's sympathy was overwhelmed by his amusement at the ever-unfolding complexities of her life.

"Yet was he not a very old man?" Wilhelm continued, thinking out loud. "As I recall, while credited with many heinous deeds, he was well into his sunset years."

"Aye," Vincent said. "So how was it he died?" he asked curiously.

"Like your brother, he was struck down dead on our wedding night."

"And what do you mean by struck down dead? Exactly?"

The strange light in his eyes gave Roshelle pause. These questions made her nervous, so nervous. "Well . . . I—"

"Yes?"

"I do not know exactly. I was awaiting him for the marriage bed and, and when he came in and his eyes fell on me, he grabbed his heart as if with a seizure—"

Laughter exploded from the men in the crowded room, startling her into speechlessness. "And you think the old man's demise owed itself to the curse?" Bogo asked. "That it had nothing to do with the grandiose pretensions of an old man's excitement?"

More laughter sounded. Roshelle listened with confusion, resisting the urge to cover her ears. She didn't know exactly why she even should be embarrassed! "What do you mean by that, by grand pretensions?"

The room roared with laughter again. Vincent nearly lost the sip of water in his mouth, laughing more when Wilhelm said, "Well, how could she know that, if indeed all the men who try are struck down dead!"

" 'Tis like this, milady." Bryce stood up. "An old man is like a drunken one: the mind might be willing but the flesh shrinks from the task—"

Her large blue eyes jerked from one face to the next until finally settling on Vincent's. She could not comprehend the strange light in his eyes or the smile on his lips, though it somehow made her desperate to make him see. "What about the night I was accosted by those outlaws?"

"Indeed? I believe I rescued you."

"Aye. The curse brought you to the door just in time—"

"As I recall, your screams brought me to the door."

" 'Twas the curse that put you in a place to hear my screams! Just as the curse gave the Duke of Normandy a heart seizure, my second husband apoplexy. Just as the curse pushed Lord Edward to his death—"

"Was not my brother drunk that night, as he was every other night I have known him?"

"Well . . . ay, but 'twas not his drunkenness that made him fall—"

"This nonsense is preposterous—there be no other words for it," Bogo declared, motioning with his hands as he spoke. "Rather than believe Edward tumbled to his death from drunkenness, you would have us believe that some magic words, uttered many years ago, manifest now and do not just change reality but have the awesome power to kill men?"

Roshelle's chin lifted and her bright blue eyes narrowed menacingly as she listened to Bogo's charge, an indictment of her wits, or lack of such. "All I will say is the world is full of miracles and wonders. I do not ask you to believe anything, past the truth that no matter how it happened, I did not do it willfully—"

Cisely stepped forward, clasping Roshelle's hand, and cried, "And even if she did, Lord Edward deserved it!" Her tear-filled eyes seemed to plead for understanding, desperate as she was to defend Roshelle. "Milady had no one to defend her here at Reales. She had no choice but to try herself. You don't know how she suffered him! He was a terrible, wicked man . . ."

These were the bravest words Cisely had ever uttered, and they sounded with impact. No man there disagreed with that, though most of the men returned to the curse and French madness. Everyone seemed suddenly to be talking at once. Bogo heatedly began explaining to Wilhelm the danger of these heretical beliefs, even from a secular framework.

Roshelle squeezed Cisely's trembling hand tightly, and knowing the courage it took to defend her, she felt a surge of love for her friend. And somehow the surge of love made her think of the imminence of her death. Her face drained of its high color, she felt a cool numbness of limbs and she realized with sudden clarity how desperately she wanted to live. Dear Lord, she would fall to her knees and beg the duke's mercy . . .

Gradually the room grew quiet again as, one by one, gazes turned to Vincent, awaiting his direction. Yet he seemed suddenly preoccupied. His long arms braced on the table and he appeared to be studying the tabletop, his expression concealed from view as he obviously deliberated on some weighty matter.

A weighty matter indeed. For several long minutes he struggled to believe something. Could the men of France be this feebleminded? Was this the reason the lady remained to this day unmarried, leaving the vast wealth of her lands without the guiding hand of a lordship? No man would brave the curse—

Which could only mean that standing before him, incredibly, was a girl in fact; she was a twice-married virgin!

Anxiously Roshelle watched his response as he looked up with an expression of awe and wonder and an unholy kind of amusement. She slowly shook her head, frightened senselessly by that look. What thought made him look so? Was it the idea of her death?

"Well." Vincent drew a deep breath and held it, pausing as he desperately tried not to laugh. Not now. "At last I feel I understand the 'extraordinary' circumstances here. So . . . Very well . . ." He stopped again and bit his lip, nearly overcome by the humor of it. A wild kind of mirth rose in his chest; he could not control it. A wave of his hand motioned to Bogo to call Miles Hartman back, while he, with tremendous effort, tried to recover.

No man had ever been so tempted . . .

"Sir Miles Hartman." A page called the man back inside. He came at once, his expression as far from contriteness as the moon from the sun. Spitting mad, he stared at Roshelle.

Roshelle did not notice. She reached a trembling hand into her apron pocket, removing a small, perfectly round black stone. Papillion's jest of a sorcerer's stone, like rosary beads to the devout; it was her good-luck charm. Though now that the ax would fall, she needed a good deal more than luck. She needed a miracle.

Vincent leaned back in his chair, and with hands resting behind his head, he considered her accuser. "So, Miles Hartman, we have now heard both your accusation of Countess Roshelle Marie St. Lille for the murder of my brother, Lord Edward, and the lady's defense. Now, seeing as you are a good Englishman and she is French, seeing as you had served my brother in the, the . . . where was it, Bogo?"

Bogo read from a list: "The campaign of Riveriere, where the honorable soldier Miles Hartman was laid to bed with dysentery through no fault of his own; then the said soldier accompanied Edward on a minor expedition to Dublin, alas unsuccessful through no fault of his own, before again accompanying his Lord Edward here to Reales—"

"Yes, yes," Vincent interrupted impatiently. "The said Miles Hartman served my brother as well as any." His pause filled with an unpleasant contemplation of just what this probably meant. "Now you have sworn the murder of my brother was premeditated, done with malice of forethought, am I not right?"

"Aye, 'tis what I said."

"Ah, there it is—our problem."

"What problem is that, your Grace?"

"The countess claims differently. She has sworn under oath, too."

"Well, she be full of falsehoods! To save herself—"

"Aye, aye, so you say, and, well, if it were up to me to arbitrate truth in these matters, things would no doubt be different. However, the king's law does not leave it up to me, does it, Bogo?''

"No, your Grace, I'm afraid it does not.''

"And what law stipulates thus?''

"Here 'tis. King's law two hundred and fifty-seven.''

Roshelle stared with mounting confusion. What madness was going on here? Bogo le Wyse had peered into a Bible! And upon hearing this, the men of the duke's personal guard erupted with sudden groans just as the knight Bryce leaped up to say, "Not the king's law two hundred and fifty-seven! God have mercy! I will never forget when poor old Samuelson went that way, and even though he was miraculously saved, he died of pneumonia that very week—''

"Aye, aye,'' Vincent agreed, and with irritation again, as if he were taxed by the unpleasant memory of a man named Samuelson and his unfortunate demise. "While it is true that many tragedies are bought by obeying the king's law, all wise men would benefit from a brief reflection of how many more tragedies would result if we did not.''

"Besides,'' Bogo added, "life itself is fraught with dangers.''

"Prudent words.'' Vincent nodded solemnly. "So! The king's law requires all sentences involving a personage of import, title or landed gentry to be decided by a higher authority.''

Roshelle was not the only one confused by these words. Confusion marked Miles Hartman's features, then even more as he watched the group of guards mumbling and shaking their heads, gracing him with plainly sympathetic looks. He knew only one man with a higher authority and, surprised, he asked: "Will the matter go before the king?''

"Higher than that. Who is the very highest authority, the most capable discerner of truth in all the world and beyond? In whose judgment does all mere mortal fates rest?''

Miles Hartman had to think the question through. "God?''

"Aye." Vincent appeared pleased with the man's wits. "You do believe God sides with truth, do you not?"

Miles shifted nervously.

"Well?"

"Oh, aye."

"Of course you do. So on the morrow we shall adjourn to the river's edge, where you, Miles Hartman, will jump into the river and ask God to verify the veracity of your testimony by sparing you a drowning. Let us set our time for morn—"

Shock made Miles gasp. "What?" His eyes frantically searched the hall in disbelief, and fear altered his face. "Milord, I, I cannot jump into river water—"

"Why not?"

"I do not know how to stay afloat in water! I am loath to get near water! Why, crossing the Channel was nearly my end, as it were—"

"Do not concern yourself with such trifles, my good man. You have God on your side," Vincent assured him, smiling hugely. "Do you think God would let you drown when it is a test of truth, for which He stands in judgment?"

"Well . . . I, I cannot rightly say—"

"Bogo, do not all theologians agree that God is the absolute arbitrator of truth?"

"Aye, all theologians are in agreement on that point, milord."

"There you have it," Vincent said, as if that settled the matter. "You have nothing to fear. If you are telling the truth, God will spare your life. Unless . . . why, you are telling the truth, are you not?"

Miles Hartman rocked back on his boots, nervously shifting from one foot to the other, his dark gaze searching the knights as if for guidance. None came forth. "I, ah . . . oh, God, I—"

"Oh, no." Vincent appeared solemn, save for his gaze. "Bogo, I believe I detect a hint of hesitation. You'd best come clean with it, Miles Hartman, at least before you hit the cold water of the river.''

"Deep water, too, milord," Bogo mentioned. "Or so I have heard.''

"Quite a fierce current as well," Wilhelm added gravely. "The water spaniels nearly went under the day we came . . .''

Miles's gaze shot to Wilhelm, whose voice tapered off with a discouraging shake of his head. "Well, I . . . I was telling the truth . . . mostly.''

"Not good enough, Miles Hartman." Vincent shook his head. "Most of the truth suggests truth's opposite, does it not, Bogo?''

"Aye, milord. The question now is what part of your accusation might be wanting more of the truth.''

Perspiration marked the man's brow; his gaze remained fixed on the floor; his mind, on drowning. "I . . . I'm not perfectly sure about the weapon she used." Then he whispered, "If there was a weapon—''

"So the lady had no weapon," Bogo said triumphantly, knowing his part well from other, remarkably similar experiences. "Which, I believe, changes much of your testimony. It seems impossible that the lady waited to attack Edward—if she held no weapon and considering the fact that a woman's strength is useless against a knighted man's. Therefore there could be no premeditation. Which means it is also probable that you and the other guards encountered Edward as she has said, when Edward was carrying her down the stairs bent upon harming her person—harming that no doubt deserves the harsh name raping!" The thunder of Bogo's unnaturally deep voice somehow made it seem as if Miles Hartman had done the deed. "And therefore Edward died as a result of falling—due to no fault of the accused. Is that right?''

With wide, shocked eyes, Roshelle held her breath.

Miles Hartman's pause filled with the sudden understanding that Roshelle Marie St. Lille would not be punished. Yet as unpleasant as that was, it rested against the idea of the cold, deep waters of the river Reales.

Bogo's deep voice thundered again. "Is that not right, Miles Hartman?"

"Aye, aye!"

Silence formed, everyone waiting for Vincent to pass the verdict. "Let the record show that Miles Hartman reneges on his damning testimony against the accused Lady Roshelle Marie St. Lille, admitting in the presence of all that he lied, that he now corroborates the testimony of the lady. For all to witness. Miles Hartman is judged guilty of perjury, a high crime. Considering the unusual circumstances, I am inclined toward leniency in my sentencing in this matter. I dismiss Miles Hartman without pay from my service, yet with a mind on justice, I afford him the exact sum required for passage back across the Channel. And may God, acting as absolute arbitrator not just of truth but also of justice, orchestrate a fierce and treacherous storm for the day of said crossing." The men saw the humor and chuckled. "Guards," Vincent concluded, "if you would see the perjurer to the gates."

The guards rushed up to escort the man out as Vincent turned his gaze at last to Roshelle. She, too, stared at the tips of her boots, hardly able to believe these past minutes of her life, let alone understand how or why it had happened. To be given mercy by the English, a mercy she had never known them to exercise. There must be a catch or a trick—

Yet there was not.

All eyes turned to where she stood awaiting Vincent's adjudication, but he paused, and chuckled. "Never have I enjoyed a trial more. It was like listening to a well-writ comedy of the absurd, it was." The men heartily agreed, quieting as Vincent continued. "As for Countess Roshelle de la Nevers of Reales, I find her most certainly and surprisingly innocent." The men laughed loudly and Cisely cried out for joy before falling into Roshelle's arms. But Roshelle was too stunned to return the embrace. "As to what that innocence inspires in a man . . ." Vincent's eyes filled with mischief and humor. "Well, some things are better left unsaid after all."

The men rose with laughter and backslapping, the happy conclusion of a job well done. Even Henry would not be so mad now. Bogo was telling Wilhelm that the trial was indeed an amusing tale, perhaps worthy of repeating for a bored audience on a rainy night, save for the fact that it was too farfetched. "And though all the world knows of Frenchmen's ridiculously exaggerated vanities, no one, but no one, would ever believe them quite this moronic . . ."

The room started spinning. She was free! Free! Death must wear a solemn mask of defeat, for she had escaped its grasping hand today! She wanted to sing and shout and spin around and around like a child's top . . .

Abruptly, she panicked. The duke was full of cruel capriciousness, was he not? He might see her happiness and take it away! With eyes downcast, yet her heart hammering with a giddy kind of joy, she moved quickly to the doors. Cisely followed.

But she stopped. What was she thinking of? Just because he had spared her, would he do the same for her guards? Dear Lord, she must ask him! She must beg—

"Ah . . . My Grace?"

All this time Vincent's gaze had never strayed. "Hmm," he said, distracted. Then he guessed she wanted to thank him. "Ah! Now shall I hear your gratitude for my hand that served justice so well?"

The words surprised her. "Well, no," she said before she could think better of it. "I deserve nothing less. Like my people. However, it is to your sense of justice that I put the question: what of my guards? Shall they be free as well?"

"Aye," he said, the girl's boldness making him chuckle. "They are free as well."

Merciful heavens! Roshelle squeezed Cisely's hand tightly, trying not to let her joy and relief show too much, still wary that he might enjoy snatching it away. She nod-

ded and started to turn again, but a low grumble of disapproval rose from the knights.

"My Grace." Bryce stood to address the duke formally.
"Your generosity stretches too far. 'Tis one thing to set
this beautiful maid of Reales free, especially seeing as you
be . . ." He looked to the men, then to Roshelle herself,
and with a smile he said, "Well, cock-led in the matter.
Not that any man be faultin' you for that!" The men
chuckled briefly, Bryce's smile vanishing as he said the
last. "But 'tis quite another thing to let the French guards
go—"

"Aye! They must be made to pay the price of rebellion!"

"Aye—"

Vincent silenced his men with his hand and, shaking
his head, said, "Oh, no. I will fault no man for foolishly
chasing the girl to hell—indeed when I look at her"—and
he was—"their loyalty to her misguided passions is too
easily . . . grasped."

Roshelle had not moved. A visible shiver shook from
her spine up. Like a premonition. ". . . more tempting
than any woman I have known . . ." The bold comments,
the way he stared, bode ill; he courted disaster. She welcomed his attention much as a lamb welcomes the attention of a butcher, only she would be the butcher and he
the slaughtered lamb. The thought made the room grow
hot. She heard Cisely's quick, shallow breaths and she
knew if she turned to look, she would see Cisely biting
her lip and wringing her hands.

The time to leave was long past.

Roshelle nodded numbly, stupidly, and turned to exit.

She started past the dais. Yet, with one hand on the
table, Vincent lifted himself agilely over, startling her as
he landed less than a hand's length from her person.

Stopping short, Cisely nearly fell into Roshelle. For
some reason she caught Wilhelm's eye. He winked. She
started to smile back, abruptly realized the gravity of it
and looked quickly away. Wilhelm only chuckled; for no

reason he understood, the pretty lady's timorous nature appealed to him . . .

Roshelle had looked up at Vincent with a gasp. His eyes were laughing, and in that moment she saw many things about him: his ever-present amusement even now as he threatened her, his restless energy and impatience with a world that moved far too slowly for him and, more than anything, the stunning force of his will. It scared her senseless. "Beware the perfect cleft." Had Papillion foreseen this man, Vincent de la Eresman, in her future? Had he been warning her of him?

"Milady," Vincent began, "this lamentable curse of yours. I wonder . . ." The words were spoken slowly, as if with careful deliberation, before his gaze lowered just as slowly to her hand. Suddenly no one else was in the room. She hardly knew what he was saying or trying to say as her senses filled with the pleasant assault of his nearness: there was a sumptuous promise of warmth and a clean, rich scent. She was breathing deeply all of a sudden, and even more deeply as he took her hand into his and seemed to study it.

His large bronze hand enveloped her small cold one with sudden warmth. Her blue eyes widened. She swallowed, remembering the torment he had brought this very same hand. As if scourged, she wanted to snatch her hand way, but couldn't. His gaze had found hers again, and with Papillion's own gift of mesmerizing, he held her still and transfixed. Like a tiny bird caught by a snake, her heart hammered with alarm and fear, yet she could neither move nor turn away.

He brought the small trapped hand up, slowly turning it around palm side up to expose the sensitive skin of her small wrist. His thumb lightly grazed the spot before closing his eyes, and as he had done once before, he drank deeply of the sweet perfume of her skin.

Then he brought her wrist to his lips.

Tiny hot shivers leaped from the spot; her breath was released in a gasp. Which seemed to please him. "I wonder," he continued obliquely, and at last came to the question, "at what point exactly . . . does a man die?"

The laughter of his men sounded distant and far away, but it made her see his own racing amusement in that light of his eyes. Fury immediately greeted his laughter. She snatched her hand away. One reproachful look at his men subdued their rancorous amusement before she turned back to Vincent. "No bolder beast ever walked the earth! And, my Grace"—she spat the title—"I dearly pray you—unlike your doomed brother—have the good sense never to discover the answer. And not because I would mourn your death!"

With a lift of her skirts, she fled the room, chased by the sound of his laughter. No bolder beast ever walked the earth indeed!

"Ah, you lecherous bastard!" Wilhelm scolded Vincent as soon as Roshelle and Cisely were gone. "Need I ask what no-good thoughts run through your head? You who have always preferred the well-traveled path with all other women! You who once said forging a path where no one hath been before is like owning a piece of the holy cross: its cost is great, if not prohibitive, while its rewards exist only in the imagination of fools."

"Aye, that is true, my friend." Vincent smiled back. "Or was true until this night, when it seems the heavens themselves offered the challenge, one I could no more refuse than my next breath."

"Do reflect, your Grace!" Bogo exclaimed with a wicked light in his eyes, too. "What if it's true? Have you no fear of hubris, offering this mortal challenge to the gods? Death be not far indeed—"

"Aye." Vincent laughed. "But never has a death seemed so sweet."

Yet all of the laughter and the jesting disappeared beneath a nightmare that played in his sleep that night. It was a terrible dream wherein Roshelle called to him from far away, atop a great high tower made of white stone. A surge of desperation filled him, desperation to take her away in his arms and carry her back to the solid earth of the world, to hold her slim softness to him and press his lips to hers one last time. He began climbing and climbing and climbing. Climbing until his muscles ached and perspiration drenched him, until he felt his next breath would be his last, and just as he felt his fingers slipping over the smooth cold stone, he reached the top and saw her there.

She looked more beautiful than ever: shrouded in white cloth from head to toe. A gold band fit around the cloth that covered her head. She was shaking her head. A haunting sadness clouded her lovely blue eyes and that sadness struck his heart and filled him with fear, even before she said, " 'Twasn't meant to be in this lifetime. Forever, I love you forever. Hold my love in thine heart, to cherish in memory . . .''

"Nay, Roshelle!''

Yet his fingers slipped and he was falling . . .

Chapter 7

"**S**o what say you?"

Vincent hardly heard Wilhelm's question as they returned to the keep from the stables. He was thinking of roses. The faintest trace of the blossoms' scent lingered in the still night air. He inhaled it deeply. Of course it was impossible—a month or two too early for blossoms. He must be imagining the scent, and the thought made him smile. "I was told the girl is planting a rose garden over there, outside the wall where the moat was—that she was heard saying it was the only concession she'd make to me. I was told she loves roses."

Wilhelm shot a critical glance at Vincent. "Vince," he warned, his hand shooting out to stop him where he stood, " 'tis not like you to lose your mind like this. Here I am talking about the threat to your life—your life!—and your mind goes traveling to the girl! Again!"

Vincent did not deny this. "Aye, again and again. 'Tis not enough that she fills my dreams, but now she begins to steal my every waking thought . . ."

Wilhelm shook his head impatiently. "Listen to me: we must do something first. You know the knights have heard it said 'twas he, this grand Duke of Burgundy, who set that band of mercenaries upon the hapless Count Valentine, and all for a parcel of land one hundredth the size of Suffolk. And these merry men cut the poor fool into little pieces, which were sent in a bag to his widow—"

"Ah, in time, Wilhelm. I will know what to do in time."

"Oh, aye, 'tis just like you to ignore—" Wilhelm stopped suddenly, motioning to Vincent for quiet. Crickets hummed in the still and quiet night. In the far distance came the sound of a card game from the ranks outside the walls, and closer still, the scrape of hot iron from the armorer and that man's call for more wood. The whispered sound came again. Wilhelm's gaze swept the battlements, then stopped, and he pointed to a lone guard who slept in the shadows beneath a torchlit battlement.

Vincent issued a short, high whistle.

Footsteps sounded. Another guard emerged from the darkness, rushing to where they stood. "Milord?"

Vincent motioned for silence. The guard looked around in confusion as Wilhelm tossed a coin and Vincent called it. "Curse you, Wilhelm—I begin to think your coins are crooked."

"Poor loser, you." Wilhelm took the bow from the guard, drew an arrow from his pouch and set it to the string. The sound of the arrow flying through the air was shrill, and it hit the slumbering guard's bonnet with a loud ping. The man woke with a start and jumped to his feet, gasping and looking frightened before Wilhelm's laughter drew his gaze down to the courtyard below.

Wilhelm returned the bow and, still laughing, turned toward the hall entrance. Only to realize Vincent had not followed. Vincent was staring up at the light pouring out from a window above, a mischievous grin on his face.

Wilhelm knew that grin.

Though Vincent was kept informed of Roshelle's activities, he had not seen her for a week. The girl took extraordinary measures to avoid him. For good reason, especially if his dreams were a measure of his intention. "Perhaps I'll join you later, Wilhelm."

"Aye. And if ye die before ye wake, at least 'twill save the duke the trouble of killing you. I'll make the lady pay the burial fees."

They parted laughing.

The chamber doors were ajar. Soft light from a dozen candles streamed through the door, and inhaling the sweet fragrance of her rooms, Vincent knocked gently. The enticing scent acted like an aphrodisiac, which was the last thing he needed with the girl. A whispered voice came from inside. He knocked again. Still no one answered.

Most men would mind her privacy and, before stepping inside, grace her with the announcement of their presence. Yet no one had ever accused Vincent of slavish observation of propriety. And he was definitely not one to resist the temptation of catching Roshelle unawares. Anticipating the treat, he stepped quietly inside.

As always, the girl surpassed his wildest expectations and he drank in the sight of her with a sharp gasp, his eyes darkening with pleasure. Hard, hot desire shot through him. Gripped by it, he clenched his fists and leaned back against the door as if for support. For a long moment he could not move, as he tried to temper the sudden race of his pulse.

With her side to the door, Roshelle spent several long minutes trying to convince the cat sitting on the shelf above her to taste a concoction. "Last time was a mistake! By the saints, I swear this will not be as bitter. Just taste— molasses, sugared ergot, a splash of nectar and cumin butter . . ."

The girl's comeliness played an alluring melody on his mind, and at times the song seemed to shepherd his every thought and move. Yet never more than now. Bathed in candlelight, she wore only a thin cotton nightdress that left her thin arms and long legs bare to his gaze, while its transparency hinted at the slender figure beneath. The outline of her high lovely breasts was enough to arouse him, more than enough as he imagined slipping the straps from her shoulders and cupping the softness of her full breasts as he touched his lips to her mouth—

Watching a hand and the small spoon coming at him, the cat reared in an arch before settling back down, swinging his tail neatly around his paws. "Ah, Moonshine, you are no good to me tonight." She shook her head. "And where might Joan be, I wonder? 'Tis not like her to dally . . . If only I had some roybra left!" She poured a mixture into a wooden cup, smelling its aroma and then searching the shelves above, her long unbound hair swinging over her hips as she did so. "But if I mix a smidgen of rotted pumpkin with olieribus, I think 'twill provide the same outcome. Severn, the candlemaker, has a pumpkin growing in his vineyard—"

Noisy screeches came from the window as Greyman suddenly made an appearance after a night of hunting. He swooped inside, circling the room to approach his mistress from the right side. Roshelle turned to the bird with a smile just as Moonshine rose with an alarmed, frightened hiss. "Stop, Greyman—"

Too late. The mean bird dove at the cat for fun. The cat leaped into the air, knocking the concoction off the ledge. Roshelle cried out as the sweet mixture splattered over her face and chest.

An angry melody of French swearing filled the room. Roshelle angrily swung at her bird, who flew back just out of reach. With a pleased screech, Greyman settled happily on his perch.

"You beast! 'Tis brutish to frighten poor underlings for sport, it is! You no-good barbaric— Why, look! Just look at what you've done—"

Vincent bit his lip hard to stop his laughter from sounding, his amusement dying the instant Roshelle moved to the dressing water. The straps fell off her shoulders. The chemise gathered at her small waist as she wrung out a cloth. The cool moist cloth came to her face first, then to the slender arch of her neck, before circling her round, full breasts.

"Roshelle . . ."

A husky voice whispered her name, and then she heard, "You would not be needing my assistance with that, would you?"

All movement came to an abrupt, instant halt. 'Twas not really him. She was dreaming, that was all. Aye, she must be losing her wits, collapsing under the pressure of her grief and the disillusionment of the failed rebellion, a burden weighted now with the dangerous teasing light in those remarkable dark eyes. She had begun imagining his voice in her solar chambers—

Boots sounded softly against the stone floor.

The wet cloth dropped from her hands. She swung around and gasped. Instinctively she crossed her arms over her naked breasts. A blush suffused her cheeks as her blue eyes widened.

"Might I help you, Roshelle?"

The rich timbre of his voice passed through her like a caress. A hot rush of chills shot up her spine. She swallowed, slowly shaking her head as each step he took brought him closer to her. The ridiculous question mattered not at all, for she could barely comprehend the words, let alone discern the meaning—he might have just asked her to describe Plato's philosophy in half the length of an hour. All she knew was the danger of her situation.

Slowly, with mounting alarm, she asked, "What are you doing here?"

Vincent had even more trouble comprehending the question, simple and reasonable though it was, as he saw the inadequacy of her arms at providing complete coverage. "I had come to speak with you. At least originally." A lie, and one he knew the moment he uttered it, and he smiled.

Her blue eyes narrowed with suspicion. "In the middle of the night? Unannounced?"

"I saw the light in your window as I returned from the stables. There were no servants about to make the announcement. I found your door open, and not wanting to wake your maid when no answer came to my knock, I stepped inside."

Unmasked suspicion still marked her lovely features. She glanced at her saber, resting in the corner of the room.

His gaze followed and he laughed. "No, not that. Anything but that! Besides, I am unarmed—"

"That is your second mistake!" She started toward the weapon. His next two steps stopped her as they placed him in her path. A mistake, hers. She gasped and knew the mistake as the sudden silence in the room rang like an alarm in her ears, his nearness banishing every thought from her mind.

They were alone.

The silence stretched and lingered, and seemed to magically magnify each small movement. He could quicken the pace of her heart from across a crowded room; standing so terribly close only heightened his effect on her: her heard pounded as if she were running, and she was intensely aware of each breath she took . . . and of her nakedness.

"Look at me," he commanded huskily.

Slowly she raised her blue eyes to his face. This was her second mistake. His eyes darkened as she watched, but he seemed strangely preoccupied, as if his thoughts had flown many leagues from the room. A gentle hand reached to her long hair, the intimacy of the gesture expanding her fear like a cloud brushed by wind on the horizon. She blurted, rather breathlessly, "Do not think that because I have no guards, I am incapable of defending myself!"

The statement drew him back for a moment. Warm humor filled his gaze, replacing the darkening light there. "I'd never think that." Gently he brushed the stray wisps from her face as he considered her; then he combed through her hair with both hands, stopping at her shoulders before returning again, a movement that was somehow both soothing and stirring.

Her impossibly long hair was thick, and as smooth as silk. He lifted the bulk of it to his face, drinking in the scent of rose water. Yet there was a mystery in her hair and he asked: "This white streak that marks your hair, if not your life—you were not born with it, were you?"

The question was asked as if they now chatted amicably from across a supper table. Yet no one had ever asked that question. People assumed the white streak marked her fate like the curse, separating her from a common life. Yet it had been only an accident.

He seemed to sense this. He separated it from the rest of her hair, his fingers streaming over the long streak of white. "I would know how it happened."

"A childhood mishap," she answered softly. " 'Twas just after Papillion took me to live in the forest house. I was always underfoot and he spilled a drop of scalding liquid there. Forevermore the strip of hair came in white."

Only as a grown woman did she begin to question if it had truly been an accident. She knew Papillion never had accidents . . .

Vincent nodded, though he had hardly heard, distracted as he was by the rounded fullness of her bosom, the rosy pink tip peeking through her arms, the weight of her hair in his hands and its sweet, delicious scent. She swallowed, wanting to pull away, but she forced herself to remain perfectly still, afraid beyond reason that he would restrain her.

Which he noticed. "Roshelle," he said with a hint of humor as he slipped a large warm hand over her breast, where he felt the wild race of her heart. The hot, tingling sensation made her gasp with a strange pleasure. "I am scaring you. Why, I wonder?"

Slowly she shook her head, desperate to break the spell, but his unerring gaze held her still. She could not for her life respond. A hand lifted to her face, where his fingertips brushed along her hairline before he traced a line, light as a feather, over her mouth, where he would kiss her. "Does the curse make you afraid?"

She started to shake her head. " 'Tis you who should be afraid!"

The exclamation held urgency, and a hint of sadness. He studied her lovely blue eyes, searching for an answer.

"What are you frightened of more: that I will be struck down dead or . . . that I won't?"

The answer would be "Both," but she barely heard the words. The lure of his voice, the touch of his hand, the compelling warmth of his body all neatly dissolved her will. "Shall we find out, Roshelle?" The question sounded whisper-soft. "Let me put it to the test . . ."

She could not imagine a worse idea.

Her heart pounded in sudden panic and she started to shake her head and back away, but before the message reached her unsteady feet, his strong arms encircled her. A quick, sharp breath came in a gasp as her rounded fists felt the warm, hard muscle beneath the rich velvet of his tunic. His hands slid along her back before sliding lower, cupping her buttocks. Her flimsy chemise fell to the floor.

She was naked.

She felt the slow caress of his hands on her bottom. A hot lick of fire shot through her, and she gasped, then gasped again as he lifted her gently to the tip of her toes. She felt the press of her breasts against the velvet fabric of his tunic, and another shudder passed through her, one that made her cry out in alarm, "Oh, no, no—"

"Yes and yes," he whispered as he lowered his mouth to hers. Her blue eyes widened dramatically, only to quickly close as he bent his head further and she felt his firm warm mouth on hers. Any last thought of fighting him vanished the instant she felt the shining pleasure of his kiss.

The sheer wonder of it seized the whole of her. He dared, she couldn't believe he dared! No one had ever kissed her before. Not even Millicent de la Nevers during the heady days of his courtship, when he swore to her the curse would not matter. Edward had tried, but had been killed for trying. No one else had ever dared.

Fear blended with the warm sensations washing over her. It was a potent mix, yet she was still unable to overcome the terrible certainty that any second he would be struck dead where he stood—

Sensing her fear, he broke off the kiss, and stared into her lovely upturned face with both amusement and curiosity. His one arm still held her against him, while his other hand strayed along the slender curve of her back to gently comb through her hair as he waited until her blue eyes opened to him. "Roshelle," he said as his thumb gently coaxed her lips into parting, "you kiss as if it's your first time. Don't tell me no man has yet taken you through even the preliminary paces?"

Confusion drew her brows together, and, lost in a heady mixture of sensations, she traced her tongue over her lips to soothe the strange tingling sensations there. Then she looked up at him, an alarmed expression in her blue eyes as she cried, "Have you no fear at all?"

"Right now my only fear," he confessed, "is that you might pass from my life without my having tasted your lips . . ." The words were whispered as his fingers traced her lips. He kissed the corner of her mouth where her lip trembled once, before gently kneading her bottom lip apart. She gasped with surprise as he gently brought her head back further to accommodate him.

It was a kiss that was her undoing. She couldn't breathe, she couldn't think to breathe and she wondered wildly why she wasn't fainting as her mouth, her mind, her every sense and fear melted beneath the sensuous press of his lips. The kiss deepened as he added more pressure, slipping his tongue into her mouth and exploring it to full measure. Then she couldn't think to realize she was breathing hard as her head swam dizzily and her mouth was filled with a taste like warm sunshine. A great burst of heat from deep within herself came with a frantic rush of chills and she felt herself sinking slowly into his arms, which were suddenly holding her up.

His entire being greeted the soft pliancy of her slender curves. He broke the kiss to let his lips graze over her flushed cheeks and the satin arch of her neck. "Roshelle, Roshelle, you taste like a sweet summer nectar . . ." Chills erupted from every place his lips touched her. His hands slid along the slender curves of her waist, over and over. "Here . . . put your arms around my neck . . . Better . . . much better," he said as he gazed at her nakedness. "My God, you are beautiful, sweet and beautiful and sweet again . . ."

His thumbs gently teased the sides of her breasts. She gasped with another hot rush of chills. The peaks of her breasts tightened like tiny flower buds fed by warm spring rain. He caught a small, delicious little pant in his mouth before he was kissing her again.

The next kiss frightened her to the depth of her soul. She had never been carried so far, not even in the secret place of her dreams. She imagined the sudden strike from the heavens, the rush of guards into the room, frantic explanations that would bring Henry himself to Reales to personally watch the slice of the guillotine's blade.

She twisted her mouth from his, and drawing a gasping breath, she cried, "Oh, no . . . please!"

He kept his mouth dangerously close. "Please what, Roshelle?" The question was asked as he took her clenched fists and gently brought them behind her back, and his lips lightly caressed the place on her neck where he knew to find the flutter of her pulse, which was escalating along with his. He also discovered an incredible sweetness there. "What is this?"

Trying to guess what he meant, too weak, confused and frightened to even begin thinking how to fight him, she arched her back dramatically, with a foolish intent to escape the caress of his lips. Only to realize she actually offered herself to his mouth as he moved his lips in compelling little circles, lower and lower. She felt his warm laughter against her skin as he said, "Oh, dear Lord, save me . . ."

Her exact thought.

Her blue eyes closed with a pained gasp of pleasure and a queer kind of embarrassment as his lips circled the rosy pink tip of one of her breasts, circling, then gently sucking, her small gasps telling him when he had found the right movement.

Chills shot through her like hot dashes of fire. The sensation was feverish and tantalizing, and far too much for her untrained senses. Just as she felt certain of swooning, sinking into thick warm depths from which she'd never emerge, his lips returned to her mouth. A strong hand gently cupped her breasts and soothed the hot, singing sensations there, but the heat spread to a mounting vexation between her thighs. She could hardly understand what was happening to her. Without realizing what she was doing, she pressed her supple form seductively against his length.

That did it. He knew he traveled too fast for her untutored senses. He tempered his response, easing the pounding pressure of his lips from hers. He was, if anything, an experienced lover; he knew as many ways of kissing a woman as the sun had of shining, and the kiss changed, slowing, becoming mercilessly unhurried. This did nothing to ease the pulse of her blood, even less as she felt the tease of his tongue on hers, the slow caress of his hands riding the curves of her hips. "Roshelle, Roshelle." He said her name over and over as he caught her small, quick gasps in his mouth before, just that quickly, he lost any semblance of control and was kissing her again.

He tilted her head back even farther and widened his lips as his tongue swept into the incredibly sweet moistness. He groaned deep in his throat, the sound lost in their joined mouths. His hands slipped up and down the slender curves of her back as he was teased to distraction by the press of her breasts on his chest, wanting to see, feel, taste her naked flesh beneath him—

"Kissing is very nice. Very, very nice . . ."

For a long moment Roshelle thought the voice was her own, foolishly confessing the understatement of the century. Then she knew. It was Joan's! She tore her mouth from the duke's and pushed with all the force of her being.

The sudden violence took him by surprise, and he could not catch her in time.

Roshelle stumbled back, landing on her bottom. Naked as the day she was born. Greyman squawked noisily, his wings flapping wildly as if with applause. The hearty sound of his lordship's amusement was far, far less humiliating than the single terrible thought that gripped her: she had let him kiss her. Not only that, but after one stolen kiss, she had welcomed the next with the stupid idiocy of a flower welcoming the sun.

All she needed was two dead lords of Suffolk!

Joan hurriedly rushed to Roshelle's aid. Roshelle came to her feet and, in the rush of emotions, failed to notice the pretty blush on Joan's cheeks, the tousled long ropes of her hair or the disarray of her dress, alarming things when placed beside what she had just said about kissing. All she noticed was the maddening light of laughter in the duke's eyes.

She grabbed the discarded heap of her nightdress and covered herself.

Vincent said a disarmingly casual "Good evening" to Joan, glancing at her with some small interest. He noticed all that Roshelle had not and frankly wondered at the peculiarity of her interruption until he heard, "If you ever, ever kiss me again, I won't wait for the curse to strike you dead. I'll do it—"

"I know. You will do it yourself." He turned to leave, laughing. "Roshelle, I look forward to it. And who knows? Perhaps the next time I kiss you, we will find the, ah, exact point of my danger."

"You mean demise. And I don't believe you will be forewarned!"

Yet it was too late, far too late. The sound of his amusement echoed all the way down the hall. Roshelle quickly slammed the door on it, only to discover, in the room's sudden silence and emptiness, how much harder it was to rid herself of the lingering memory of his kisses.

A trembling hand went to her lips as she paled at the

thought. She was shaking like doomed leaves whirling in the autumn wind. Her nerves felt stretched and taut, and a terrible restlessness and disquiet seized her.

She whispered with frightening certainty, "Joan, dear Joan." Her hand went to her head in distress. "I am in trouble . . ."

"Bless the lord who saved you."

The Archbishop of Flanders nervously shifted in his seat alongside the Duke of Burgundy, casting furtive looks at a group of near naked men who played dice upon the high altar in the Cathedral of Flanders, then glancing at the Abbot of Fools. Wearing the priestly vestments turned inside out, and newly bald for the festivities, the Abbot of Fools stood on a makeshift pulpit singing a mass made of equal parts ribald song and gibberish as the people gathered around, laughing and eating blackened soup and sausages. The noise rose to deafening levels; the archbishop could hardly make out the man's comedic presentation because twelve scantily clad maids danced lewdly in a circle around the Abbot of Fools.

Best not to watch that, he realized too late.

The archbishop drained the goblet and held it out for more, trying to tell himself the Feast of Fools celebration unfolded no differently in Burgundy than anywhere else in Christendom, that all was as it should be. The people needed this one day to mock and ridicule all that was holy; they needed this one day set aside during the high holidays at Passover to celebrate in burlesque the old and familiar rituals of the church; they needed this one day to release the natural brutishness that often hid beneath the veneer of obedience to God and church.

The good man drew a deep, even breath, trying to slow the pounding of his heart. Then why did his heart pound so? Why did he feel so . . . so anxious?

This pervading sense of unease no doubt owed itself to the Pope's dispensation that let the Duke of Burgundy hold the Feast of Fools inside the cathedral rather than in the great hall. No doubt. Unfortunately, the duke's workmen still labored to finish minor repairs in the great hall, and were unable to complete their work by the time of the feast. He wiped his perspiring brow, cast his gaze down and desperately sought the humor in the Abbot of Fools charade.

No relic or article of the church was too sacred for the ridicule of this Feast of Fools day: presently the elected Abbot of Fools—a commoner, Jean de Berry, a baker— bowed as the audience burst into drunken applause at the end of his gibberish mass. Someone threw his blackened soup at the Abbot of Fools, then another and another. A thick mess struck the statue of the Virgin by accident, causing the archbishop a small, pain-filled gasp—

Mon Dieu! The bishops and priests at his side stared with shock or looked away, murmuring miseries, and strangely, all appeared as uncomfortable as he was. Priests usually found as much fun and humor in the Abbot of Fools as the people. Yet not so today, not here in Burgundy. He looked at the Duke of Burgundy, waiting to see if he would speak out against the defamation of the Virgin's statute.

He did not. The Duke of Burgundy sat calmly and regally on his throne. The grand duke wore robes of a shocking red and gold, the costume of the Pope of Fools, and watched the turmoil of his court from behind a mask. The whitened side of his mask revealed a grotesque caricature of Pope Benedict, and on the reverse side, a startlingly sinister horned god, this used only to express extreme pleasure at the burlesque show before him. A wreath of black roses crowned the elaborate mask.

The deafening noise became a backdrop for troubling thoughts as the archbishop studied the courtiers surrounding the duke. They wore elaborate costumes in a shadowy spectrum of dark reds and black, gold and silver, their contorted, even hideous masks depicting the whitened caricatures of the saints. Count de la Flabreir appeared as a bloodied horror that could only be Saint Sebastian; the

Count and Countess of Ramsey Las of Bourbon, as a mad, crazed-looking Saint Brigitte and her pope, Nicholas I; all among various other obscene distortions of the saints. The longer the archbishop stared, the more sinister they became—

A chill raced up his spine.

As if aware of the archbishop's scrutiny, Rodez chose that moment to turn to him with an inquiry couched in politeness. "Are you not enjoying the show, your Grace?"

Perhaps he only imagined the derision in his tone. The archbishop spent several long moments attempting to discern whether the duke smiled or no, as if that might shed light on his motive. "Well, I, I am enjoying it as much as it is possible for me to do so, as much as a hawk enjoys the hood. Perhaps if the repairs in the great hall had been finished in time and the celebration were not held here in the very cathedral—"

The archbishop found himself abruptly staring at the leering grin of the horned god as Rodez replied, "Ah, but the sacrilege was bought with a papal dispensation, which, of course, you know. Condoned by the one 'true' pope himself." He turned back to the celebration, adding, "I must say the cathedral gives the celebration previously unreached dimensions."

The archbishop abruptly realized he still nodded as if in acquiescence and he stopped, his entire being abruptly focused on the word "true," the one word that underlined his own personal struggle more than any other. Like so many others, he had never, but never, questioned the authority of the church, its most noble aspiration to lead humankind to the kingdom of God. While the church was run by mere men, and men had their failings and faults and sins, some of these damning and leading to corruption, the church itself was the physical manifestation of God's own hand. Or so he had always believed until the world began reaping the result of the great schism between two competing popes.

Two popes in one world. All because over a hundred

years ago the Pope had traveled from Rome to Avignon, bringing with him half his bishops and court, and leaving half behind. Upon Clement's death the Roman clergy elected one pope, the Avignon clergy another, and to this day neither successor would abnegate his seat to save the church.

Now the great schism lay between the Roman Pope and the French Pope Benedict in Avignon, and each side pressed the world with its claim of rightful pope, forcing countries to choose sides against one another, forcing bishops to fight bishops, priests to fight priests, lawyers to fight lawyers, men to fight men. The schism, like no plague or war or famine, brought unparalleled chaos and tumult to earth. A great, widening black hole opened in man's already dismal spiritual prospects, a hole filled with warriors desperate to lose their lives for the "righteous" pope. This resulted in the poverty of spiritual leadership as bishops seemed only to argue interminably over this benefice and that tithe, while greedy priests ran from town to town collecting coins so that now 'twas popular to say, "The gates to heaven do open, but only for a coin or two." The most pious and devout became consumed with rage, a rage often carried unto death in one of the many battles.

A wave of despair washed over the archbishop as he sat and watched the proceedings. What was happening to him? Was there no hope for salvation? *Mon Dieu*, was this what they were reduced to? A Feast of Fools?

While the archbishop lamented the state of affairs, Rodez searched the boisterous crowd for the sacrifice to the black rose. A darkly shrewd gaze surveyed each person in the great torchlit church from beneath half-closed lids, a dispassionate expression permanently planted on his long pale face, but hidden now beneath the mask of the Pope of Fools. The drunken noise rose with laughter and gaiety: pestilence, bankruptcy, war were not enough to dampen the ardor with which the people pursued their pleasures on this day, and as the wine flowed, the noise grew ever louder.

A familiar spirit hovered nearby, begging, threatening, pleading for him to repent before it was too late. Sensing it, Rodez laughed, the wild rancor of the celebration fading in his mind as he stared off into space as if he could see it. The black rose had always inspired fear in Papillion and he felt it now, the old man's fear of what he could never control. It surrounded him, his fear—palatable and thick and sweet to his lungs. He remembered the old man's fear, as his own youthful powers had surged and grown like a wild weed in the heart, had sparked his own early interest in the occult arts. Just to see the omnipotent old man afraid of anything was a strange kind of thrill. Even now he felt the spirit recoil from the noise and defamations and sacrileges of the people.

You old fool! You always tried to hide this fear from me, and yet I had only to look in your eyes. I had only to look in your eyes. With the pathetic desperation of a condemned man, you tried to explain it all away with your precious science and philosophy: "Ah, let us pull this darkly sinister ruse into the harsh light of scrutiny," you would say, but then later, "Well, surely if only I had some cassia or senna. But you see, Rodez? 'Tis only a reaction to the compound. It has nothing to do with that chant or a goat's heart . . ."

All those explanations, like the last echoes of a hanged man, sounded too loud, stretched too far, tried too hard. The harder you tried to convince me, Papillion, the more you yourself came to doubt. The experiments became ever more grand and ambitious, with ever more incredible results, and all the while your excitement and terror grew. Then came your first dream, the start of your increasing power of prophecy. And your precious science could never touch that, now, could it?

Yes, you failed, Papillion. You failed! How could science explain the dream in which, before you had even fallen in love with Roshelle's mother, before the girl had even been born, you held a blossoming white rose to the sunlight, marveling at the beauty you possessed? Yet the fire started in your hand, and in horror you watched the flames consume the blossom until it turned black.

The black rose, you had foreseen its triumph.

For the girl was born and surely without your consent, she was christened Roshelle—the White Rose. How wonderfully ironic. And only then did you begin to understand the nature of the battle, but it was all too late. Much too late.

"You fool! Did you really think banishing me from your life would stop it? It was too late by then, far, far too late!"

The vicious outburst drew masked gazes. Masks dropped as people looked in the direction of where Rodez shouted, only to find themselves staring into empty space. The masks returned as gazes returned to the masses below. No one commented; everyone, especially Terese, pretended that nothing unusual had happened.

Yet suddenly Rodez gripped the banister as an image burst in his mind: the image of the sacred text exploding into flames just as his hand enclosed over it. The terror of that moment seized him. He felt the steady escalation of the pounding of his heart, a wave of panic as he relived it—the moment he lost the only love he ever knew. Angelique . . .

How strange, too, it seemed so pitiful . . .

"I might have killed you then, Papillion," he whispered with feeling, "forced my knife through the soft flesh of your throat, but I didn't. Death was too merciful for you . . ."

"Milord." Terese beckoned nervously, but, aware of their friends' interested stares, she forced herself to say only, "Such a thoughtful expression. What are you looking at?"

With a slight jerk and feeling startled from a dream, the duke suddenly saw Terese. He relaxed. "Why, I am searching for our sacrifice, my dear."

"Milord! Did Mary not tell you? I have found her. She's perfect, too. Here, let me find her."

Terese turned toward the archbishop in the pretense of searching the masses and Rodez smiled at her trick. She wore the robes of the Virgin; the carefully chosen material at first appeared chaste, drawing the eyes with a promise, yet leaving it maddeningly unfulfilled. Unless one stared long: as if by magic, the longer one stared, the more one saw, until the robes became a transparent shroud over the lascivious, voluptuous curves of the most enticing woman in all of France.

Several years ago, when the duke had been about Tournay, examining his troops for readiness, he had come across a common scene: a young peasant girl flat on her back with legs spread indulging a man, while two others waited. She had immediately caught his knowing eye: with her shoulder-length, tousled blond hair, her sparkling almond-shaped eyes, the ripe, naked curves of her youthful form. He had glimpsed in these raw materials what he could make of her then: the most ruthlessly seductive and beautiful creature in France. He had her immediately removed to Burgundy to initiate her instruction, discovering in a year or so that his apt pupil had far exceeded his initial expectations.

For no man alive could resist Terese's seduction. With a little help from him, she married into the landed class, first Baron Philip de Comines; then, upon his untimely demise, Count Bercuire, who—how unfortunate!—had died in one of the more minor skirmishes with the Swiss. Or so it was said.

Terese then pursued what was her greatest challenge and what became her greatest triumph: the seduction and marriage of Lord Edward of Suffolk. Few could resist Terese's sheer provocative powers, and Lord Edward was certainly not one of them. It had taken her only three months to get him to break with his famous brother and marry her, secretively, unannounced, in the middle of the night, on All Hallows' Eve. A date that had left them all laughing.

Terese had had the child just in time. The power of the black rose was growing stronger with each passing night. It would soon swallow the last of Papillion's power on earth. Now Rodez knew how she would get him the sacred means that would convince Roshelle to offer herself to Vincent de la Eresman, the Duke of Suffolk, an offer that would kill him just as surely as it had killed his brother. And those death bells would land Rodez himself nothing less than the duchy of Suffolk.

I said I would use the curse against her, Papillion . . .

Rodez pretended not to notice as the Archbishop of Flanders fixed his gaze on Terese's person, then suddenly finished the wine in his goblet. Another two minutes and the poor wretch's hands would be atremble with temptation—the effect she had on all of his sex. Her seductions accounted for half of all dispensations in Burgundy, many of these from the lofts of the bishops themselves. Her effect was unaccountable by her beauty alone, though she was no doubt beautiful: tall and voluptuously proportioned, blond hair framing her oval face, unnaturally pale skin, richly pouting lips in the perfect shape of a budding flower—Frossant's words, not his; he still laughed when he thought of those words!—and carefully thinned brows over almond-shaped gold eyes, eyes shining with the bountiful pleasure brought by her senses. A single dark spot sat on her chin, like the signature to a painting that was intriguing and ripe with promise. The black rose sat magnificently against the white skin of her bosom, and while the bishop's gaze kept darting there, the duke had little doubt the man had yet to notice it was not the traditional gold cross.

The archbishop coughed, trying not to stare, but the material of the lady's gown held his gaze, so, against his will, he stared. A cruel trick; he almost didn't believe what he saw: as the gown became transparent, he made out the black outline of two hands on her naked bosom. The jest was on him.

She was laughing at him. ''Something wrong, your Grace?''

Terese turned her gaze away to follow the archbishop's. His eyes were on the opening of the cathedral doors. A dog raced into the church toward the altar. The dog sniffed as if searching for something, a scent leading the creature to the very altar where the men still played dice. Before anyone realized what was happening, an enormous black dog appeared, quickly finding the bitch at the altar. A brief dogfight ensued. Wild screams and hoots greeted the next sight, one that made the archbishop abruptly stand. The other bishops followed, staring with shocked, reddening faces at the bizarre sacrilege of dogs copulating on the altar. The archbishop tore his gaze from the sight and turned with an accusation to his host.

Only to find the leering grin of the horned god.

He quickly led the clergy out.

Terese noticed the strange light in her lord's remarkable eyes again. *Mon Dieu!* Each day he lost his thoughts more and it scared her. She'd have nothing without him; she could not live without him. He was like air to her lungs . . .

She followed his gaze below. She saw nothing amidst the chaos and mayhem of the dancing, flailing bodies, the wild cries and rancorous laughter. The girl who would be sacrificed danced seductively in a circle around the rutting dogs at the altar. Terese's eyes sparkled with the pleasure of watching her—Rodez had whetted her appetite for uncommon pleasures indeed. Intoxicating it was, and her heart started pounding like a slow, savage drum. She wanted to be in it . . .

''I need you to do something, my pet.''

''Yes, my life, *mon amour* . . .''

''There is a bishop here, a man named Rapondi Dino.''

''And what is special about this bishop?''

''The honor of protecting my brother's precious seal. He alone is entrusted with the precious plates of Orleans, and if I should get these plates, I could have my goldsmiths make a seal that would be placed upon a letter that would convince a certain young woman to offer her virginity to a man—who will be struck down dead for the pleasure.''

Her eyes found him filled with humor. "The Duke of Suffolk could not be so foolish as his brother?"

"Indeed, apparently he thinks the curse is little more than a measure of French foolishness."

"He is the fool!"

"The world is full of them, my pet. Now, Terese"—he pointed out the man Rapondi Dino—"there he sits. I understand he enjoys a strange trick done with ropes . . .''

Chapter 8

Blue eyes like Roshelle's. The ring, too.

Joan tried not to stare, yet her gaze kept darting to the open grassy field of the courtyard where Bryce and the lord fought with swords. He was covered with sweat. Like before.

With an empty bucket in hand and a saint's patience, Joan waited for Bryce's attention. Last night he had made her happy. Happy with a bright sun bursting inside.

Bryce parried, swung, hit.

Blue eyes like Roshelle's.

"Joan! Joan, hurry over with the water!"

Roshelle's voice called from the newly planted herb garden nearby where she and Lorette, a kitchen maid, knelt in the rich brown soil pulling weeds. Cisely sat prettily on a quilted blanket on the lawn nearby, sewing, refusing absolutely to sink her hands in soil. Instead she contented herself with stitchery—a lady's work—while chatting merrily about Wilhelm.

Wilhelm this, Wilhelm that, conversation Roshelle swore she was neither interested in nor wanted to hear, though Cisely seemed unperturbed by Roshelle's disinterest, disinterest rapidly becoming ire. Indeed, Cisely failed to notice the hardening line of Roshelle's mouth as she worked.

"Wilhelm says his family, the Dirletons of Scotland, have been connected to the la Eresmans of Suffolk for over a hundred years. Imagine that! Apparently Vincent's family sells Suffolk's wealth—which is great indeed, he says—

on his family's merchant ships. Ships that sail throughout the world and oh, my, you should hear the good man's tales. Wilhelm does not care for life on the high seas, being susceptible to seasickness and melancholy at sea, so he has made his way in the duke's personal guard. He has done very well for himself, too, and since he is the last of five sons, his father did not mind his choice overmuch. And did I tell you, milady, how his first wife died after giving him two healthy sons? One of his sons is a novitiate at Cambridge, while the other lives on and loves the sea, sailing since he was ten with Wilhelm's brother on one of those fine ships." She set down her stitchery and said dreamily as she looked up at the sky-blue heavens, "Do you know what else Wilhelm says? He swears that, except for the English lake land, which is very near Scotland, there really is not a prettier land in all the world—"

"That be just what Merwyn says," young Lorette said with a soft smile. "He said that someday he will take me there, to this great English lake land. Merwyn says—"

Roshelle tossed down the hoe. "So help me Mother in Heaven, if I hear one more 'Merwyn says' or 'Wilhelm says' I shall scream. Enough of it—both of you. I would remind you they are English. English—"

"Wilhelm is not English! And why, why, the Scots have often fought on the side of France—"

"A long time ago! A very long time ago, and certainly not of late. Now the Scottish knights are little better than Henry's handmaidens. Besides," Roshelle said crossly, "Wilhelm lies so closely with the English, he might as well be one!"

Inexpressible anguish appeared on Cisely's face and her lips trembled. Roshelle tried to soften her tone, but the gravity of the situation made her strict. "Cisely, put him out of your mind. 'Tis not proper to maintain a liaison with a man you can have no future with—"

The sudden pain in Cisely's eyes took Roshelle aback. Cisely rose, her short dark curls shaking, and without a word, not trusting herself to speak her mind, she took her leave.

Stopping her labors for a moment, Roshelle stole a glance across the courtyard to where Vincent and another, that man Bryce, furiously engaged in a sword fight, the loud clang of metal resonating off the stone walls like furious church bells calling the faithful to task for their sins.

"Just look at him," Roshelle said in a heated whisper as they fought. Bryce lunged forward and, catching Vincent as he turned, swung hard. Vincent's sword flew into the air, landing a good ten paces away. The men applauded loudly. Vincent bowed obsequiously to his knight.

Anger bristled through her.

There he stood laughing—just as gay as you please!—his hands on hips, his feet apart. A bright red mouchoir circled his head, and his hair fell unbound to his shoulders. He wiped the perspiration from his face and neck with the cloth slung over his shoulders. Naked to the waist, he wore only breeches, belted by a metal-studded strip of black leather, and tall black boots. It did not even matter to him that he had lost! He was still full of self-congratulations! More prideful than Satan, arrogant, cocksure—

The precious seeds were freshly sprung, but so were the weeds. Roshelle seized one and with a violent pull, ripped out its roots to vent her anger. Weed after weed followed. 'Twas not fair to put her womenfolk amidst all these Englishmen. There was no hope for it. None!

As if being practically English weren't damning enough, Wilhelm had not a parcel of land, his family essentially as nameless and as titleless as the piggery man. There were other things, too: Wilhelm was as big and gruff as a bear waking from months of winter slumber, while Cisely was delicate and fair and slight, and God forbid the man ever got her with his child! Why did the first man Cisely ever took a fancy to have to be practically English?

"Curse all! What is taking Joan so long? She's so featherheaded these days! 'Twill be snowing by the time she returns. Lorette, run off and see what's happened to her.''

"At once, milady."

It was all his fault, everything was all his fault. Curse the day she ever heard the name de la Eresman! He and his merry band of men were not just seducing her womenfolk faster than hungry crows on a row of corn, but he audaciously tried to redeem English honor among the people, practically bribing them into acquiescence and obedience. This past week Alicia, a peasant woman, had come down with a strange fever and flux. The fever had left by nightfall, but it had dried her milk. Her youngest child was but a month old, his wails weakening with each passing hour. No goats or milking creatures were left in all of Reales. Desperate, never expecting him to help, she had sent Cisely to ask Lord High-and-Mighty the favor. Six hours later the captain of the English guards had appeared at the woman's cottage with a nanny goat slung across the front of his saddle.

She knew why the duke had extended his help! Just so everyone would talk about how noble and kind he was! Just to buy the people's favor!

The situation had worsened. He'd had the brashness to absolve all peasants of their feudal debt until the fall harvest of next year, and then, then he'd reduced the amount owed by half and the rents by three-fourths. Three-fourths; she still could not believe it. Singing had broken out on the streets. More singing erupted when literally hundreds of creatures—sheep and cows and pigs—had arrived from Suffolk to help provide enough manure for a bountiful harvest. Then he had his men—men of arms, no less!—helping the peasants and village farmers till their soil. Like lowly cotters! Some of his men were even clearing back the brush and forest for the poorest families to plant even more rye and barley and wheat. And his men were spending coins in the township as if it were their very own England. Already five traveling minstrels, a dozen merchants and two moneylenders had arrived in Reales to catch these coins, spending their own, and suddenly the people were bustling with industry. The mill, the tailors, everyone had new business. Phillips, the bootmaker, had apparently taken on an apprentice to help with his new orders, and really, it would all be quite wonderful if only he weren't . . . English!

He only did it to keep the people content and docile, like feeding the pigs before slaughter. Just as he had stolen kisses that night, utterly undaunted by the consequences. She had to do something, she just had to. Somehow she must convince him these kisses would lead him to a certain death . . .

Yet how? How?

Dear Papillion, what should be done?

A warm spring breeze blew across her cheeks, lifting roan-colored strands from her furrowed brow, which softened as she remembered his kisses. How bold he was! He had stolen her kisses! She had been naked and—

The garden hoe fell from her hand and she reached to touch her lips, the memory of the pounding sweetness of his kisses sweeping her with heady emotions: she felt hot and cold and shaky all at once.

His tongue had swept inside her mouth . . .

With a taste like late-summer apples and warm sunshine, his kisses had brought an avalanche of hot chills and pleasure and then, then his mouth, his tongue, had come to her breasts—

Her arms crossed over herself and she blushed, her blue eyes darting to either side, half expecting to find people pointing fingers at her. Her breasts! Did all men do that? Would any other man in the world do that? He must be darkly, wickedly, carnal! For the first time in her life she had wanted to ask Cisely if such a thing was, well, common; if all men did this. After all, Cisely had been married and bedded, and she had wanted to ask if her husband had done that to her, and if he had, if it had filled her with a thick, hot pleasure . . .

Somehow she could not imagine Cisely and a man . . .

She had always felt so worldly-wise, and while destined to be forever a virgin, she had known everything about the physical aspect of being a man and a woman. Indeed, she had once seen the secrets of a human body in a dissection! She had been bedside at thirty-four births! She knew all about copulating, or so she had thought, but never, never had she imagined that a man's kisses might make a woman hot and weak and, and filled with yearning—

The memory shot hot crimson color to her cheeks. As if his kisses were not torment enough! She and Cisely had been cleaning the stained-glass windows in the great hall as Vincent and his men supped. She had been listening intently to their conversation, most of it concerning their king and counselor and the capture of Lord Darmeth and Lord Somerset as they conspired against Henry. The conversation had excited her, indicating Henry's ambitions were receding, that he was too involved in his own domestic crisis to push any further into France with another godless campaign. Then someone asked if it was true, if Henry was looking for a gentlewoman to be Vincent's next wife.

"Oh, aye, Henry is always looking for the woman who would be my wife." He paused, his darkly intelligent eyes traveling across the room to find her sudden stare. "Yet he has had no luck finding her. For this woman who would be my wife is as rare a creature as the winged goddess of Athens."

The room fell silent and the men smiled as they followed Vincent's gaze to find Roshelle's interest. She swung back around, pretending she had not heard and was not listening, and wondering wildly why her heart began a slow, escalating thud. As if she cared at all about his next wife!

She did not!

Then Bogo had commented dryly, "My poor Grace, there be no such thing as picking out the best woman or even a good one—'tis only a question of comparative badness."

The men laughed, but Vincent disagreed. "Comparative badness? I think not," and he added in that rich, compelling tone she remembered so vividly, "For the woman I shall marry will be graced with the virtues."

As if the heavenly sun depended on the sparkle of the glass she cleaned, she put all her strength and vigor to her task. A cramp had shot up her arm. Still she scrubbed, desperate to escape the heat of his stare, the more disturbing idea of his new wife, this rare bastion of virtues. By the saints, what did she care? She cared nothing for this man who braved the curse, who had brought her to her knees before him, who—

"Ah!" Wilhelm exclaimed. "Do tell! I would hear about this good woman you would marry. What goodness be in your Grace's mind?"

Against her will she had stopped, turning to discover the strange warmth of his stare upon her. How could it affect the race of her heart? How? The way he stared, as if there were no one else in the room, as if he were thinking about kissing her again—

"Why, the goodness of heart," Vincent responded easily, and seeming to speak to her, he said softly, "This woman who would be my wife shall have the spark of heavenly fire in her heart; she would be blessed with the virtues of compassion and kindness, and with my love, this spark will kindle and beam and blaze in my home."

The poetry of his words brought silence again, his men smiling as Vincent pushed his chair back from the table and rose. She had grasped the upper rung of the ladder as if for support, trying to look nonchalant, looking panicked instead, then more panicked as he began to stroll toward the ladder.

"I'd not like a dull wife either; I should rather want this woman to be more clever than most, learned of numbers and the languages—to aid rather than hinder me in my many efforts."

"Intelligence and women," Bogo had said. "Now, there's two mutually exclusive terms."

"Quite the contrary," Vincent had said with a warm chuckle as his men laughed. "I have met a woman whose intelligence shines, sparkling like light through crystal with her every deed and word, and while 'tis true, this impressive intelligence sometimes serves her ill, 'tis nonetheless very apparent."

She had swallowed, nervous and alarmed without reason, for all he did was stare, slowly strolling toward her. It was as if he spoke of her. The idea was preposterous, and yet the way he stared . . .

"And, of course, her beauty would manifest itself physically."

"Oh, aye, of course," Wilhelm had said.

"This woman who would be my wife would have to be more beautiful than a thousand others—"

"To aid in your well-known difficulty in keeping your marriage vows," Bogo interrupted with a roll of his eyes, and the men laughed again.

"Aye," Vincent agreed with a smile, and his eyes—dear Lord, those eyes—traveled over her, as potent and powerful as his most silken caress. She had completely forgotten her pretense of disinterest, because her interest was as loud as the pounding of her heart. "To keep my eyes from wandering elsewhere. In fact," he said, and then he stood less than a hand's length away, staring up at her with his remarkable eyes. "Her beauty shall send my desire a thousand miles out and more."

"Huh!" Wilhelm laughed. "She must exist only in your imagination!"

"Oh, no." He shook his head, and Roshelle, unable to bear what his manner and words and gaze were saying to her, turned away and therefore missed the wicked light of his barely contained laughter. Instead she wandered blindly into his carefully spun web like a hapless bumblebee.

"For every night this woman walks in my dreams . . ."

That made her spin back around on the thin ledge of a ladder rung, clenching her cloth tightly in her hands, her eyes wide, frightened and daring him to say a single word more.

Which he did. "She is tall." His gaze traveled up from the tips of her slippers to the top of her head, as if assessing her fine height. "Made of softness, her waist as thin and narrow as a lad's, but the rest . . ." His eyes fixed on the embarrassingly rapid rise and fall of her bosom as she stared back at him in horror. "Ah, the rest is an answer to a man's desire. The answer to my desire. Her lips are the color of dark red wine, her hair is long and glorious and rich." He caught the long rope of her hair in his hand, studied it for a moment, turning it around as he stroked it. "And when it's caught in the firelight or sunlight, it seems ablaze with colors of gold and red."

Horrified, moving in slow motion, she took back her hair, staring, unable to believe he'd make his sentiments public like this. Dear Lord, she had thought, he is falling in love with me! Yes, she had thought that—

"But more than anything," he said, lowering his voice and locking his gaze to hers, " 'tis her eyes that I see in my dreams . . ."

The cloth floated slowly down to the floor while her hands came to her hot cheeks, and still his gaze did not waver. He spoke far more boldly even than these words.

"And when I look into those eyes, I feel as if I am pulled into the warm depth of her soul, and a wild and wondrous winged thing it is . . ."

Just as she was about to literally fall into his arms, his brows crossed as if he were considering an amusing curiosity. "Why, milady," he remarked, "the way you're all a-blushing, it is as if you think I am speaking of you!"

For a mercifully long moment she hadn't understood the exact nature of his trick. Yet the roar of laughter from his men felt like sudden death drop into icy cold water. Then she could not deny it quickly enough, forcefully enough, long enough, and the whole time she stammered away like an incoherent idiot, he only laughed. Laughed himself silly. Indeed, she suddenly realized that the situation was like Satan before the angels: nothing on heaven or earth could make him stop laughing. Not even the threat of his death . . .

Oh, what a fool she was!

With sudden violence Roshelle picked up the hoe and swung it into the moist earth, then swung again. He had purposely made her the fool with those honeyed words! He had probably rehearsed it a hundred times! He had probably laughed himself silly every time he thought of reducing her to such speechless, blushing idiocy!

Dear Lord, I am in trouble . . .

Tragedy waited in the not-so-distant future. She felt it like the air before a summer lightning storm; she felt it moving toward her. She did not know what to do. A hand went to her forehead to slow the spinning thoughts: the curse and its threat and how to stop him before it was too late.

A loud mule cry sounded in the distance, but so lost was she in unpleasant thoughts, Roshelle did not at first hear. What was wrong with Charles? Each letter from Orleans brought news of the worsening situation. Charles's health continued to deteriorate; each day he became more despondent, fraught with anxieties and unnatural fears. As his kingdom crumbled, so did he. He needed her so badly! She should be with him! She could help him, and if he got strong again, then he surely would be able to rally the knights, initiate the final offensive and push the English from their shores. Now was the time! Henry was consumed with his own domestic crisis, so there would be no help from England. If only she could get to Charles to speak with him, to help him convince his legion of impotent old chancellors . . .

If only . . .

No, do not think of that—

The mule screamed again and riveted Roshelle's gaze on the castle wall. Seymour, her old mule. Forgetting Charles, the curse, everything, she jumped to her feet and started running. With a lift of her skirts, she flew past her watching woman at the oven house and toward the gathering of fighting knights. Vincent caught sight of her: the pale violet skirts raised above slender calves and billowing behind her with the urgency of her flight, a heart-stopping look of anguish and love on her lovely face, and for one wild moment he imagined she was running to him.

She ran past him.

Roshelle stopped just outside the gates of the castle wall that surrounded the courtyard and looked around. Forty paces away from where the men had begun constructing a new and bigger mill, a mule, her mule, had stopped, refusing to take another step. Men gathered around the beast, beating, kicking, pulling, shouting, but to no avail. A whip manifested at one man's side.

She raced to the spot. The group of men stepped back for the crack of the whip. This was the last haul and both men and mule could quit once done. That is, if they managed to force the dumb ass to pull the cart to the river's edge, where the mill was being built, before they killed it.

"You goddamn stubborn ass! Get!" Bower, the foreman, raised his arm and with all his strength cracked the whip across the creature's back. The mule neighed in a loud cry but otherwise did not yield to the other man pulling the lead.

"Stop!" Roshelle burst through the crowd. "Stop!" She grabbed the reins from a man, turning to the foreman with the whip in his hands, meeting his surprise with determination and a prick of anger. "I do not abide the beating of creatures at Reales. Under no circumstances—"

Bowers looked incredulous; English pragmatism met French idealism—beautiful as it was—with a simple, outraged "You what?"

"You heard me! I do not abide the beating of creatures at Reales. 'Tis bad enough I am forced to watch the ruin of the castle stone by stone, but I will not abide any brutality to the poor creatures forced to do your work. Besides," she said more softly as her hand went to calm the animal, "he does not know better. Whereas God gave man his brain and hands, a lion sharp claws and teeth, the falcon keen eyes and strong wings, He gave the mule his stubbornness. 'Tis the poor beast's only defense."

The crowd of men stared as if she were stupid, their gazes swiftly searching the surrounding area for someone to step forward and put the lady in her place. Roshelle continued to calm the frightened Seymour; no hands were more gentle. Fear still shifted his small eyes, but he soon leaned against her, nuzzling her hand. "Aye," she said softly, too certain of her principle to be embarrassed by the men, "stubbornness is nature's way of protecting the poor things from abuse and overwork. The whip only terrorizes them, nothing more."

The mule nudged her as if in complete agreement.

Bower rocked back on his heels, the whip swinging under his arm as he crossed his thick arms across his bare chest. Aye, there be some humor here for sure: the mule and the lady, it sounded like a yarn his wife spun for their five bairn and he'd laugh, he would, if he weren't as tired and hungry and thirsty as the damn arse himself.

"Oh, but of course," he said in a sarcastic pretense of courtesy. "No whips for the poor beast, stubborn, as ye say, through no fault of 'is own. Fine. How, then, does milady imagine"—his tone of voice changed considerably, "we should get the poor misunderstood beast to there—"

A demanding finger pointed to the river.

Watching now from the crowd, Vincent tried to keep his laughter from giving away his presence. It was hard, harder still when Roshelle replied with all patience: "One must always ask for a creature's cooperation."

"Ah! Of course. Ask him. Daft of me to even put the question. Just ask him!" He turned his smile on the mule, and with sudden showmanship, he bowed. "Please me good and kind, Monsieur Mule," he raised himself from the bow, making the growing crowd laugh. "Would ye please oblige me by walkin' the short distance to the pile there? I be forever in your debt."

The mule did not move.

"I do not think 'tis working, milady."

The men laughed. Roshelle remained undaunted. "Well, of course not. He is a French mule. He does not know your English tongue."

Bower rocked on his heels as laughter erupted all around. "Not a common mule, then? Only knows the courtly French, does he? And all this time I was thinking he was just a dumb, stubborn arse!"

"Oh, no, he is as smart as any. True, I would not say brilliant—"

"Ye wouldn't? Well, 'tis a problem, then. Ye see, I am but a common man from Suffolk. His Grace, as good as he be, hath never asked me to join him at court, and so I have never learned your silver tongue. Or Latin. Or Hebrew or Prussian or any other of the hundreds of languages created at Babel. I fear I only know a common man's English." His smile was all condescension as he inquired, "But mayhap milady herself could help me out here. Do ye think ye could ask your dear friend"—his hand swept in deference to the creature—"Monsieur Mule, if he would mind very much obliging us?"

The men laughed and Roshelle, knowing of course it would not be any fun if she couldn't, smiled with a curtsy. "Oh, but of course."

With laughter in his eyes, Vincent watched with the others as the girl turned to the mule and in her high musical voice whispered soft French words in the creature's ear. A shiver raced over the mule's strong back. She released her breath in his nostrils, petted and coaxed him. Vincent sighed as not a man stirred, each one as mesmerized as the mule. The words became a pretty song, and with the reins held loosely in her hand, she started forward. The mule obliged with a happy flick of his tail.

Watching the parade at Vincent's side, Wilhelm laughed, too. "That mule is not the only male eager to follow that voice!"

Vincent bit his lip and nodded, his eyes lit with laughter. From the looks on the men's faces, it appeared only too true. With all the boundless charm packaged so alluringly, no man or beast could ever resist. Least of all him. It was not just her beauty or her passion, it was more than anything the girl's heart—the very beat and pulse of her soul.

The emotions she evoked from him felt so strange and novel and wonderful. Love was certainly not new to him, or so he had thought. Bogo was fond of saying, "My Grace falls in love with the same regularity he wears out boots . . ." That was true, or had been true, but those loves now felt so different and this love so new.

Yet why did that nightmare of the white tower plague him?

At the end, and to the hearty applause of the men, Roshelle curtsied and Bower bowed. Her blue eyes were laughing until the very moment she met Vincent's gaze across the crowded area. He saw first her confusion, then a sudden flash of fear and alarm and horror.

Then he realized she wasn't staring at him at all.

His gaze followed hers across the distance to the castle gate, where Bryce stood with his hand in the maid's, Joan's. Bryce was smiling from the show; Joan was smiling because Bryce was smiling. Bryce leaned over to kiss the maid's cheek. Roshelle's eyes widened with disbelief.

Vincent quickly disbanded the crowd of men with a nod of his head and rushed to Roshelle's side. She didn't notice. Squawking chickens scattered from her path as she marched toward Joan and Bryce. Noticing something terribly amiss, guessing what it was, Cisely, too, rushed to Roshelle's side.

"Roshelle, please . . . Let me explain—"

There could be no explanation that would soften the anger pounding with fear in her heart. Roshelle shook her head, not trusting herself to speak to Cisely. Cisely, who obviously had kept this from her when she knew. She knew what it meant.

Roshelle came to the couple at last, not even glancing

at Joan. Instead her blue eyes were an indictment of Bryce; she stared as if he were the lowest, most vile creature she had ever seen, and he was. He was. At last she turned to Joan. "Joan," she said with soft urgency, "get you to my chambers."

Joan did not at first hear, so transfixed was she upon Bryce's eyes. Then as the words finally penetrated her mind, she simply shook her head. "I will stay."

Roshelle acted instantly. She grabbed Joan's shoulders, but the poor lovesick girl peered around Roshelle's worried gaze to smile back at Bryce. Roshelle clapped her hands in Joan's face. The sudden noise jerked Joan backward, and she came abruptly to attention. "Get you to my chambers, Joan! Now! And wait for me there."

Roshelle had never used that tone of voice with Joan before. Never. Roshelle's anger shocked Joan, then confused her. Cisely, too, appeared stunned. Then Joan's gaze dropped uncertainly to her feet and she nodded quickly, obediently, before rushing away. She stopped several paces beyond, turned and rushed back. She lifted a flower chain from her neck and placed it over Roshelle's before kissing her cheek. Then she waved a fare-thee-well to Bryce and disappeared into the courtyard.

The men watched Joan until she was gone, their smiles disappearing as they turned back to see the fury shining in the blue eyes fixed now on Bryce. Dear Lord, Vincent thought, staring, she was beautiful, even with the fury brightening her cheeks and changing those eyes. She wore a violet gossamer panel over a white short-sleeved chemise, all loose, unbelted and flowing, trimmed with a magnificent design of embroidered bright purple birds and wildflowers. She wore no surcoat and no caul, unless one counted the rather elaborate crown of her half-lifted hair. Yet from the fury in her eyes, Vincent guessed the problem.

Like a mother cat, she was.

He watched the small pale hand clutch the cross around

her neck, and why this bothered him, he'd never know. As if she used it for her heavenly appeals, the madness of her magical thinking, he supposed. She gave him the briefest glance. Few maids, highborn or otherwise, could remain unintimidated by the sheer size and force of the masculine presence surrounding her, but not so Roshelle.

For her blue eyes had found Bryce again.

Bryce met her stare evenly, undaunted as only a knight could be, though mystified. He asked slowly, exercising his own caution, "Do ye have words for me about the lass, milady?"

"Indeed I do. And these words be simple and to the point: if you ever touch Joan again, so help me God, 'twill be the last thing you ever do."

"Temperance, milady." Bryce's gaze narrowed a fraction as he, too, warned, " 'Tis no idle thing to threaten a knight of the Suffolk guard."

"Not one word from me should you consider idle, sir!"

"Huh! Then what be your complaint? State your objections plain, for I cannot fathom a one."

"Aye," Vincent said, "I, too, would be interested to hear your objections to my good man's courtship of the maid."

Her blue eyes widened incredulously. "Be you deaf, dumb, blind? For that be the only excuse for failing to grasp that the girl is simple!"

Yet that was hardly the main reason—

"Oh, that!" Bryce exclaimed with a pretense of surprise. "Well, if that be all, rest assured, milady, I do not fault Joan that."

"Grand of ye, Bryce." Wilhelm nodded as if his generosity were a fine and noble thing indeed.

"You do not fault her—" Roshelle stopped, aghast that he would make fun of this. Slowly, with mounting ire, she said, "Joan has no mental reasoning—"

"Roshelle, sweetling," Vincent broke in, thinking to point out a fact. "I know of few men interested in a woman's reasoning facilities."

"Seeing as they have so little," Wilhelm added, pointing a finger at his head, as if Roshelle herself might need a visual clue to grasp the subject. Then he winked conspiratorially at Cisely and received a fetching giggle, one she quickly stifled. "A good thing all around."

"That does it! I will not condescend to listen to you make jests of Joan, or my sex, or to you calling me that name!"

"Call you what name?" Vincent asked.

"That name!"

"What name is that name?"

"You know what name."

He pretended ignorance. "Your Christian name? Roshelle?"

"Oh, never mind!" A hand spanned her forehead, a gesture of extreme frustration. She did not know how he always managed to pull her off a subject, especially when it was a grievous subject. She started anew. "This is not the point—"

"Ah, milady, I mean no harm to the maid," Bryce interrupted with a small measure of contriteness. "In truth, I have not in all my years met a soul so sweet or good as the maid Joan—"

"Do not describe Joan's goodness to me!"

"Well, I care for the girl and—"

"A false sentiment at worst," Roshelle snapped in renewed fury, doubting his sincerity. "A convenient one at best, and how both grate upon my ears like the howl of demons! They are convenient, no doubt, when you seek the easiest prey for your lust! And I will not have that," she swore with soft viciousness. "She is but a child, which makes your seduction little better than a raping—"

"Raping?" Bryce's face reddened with the accusation, and for a moment he could not answer. Vincent started to step in, but Bryce held him back, wanting to answer the accusation himself. "Milady, you grievously do me a wrong by accusing me of this heinous deed, of my wanting the maid Joan only to vent my lust. And you cannot assume to know my mind, let alone my heart. True, I am a man, and as that sorrowful creature, I allow there be a truth to what you say, but only a half-truth and one that needs—nay, demands—to be set beside my feelings for the girl. And these are simple, too: I find more happiness and ease with the maid Joan than with any other woman I have known. Her simple mind is an unexpected joy to me; unlike other women, she has no demands, no grievances, no mire of complexities I have to muck blindly through. You know her! She is all happiness and soft sighs, laughter and pleasure. Do not doubt that I care for her, and deeply.''

Roshelle stared at him for a long moment. In the heat of the moment she first tried to disbelieve these soft sentiments, but her intuition would not let her. He did care for Joan. As everyone who ever knew Joan cared for her—

Dear Lord, help me here . . .

The only point that mattered was Joan's absolute safety, and Joan was only safe when she was within arm's reach. This man would take her away, or try to, if she did not stop him. She had to stop him. Despite the hefty price she had to pay in order to protect Joan, she would never forsake her. 'Twould be far easier to slit her wrists than to forsake Joan to the beast of Burgundy.

"Someday I shall come for her . . .''

Sudden fear and sadness came to her eyes, and Vincent was transfixed by it. 'Twas the sadness and yearning he saw in his dreams when she stood at a white tower. What on earth caused it?

A colorful robin crossed overhead and her blue eyes lifted to it. Papillion had once foreseen man with wings. A fanciful idea, and yet a man in Venice had drawn a picture of a machine that would make man fly like the winged creatures . . .

Papillion, help me . . .

She could only begin again. "I am sorry, but I fear even love does not matter—''

"No, of course not,'' Vincent agreed, nodding as if she walked a wise course and he with her. "Love matters not at all.'' He shook his head. ''No doubt poor Joan is too feebleminded to know her feelings, indeed if she even has any feelings.''

''Well, that is not true!'' Roshelle naturally took affront to this. ''Of course Joan has feelings, just as everyone has feelings, and of course she knows what those feelings are—''

''Surely you do not imagine Joan could fall in love with a man?'' Vincent now looked perplexed.

''Well, I do not know . . .'' The image of Joan's face as Bryce blew her kisses emerged in Roshelle's mind. ''I suppose she might—''

''Ah, then,'' Vincent said smoothly, trying to follow her reasoning, ''such a love could not be lasting.''

''Do not be so sure of that—Joan is the most loyal person I know,'' Roshelle said, casting a mean glance at Cisely. ''And her loyalty is far more tenacious than any—''

''Milady, then what be your objection?'' Bryce wondered.

''Well . . .'' She searched for another excuse, but her mind somehow fixed on an errant curl draped across Vincent's forehead, the lick of dark hair so reckless and, well, beguiling somehow. Why did he have to be so handsome? Perhaps if he were balding, short of stature or corpulent of frame, it would be easier to fight him . . .

''Yes?'' Bryce pulled her impatiently back to the subject. ''What be milady's objection?''

The idea occurred to her from seemingly out of the blue. ''What if, God forbid, you get her with child?''

Bryce appeared insulted; indeed all the men abruptly straightened. ''Milady, you do me dishonor. I have never abandoned my dependents.''

''Indeed,'' Vincent added with a sharpness to his tone, ''I would not have a man who mistreated his dependents.''

Roshelle turned from one face to the next, the voracity of the sentiments writ in their voices and eyes. ''But I am thinking of Joan! She cannot care for herself, let alone a child. 'Twould be a disaster. No.'' She seized on this believable excuse. ''Out of the question—''

''Aye.'' Vincent nodded, pretending to see her point again. ''You would not want to help Joan care for this child. 'Twould probably be a great burden to you. You probably do not care for children at all—''

''Roshelle loves children!'' Cisely appeared aghast at the idea. ''All children! Why, half the children of Reales think of Roshelle as their mother. Have you not seen them following her about? And, why, she is even named godmother to at least a dozen—''

''Of course I love children, children being God's greatest gift to life, anyone's life, a joyful blessing, but—''

''Oh, Roshelle, do reflect!'' Cisely reached for her arm, the very idea swaying her gentle soul. ''What if Joan did get with child? Would our hearts not love this child as our own? Would we not help Joan raise the child to a goodly Christian life?''

Fingers went to her forehead in frustration. ''This is not the point, Cisely, as you, of all people, well know!''

''Yes?'' Bryce questioned, all patience still, thinking Roshelle's confusing point—if there was a point—was the very reason Joan's simple mind was such an unexpected blessing to him. ''And so what be the point? Do ye have another objection?''

The image of Joan being left alone in the rain emerged in her mind, a warning. ''Yes, I do. I object to, to . . . My objection is—''

The thought disappeared as she found herself staring at an angry scar on Vincent's shoulder. Two fingers thick, the red gash ran from his shoulder blade down his chest. Her blue eyes followed the line with a queer fascination, seeing where it picked up on his arm, forming a savage dent in the smooth bronze skin covering the hard rock of his muscle. He was so strong, a skilled, seasoned warrior and so tall, too—

She shook her head to rid herself of the unpleasant train

of thoughts. She simply could not step near him without losing her mind! Now what was she saying? "Oh! My objection is, is—"

Then Vincent observed with some small alarm, "You seem to be repeating yourself, milady."

"That is only because you keep interrupting me!"

Vincent appeared greatly offended. "Why, I have not interrupted you once."

"You are doing it now! This very minute—"

"Quite the contrary, sweetling." A dark brow rose. "I am standing here in all innocence, eagerly awaiting your words."

Roshelle seized on this. "There, you did it again!"

"Did what?"

"Called me that name!"

"What name is that?"

Trying not to laugh out loud, Wilhelm braced, watching as the girl's frustration built. He half expected to see her arms start winding like a mill as she set about landing a hard blow to Vincent's face—which would be a grave mistake. Breathing deeply, she glared at Vincent.

"The point is, the only point that matters is I do not want your men coupling with my women, your army pillaging my country's land, and most of all, I do not want your vile presence in my home!"

"Vile presence?" Vincent appeared quite shocked by these words, though a wicked light betrayed his true sentiments and he bit his lip to stop his laughter. "Now you would call my presence vile? Why, how strange!" He leaned closer, briefly motioning to the others as he steered her a few paces away so as not to be overheard. "You did not seem to find my presence in your chambers very vile that night. As a matter of fact, sweetling, I remember, rather vividly, you, too, were all soft sighs, atremble with the pleasure of my kisses—"

Horrified color shot to her cheeks. Her blue eyes darted quickly around to ascertain if anyone had overheard this.

Yet everyone pretended extreme disinterest in their impassioned exchange. Wilhelm had led Cisely away toward the well water, while Bryce seemed suddenly consumed with his effort to pick dried mud from his boots with his dagger. She turned back to see Vincent's amused—very!—smile.

"You have the audacity and mean spirit to remind me of that night, a night that with every breath I draw I try to forget—"

"Yet you cannot, can you?"

"No! I cannot—though not for want of trying! And I warn you, milord, do not delude yourself. 'Twas not because of the sweet seduction of your kisses—"

"No?"

"No! 'Twas that I was mad, out of my mind with fright! I can only reason that you so scared me, I, I lost my wits and, and fell victim to some manly spell that preys upon innocent maids—"

"Indeed!" Vincent's gaze lit with laughter and pleasure. "While I would not use those exact words to describe the acquiescence of your kisses, they are indeed apt. And think of this, milady. Each and every time more, you will be less afraid and more—"

"Do not say it! I will not! Never! But even if I were a willing partner in your seduction, I must make you believe, you must know, 'twould mean your death!"

The impassioned declaration made him release her arms, but only so he could throw back his head and laugh. Stunned, she could only glare up at him, her blue eyes shimmering with fury and fear and something else, something very much like excitement. Which he saw. "Oh, my love," he said, leaning forward, laughing still, "I have said it before and I see I shall have to say it again: death has become an absolutely irresistible temptation—a temptation I march blindly and verily toward!"

"You are mad, just mad!" Roshelle's fists tightened and she swung around and marched away with all the dignity she could muster. Away from him, his men, his army, most of all his laughter. A sound she knew would haunt her, and probably for the rest of her days—as short a time as that was likely to be!

Chapter 9

Roshelle sat at her writing table, quill in hand, furiously scribbling an urgent message to the herbalist in Rouen. The Duke of Suffolk needed his ardor dampened, 'twas the only thing she could think to do. The potion had worked on Edward, so she saw no reason to doubt its effect on his older brother. She needed some ergot, and while she had no coins to pay for it, she thought to appeal to the monsieur's charity. She had to fix the duke a potion! It seemed the only way to avoid disaster.

For she could not leave Reales.

A knock at the door sounded.

She looked at the door and she stiffened. It was him. Again. Here to torment her with his kisses. What would she do? What could she do? It was painfully clear she had not the armor to fight this kind of attack—

An insistent knock followed.

The quill dropped. She stood up, staring at the door in horror. She swallowed. "Who stands there?"

"Your servant, milady. I carry a message from Bishop Rapondi Dino, of the Orleans court."

"Saints alive!" Roshelle rushed to the door, pressed the latch and opened it. A young page of Vincent's retinue stood in the hall. He could not be the messenger from Orleans, who was no doubt watering and feeding his horse, perhaps even accepting refreshments from his English adversaries. She had to hurry if she wanted to give him a message to take back to Orleans.

"Eveningtide, milady."

She nodded curtly.

He handed her the sealed parchment. She nodded again as she shut the door. For a moment she stared at the parchment without opening it. What ill tidings could come from Orleans now? Charles's poor health or worse—

She ripped the bishop's seal and unfolded the message. She skipped the lengthy formal address to read the main text:

We most urgently appeal to you, our young Countess de la Nevers, in France's struggle against her English invaders! As you read these carefully penned words, a new army is amassing under the orange-and-white banner of Orleans. Charles, the young and noble Dauphin, will lead these brave knights in an advance against the English strongholds throughout Brittany—

Roshelle stared at those last words, reading them again and then once again. Charles amassing an army? It did not seem possible. It seemed even less likely that Charles meant to lead men of arms against the English himself! He must be getting well at last! Why had he not written her?

Because of his fear of interception of his penned words!

With her heart pounding with new fervor, she read the rest:

Be forewarned! Thy time has come!

Now is the time we must gather all our weapons, large and small, to wield against the English, and so we ask of you a great sacrifice. This sacrifice is nothing less than to rid the English army of its villainous leader, the Duke of Suffolk, Vincent de la Eresman. You know to what weapon we appeal: we appeal to your wholly unique, God-protected chastity. In secret meetings his Holiness and revered leader of the Christian world, Pope Benedict, hath decreed His design meant for you to use your chastity now, to free all of France! We are depending on you, so young, pure and chaste, graced by the heavens and celebrated by the people, to exercise the curse and rid the English of their greatest champion—

The parchment floated unnoticed to the floor.

Color drained from her face as her blue eyes sought and found the candle on the table. Her thoughts raced to the near future: she had always known it would come someday. Now here at last was the sweep of history she awaited. The amassing of a brave, valiant and victorious French army, thousands of men of arms led by their true king, Charles. There would be a great battle, the final battle to return France to its rightful citizens.

A battle in which she must do her part.

She must use the curse to murder Vincent de la Eresman.

It would not be hard. He had made perfectly clear how verily he would march to his death. She had no illusions about it; she would go to his chambers, he would play his game of seduction, an act of violence would follow: a sudden intrusion of another knight bent on his murder, a heart seizure or sudden apoplexy—something that would kill him.

As the curse had killed so many others.

The idea of his death left her feeling so strangely cold. Why? She hated him, his English heritage, his strength and power, his unearned, undeserved lordship of Reales, did she not? Would not his death be welcome? Was she afraid of being killed in the tidal wave of bloodshed?

Why was she so frightened?

She clasped her hands together in horror when she realized they trembled.

Think! It mattered not at all what she felt! All the men

and knights of France amassed nearby even now, preparing to boldly spill blood and lose their lives, and all of those brave souls depended on her to do her part. A part that Benedict himself decreed had been ordained in the heavens! God Himself gave her this precious weapon to use against the duke! 'Twas meant to be!

Roshelle forced the sudden whirlwind of emotions back. There was no room for sentiment here. She had to do this! For France! For a France governed and led by the rightful heir, Charles.

She knelt down and picked up the parchment. Very carefully she stepped over to a candle. The parchment went up in flames. She set it in the metal basin and as she watched it turn to ashes, a curious numbness swept through her limbs like a tonic. The last time she had felt that numbness was on her wedding night: the first time the curse had worked its awesome power to steal the very breath of life from a man.

And so it would again.

Roshelle slipped quietly through the door to his outer chambers. The door closed softly. She stood still for several seconds as her eyes adjusted to the darkness, until, like a cat, she saw the dark outlines of different shapes in the room: two trunks, a chest of drawers, sword shield and halbert hanging from the wall, the pallets from which the soft sounds of his servants' slumber rose. The only light came from beneath the door to the inner chamber.

He was awake.

She stepped silently to it. A pale hand touched the latch. Closing eyes, she mutely whispered a brief prayer for courage, then gave the latch the weight of her hand. The door opened and she stepped inside.

A cool spring breeze blew through the open window. Atop the large stone hearth, candlelight flickered above the dance of a bright fire. Vincent stood at the window, staring out at the darkened landscape of the night, and as her eyes encountered him the brief moment before he turned to see her there, she felt her heart skip a beat. He wore only loose cotton leggings, rolled at the waist and cut off at the knees, that was all. One outstretched arm braced against the stone wall; the other arm rested on his raised knee and held a goblet. She knew the cup would have only water or goat's milk in it, for one of the eccentricities of his remarkable character was that drink—common ale, as well as wine—apparently gave him a headache. His handsome face held the thoughtful expression of a man contemplating the world he had made, and for one brief moment she thought of all he had done for the poverty-stricken land of Reales.

Would Charles or his liege lord be as good?

By God's grace, he would . . .

Something alerted him to her presence: the sound of her sudden sharp intake of breath or the barely perceptible trace of her perfume. His eyes found her and for a long moment, a full minute or even longer, he stared, just stared.

With the front ends held simply back by a ribbon, her long auburn hair fell unbounded and unadorned down her back, cascading over a plain white cotton nightdress. Her wide blue eyes were full of fear and uncertainty, two things he did not have to wonder about.

"I wondered if you would come."

The words meant nothing to her, less than nothing as he drained the goblet and set it down. For in the span of a moment she was consumed with fear. A fear that choked her, claiming her where she stood, subdued at last by the idea of the waiting French army.

As God is merciful, it would be quick!

With the loud pounding of her heart, she wondered wildly if she should say something. She steeled herself against the intensity of his stare and tilted her chin up, her eyes narrowing as if she were a warrior princess with sword in hand. "I . . . I have come to endure your challenge to the curse . . ."

There, she'd said it—it was all but over. He would kiss her, lay her on the bed and then, then—

He would be struck dead.

A cold dread filled her, and she trembled. More so when she heard a soft, low chuckle, echoing her hollow words with mockery and scorn. Something awful sprang into his expression, reflected even more in the light shining in his eyes. A warning sounded in her mind and she realized suddenly how he threatened her. To make her afraid? Aye, something dark and threatening loomed between them. Instinctively, like a fawn caught within eye range of the archer's bow, she started to bolt, but too late.

He suddenly stood in front of her. A long arm reached past her and shut the door. He stood so close, his height towering above her. A strange heat and violence radiated from him, trapping her like the eyes of a snake. She couldn't have moved if her life depended on it, and having no choice, it seemed, she lowered her eyes as if shutting out her vision could transport her away. A hand came to the string of her nightdress and lightly toyed with them.

He stared at the plain dress, it said so much. Long, loose sleeves covered her arms; a string gathered the garment at her neck before it dropped to the tips of her toes, every inch of her covered in thick cotton. Like a child's nightdress, one wildly inappropriate for her intent.

Praise be the fates that made her want him dead!

"So," he said easily, torn between laughing out loud and dropping to his knees in gratitude to Papillion, fortune, fate, for the gift of this night. "You offer yourself to me. Like a condemned man's last meal, you will give me the taste of a sweet treasure before ending my life!"

The words somehow made the idea seem ridiculous. Only because he did not believe. 'Twas this very pernicious lack of faith that would cause his death!

"Aye," she said.

"You little fool."

Her blue eyes shot to his face. He wrapped the string of her gown around his finger, as if it were a noose on her neck. Then he pulled it. Both hands came to her neck to part the dress from her shoulders. A soft cry escaped her as her hands flew to his as if to stop him.

"Which is it, Roshelle?" he asked in a compelling whisper of words. "Shall I stop and live to see the sun rise on the morrow? Or shall I play this game and march verily down this sweet, mercifully dark tunnel that ends in my death?"

She could not answer, yet distress marked her face. Heat gathered where his hands covered her shoulders. Small chills raced from those spots. She felt confused and scared of so many things, she could hardly separate and make sense of any of it: his inexplicable anger; the threat of his strength and power alongside memories of what would come, what was coming; the play and passion of his kisses and tender play of his hands; and all of this was shadowed by the threat of violence. The vengeful force sat between them, waiting for the bold touch of his kisses and hands, and its waiting threat would keep her from succumbing to his kisses. She would remain as cold and hard as a wooden doll. Surely! She would hardly feel a thing . . .

As cold and hard as a wooden doll.

The thought let her slowly lower her hands to her side and she braced. As cold and hard as a wooden doll. He parted the cloth from her shoulders, sliding it over her arms. Heat shot to her cheeks and she closed her eyes in shame as she felt the warm fix of his gaze on her naked bosom.

"My God, you are beautiful . . ." Then she heard the deep timbre of laughter. "A treasure worth dying for, indeed."

She drew a sharp, surprised breath. He would still amuse himself! She looked up at his face, letting him see her anger, a victim's anger, as if this pained her. Only to see his expression, mocking and amused and somehow challenge, daring her to protest.

How badly she wanted to wipe that amusement from his handsome face!

She did not. She kept herself very still but closed her eyes and drew a small breath as his large warm hands slipped beneath the cloak of her hair—how he loved her hair, so soft and thick and satiny velvet, he marveled—and then grazed her slender back, riding up and then down again, and with a touch as light and stirring as ten feathers.

His hands came to the gown, trapped at her elbows. As cold and hard as a wooden doll, she kept repeating in her mind, over and over as she felt his hands slip beneath the gown, and yet the hammer of her heart as she endured the slow and thorough caress beneath the heat of his gaze felt like a symphony of sensation. A symphony! Dear Lord, she should not feel a thing, she should not feel a thing . . .

He understood her distress all too well, and he'd see it increase tenfold. She would not escape with impunity. Not when he felt the drive of his pulse from the all-too-potent effect of her form shrouded in soft candlelight, and indeed, she looked more beautiful than a thousand others. His pulse raced fast and faster still as his hands came to her small, narrow waist and the feminine flare of her hips, where he savored her sculpted softness. Then his hands circled her back and he gently brought her against him, letting her feel the rock-hard outline of his desire.

A small cry of distress stopped in her throat.

He towered over her, his unconventional height as threatening somehow as an unsheathed sword raised in anger, and with the hot press of his body, she felt another surge of naked fear, a maiden's fear. Before she could think better of it, before she could stop herself, she raised her arms to protect her modesty and shook her head.

Again he just stared, his stare a challenge. She could not meet it and her lids lowered as if they were a curtain on her heart. His large hands came over hers, bringing her hands not just to her side but behind her back as he pulled her tight against him, their bodies firmly aligned.

The pleasure of the heavy softness of her breasts on his

chest caused a sharp intake of breath, released in a whisper as he lowered his head to hers. "Roshelle, Roshelle." He let his lips graze hers, demanding without words that she hold perfectly still for what pleasure he'd take, and she did; only the anxious pounding of her heart moved in her still body. His warm, firm lips rocked over hers until he heard her gasp and felt her shiver.

His hands lowered to her sides, traveling back and forth in a sea of sensations, stopping beneath her breasts, where he was teased by the length of cloth between them. He pulled it all the way over her arms and it dropped around her ankles. Venerability, intensely felt, came with her complete nakedness, growing as his gaze found the beauty thus unveiled. She crossed her arms over herself. "Oh, no, Roshelle . . ." He took her clenched fists in his hands. "I will humor no modesty tonight."

Her cheeks burned with color as he stared, his gaze traveling over the straight, slender shoulders, the oh-so-generous lift of her full, rounded breasts. He reached a hand to the silken side that narrowed to her small waist, then moved over the sensual flare of her hips and the long shapely lines of her legs.

She tensed, her flesh recoiling from the warmth of his touch as if it were scalding water. It was all she could do not to bolt, and as the moments stretched beneath his unkind scrutiny, she wondered above the furious pounding of her heart what, please to God, was taking so long.

Then she heard him say, unbelievably, as his lips rocked gently over her forehead, "Ah, Roshelle, I wonder, is it really my death that you want?"

The startling words brought her blue eyes up with a shocked gasp, and he had to bite his lip hard to stop from laughing out loud at the moral indignation there. She cried, "You are filled to full with conceits! To imagine that I might welcome this, this torment! Know this: I . . . I am a most reluctant player here and your, your every touch is a tribulation to me!"

A wicked kind of amusement filled his eyes, and absolutely no pity. "Such a violent protest—shall I humor the pretense and pretend it's true?" The question was asked as he swept his hands along her back to cup and hold her bottom, a movement intimate and so possessive, she felt heat spread from the tips of toes to the roots of her hair. "Or, Roshelle, perhaps I should show you how effortlessly I can change this reluctance and turn your tribulations to a celebration."

The words brought a kind of heartfelt agony and she cried, "How can you laugh in the face of your death? How?"

"Here, I'll show you, love."

And he did. From behind, he reached his hand around a handful of her hair, gently tugging so her head tilted up for his kiss. At first he teased his lips over hers, testing their softness until she gasped. Then his mouth came over hers, hard. Fear engulfed her, growing as his lips seemed to ruthlessly devour her, a kiss given with as much pain as pleasure. It stole her breath and her will, and she tried weakly to steel herself against the force of this kiss, she tried to conjure up the triumphant image of a waiting French army, but the very thought burst into a sea of bright gold-and-orange suns beneath the warm, firm lips and the stunning intrusion of his tongue, a taste like liquid fire . . .

Her head spun like a child's top beneath the dizzying onslaught of sensations, and somewhere in the passion of the kiss he had released her hands, so that she realized all of a sudden that they lay against his chest, opening and closing with the frantic beat of her heart. She was breathing hard and fast as he broke the kiss to stare down at her changed expression.

Her blue eyes were closed and she felt a wild race of tremors as his lips grazed her lids, her forehead, the corner of her mouth where her lips trembled. "Kiss me again, Roshelle," he whispered against her ear, gently taking the sensitive lobe between two teeth. A hot tremor of shivers coursed through her and she gasped as he said, "And see if I won't trade my life for another."

His finger lightly circled her lips until they parted with another gasp and she opened her eyes, only to close them again as she felt the sensual press of his lips. His hands held her head with a gentle but firm restraint, forcing her head back to accommodate him. And he wanted more. The kiss changed as he molded her mouth to his, teasing her with the skillful play of his tongue, moving in tantalizing slowness over every height and hollow.

He broke the kiss to let her draw a deep breath. "Look at me, Roshelle." Her blue eyes, darkening with passion and drawn from his dreams, slowly lifted to him with confusion and fear and passion. "You are confused now?" he asked. He let his lips lightly graze the place where hers trembled, savoring the sweetness of her small breath and mouth. "And very frightened. Roshelle, Roshelle," he whispered, then let her feel the light lash of his tongue on her ear. Like a hot little lick of fire. "I will answer your confusion by increasing your fear."

The fear he spoke of trembled through her. She felt a tingle of the rough cotton of his breeches on her abdomen, the threat of his hard, aroused manhood. Her senses reeled and against her will, she felt that melting warmth rising to greet him. His lips found her closed lids before he let his mouth lightly brush her forehead as he drank in the sweet scent of her. He called her name against her ear. Shivers, she felt a rush of tiny shivers, a feverish trail where his lips touched her skin. The pounding of her blood drowned out the crackle of the fire and his own changed breathing. His lips met hers with a promise calling to the very core of her being. So tenderly did he first kiss her, she felt a strange sense of wonder, mixed potently with some small distress. But her distress was quickly soothed as the sensual press of his mouth deepened, fueling a tingling warmth surging from deep inside, growing, spreading, until—

The pleasure magnified as his tongue skillfully entered her mouth, sending her into a soft swoon, melting and helpless. Yet he was holding her now. He had taken her small hands in his, bringing them behind her back and lifting her as he did so, gently aligning her soft curves to the hard outline of his body.

She didn't know when or how he did it, but somewhere in the space of that kiss, as her senses soared, then swooned, he had separated her from his body. Then he reached his arms around her back again, feeling only the slender shape beneath her long, loose hair as he pulled her against the full length and measure of his desire.

The shock of it sounded a long, loud "No" in her mind and she tried to pull away. Only to abruptly feel his arms tighten around her. "Don't," he said. "That's part of my pleasure."

The hot, burning part of him brought fear pounding with her pulse and she started to shake her head, but then she could not think, not as his moist lips found the soft hollow of her throat, the line of her neck and the curve of her ear, where he whispered her name over and over. She felt hot and cold all at once. The artful tease of his mouth and tongue sent small, hot slashes of pleasure through her until her breath came in tiny little gasps and an involuntary whimper escaped from her.

"You move so slowly . . . 'Tis a cruel torment to me!"

The exclamation made him chuckle. "Beg no sympathy from me, Roshelle. For if killing were made easy, there would be no human history to step into . . ." And before she could reply, he swept her up in his arms to bring her to the bed. She stared up at him, simmering with a dazzling mix of mounting fear and newly awakened passion as he laid her on her back against the soft folds of the dark velvet bedspread. "Let me see how I might draw out, magnify and prolong thy torment."

Blood rushed hot and fast through her veins. A strange burning sensation filled her, as if his heat penetrated her very skin and, to her wild alarm, her very loins. Futilely she tried to steel her mind and rally her defenses against the pleasure of his lips, his hands, even the anticipation of his touch, and in desperation she grabbed his strong forearms as he came partially over her, as if unsure whether to draw him closer or push him away, and she said in a cry, "Why do you persist? When you know—"

I am trying to steal your life.

She did not have to say it out loud. He answered anyway. "Why do I persist?" The question repeated itself in his mind and he said nothing for what seemed an eternity as he studied the beauty of her naked form bathed in firelight. Then he closed his eyes, trying desperately to restrain the surge of desire he had never known before, managing only, when he opened his eyes again, to see the slight tremble of her lips. He lightly kissed the corner of her mouth where they trembled.

Leaning on an elbow, he took one of her small hands in his. He gently took each finger in his mouth, his eyes never leaving her as he whispered, "If I believed in the power of this curse as I know the sun will rise on the morrow, as an absolute, unalterable fact, I still would neither offer impunity nor take it. Not when your lips wait for mine." He touched her lips, kneading her bottom lip between his teeth until he heard her gasp and she trembled with its gentle eroticism. "Not when your naked beauty lies before me, begging for my touch . . ." His hand grazed the beckoning curves as if sculpting her very softness, lingering beneath the flattened mounds of her breasts, until her blue eyes closed on a sigh. The callused tips of his fingers brushed the petal-satin of her skin above her breast, over and over, until a hot congestion gathered there and each breath came with a conscious effort. "Nay, death is no distraction, Roshelle, not now, not when my need for you pounds through every part of my being . . ."

"Vincent . . ."

His name was uttered in whispered agony. Agony the moment his mouth claimed hers. Like a finely built crescendo, the kiss deepened slowly, and she couldn't resist or think or breathe. There was no thought past the lips on hers, the heady flavor of his mouth, the sweep of his tongue on hers, the feel of his body on hers. She had never felt this, anything like this, except—

Except in her dreams. He had kissed her before, not once but many times, in the secret world of her dreams. The knowledge, the very force of what was overwhelming her, struggled up from the sweet onslaught of sensations and she knew at that moment that a part of herself would die with him, a large part of herself . . .

He drew back, only to let her feel his lips elsewhere, everywhere. Shivers erupted in full force. Shimmering heat swept through her. The pounding of her heart became the pounding of her blood. As if needing a lifeline, her hands were suddenly clinging to his head, her nails scraping through his hair, and only in the furthest recess of her mind did the thought persist—

He would be struck dead, any minute now, he would be struck down dead! A violent tremor shot through her, one he completely misunderstood. She stiffened dramatically as his hands came over her breasts, scared, just scared by the caress of skilled fingers. The palm of his hand slowly circled there and he was whispering her name, again and again, as his lips and tongue teased the most sensitive lobe of her ear. She tensed with a rush of chills. She shook her head in a mindless kind of negation as his hand continued to circle in erotic patterns, sliding over her side to the curve of her hip and thigh, then back again in ever-deepening strokes.

Dear Lord, 'twas coming . . .

His desire mounted, driving hot and fast and far. He went weak with it. My God, she felt so soft, slim and warm. Passion overwhelmed his mindfulness of her innocence; the demand of his desire became like a flame, consuming and devouring. "Roshelle, I want you . . . I want you . . ."

And he was kissing her again.

Chills rushed between her legs, alternating with the slow explosions made of her blood, and as her passion rose, sparked, flared, so did the fear, the idea that at any minute something unspeakable would happen. She didn't realize she was whispering "No" over and over until his mouth covered hers and he was kissing her again.

The kiss was feather-light at first. Until she felt his tongue traveling over her lips until they trembled and opened and he caught her mouth in a hard, exploring kiss as he let her feel his weight. The brush of their bodies brought another rush between her thighs, a growing heat there, and suddenly, without realizing it, she was kissing him back, her lips clinging to his of their own volition, burning and aching as he broke away.

Like a brush with fire, his lips left her mouth to travel to the arch of her throat. She gasped again with this play of his lips, the tiny spark like shivers he left there, but his lips moved lower still until she felt them on her breast.

She tensed with the hot pleasure of it as his lips moved softly back and forth over a nipple. A helpless whimper escaped her as his tongue swept around the tightening bud, stroking the secret wellspring of her desire and making her heart pound in the deepest part of herself. A feather-light hand replaced his lips as he managed, "My God, you are so soft . . ." His voice trailed off as he dragged his lips to her other breast. "God, Roshelle, I want you so badly . . . I fear—"

A feverish love cry interrupted him and he forgot what he was saying, indeed that he was even speaking, as he moved his lips over her nipple, again and again, drawing first softly there, then not, her soft, shocked gasps of pleasure answering him when she could not, and somewhere beneath the scattered fragments of her consciousness formed the pressing question—

Why did God mean to torment her like this first?

And she knew. The answer was, to punish her for taking his life. The curse, the weapon she used to alter the course of history and free France, came with a heavy price. A heavy price indeed, as she knew now what she would never have in this life. The idea brought a pained cry to her throat, disappearing as he called her name in an impassioned whisper and she felt his hand come to her other breast, drawing small circles around it, as if to encompass the maddening sensations before sliding over her side, pausing above the tuft of dark hair on the tempting point of her thighs. Heat gathered beneath the tease of his fingertips before they slipped over the velvet moistness of a place where no one and nothing had been before.

A great, voluminous burst of warmth overcame her as he slowly fanned those flames. She cried softly as the sensations washed through her, and arched her back, as if offering herself to him, the movement rewarded with a deeper probe, another burst of voluptuous warmth, carrying her farther and farther until she heard his name on her lips, again and again. She felt that she stood on a great high cliff . . .

The pleasure of his possession seized the whole of him; he was mad with it, with her, the taste and scent and feel of the small body beneath him, the welcoming moist heat of her sex, the pleasure that was changing her beauty, and he neared his end. His mind filled with the heady anticipation of the feel of her hot, tight sheath around him . . .

She shook her head weakly, until she felt his mouth return to hers with a kiss of savage sweetness. Yet her dazed consciousness rippled with alarm as she felt the smooth, hot pressure of him slide back and forth over her sex. He broke the kiss and lifted partially up to stare into the terrified pools of her eyes, and he said, "Your curse, Roshelle. Say it never was . . ."

"Nooo . . . I do not know . . . You should be dead . . ."

She shut her eyes tight and suddenly fate spun the vision, the certainty of his hot blood spilling over her naked skin. She screamed, loud and long. He was staring at the terrifying shape of her madness and it shocked him. Before the chills on his back stopped, before he drew his next breath, a violent wrench tore her slim figure from him. Instinctively, but slowed by the race of his blood, his arm snaked out to catch her. Too late by many meaningful seconds.

Through the candlelit darkness he stared at the corner of the room where she curled herself into a tight ball. Her eyes shone like a cat's in the dark, and he gasped upon seeing the fear and confusion in those bright, terrified eyes.

Dear Lord, did she want him dead that badly?

His desire was still hot and strong and consuming, a kind of madness that made him consider carrying her kicking and screaming back to the bed, and yet as he considered that scene, all he could see was the terror shining in the bright blue eyes.

He cursed viciously.

Cursed himself for letting it matter. For it did matter. In that moment he confronted the idea, the knowledge, the certainty of how very much it did matter. He closed his eyes in a desperate effort to control his changing desire, and unexpectedly, the image of Roshelle standing in the white tower swam dizzily through his mind. The terrible sadness in her eyes was there as he felt the scrape of his fingers and he fell away from her . . .

At first so terribly amusing, the curse had seemed like a great gift of the gods, and indeed, as the man Papillion had surely intended, it had kept her safe until he came into her life.

Yet now the charade had gone too far, much too far.

All the wealth and warmth of his desire had not dissipated but rather changed, transformed to violence. He would not let her know that. It took him several long minutes to control his emotion enough to lay hands on her safely, without the very real fear of hurting her. Then he pulled on his breeches and found her fallen gown before approaching the place where she knelt.

She felt her heart pound fast, then much too slow, and her pulse still ran hot and thick with the lingering heat of his pleasure, while her senses felt strained, saturated with a druglike lethargy. She tried to pull herself above it long enough to think. To think anything past the physical pain, a pain so deep, so strong, that her dazed mind could not recognize it as disappointment.

All she knew was it could not be so, and yet he was standing there, still very much alive! Thoughts spun fast and furiously around the idea that the whole of her curse and her life was little more than a ruse, a trick, Papillion's jest to the world in an effort only to keep her safe. She could not believe it. It could not be true! The whole of the French army waited for the duke's death, and she had thought, she had been certain, God Himself had ordained the deed—

"You should be dead!" she cried in sudden desperation. "I do not know why you are not dead!"

"God curse you, girl!"

His voiced thundered above her, jerking her into a trembling wave of confusion and fear, and she cried out as his arm snaked around her, lifting her to her feet. "Come, Roshelle," he said as the cool folds of her gown came over her head to cover her nakedness, and she felt his hand pull the heavy weight of her hair out from beneath. "Let me tumble this castle of cards once and for all and show you the full extent of the fabrication and farce you live in."

Chapter 10

W hen her knees collapsed, he cursed again and lifted her into his arms. Quickly he carried her through the darkened waiting room and into the torchlit hall. He leaped down the spiral staircase and through the halls and corridors until finally they were in the courtyard. Confused and frightened and not knowing what he meant, she saw suddenly that he headed for the stables. "The stables? I do—"

"I want you to meet someone."

The doors were open. Torches lit the inside. A number of guards of Suffolk stood around a small barrel, turned upside down to support cups and cards. A few of the men rose upon seeing the Lord of Suffolk carrying Lady Roshelle, others did not, but all watched with interest.

Vincent carried her over to a man, chained and bound to the wall. He was asleep. The duke set her on her feet and, still clasping her upper arm, kicked the man hard with his bare foot. He woke with a start.

"This is the sorry man who brought you a message today." Then he addressed the frightened man. "Tell the lady the name of thy master."

The man looked up, his gaze riveted on the tall, princely figure of the duke, and in a pained, raspy voice, knowing he was doomed in any case, he produced a name that made Roshelle regret her next breath.

"My master's name be the Duke of Burgundy."

The name spun through her mind. The Duke of Burgundy, dear Lord. A hand went to her pale forehead; she felt her knees buckling with the magnitude and meaning of the name. But the seal—

A trick, another in a long list of his wicked tricks. He must have killed the seal keeper or tricked him somehow. There was no French army, no brave French knights, no sword risen from Charles's hand. 'Twas all his jest, his wicked jest. The image of the Duke of Burgundy's face contorted with amusement at the idea of her offering her virginity to Vincent de la Eresman—

"He was trying to kill you, and I, I was his agent . . ."

Violence strained Vincent's muscles; he felt a murderous rage and he struggled hard to control it. "Aye!" His gaze came to the man's smirk, and as if he were swatting a fly, his bare foot landed against the man's jaw. There was a sickening crack and Roshelle screamed as the man dropped forward like a puppet without a string.

Wilhelm stepped through the doors, and hearing this, he motioned for the guards to disband. In a sudden rush of movement they rose and moved quickly through the doors. The last men out shut the doors, letting Cisely slip inside at the last minute, pinching her nose until she saw. She took one look at Roshelle's abject distress and rushed to her, but Wilhelm caught her arm, stopping her.

Vincent turned back to Roshelle. He towered over her, his eyes filled with fury, and she dropped to her knees and lowered her eyes.

"And do you know why he wants me dead?"

She shook her head, afraid, just afraid.

"Because he sired a bastard with that whore who married Edward! His bastard and whore stand to inherit my duchy. My life, Roshelle! And believe! He will not rest until I am dead."

She looked up at him, shocked.

"And the only reason I am still alive is because he is so foolish, so utterly idiotic as to be struck by this peculiar French madness, this belief that your precious virginity has the awesome power to kill men." Crushing hands came over her thin arms as he lifted her to her feet, stopping just short of shaking her senseless. "And, curse you, girl, when I think of the megalomaniacal arrogance necessary for you to think you were killing me tonight, 'tis all I can do not to knock you to the ground and part your thighs so you can feel the merciless hard stab of a bit of a man's flesh, and with it, a woman's humility—"

"Vince!"

The urgency with which Wilhelm uttered his name cut through his fury and made him absorb the stark terror in her eyes, terror mixing with shame and tears. His hands lightened their grip on her arms, and then he released her altogether as Cisely suddenly surrounded Roshelle, dropping to her knees.

Vincent swore softly. Wilhelm made use of the wine left by the guards and handed him a cask. He drank a mouthful, spat it out, then brought the cask to his mouth again and swallowed the bitter taste, knowing of course it would have no discernible effect. Not tonight. Thank God for Wilhelm, though; his presence would at least keep her safe from his fury.

Roshelle heard the intake of his breath as he finished at last, then felt the return of his cruel appraisal. A horse neighed in the background, restlessly shifting its feet, interrupting the still and quiet night of the stables. She tried to focus on the sound of the crickets laid against the quiet of the dark, desperate to still the emotional rage in her breast, but it swelled, cresting, as if the weight of these past terrible years were crashing down upon her.

The Duke of Burgundy existed only to torment her. She had lived through four years of his torture, nothing but the trials and tribulations of his endless tortures, and now the curse, the curse that had always kept her safe and separated her from all others, now this, too, was gone. Or was it?

She did not understand what was happening . . .

Vincent tried hard to ignore her tears; he would use this to make her see at last. "So, my dear young Countess, you are nothing more than his pawn in this little chess game to get me killed.''

Almost the exact words she herself had once said to Louis, the day it all started. She wished to God that were true, but it wasn't. She meant so much more to him. Papillion, when will it end?

"He will try to kill me again. And soon. He is my enemy, Roshelle. The lines are drawn. You must choose your sides and choose carefully."

Kneeling still, she looked up at him. In desperation she pleaded, and it was a lie. "I do not know what you want from me."

"I need to know about him. Everything about him."

"There is nothing to say . . . I—"

He swept down on her again, lifting her up. His eyes were ablaze with fury and he said, "You can start by telling me how he threatens you."

Vincent watched the unnatural fears spring into her eyes. She shook her head, panicked. "You are wrong! There is no threat! He has my lands and that is enough for him—"

A hand came to her mouth. "A lie. I know you, Roshelle, I know thy spirit, for I have touched it. You are like a caged winged creature; I have felt the longing in you to be free, to be gone. You would have left Reales long ago. Somehow he keeps you here—"

She shook her head. "Please, just let me go!"

The fear magnified many times. "Why? Do you imagine he has spies here, that they are listening to us as we speak?" He watched her wide, frightened eyes sweep the dark space, jerking from one shadow to the next. A barn owl flew from its perch with a screech. She shuddered.

"I see. I should have known. A threat to you would not work. Your unnatural courage again. He threatens someone you love—"

"Tell him, Roshelle!" Cisely begged on her knees. "They will help us!"

"Hush!" Roshelle looked at Cisely. "He cannot help. No one can help."

Wilhelm heard this with mounting alarm, Roshelle's terror making him want to kill the man responsible. "Be it you, Cisely? Does he threaten you?"

Cisely shook her head; she, too, was crying now.

Vincent looked from Cisely to Roshelle and back again before he realized. " 'Tis the maid Joan. Which is why you objected to Bryce's courtship of her."

"Dear Lord," Wilhelm said, thinking of Bryce, of his simple sense of justice and right, the kind of man who never saw a shade of gray. "The Duke of Burgundy is reputed to be the best swordsman in France and the Continent beyond, perhaps in all the world. Now Bryce be good, but—"

"Not that good," Vincent finished. "And his damnable fearlessness, too."

"Aye, a fearlessness that oft made me wonder if he was as simple as the maid he loves. We must keep it from him."

"Aye."

The suggestion of a sword fight, that the fate of Rodez might possibly be decided with a sword, brought anguish to Roshelle as she remembered a day long ago, just after her tenth birthday, when three knights came to Orleans to present Rodez with a challenge. They were only three of probably dozens of men with a grievance, and the only thing different about them was that they had the courage to offer the grand duke a challenge. For he had split with Papillion by then and had come into not just his inheritance but his full, awful power. With Charles and Louis, she had watched the match. Watched with unrelieved terror as first one, then another of these brave knights was slain. Just before Rodez's sword pierced their hearts she saw the strike of horror on their faces. Desperate to help, she had closed her eyes, and thinking she could somehow save the doomed man, she cast her thoughts into his so she could wield the sword with his strength and skill. And with success at first, the swordsman seized an advantage. Rodez was tiring, weakening, and if he could just—

Suddenly Rodez's face transformed into a woman's. Numbing horror gripped the good knight as he saw this, the lovely face of a woman he had once loved, and in the same instant Rodez lunged, his sharp blade piercing through heart and flesh, and she had screamed . . .

"Roshelle, Roshelle." Vincent thought he understood the anguish on her face. "You must know I would extend my protection to your women, to Joan, that I would never let him hurt—"

"Nay, you think so. You think 'tis a matter of swords or bravery or battle. If only it were so, if only it were me. You do not know yet how diabolical he is. And he promises me that someday he will come for her. Someday . . ."

"The day you leave Reales," he had said. "Or the day she leaves . . ."

"Why does he? When he has your lands—"

"He torments Roshelle for the same reason. Everything he does is for one reason and one reason only," Cisely said in a distant and forlorn whisper. "Revenge. He will spend his life exacting revenge against Papillion, and therefore Roshelle, because she had the extraordinary blessing and curse of Papillion's love."

Vincent studied the sadness and hopelessness in Roshelle's eyes, so like in his dream. 'Twas the rhyme and reason of his dream. A dream to warn him of this threat. Yet the white tower, what did the white tower mean?

"You see," Cisely answered his confusion, whispering still as if it were dangerous to speak of it out loud, "Rodez had once been, like Roshelle, Papillion's student. Yet not at all like Roshelle. For some reason, perhaps the perversity of Rodez's nature, all of Papillion's teachings became twisted, changed, used in his relentless thirst for the power of the occult—which Papillion condemned. I remember their fighting spilling through the halls of Orleans, a tension so thick—" She shook her head. "It became a battle of wills. Louis always said that Papillion knew what he had helped to make and he was desperate to change Rodez before he lost him completely. But it was too late. From the first day of their liaison, it was too late. In the end Papillion had no choice but to banish him from his life, and forevermore he was banished.''

Wilhelm did not understand. ''Blood for banishment, but—''

''Nay,'' Roshelle said, '' 'twas only the beginning, a beginning that ended the day Rodez tried to kill Papillion. I was there. I saw it. The jeweled knife at his throat and, and then it was as if he decided, he suddenly saw death was not enough—'' A violent shudder passed through her and Vincent thought she was going to faint and he caught her up again in his arms. ''The Archbishop of Orleans sought Papillion for over a year, you see. Since the night of my wedding feast. I had not been there when it happened, but I have heard the story many times, tales of black magic: cups and bowls secreting a foul-smelling soup, spilling all over; bewitched creatures appearing everywhere, cats and dogs and insects and birds; and bishops falling into possession.'' She shook her head. ''Papillion could make miracles, aye, but he would never condescend to a magician's simple tricks, much less tricks tainted by the occult arts, all those stunts that horrified the good lords and ladies in the hall. And yet everyone assumed he was responsible. 'Twas Rodez who orchestrated those horrors at my wedding, knowing full well that the church would blame and persecute Papillion for them.

''Until then Papillion had always happily coexisted with his church fellows, and though there were some priests who were jealous and suspicious of his ways, there were always many more who loved him as a friend and teacher.'' She shook her head sadly, remembering the betrayal of so many. So many. ''Of course, Papillion made fun of the archbishop's summons,'' she continued softly, her voice carrying no emotion, yet weighted with unmasked pain as she spoke. ''So whenever the archbishop's men showed up at the forest house, Papillion would be seen lecturing or ministering in Orleans—sometimes from the very steps of the archbishop's house. It got to be an amusing charade of cat and mouse, one that kept the entire court amused for over a year—Papillion's cleverness in duping the foolish old archbishop and his bumbling band of men time and time again. How we had laughed. We all thought, we *knew*, there was nothing he could do to Papillion. Papillion was protected and loved by everyone at court—by Charles, his family and counselors, and though Louis was gone to the Tower by then, his stamp still sat on every decree of Orleans. Everyone, all at court and half the church, loved Papillion. As if love was a force to contend with, as if love mattered at all . . ."

A small fist clenched against his bare chest as she said the last. "At last, as he tended a dying friend's deathbed, they came and he was taken away. Within the next twenty hours he was tortured and tried and killed as a heretic of the Christian world." The image of Papillion's tortured body floated into her mind and she felt suddenly dizzy—

"Roshelle—"

Tears sparkled in her blue eyes, and she tried to banish them. "Roshelle." He stood over her, peering down through the darkness at her pain-marred face. "What happened then? He did not stop?"

"Nay. He will never stop. He exists only to bring destruction and death to anything and anyone Papillion loved! To anything Papillion's love ever touched. To torment me . . .

"I remember Papillion's garden, a secret place of flowering blossoms from Passover to Michaelmas where they say my mother oft walked. Papillion kept the roses for her memory, long after she died. He always planted roses, simply because she had loved them so. When he was torn from me, I, like a cotter maid, spent weeks planting the seeds and tilling the soil. I wanted it to blossom again. And it did.

"I remember the day the roses blossomed in a rainbow of colors between red and white. A sad kind of joy burst in my heart! Life and love renewed and begun again. That day I stood in the middle of the garden, drinking in the simple beauty and breathing the heavenly scents of the roses, and I felt his love all around me again. Until I looked up. Rodez stood there watching me. I panicked. I did not know how he got there. There was no announcement in Orleans of his arrival from faraway Flanders, and yet there he stood. He said only, 'Behold your fate, Roshelle,' and suddenly, as I watched, a fire grew. The roses caught a flame. All around me the roses burst into flames. Their petals turned to brown and finally black . . .''

The expression in her eyes alarmed Vincent and he said with feeling, "Roshelle, 'tis but a dream you tell. 'Twas only a long-ago nightmare—''

"Aye," she surprised him by agreeing. Papillion had once asked her what the difference was between a needle prick in a dream and one when awake. Nothing really. For they both bring the same pinch of pain. "I have sometimes thought it must be a dream, that it could not have happened. It seems so long ago, too . . .''

He glanced at Wilhelm, who nodded, both men seeing that, whether dream or no, it did not matter to her. She lived in another world, a dark world of magic and miracles and sinister shadows, and what frightened Vincent the most was the idea that nothing and no one could pull her out from this world and into his.

"What did Papillion do to him?"

"Papillion kept him from love, or so he thinks. Papillion believed Rodez just used it as an excuse for the black seed he let grow in his heart; hate demands a focus, and Rodez found his." Her blue eyes retreated as she remembered how, at the forest cottage, she would catch Papillion staring out at the distant landscape but really seeing his memories. Tears would come to his eyes. Only later did she know he was remembering Rodez as a boy. "I should have known," he'd whisper. "I should have seen it coming, growing and taking shape before my very eyes. Sometimes I think I did know, I did see, but 'twas too terrible to confront . . ." Then he'd draw her into his arms and he'd say, "The love in thine eyes, Roshelle, the love that pounds in your heart and shapes every movement of thine hand, it is my gift . . ."

"Roshelle." Vincent's voice drew her back to the difficult subject. "What happened then?"

"I do not know everything. I know it started when Rodez fell in love, for the first and last time, he knew love."

"With this woman Terese?"

"Oh, no. 'Twas with his wife, Angelique."

"His wife?"

"Aye, a long time ago now—"

He had heard about this. "Wilhelm . . ."

"Aye." Wilhelm nodded. " 'Tis said that years ago Rodez Valois abdicated on a marriage contract with that Spanish duchess, Anna Marie Guardairia, the one who later married Frederick of Austria, and he did so to marry a poor baroness. This young girl had nothing, no dowry to speak of, only a few parcels of worthless farmland to the north of Flanders—or so 'tis said."

"Aye," Roshelle agreed. "He loved her that much. Angelique would never be content to be his mistress. She would have no liaison with a man except with the sacrament of marriage. So he tossed away a fortune and bribed the church to find reasons for breaking his marriage contract. And then he married her."

"What do you know of the woman?"

A distant look came into her eyes again. "I only met Angelique once, but once was enough . . ."

"Enough for what?"

"Angelique, you see, was touched."

"Mad?"

"Nay, milord. Or not exactly." Roshelle shook her head. "Angelique was touched by God's grace; the holy spirit lived and breathed through her soul. She was not meant for this world. I remember Papillion was very upset when Rodez announced his plans . . . I was so young then, but I still remember Papillion said that Angelique's blessing would be Rodez's curse in this world, or so he would think . . .''

"Does she live with him now, his whore underfoot?"

Roshelle shook her head. "Shortly after her marriage to Rodez, she took a vow of silence. She lives the cloistered life at the Abbey de la Sainte-Chapelle but rumor has it that she went mad, that he made her go mad, and all because she would not love him more than God."

"Yes?"

Her blue eyes filled with the fear of it. "There is a secret Papillion knew, a terrible secret, a potion or a spell, I do not know. But Rodez wanted it, for this secret had the awesome power to separate one's soul from God."

Vincent's brows furrowed as he exclaimed, "That is such nonsense!"

"Is it?" She shook her head, a profound sadness in her voice, for she understood so well. "I think not. For even if it were a thing that exists only in the mind, it is still too awful to contemplate. Do you not see what it means? Rodez saw himself as warring with God—with God!—for Angelique's heart. To live against God is to live without Him, a fate so terrible that the only way priests relate it to simple minds is through these endless descriptions of the terrors and tortures of hell." Her voice was filled with emotion as she said, "Papillion chose death before he gave the secret to him, and as Rodez held that dagger at his throat, Papillion set it to flames."

Vincent stared at her for a long moment, still hearing the emotion in her voice. Whatever the story meant to her, it explained much. The ruthlessness of this beast in Burgundy, he saw, knew no limits. He would have to choose the battleground carefully; there could be no mistakes.

"I know what you are thinking," she said with anguish. "You are wrong! Wrong! You see an enemy and you think of a battle—its victory determined by strength and skill and courage." She searched his eyes through the darkness, the fear of him changing the look in her eyes and startling him with a glimpse of what she had lived through these past years. "You cannot fight him! For in his battles the victor is never in question. Now, now you are doomed as well. Doomed—"

Emotions swelled through her again, for she suddenly understood what his life would cost her. The tragedy of the future spun dizzily through her mind, and, desperate to escape, she tore herself from his grasp, cursing the first day her eyes came to behold him and every day since as she ran from the dark walls of the stables into a still darker night.

The roan-colored stallion tossed back his head to loosen the lead, then returned to the grass. The giant of a man smiled. Fastest horse in Flanders, a personal gift of the duke. In case he had to leave in a hurry.

With the Duke of Suffolk's head . . .

Though that was not usually his way. As he had had to explain to the Duke of Burgundy, not wanting to think of what the man might want with a head. But for that much gold, he would get it if he could, but he'd be damned if he'd risk his neck in the bargain. "Ye might just have to be satisfied with a nice, clean death, plain and simple."

"My satisfaction is guaranteed," the duke had replied.

The man's dark eyes swept upward to the misty gray sky. The morning sun shone just beyond. The mist would be gone in an hour, offering him a sweeping view of the castle, all the comings and goings, and like he'd done all day yesterday and the day before and the day before that, he'd stare at the view until darkness, waiting. Just waiting. He was ever patient. 'Twas only a matter of time before the grand almighty Duke of Suffolk rode out for a hunt, a bit of jousting or to put his famous war-horse through the paces.

The man withdrew a sharp dagger from a leather bag that held steel-plated arrows, a halbert and his illustrious sword, and with knife in hand, he began whittling away on a stick.

'Twas only a matter of time . . .

"Milord!"

Wilhelm nudged Bogo and cleared his throat, nodding toward Vincent. Bogo looked up to see why he had lost Vincent's attention. All gazes followed the duke's over the battlements, where a groom held the reins of a magnificent mare. Roshelle took the reins in her hand before lifting them over the mare's head, and without the groom's hand, she agilely leaped onto a bare back.

Shrouded in the morning mist and atop the fine creature, Roshelle appeared as the sad and doomed princess of many a knightly tale. A cloak of midnight blue covered her head and spread behind her. The mare tossed her head, fighting for the bit. The girl ran the horse in five quick circles before she leaned forward, soothed the animal's tousled mane and whispered into her ear. A slippered foot kicked the mare's side, and horse and rider leaped into a gallop.

A strange vision filled Vincent's mind as he watched, like a memory misplaced in time and sent to counter the force and fear of the vision of the white tower: he saw Roshelle riding up to him, stopping as his hands reached around her small waist to lift her into the air from the saddle. To the music of laughter mixed with joyful tears, he spun her around and around in the air before lowering her to the ground for his kiss. A kiss without end . . .

He drew a sudden sharp breath, the force of his desire momentarily stunning him. He shook his head to rid his mind of it and closed his eyes, but it seized him physically. She had been away from the castle all this past week, staying at a poor cotter's hut to tend a young boy who had caught his foot in one of Edward's abandoned and forgotten fox traps. Vincent had been told that Papillion had taught Roshelle everything he knew about healing and the medicinal arts, while keeping her mercifully ignorant of anything connected to the occult. Apparently this skill had saved the boy his leg. Yet her absence had shown Vincent exactly how far they had traveled.

"Bogo?"

The small man paused before answering, aware of a sudden tension, that Vincent would say something of import. "Aye?"

"I need you to take a message back to England and personally address my king."

He exchanged confused glances with Wilhelm. They had just sent Henry a message regarding the escalating tensions and suspicions surrounding the Duke of Burgundy. "What is so important that it cannot be said on a parchment, milord?"

"I need you to beg his Majesty's permission, to plead my case."

With caution and dawning comprehension, Bogo asked: "A case involving the young countess?"

"Aye . . ."

For he would marry her now.

It would be a problem for Henry. Love and marriage were a rare combination in his exalted class; Henry would never find that compelling. On the other hand, the marriage of lands, French to English, would please Henry greatly; he would see it as a tremendous boost in his quest for the French crown. Yet such a prize as Roshelle would not come for nothing: even if the Duke of Burgundy could be made to agree, he would no doubt want concessions Henry could not, would not make. Unless Vincent made the appeal to Henry as his friend rather than as one of his vassals.

Then Roshelle would have to be told.

He could not guess her response. All the violence and fury had left the night he'd seen her fear and grasped the nature of these past hard years of her life. Years in which she had lived with the illusion her love would kill the man she gave it to. The illusion he had shattered. Or had he? Did she know the curse never had been, never was? Or, dear God, did she still have doubts?

Wilhelm stared at him in amazement, a strangely solemn amazement, but Bogo did not hesitate long. "I shall begin the preparations at once." With a short bow he withdrew.

Roshelle and mare disappeared into the mist atop the hill and Vincent turned to meet the solemnity of his friends' gazes. "Richard," he said to his squire, "saddle my horse."

"Aye, milord."

"Oh, no," Wilhelm said, shaking his head to send his red mane falling over his shoulders. "Not without guards, you don't. Owens, saddle me up, too. That lone knight stalking the place still has not been caught—"

"Stay where you stand, Owens." Vincent contradicted Wilhelm's order. "You can believe my intentions call for no company. Besides, that knight has not been caught because he is no doubt many days gone from the place, an innocent traveler—"

"Huh! Innocent? Then why did the bastard hide tail and run? As innocent as the whores of Babylon. And your intentions will no doubt lay the girl's backside to the ground with her eyes closed and yours on only one thing. So I will go with you just the same—"

Vincent lost his patience with his friend's last words. "And I say you won't."

The black stallion crested the top of the hill. Vincent drew hard on the reins to stop, turning the stallion around to absorb the view. The morning sun burned through the thin layers of fog, and the whole of the Reales Valley emerged below. The five towers of the castle jutted up from the gold-and-brown tents of the army surrounding it. Nearby, nestled in the hollow of the tree-lined valley, were the thatched roofs of the township; the two muddied roads of the town formed a perfect cross from this spot above. Behind this, the river raced toward its mother water, the ocean. In the far distance, the thatched roofs of the village cottages appeared scattered about the patchwork of the plowed fields. It was an arresting view, for only from above could one see how many fields that had once been left to weeds and encroached by the forest were now newly cleared and planted.

Did you look back from atop the hillside, Roshelle?

He turned his stallion to the east and held him still as he searched for her path. He saw nothing but the mist-shrouded forest of beech. He waited for some sign or movement to give her away. Nothing. She had just disappeared.

After over an hour of tramping through the thick, carpeted forest, Vincent finally gave up his search and was turning back toward the castle when, a few dozen paces away, the sudden shrill cry of a bird overhead drew his gaze to the heavens. He spotted the bird through the tree-tops at once. Greyman. The falcon circled not far away. He turned his stallion toward the place.

Within minutes he found her.

Time stretched and lingered, marked only by the subtle play of illumination and shadow over the place where she knelt in prayer. A stream of golden morning light poured through the towering beech trees to fall on the carpet of bright violet bluebells all around her, the flowers blooming in urgent brilliance before the leafy canopy above them grew too thick. The air filled with their sweet fragrance. A dragonfly danced a circle around her. A group of wood warblers chirped from a nearby tree, the only sound violating the silence.

He could not move; for a long time he could not move. He had always been a man of action and deed, war-hardened and calloused to the continual march of human folly around him, and much of that folly derived from the pretensions of the religious. He had little patience for it and, with few exceptions, he viewed the plain idiocy of most of the religious teachings and practices of his time with a bemused, if not cynical, eye. Those few times he encountered the truly reverent were inevitably through the written word: especially those of the Greek philosophers,

Thomas Aquinas, one heretical monk of the Moslem faith and two of the Hebrew faith, but that was all. Until now.

He quietly slipped from his horse, but his gaze never left her, as if he, too, were drawn into the profound sanctity of the moment. A mysterious air surrounded her, indeed, seemed to emanate from her as she knelt there on the forest floor in a marvel of perfect stillness. That he had happened upon a secret moment was obvious; that it was sacrosanct, even more so. He wanted badly to honor it, to turn away and leave her moment inviolate. Yet another, stronger force compelled him to stay. A thing greater than simple curiosity.

He did not know how long he watched her, but gradually the light cascading from above shifted, changed, and finally disappeared altogether. She knelt in a shadow. As if this were a cue, she seemed to suddenly wake and take stock of her surroundings before she fell back on her heels and covered her face with her hands.

The sound of her tears came to him in a whisper . . .

He drew a sharp breath, released in the sound of her name. "Roshelle . . ."

She came to her feet with a gasp, turning to see him there in the same motion. Her blue eyes widened, staring as if questioning the very reality of his presence. The strange aura around her lingered still; she looked otherworldly somehow, angelic and, dear Lord, so innocent. Her vulnerability was a thing felt, and powerfully. The blue pools were moist with tears, large, and haunted with that strange sadness. The thought of lowering his lips to taste those tears brought another heady rush of desire through him, and for a moment he went weak with it.

"Roshelle . . . what has made you cry?"

The question was whisper-soft. She shook her head, still unable to speak. The sadness gathered in her throat, waiting, threatening with the first spoken word. She did not want him to see her like this. The mystical revelation still trembled through her, the joy of it retreating, dissipating, like a dream upon waking. Sadness and longing filled the empty space, leaving her defenseless, like dandelions beneath the breath of wind.

Delicate blossoms crunched beneath his boots as he came to where she stood, the soft sound loud in the stillness of the forest trees. She met the intensity of his stare as he stepped in front of her. So close he almost touched her.

"Non pas maintenant . . . s'il vous plaît . . ."

Not now, please, his mind translated, and yet he knew he could not honor the plea if his life depended on it. She was shaking her head. The tempo of her heart escalated; her senses filled with his nearness, more potent somehow with the exposure of her emotional fragility. His hand came to her face and her eyes lowered as cool fingertips brushed along her hairline. She fought the urge to turn her face into the warmth of his hand. A lone tear slipped down her cheek. His thumb tenderly caught it, banishing the sweet drop in a gentle caress across her cheek. "Roshelle, tell me . . ."

She looked up to see the compassion in his gaze. For a moment it startled her and then she wondered why. There seemed to be no limits to the reach of his compassion.

'Twas an English duke who lifted the people's burden, who stared at her now with unmasked sympathy and concern. 'Twas an English duke who promised her safety at last, whom she longed so desperately to believe. 'Twas an English duke who made her heart leap and pound with a strange fluttering excitement and fear the moment she saw him. 'Twas an English duke who appeared each night in the secret place of her dreams, who carried her so far that she was forced to question the reality of the curse . . .

The unnatural ivory of her skin begged his touch, its paleness accenting the red-brown plaits of hair that haloed her lovely face. "Tell me," he said, cupping her chin in the palm of his large hand, marveling at the poetry of her tear-washed eyes. "I would know this burden of your heart. Is it his torment again? Rodez?"

She could not speak. She shook her head, her lashes

lowered as if to hide her secrets. He would not have her
retreat, though. "You were praying, for . . . for—" His
brows drew together as he guessed in a whisper, "For that
man you loved. You seek him through prayer."

Her blue eyes found his. Another time she might have
been surprised by his understanding, but not now. Not as
her mind, her heart, her very soul remained firmly fixed
on the miracle brought by her forest prayers. For sometimes when she prayed, she was graced with the miracle
of love and light, and she felt Papillion's love cascade over
her like a warm fountain of light, and for those precious
moments she knew peace.

Peace. Her soul felt like a weary and bedraggled beggar
who had traveled so far, for so long, the simple comfort
of a fire and a warm cup of milk to wrap his cold hands
around was only a distant memory. A very distant memory. Yet all this past week she had found a different kind
of peace: as she tended the little boy, Paul, as she worried
over his fever and blood loss and swelling, all the medicines and their mixtures, she barely had time to think of
Vincent, or of warring countries or curses or evil threats
of unspeakable torments. Aye, a different kind of peace,
it was but precious . . .

The miracle was gone now, dissipated into the waking
light of day, as if it never was. Now she felt only the
longing, a terrible longing to get it back and hold it, the
peace and freedom from the endless circle of her tired
thoughts.

"Aye . . ."

He stroked an errant strand of hair curling on her forehead, and she was strangely conscious of the gesture.

He saw the truth then. "You are afraid."

Her blue eyes darkened with a worry as she nodded,
tears brimming in her eyes. She never knew exactly what
happened next. He stood up, drawing her against him as
he did, enfolding her into his warmth. A great warmth.
She felt the unnatural strength of him, the relaxed muscles
of his thighs, his hips on her stomach and a muscle-

encased rib cage before, in a single fluid motion, he lifted her into his arms. She started to protest but he stopped her. "Roshelle, no. I'm just taking you to that oak tree there. See it? That's all . . ."

The next thing she knew, he sat against the trunk, his long legs stretched in front and she upon his lap. Her arms were neatly folded against the wide breath of his chest, her face and tears buried against the swift, steady beat of his heart.

For a moment he struggled without success to temper the soaring effect she had on his senses. He smoothed the crease on the side of her forehead over and over while she cried against his chest. Cried so softly, he knew only from the small, irregular breaths that teased the skin on his chest. Each inhalation brought the sweet taste of her perfume and he closed his eyes, breathing deeply and trying to steer his thoughts from the mounting heat between them. The mere thought of her inevitably registered physically; holding her on his lap played with fire.

"Roshelle . . . look at me."

Tear-filled blue eyes lifted hesitantly.

She saw his answer to her doubt and fear in the warm caress of his gaze and, *mon Dieu,* how she wanted to believe him! He withdrew the pins that held her plaits around her head, yet she did not know it until first one, then the other swung free and his gentle fingers began unwinding the braids and still their gazes were locked, the key tossed away. The desire in his darkly intelligent eyes charged the air around them, like the air before a lightning storm. She swallowed, abruptly conscious of the rising tempo of her overworked heart and pulse, and even more when he said, "I want you, Roshelle." His fingers combed through the long unbound hair that spilled over his arm to curl on the forest floor. He traced a line around her ear and neck. Shivers rushed from the spots. "With each and every breath I take, I want you." He leaned over and gently kissed her lips once, withdrawing a bit but keeping his own dangerously close.

She felt a tremor of fear, her thoughts begging the question for the millionth time: what if he was wrong and the curse was as real as a sharp-edged sword? What if he had not died simply because Rodez's wicked intentions had stopped it, as if Papillion's magic would not work for Rodez's gain? What if—

"Don't, Roshelle," was all he said, all he had to say. She wanted so badly to believe him and she closed her eyes, as if to make it so as he said, "I mean to kiss you until my head swims in the sweetness of this perfume." His large strong hand went to the laces at the bodice of her gown. "I mean to kiss you until I have felt and awakened every inch of this body. Again. I mean to kiss you, Roshelle." He let his lips gently caress the spot on her neck where the shivers raced. "Until I feel you trembling beneath me, until your cries need only my answer. My answer . . ."

Tiny sparklike shivers rushed from the spot where his lips teased her, and her racing heart sped blood through her now feeble veins. Her small fist curled against his shoulder, she felt but a hairsbreadth from panic. "Vincent, what if, if you are wrong—"

He laid a finger over her lips. "Enough of this. I have no mind to hear of it ever again. I will lay your every last doubt to rest on this sunlit forest floor beneath the arch of trees above . . ." He caught her curled fist and gently pried her fingers open before stroking her anxious fingertips with his parted lips. "Tear your mind from the curse and tell me, what of you, Roshelle? What do you feel when I kiss you . . ."

What did she feel? What did she feel?

And then she named the fear she lived with, the fear she had lived with all these past long years of her life: "I feel 'tis an impossible dream too beautiful to be real . . . Do you not see, or can you not see, how I am not blessed with happiness?" Then with tears, she cried, "Vincent, this was not meant to be!"

The words landed like a blow to his head and for a long

moment he just stared at her tear-filled blue eyes, eyes that held the haunting sadness he saw so many times in his terrible vision of the white tower. He tried to deny it. He knew she lived the whole of her youthful existence burdened by her compassion, compassion that separated her from others and made her know the suffering caused by the cruelty of their world: all the wars and bloodletting, the suffering of the impoverished masses, death, especially Papillion's death, and always the shadow of the Duke of Burgundy's hand—but it did not mean, it could not mean— "Roshelle, my dear, sweet Roshelle, fate is bent by will, our will, nothing more . . ." She started to shake her head but he stopped her. "We have this moment, Roshelle. This one moment now. Kiss me, Roshelle. Kiss me now and let the world fall away as if it never was . . ."

His splayed fingers held her head still and he watched the sadness disappear beneath her closed lids as his mouth came over hers. A kiss of promises, promises of things that could never be. She felt and remembered, felt and remembered the sensual promise of his lips and, dear Lord, how she wanted to believe! Promises manifesting in an enticing taste of warmth, a gathering heat deep inside herself, like a small ball of flame, while his finger traced a slow, soothing line over her hairline, pausing to toy with the sensitive earlobe, his touch leaving a feverish trail that sparked tiny shivers and heated serums.

Her lips became soft and pliant, as if to shyly greet the sweeping pleasure of it, and without realizing it, she answered the question, rewarded as he deepened the kiss more. His arm cradled her head like a child's, which was absolutely necessary to steady the spinning sensations of his kiss. He broke the kiss, allowing her to draw quick gasps of air as she felt the melting heat of his lips on her cheek, her closed lids and her thin brows before he returned to her lips. "Your mouth is a sweeter intoxication than every promise made of heaven . . ." With an effort, he tried to slow the pace demanded of his desire, a thing that, until Roshelle, had always been as natural for him as breathing. Until Roshelle . . .

Desire softened the delicate lines of her face where he ran his fingers. Gasping for breath and her head spinning, she produced his name and uttered it like a secret wish spoken to the first shining star in the night. "Vincent . . ."

He answered by returning his lips to hers again, more insistently now. His free hand had fallen to her waist, testing its narrow curve before riding the sensuous flare of her hips up to the soft, voluptuous mound of her breast. He felt the wild gallop of her heart before testing its softness in the whole of his hand, sliding back and forth, his thumb teasing the tender peak to a tiny hard knot of fire beneath the thin cloth of her gown.

Deftly his fingers began working the laces.

A small involuntary whimper escaped her as his large warm hand slipped beneath the bodice of her gown and his warm, firm lips broke his kiss to find her neck. "Soft, so soft, like moonlight on a summer's eve . . ." Shivers rushed, gathered, exploded and she cried softly, her next breath pressing her fullness into the enticing warmth of his hand, which he expertly used to advantage. Then his lips gently kneaded hers, his warm breath sending sparks like fire through her before he was kissing her again. The kiss answering her desire, stroking it, soothing it, only to spark its flames to greater heights.

Unlike before, he was so gentle now. There was no threat or cruelty between them. Unrestrained by fear and free of thoughts of death, for one wild moment she began to believe in the miracle and gift of their passion . . .

Breaking the kiss, he lowered her backside to the cushion of bluebells, his arm still cradling her head. A beam of sunlight caught the long auburn hair spread out in ripples of silken color from her plaits. Her blue eyes opened to him, darkening with newly awakened passions.

He closed his eyes for a moment, desperate to find some measure of control. The magnitude of his struggle surprised him, for while her innocence called to all the gentleness he owned and then some, his desire felt like an unbridled, unrestrained force, dangerous for her and absolutely the last thing he would let her know. An untried virgin still, he reminded himself, drawing on all the gentleness of which he was capable and more as he kissed her neck and ear and closed lids . . .

He needn't have feared. A quivering restlessness pulsated through her, so powerful and urgent she could hardly think. The blood pounding in her head drove away the lingering remnant of any last doubt. "Vincent . . ." And her hands curled around his neck as she brought her trembling lips to his mouth and she was kissing him, wanting him . . .

Deft fingers unclasped her cloak, spreading it out behind her. A strong, firm hand gently lowered her back and the kiss was without end. The molding of his mouth on hers and the sweep and taste of his tongue felt like a savage, primitive power descending on her mind, body, soul, claiming all as his own. A sea of bright, shimmering colors exploded in her mind, shimmering into the heat sweeping through her, then more as he let her feel some of his weight and his hand came over the small arch of her backside, gathering her tightly against his length.

He wore breeches, belted at the waist, and a shirt like a sailor's garb, but the cloth was cotton and she felt the hard outline of his body beneath the press of his belt. Each spot tingled beneath the pressureless play of his warm breath, changing with the gentle caresses of his lips. His kisses sparked tiny explosions of shivers and she gasped, twisting intimately against his warmth. The small writhing body made him bury his face between the gentle swell of her breasts as he released a husky groan.

Then he molded his mouth to hers, teasing her with the skillful play of his tongue, moving in tantalizing slowness over every height and hollow. The kiss fueled the thick, hot pleasure spilling into her, drowning any last thought beneath the roar of her blood pounding in her ears.

The kiss broke, offering a brief respite as he caught her

lower lip gently in his mouth, kneading its soft resiliency while she drew shaky gasps of breath. He was saying her name, whispering, stopping only to caress her lips as his hand brushed over her side, discovering and exploring her most sensitive spots and she braced, dizzy with anticipation as his hand stopped beneath her breast. He skillfully let it build until the tension made her twist and she uttered a soft cry as if for help, answered at last with his gentle massage of the voluptuous rise.

The pounding of her heart pulsated through her. He lifted partially up and she felt his gaze on her, as warm as a caress. A changed tempo of his hand made her gasp, a gasp he caught in his mouth. His mouth rocked over hers with beguiling eroticism. He took her hands in one of his and held them back to the ground before he heightened the hot spinning sensations in her breasts by taking her mouth again. She melted helplessly beneath the driving agony of the kiss, a kiss that did not stop as his free hand drifted over her side and down her flank and up again where his palm traveled in a slow, hot circle over one breast, then the other, letting the pleasure slowly penetrate her dazed senses.

She gasped slightly as the touch changed, rotating light as a feather over one rosy pink tip until she whimpered. He answered the secret wish and gently kneaded with the full warmth of his hand as he pulled her back into his arms and he was kissing her again.

The kiss had nothing to do with gentleness and everything to do with the unleashed force of his desire, encompassing the last of her uncertainty and its resistance. Gone. The curse and death, warring nations and every last injustice was gone, banished by this kiss. All she knew was the spinning carousel of hot sensations, the start of a dream too beautiful to be true . . .

The kiss drove an avalanche of desire through him, the demand of it growing, devouring as his free hand slipped beneath her gown at her waist, sliding over the sculpted softness of her hips and thighs, then back again and over and over in ever-deepening strokes as his lips drifted to her arched neck, over her shoulders until, drawing breath hard and fast, she felt them on her breast.

The pleasure of it seized the whole of her body. She twisted maddeningly beneath him, but he hardly seemed to notice her struggle. A whimper grew in her throat as his lips played there. She was flushed and breathless, her consciousness fragmented to every sensation erupting through her body. She was lost—

A loud, shrill sound crashed into her mind. She stiffened, her consciousness collecting, riveting on the urgent cry. The clang of death bells echoed in her mind as he abruptly freed her hands and lifted himself up with a soft vicious curse. A cool shaft of air hit her like a blow, and her eyes flew open to see the screeching bird flying frantically around Vincent's head.

"Greyman!"

The falcon dove at his head and instinctively Vincent swung at him. The frantic bird lifted up and away with wild, loud screeches of alarm, and in that instant Roshelle knew. "Nay," she said in a whisper, her brows slanted in confusion as her eyes darted to the surrounding wood and she screamed.

A slight thud sounded on top of an unnatural gasp. She looked upward to see Vincent's handsome face contorted in sudden agony. For a moment she stared in confusion until a blood-red color sprang onto his shirt and she screamed again.

An arrow had hit him from the back, piercing all the way through the side of his waist. She stared at the horror of the tip pointing out from near his stomach. She screamed as, like a lion with no more than a thorn in his paw, Vincent rose and turned simultaneously with an angry shout. Just as another arrow struck his head. Roshelle heard a whistle before it plunged into the tree trunk behind her. Desperate, thinking only of her, Vincent fought the swirling black-and-gray colors exploding in his head, but they suddenly burst into red colors and he felt himself falling, falling from her as from the white tower in his dreams . . .

The man watched the lady collapse at the duke's side with a frantic call and he exclaimed out loud, "Holy demons in hell, that be a close one!" A wide grin spoke of his pleasure.

Roshelle knelt over Vincent's form, an anguished cry on her lips. She stifled the panic. Papillion had trained her to the trick and she didn't think, only acted. Blood poured through the pierced flesh, quickly soaking Vincent's shirt. She had to remove the arrow, tricky business, and one requiring a sharp knife and a fire, which she didn't have. She first ripped the hem of her gown in one neat, long strip, then carefully started wrapping it around his head wound to stop the bleeding there. He would die, she knew, of course . . .

The curse would make him die . . .

Quickly, desperately, she stifled the thought. Not now. Now she must try to save him. She needed help, a knife . . .

"Leave the bastard to die, *ma petite* filly."

Dark blue eyes lifted to the giant of a man standing less than three paces from where she knelt. He spoke French, a low, guttural French. It sounded strange on this man's tongue, and in the space of the moment she realized why. He was from Burgundy.

The knowledge registered dimly, disappearing as the nature of the threat crashed into her dazed mind. The man wiped his sleeve across his mouth, his eyes fixed on the sight of her. She pulled the parted gown tight across her front. "The bastard was taking such a long time about it," he swore, the word jerking her slightly. He looked around, confronting only the quiet of the forest. Greyman flew high overhead now, crying from the distance, but neither man nor girl noticed him. "I do not think he will be missed for a while, huh, *ma petite?* Besides, unlike him"—he motioned with his head to where Vincent lay, and laughed—"trust me to be quick about the business."

The man was smiling at her as if she were likely to be

thankful for his intentions. She encountered the horror of his smile with a tiny shudder, and in the same instant he lunged at her. She was ever quick. On her feet and turning, she left his hands grasping at thin air. His curse disappeared in the loud fear she put into her scream.

He caught her some distance away and she was still screaming, louder as his large, filthy hands came to her waist. He spun her around, laughing as he threw her to the ground, and hard. So hard, she lost her breath and darkness momentarily spun amidst tiny pinpoints of light in her head, her consciousness returning as he straddled her and she felt his weight on her stomach. The next scream died without sound, for she couldn't breathe. With the desperate energy of a drowning person, she clawed at his bearded face and belted doublet. He only laughed as he grabbed her hands and pushed them to the ground above her head. Holding them there with one hand, he pulled open her gown. The sight of her full, ample breasts caught his breath, and he nearly lost his sap right then, her ceaseless frantic cry not helping at all.

His shaking hand quickly fumbled with his belt. Urgency made his hand all aquiver, and needing both hands, he released hers. Instantly they flailed at him again with nails bared like a distraught kitten's, and he cursed her as he bounced his weight once to stop her. It knocked the wind from her heaving chest to her throat; she felt bile rising to make her sick, choking her as greedy hands suddenly were on her breasts.

A dark shadow came over the man and there was but the briefest sound of masculine disgust before he felt savage hands pulling him into the air. He screamed in a howl. The only reason Wilhelm let the man live the two seconds more that it took to pull him up before he thrust his long knife through his back was because Wilhelm did not want Roshelle to have the giant's weight on her when he died. Roshelle screamed as other gentle hands came to her person, and she covered her eyes just in time to keep the gruesome sight of his death from her mind.

She collapsed into a breathless wash of choked tears. Bryce held her tightly in his arms until she caught her breath. " 'Tis over, milady . . ." Greyman flew overhead, finally landing on her shoulder as she tried to collect her torn senses. His claws stretched through her gown but she did not care. Trembling hands quickly worked the laces of her gown, but Bryce's strong hand still held her up by the arm.

Wilhelm withdrew his knife and let the giant fall where he died. He bent over to wipe the blood on the man's clothes, and as other guards came to take the body away, he uttered, "Light a fire. He will burn."

"Aye."

"Where is he?"

Roshelle heard the fear in Wilhelm's question; he assumed Vincent was already dead. She immediately rallied her dazed defenses. "He's fallen over there. Quick. He is in dire need."

She led the men to the place in a rush and stood back as they knelt in a circle around the duke. For a long moment she closed her eyes to the horror of the reality all around her: he had died or would soon die, just like the beast who slew him and because of her curse. Her curse had killed him and she was responsible. She had not stopped him because she had not wanted to. She had so desperately wanted to believe him, with all her heart and soul she had wanted to believe him and so she had. She had killed him, just as surely as if she had strung and aimed the crossbow herself . . .

"Here, Bryce, we must pull it through. Keep him to his side and we will use one hand each and all our strength to make it fast," Wilhelm said, as anxious and nervous as a newborn colt. "Now turn your head, milady," he said, quite forgetting who she was. " 'Tis nothing a lady should see."

The comment abruptly woke her from her awful train of thoughts and she opened her eyes to the dying man at her feet. For a moment she was too horrified to speak;

then, as her wits returned in force, so did the unquestionable authority that was as natural to her as breathing. "Get your hands off that arrow!" She fell in between Bryce and Wilhelm, forcing Greyman off her shoulder with an angry screech. "Nay!" Roshelle's hands came over Wilhelm's, stopping him just in time. "You cannot do it that way! Have you no sense? *Mon Dieu,* if he does not die anyway, he surely would if you use brute force to get that arrow through—'twould splinter and leave a hundred tiny pieces inside that would inflame his flesh and kill him with a fever. Indeed, a knife, a water cask, and I need a fire started . . ."

No one moved at first, so shocked were they by a woman undertaking such a thing. "Milady, I do not think—"

'Twas as far as Wilhelm got. "A knife before he bleeds to death!" While she waited as the men suddenly dispersed to do her bidding, she found the discarded strip of her gown. She tore off another strip and soaked this in the water someone just handed her.

Sanders cleared away the brush and grass for a fire. "How big, milady?"

"Small, 'tis all I need." She gently wiped the blood from Vincent's head and face as best she could for now before expertly wrapping the dry strip around his head wound to stop the bleeding. His breathing seemed deep and slow. A skillful knot tied at the exact place of the wound added just enough pressure to stop the bleeding.

Then she carefully began removing his bloody shirt. Wilhelm helped with his knife. She tore another strip of cloth from her dress and used it to clean the blood away from his wound. Yet it bled profusely; he would have to have dozens of stitches. If he lived.

The thought momentarily put the tremble back in her hands. With an effort, and using some of Papillion's teachings to control her mind and thoughts, she banished it. She ordered a man to return to the castle to instruct Joan to prepare a sickbed. "She will know what that means."

The knight nodded and quickly left, no one questioning her authority now.

She rose and stepped away to spread the blanket one of the men had brought over the grass of bluebells. "You and you." She pointed to Bryce and Tyrone. "Lift him as gently as you know onto the blanket. He will need to be wrapped as soon as I am done. And keep him careful on that side." Everyone stood back as they did. Once done, she knelt down and asked for the knife.

Slowly, hesitantly, Wilhelm handed her a knife.

"Nay, not that one. 'Tis soiled by the beast's blood."

"Aye, but 'tis my lucky knife!"

She shot him a glance. "Lucky for killing—not, methinks, for saving."

Wilhelm supposed she was right and nodded to Bryce. That man held up a clean blade. She took it in her hand, tested its sharpness by pricking her finger. The finger went to her mouth as she began a thorough examination of the arrow from both sides.

"Is the fire going?"

"Aye, milady."

What she did next would live forever in the men's minds, for it was so simple and obvious and sensible, it seemed a wonder they had never seen it done before. Carefully wiping blood from the place, she first cut off the point and the five inches of the arrow sticking through his side, so that there would be far less to pull through. Then she used a burning stick to light the short end.

"Why are you doing that?"

"The flames will make certain no splinters get caught in his flesh, while also reducing the chance of a festering. No one knows why fire kills disease, but it does. Papillion said 'tis the reason a body makes a fever."

A small flame started traveling down the cut arrow. With the strength of one hand only, she wrapped her sure fingers around the other end and then, with a prayer to the Holy Mother and waiting, just as the flames touched his skin, she pulled it gently through his flesh.

Gasps of amazement followed as she pressed the cloth to the hole in his side, exerting pressure to stop the bleeding. " 'Tis not over yet," she said. "Let us get him to a sickbed." And with tears filling her eyes, she added, "And may God above listen to my prayers."

Chapter 11

Ten men had tried and nine had died.

The fact rang loud and long in Roshelle's mind as she knelt at the bedside of the tenth man in the candlelit room, staring at the slow and steady rise of his chest and waiting for the sudden exit of breath from his body—the exact moment of his soul's ascension.

He would die before the dawn, she knew.

They had all died . . .

She kept his fine large hand against her cheek, wondering if a rising heat would steal his life.

The rhythmic sound of Wilhelm's soft snores mixed with the fainter ones of the duke's vassal, the man Fossy in the outer chambers. They were all asleep now. Wilhelm slept in a chair, while Fossy slept on a pallet just outside the open door. Neither man believed Vincent would die, though, suspiciously, Wilhelm would not leave his side until he woke again. Nor could Wilhelm conceal his worry.

Fossy had been truly shocked by the idea. "Ye think his Grace will faint away from these wounds? Because of your curse? Huh! Whatever your curse does to ordinary men, 'twill not be able to harm him—well, aye," the old man said after Roshelle pointed out that it had already put an arrow in his back, stole his consciousness and laid him to bed. "I see him lying there wounded, but I tell ye, I have seen him suffer wounds ten times as bad and rise to dance the streets by morning light. These are but scratches to his Grace! For God's sake, Wilhelm, set the lady straight. She is trembling with fear and paler than a sheet of sail . . .'' The worry in Wilhelm's eyes remained even as he tried to reassure her. All she knew was that the curse was tested nine times now. Ten men had tried and nine men had died.

The number would be ten by morning light.

How cruel fate was to her! Since her first wedding night, she had believed her heavenly decreed chastity was a great gift—God's own grace. She had felt blessed with the gift! To keep her safe and make her strong! Because her life was for the people, and she was an instrument in their delivery to a peaceful, better time . . .

Until fate's cruel hand had given her a taste of his passion. One taste so that she could know the price paid for her precious chastity, and so she would spend the rest of her life with regret. The sweetness and pounding pleasure of his kisses laid alongside the memory of his grave and, dear Lord, how could she live with the knowledge—

The knowledge she had buried him?

And she had known what his life would cost her!

The room blurred again. She dropped his hand to cover her face. A wave of despair washed over her, so strong and fierce it manifested in a small, wounded cry. She did not want him to die! She would give her life to save him—

Not an idle trade. The moment the thought came into her mind, she knew it was true. She would give her life to save him . . .

A pale hand went to her mouth and her lips trembled slightly and she closed her eyes. Her cheeks flamed with sudden color as she thought of his kisses, the taste of his warm, firm mouth on hers, the press of his body, the skillful tease of his hands on her form and, oh, God, then, then his death felt like a cold gust of wind. A cold gust of wind extinguishing the warm light that had magically appeared in her life, leaving her alone again, stumbling through the darkness, filled with a strange longing and despair for something that never was and never could be . . .

How could this be? The force of her emotions made no

sense to her, for just a dozen fortnights ago the name Vincent de la Eresman meant nothing more to her than the name of the older brother of the hated Lord Edward of Suffolk. Now it sung in her heart, mind, her very soul like music and, dear Lord, why had she let him kiss her when she'd known, she'd known he would die for it! Because the touch of his lips tapped the very beat and pulse of her heart . . .

Tears slipped unnoticed down her cheeks. Or so she thought. Until she felt the brush of his finger on her face and heard her name. "Roshelle . . ."

He might have called her from the great beyond. She jumped visibly, staring with a great shock. His dark brows drew an expression of wonder. "These tears are for me . . ." The shock of his voice kept her immobile, her reaction rendered in widening eyes, more as he turned on his side to reach his hands under her arms. As if her hundred or so pounds were nothing more than a feather's weight, he pulled her effortlessly across his chest to rest on his other side. The side that was not inflamed with an angry red hole and over thirty stitches. The blue-gray skirts of her gown fanned over the bed. She swallowed, hardly able to believe this. A gentle hand came to her face. He dampened his fingers with her tears, then brought them to his mouth to taste, a gesture connected to the rising pace of her heart.

"Why, you thought I was dying."

This was said as if it were a truly fantastic idea, like fire-breathing dragons. "The curse, am I right?" He spoke in an unaffected whisper, apparently unbothered by pain or discomfort. Nay, what bothered him was the certain effect of carrying her so far, only to lose her again. Again. He was the one who was cursed and he swore with soft viciousness, realizing just what it would mean the next time.

He drew her small form against his length, his desire stirring despite the deep burning sensation where the arrow had pierced his side. His mind greeted her tears and what they meant, and this coupled with the sweetness of her scent—like an aphrodisiac, it was—the feel and memory of her incredible softness, the beckoning pliancy of her lips and heated love cries. All these things gathered and collected in his consciousness, quickly chasing the lethargy from his blood and galvanizing his heart with lascivious thoughts. Until her blue eyes began darkening bit by bit as her mind caught up with this unlikely greeting from a man she swore, she knew, would be dead before dawn.

She could not believe what she saw on his handsome face; she just could not believe it. Desire, plain unmasked desire, and this within hours after he had lost half his blood from an arrow that had gone all the way through and another that had scraped his head and knocked him unconscious, after he had lain still and dying for hours. She saw many things as he gazed at her, but for all of these there was no fear, no penitence, absolutely no remorse.

Slowly, in a heated whisper of words, she said, "You brush with death and yet you have the arrogance to remain undaunted! Have you no fear, no remorse, at all?"

"Remorse? Oh, aye, I know remorse . . ." His hand combed through the long waves of her hair, and for a moment he seemed distracted by it. A finger toyed with the white streak. Confusion lifted in her blue eyes as she watched this, closing them as he brushed his lips over her forehead, then let them linger at the nape of her neck. A rush of shivers passed through her, part fear and part something else she refused absolutely. She started to protest but he stopped it with a kiss. Gentle and warm, his lips tenderly kissed her, then withdrew to watch her wide-eyed outrage grow in stages, and he said, "You cannot imagine the extent of my remorse. For I can see in thine eyes what you are thinking. You are thinking such terrible things that no words will ever comfort you again. Nor will any amount of pleasure be able to overcome thy fear the next time—"

"There can be no next time!" She sat up, fury and anguish in her voice as she cried, "Fate has suspended your sentence. You have been graced with a warning. You must see this!"

Emotion blazed in his eyes and he snatched her wrist, his grip as hard and merciless as iron shackles as he pulled her back to him. "Say it, Roshelle. Why it is so different now. I would hear you say it."

Her blue eyes locked with his, filling with the pain of her declaration. "I love you, God forgive me, I love you!"

Then his mouth came to hers and he kissed her with all the force and passion brought by the emotion spoken out loud at last, kissed her as if the sheer force of his will could possibly save them from the tragedy waiting in a darkening tunnel that was their future.

Huge billowing clouds floated over the wide expanse of the east lawns of the Flanders castle, gathering above the distant mountains and threatening a late-spring rain. A moist breeze blew from the west, drying the moisture of perspiration from the Duke of Burgundy's brow as he fought his sixth and best opponent of the day. After first the news that the assassin had failed to kill the Duke of Suffolk, and now this morning, the news that he was indeed recovering well and gaining strength each passing hour, the violence of Rodez's fury would pump enough strength to fight six more opponents. He wanted the blood of a sacrifice.

For Papillion's laughter echoed in his ears.

More and more the awful driving sound of Papillion's laughter and whispers came to him, consuming him, driving him mad. He could not seem to get rid of it. It was louder at times, then fading, and he'd abruptly realize it had almost completely vanished, only to have it return louder than before as soon as his mind searched for it.

'Twas driving him mad!

Desperately Rodez searched for a distraction. The breeze lifted the heavy crimson robes of the papal entourage as they watched, smiling and applauding, and seeing them from the corner of his vision as he parried, leaped back and struck made him grimace in disgust. The malleable fools! They had arrived to investigate the bishop's allegations of his Feast of Fools celebration, only to quickly agree 'twas the bishop's own demons that had made him see things no one else had. Standing near the corpulent pigs—how well they fed off the common trough!—was a group of textile merchants from Flanders, and three of the lesser barons with their ladies, all invited to the castle for Saint Brigitte's feast so that Terese might have new prey for her games.

She needed a distraction as well. Not only had Suffolk slipped from his grasp again, but she had been pelted by the peasant masses recently as she sojourned from the protection of the castle. Apparently rumors rumbled through the peasantry that she practiced witchcraft, bestiality, human sacrifice, that her child was a demon sprung from Satan's loins, the new Antichrist.

She was afraid the peasants would storm the castle and catch her. She was beginning to be plagued with nightmares, drinking more and more. He was losing his grasp on her mind—

The echo of Papillion's laughter sounded louder, then louder still. "Stop it! Stop it!" He put sudden speed and strength into his strikes as his right hand pressed hard against his ear to stop the maddening echo of Papillion's amusement. "I'll kill you. I'll kill you . . ."

No one heard the whispered vow. He meant the words. He kept reaching the point where the only way he could stop the echo in his mind was with the blood of a sacrifice. Like now . . .

The knight was better than most. As he spun around, raising his sword to counterstrike, Rodez passed a barely perceptible glance and a nod to a nearby servant.

The duke's dark eyes blazed with sudden emotion as he lunged, swung and struck the unyielding metal from the surprised knight's hand. The man's gaze fell to the sword lying on the grass. The duke's servant rushed to retrieve it. The audience burst into applause. Smiling at Rodez's fine show of skill, the knight started to bow.

"The knight hath tried to kill you, my Grace! Look!" The servant raised the man's sword for the audience's gaze. "Behold the bared point."

Murmured disbelief rushed through the crowd as all focused on the raised sword. A young maid cried out, " 'Tis a trick! I saw thy servant take—"

The next words caught in her throat, choking her as Rodez turned his gaze back to the knight. He removed his guarded point. Magically, the knight's eyes turned into the oh-so-familiar blue eyes arched by dark wings, the blond hair turned white and Rodez beheld the man haunting his every waking hour.

"Plead your remorse before you die!"

Stunned wits turned to horrified senses, and the knight tore off his steel bonnet before dropping to his knees. "By all that's holy, my Grace! I did not bare the point—"

It was as far as his denial got. Rodez lunged, his bared sword viciously piercing the flesh. Bright red blood spilled over his hand, his senses filled with death. For a moment the women's screams drowned out the quiet laughter of his tormentor and then, mercifully, all sound disappeared in the sudden rush of activity. Women were taken away, while knights, bishops, men and lords stared numbly at the slain body. Someone motioned to a servant to call for a death cart as the duke at last withdrew his sword. With a triumphant smile, he turned away into the quiet . . .

Within the hour the trumpets sounded from the battlements as four war-hardened knights, dressed in rags but outfitted for war with bonnets, chest plates and shields, rode up to the castle wall at a gallop. They stopped at the open gates, laughing, drunk and boisterous with obscene gestures and threatening noises. A dozen Burgundian knights clamored to the battlements and peered down at the novelty of such foolhardy wits. "God's teeth!" The captain could not believe his eyes as he looked down.

"Who would dare? The bloody fools—" He called the order, not even wanting to bother the duke before getting rid of the mad ruffians at the castle wall. "Heat up the oil bins!"

"Aye!"

"You black-hearted lecher!" a tall blond giant of a man called up from a spinning spirited horse, his saddle decorated with the trophies of dozens of plaits of human hair. "Aye, you! Fetch this grand Duke of Burgundy. Tell him to come wait on a messenger of Arnaut de Cervole! The grand Archpriest of France!"

Whispered amazement rippled through the Burgundian knights upon hearing this wild man. The name was famous throughout France. The Archpriest Arnaut de Cervole was said to have once been a noble of Perigord and titled to a clerical benefice there, but having once lost his land and his way, he now commanded an army of brigands numbering two thousand. Normally these warring wretches kept to the coastal area between Paris and the sea, taking castles and selling them back to their owners for lucrative profits, ransacking villages, raping, burning fields when the peasants could not pay and looting the monasteries.

A knight called down, "Thy numbers must have swelled for you to brave an appearance here at Burgundy!"

"Aye, we've enough to take this grand castle before my eyes!" The man chuckled, his Scottish lilt thick and amazingly undaunted. "Why, we've all been pardoned by the Pope, have ye not heard? The Pope himself wined and dined the grand Archpriest, pardoned all his sins and sent us away with pockets of gold!"

So that explained their boldness . . .

The Pope himself turned belly-up to the Archpriest, demon of all men in France. The captain motioned to an anxious knight, but one of the duke's favorites. The man ran off to present this news to the duke. Pages led him up the wide staircases twice, down through the halls and into one of the outer chambers of the solar. Rapid French and a knock announced his presence, and the doors opened.

The duke sat upon a red velvet cushion before the largest looking glass in France. An ornate gilt frame surrounded the glass, reflecting the arched throat of the duke and the intensity of the barber's concentration as he scraped the long smooth line of the royal throat. Though the heavy curtains were drawn back from the tall, narrow windows and afternoon sunlight poured into the room, candles lined the tabletop before the glass, their flickering light magnified and reflected back in the mirror.

Like a king upon his throne, he was surrounded by his most cherished possessions in these solar rooms. Treasures from around the world filled the lush space around him: two gold clocks, coins, enamels, new and ancient musical instruments displayed on one wall, gold vessels and spoons, the most expensive of his hundreds of illuminated books and all kinds of curiosities in the glass case against the far wall: one of Charlemagne's teeth, drops of the Virgin's milk—to be used soon in a sacrifice— porcupine quills, a giant's bones, among many other oddities.

Yet the paintings and artwork told the story of the black rose. Like the tapestry behind him: the centaur's raping of a virgin in the darkness of the forest. Or above the hearth where a fire raged: a witch's sabbath depicting the demons and the damned sacrificing the virgin—witchcraft, he believed, was the primitive expression of the black rose.

"My Grace . . ." The knight stopped, forgot what he was saying as he caught his own reflection. He had never seen himself in a mirror before! The novelty of the experience stole his breath until he saw the duke staring back at him through the glass, the flickering candlelight reflected in his dark gaze, so that his eyes looked as if they were on fire.

Scared without reason, the knight came to the point.

The duke wore black silk dressing robes, and his long unbound hair disappeared into the silken folds. No expression first registered on the dispassionate face as the barber curved the sharp edge of his knife over the unnaturally long arch of his master's neck. The guard nervously shifted his feet, afraid the duke had not heard the alarming news.

"Indeed," he finally said as the knife came away from his skin, and the barber drew an easy breath. The voice was quiet in his mind; he was enjoying his moment's peace. "Why, how strange. I thought even those mercenaries knew Burgundy at least has always been capable of defending itself."

The knife returned to the curve of his chin, so he spoke in a low pitch, like a hiss. "Well, let's send this would-be warrior a present. Dismember the ruffians but keep them alive, then send the pieces of flesh back with my good wishes."

Pleased by the order, the knight turned to leave when suddenly Rodez's hand snaked around the barber's hand, jerking the blade off his throat. "Wait!"

The knight stopped, turned and waited.

The Duke of Suffolk, the Duke of Fools . . .

He was probably the only other noble in all of France who would bravely stand against this army before ever paying their paltry ransom, despite the fact that he housed only four hundred knights at best at Reales. At best. A bloodbath, 'twould be a bloodbath. He would send assassins—his six best knights—to take advantage of the battle. If the duke survived the war—not likely!—but if he did, his six knights could meet him on his return to Reales. He would be battle-weary and no doubt wounded as well. Rodez might double the gold prize, too, if the mercenaries returned with his head.

"Aye . . ."

And just to make sure dear Roshelle did not interfere this time, or Papillion through her, he would send her a diversion, a small distraction. He had promised to come for Joan someday anyway. The time seemed suddenly past due . . .

The knight nervously shifted his feet again. "My Grace?"

The duke turned from the mirror to the knight, and the knight drew a sharp breath of fear as he saw, without the reflection from the mirror, fire blazing in the duke's eyes. "Bring them to me. I believe I have a better idea."

"You are afraid."

Roshelle made no response at first to the familiar voice. She was standing at the window overlooking the courtyard, watching as Vincent's personal guard returned from a hunt. Over a dozen squires, pages and grooms rushed behind the cloud of dust brought by the ten mounted knights, all laughing, slapping each other on the back with their congratulations and success. The kitchen servants ran out to greet the men, Cisely among them. Wilhelm leaped from his horse and swung her into the air, Cisely laughing but holding her nose to stop her sneezes. There would be a happy feast on the morrow. Bags full of birds, hares, foxes and squirrels weighed down each man's back. Strung across a pole carried by Richard's and young Owens's back were two slain deer.

A buck and a doe . . .

Tears filled her eyes and blurred her vision.

"Aye, Joan."

"For me?"

Roshelle leaned against Joan's tall, strong frame. Loving arms came around her slender figure. Her blue eyes closed, as if savoring the moment.

Tears spilled down her pale cheeks.

She would not lie. "Aye."

For you, Joan, and for me.

Vincent had banished her from his chambers. At first his rejection had confused her and she had stood at his door, pounding, demanding he let her in and thinking it a jest, finally begging him to open the doors. Yet he had not. Wilhelm finally forced her away, without explanation.

Then she knew.

He had recovered and was gathering his strength, and the banishment was the means of saying they could pretend no more. This past wondrous month she had lived in a dream spun by this short time together, a respite from the future that threatened them, and a future she abandoned to fate. "Draw your life moment by moment, Roshelle," Papillion had once said. "Leave the future to fate." So she had drawn the one month moment by sweet moment, and he had let her play that game, so that for one month she greedily, selfishly basked in the blessing of his love.

One month to remember for the rest of her life.

Like a dream it was. The dream that could never be. The first eight days and nights she had hovered over his bed as he slept in the midst of a bouncing fever: high, then low, then high again, but always there. Yet he ate every soup and potion she made him, and woke from restless sleep with a smile, a light in his eyes that caught her breath and spurred her heart. Aye, the desire was always there, but held hostage by his convalescence.

"I want to feel your softness as I sleep, Roshelle," he'd say as he drew her to the bed, and against his warmth. "I want to taste your breath on my lips and drink in your sweet scent, I want to fall asleep with your breast in my palm, your pulse against mine . . . Roshelle, Roshelle, I love you . . ." And alone in his darkened chambers, they lay together. At times they whispered secrets through the night, secrets made of laughter and tears and no consequence at all, words that defied the future. "What else would I love in Suffolk, milord?"

"What else, what else? You would love Gregory Castle. Three stories high and made of granite and stone, shaped in a perfect square with bright banners flying in the breeze from every battlement, enough room in the courtyard for a mounted regiment and enough room in its two grand halls for a gypsy circus."

Then she would laugh . . .

"And you would love the endless stretch of emerald-green hills around it, the towering trees of the forest land,

the cool, deep lakes nearby and the arch of bright blue
sky overhead.''

"What else?"

"Greedy, are we? Well, I think you would like most of
all the village peasant folk.''

"Why is that?"

"They are all fat."

She laughed. "As fat as a goose before Michaelmas?"

"At least . . . And I would order Mason to make you
so many rich and irresponsible treats that you, too, would
soon be fat.''

"And would you still love me?"

Suddenly his eyes changed, the light there intense.
"Forever, Roshelle, forever . . .''

Then it would sweep upon them, the emotional pull of
their hearts, a thing so powerful it was only expressed with
the tight alignment of their bodies, the touch of his lips
and the caress of his hands, and she would be crying for
their lost future . . .

Vincent, I love you, I love you . . .

They never spoke of it, of what would happen. How
could they? He was disbelieving but always aware of her
waiting fear, wanting, thinking he could end it, and all
the while she only knew she would die with him . . .

Vincent, do not do this to me . . .

She had been clipping his stitches. She had just risen
and wore only a pale pink robe trimmed in lovely rose-
and-violet threads, her mother's long-ago robe. The rope
of her hair slipped over her arm and she realized the gown
had parted, for she felt its weight brush against her breast.
Just as she abruptly heard the sudden stillness in the room.
She looked up to see his eyes, and the force and magnitude
of the desire there made her drop the shears with stark,
naked fear. She shook her head, backing away. Yet he was
so strong, already so terribly strong, and he caught her
wrist. "No, Vincent . . .'' She tried to pry his hand from
her. "No, please. You know . . . you know. Please, we
must talk . . .''

''Words, love, are superficial now.''

Someday I will come for her . . .

'The day you leave Reales, for instance, that would be a day. Of course, the day she leaves Reales, that would certainly be another day. Then, too, any day I am bored might be the day . . .'

''No rain . . .'' Joan's words brought her back to the present, and she smiled. When it rained and Joan was afraid, she let Joan sleep in her bed like a young child, their fingers tightly entwined.

''No there is no rain now . . .''

''Love is happy . . .''

Roshelle shook her head. ''No, Joan . . . not always . . .''

Confused, Joan ventured, ''Bryce is happy . . .''

The darkness surrounded her, waiting like the clouds on the horizon. She felt so frightened! She had to save him, somehow—

''I am happy . . .''

''I am so glad for you, Joan . . .''

''Papillion loves Bryce, too . . .''

Papillion, where are you? I have never needed you more and yet I have never felt farther from you. Your love is gone, as if you are too far away to touch me . . .

''Papillion loves Bryce with me . . .''

''Aye, Papillion loved all good and just men . . .''

''He loves Bryce most. Bryce is blessed. Bryce has the ring.''

Mon Dieu, what could she do? She had to stop him and the only way she knew how was to disappear, to flee—the one thing she could not do—

The words finally penetrated Roshelle's mind.

The hairs slowly lifted on the nape of her neck. ''Joan.'' She said the name in a frightened whisper. ''What did you say?''

''I am happy!''

''Aye, but what about Papillion's ring?''

''Bryce's ring . . .''

Her blue eyes searched Joan's lovely face. "Where, Joan? Where is Bryce now?"

"A-sleeping!" She smiled, pleased without knowing why, that Bryce always fell asleep after loving her. "I made him go a-sleeping!"

Confused, Joan watched as Roshelle spun around and ran from the room, disappearing in a flurry of pretty green and blue of her gown. She flew down the sunlit hall to the stairs and down the spiraling case in a swirl of color, bursting into the entrance hall alongside the lesser hall and out the doors into the bright sunlight.

The courtyard still bustled with activity. Servants rushed to the kitchens with the bloodied bags from the hunt while grooms pulled off saddles from the spent horses. Pages led their masters' horses to the trough, where four hands labored to bring up more water from the well. The piggery man talked with Mason, Vincent's chef, who tossed fresh bits of meat into the trough amidst the grunting, excited creatures. A group of Suffolk knights gathered around the free well, splashing water over their hot faces and washing, while another group headed toward the newly erected guardhouse, where they slept.

She ran past these, barely noticing Cisely and Wilhelm with the group. Liana, the dairymaid, was letting Derrick carry her buckets for her, and with a heated gasp, he swung the poles to avoid Roshelle's flight. Milk slopped out, splashing to the ground. "Milady!"

"Pardon, pardon, pardon!"

Roshelle did not stop. She raced into the guardhouse, a long, two-story-high structure made of wood and stone. Vincent had built it to house his personal guard and the knighted officers of his regiment. She burst inside, stopping short at the sea of faces as all gazes turned to see her there.

Vincent leaned back to conceal himself from her view.

She looked stunningly beautiful. The crinkled rich length of her hair, the front ends plaited and pulled back, dropped down a creamy, pale-green-and-blue pleated

gown. The short loose sleeves of a thin white cotton chemise showed beneath the rich fabric of the unbelted and
flowing length of it. Yet it was not the comely gown that
drew a man's gaze but the girl in it, the anxiety and pain
that haunted her lovely face and changed her anxious blue
eyes as they flew about the familiar faces.

"Curse you, Vince!" Wilhelm had sworn at him. "Forget Henry's blessing and God's. To look at her is to see
her fear, and a dark and terrible fear it is. To make her
wait for happiness be cruel."

He saw the truth of Wilhelm's words in the faint half-
moon of circles underlining the fear in her eyes. He had
joined the hunting party without her knowing it, needing
the fresh air and sport to regain a measure of his strength.
He had carefully kept his health and recovery a secret,
meaning to keep her from fear until he received Henry's
blessing from England, but of course she knew. She had
probably known the day he barred her from his room.

The poetry of her eyes!

He held his breath, then suddenly drew sharp. Dear
Lord, how badly he wanted her! With each passing day
his strength returned, his desire seemed to grow, magnify,
like some great caged monster waiting to spring. His
dreams were spun with the image of her blue eyes filling,
not with poetry but with passion, darkening like the sea
at twilight as he laid his lips to hers and slowly filled her.

There was no fear in this dream.

"Help me," she said. "I seek the goodly knight
Bryce."

More than one man rushed toward her to help.

Wilhelm came in behind her, his gaze alone drawing
the men to a sudden stop. "Milady!" he said all a-concern.
"What brings this distress?"

"Wilhelm—I must see Bryce."

"Are ye going to press your objections—"

"Nay, not that. Please, just bring me to where he
sleeps."

Wilhelm led her down the hall and up the stairs. Cisely

followed. Wilhelm took the two ladies past empty bunks to the very back, where there were a few small separate chambers that gave a man some privacy. The doors to the chambers led to a long hall. Wilhelm brought them to the last door. He lifted the latch and swung it open.

A small window overlooked the courtyard. A cross hung on the wall, like in a monastery; there was a bunk and bedclothes, and that was all.

The soft sounds of Bryce's slumber filled the small space. Wilhelm watched as Roshelle reached a trembling hand to the covers and, as if afraid of a spurt of blood or a snake or some other terror, held her breath and with a sudden jerk, brought the covers away from his muscled arms.

To behold a finger that held a gold ring.

The miracle of it made Roshelle dizzy.

"Cisely?"

"Aye, I see it . . ."

How can it be? An English guard of Suffolk? Nay, she knew instantly, 'twas not on an English guard of Suffolk, but rather on the hand of the man who loved Joan. Papillion, help me, she had asked. And of course he had. Bryce belonged to Joan, for her protection. He would keep her safe. Roshelle could save Vincent by separating from him, forevermore; she would leave him . . .

So that he might live.

To Wilhelm and Cisely, Roshelle ordered, "Please leave us now."

Confused, thinking Cisely would tell him, Wilhelm ushered her out the door. It shut. Bryce woke to discover Roshelle kneeling at his bedside, reaching a trembling hand to his. More beautiful than an angel, he thought and was glad, for otherwise he would have thought he'd died in his sleep. She reached for his hand and held it up to the light of scrutiny, tear-filled eyes marveling at the beautiful gold ring, its intricate latticework. The stream of afternoon sunlight poured through the window and hit the ring, blinding her for a moment with its miracle. In an awed whisper, she asked, though of course she knew: "Where did you get this ring?"

"Have I missed something?" he asked, dazed with his sleep and confused. "Milady, what brings you here . . . to me?"

"Please, where did you get this ring?"

Bryce looked down at his finger. "This? Everyone notices this." He smiled, ignorant of its significance. "Why, his Majesty even admired it once. This be my lucky ring, for a warring!"

"For a warring?"

To help you keep Joan safe.

"Aye. An old man gave it to me. Just like that! Took it off his finger and handed it to me. 'Twas on my first campaign here in France, some long years ago now. On the road to Go, it was. This old man begged water from my cask and once he quenched his thirst, he . . . well, he stared into my eyes and for a moment I felt—"

"Pierced to the heart?"

"Aye," he said, surprised the girl knew what he meant. " 'Twas like his gaze cut through skin and flesh to . . . peer upon me soul." He shook his head, not at all given to such fanciful notions, and swung his feet off the bed. "Well, anyway, he hands me this ring and says to wear it always, that 'twill bring me luck in battle. I thought it so odd, him being a Frenchman and all, but then I thought mayhap he weren't French. Aye, he spoke with an accent, but then no, I realized 'twas more like an Italian accent, or mayhap Arabic. There was a twinge of merry old England in there, too, and 'twas queer, I heard that tongue afore. I do not know where. Well," Bryce said with the same surprise as on that long-ago day, "I assumed the old man wanted money for it, and while I know full well that skill and practice beat omens and charms any time, I figured it could not hurt. 'Twas so . . . so strangely beautiful! Never seen latticework like this. And by the saints, I be damned if it does not make me feel lucky the moment I put it on. So I handed over a gold piece to him, but here's the odd part: the old man just shook his head, said a fare-thee-well and continued on his way.'' Then he asked, "Milady! These tears? What makes you cry?''

She shook her head, unable to speak.

"Well, then, what does it mean to you?''

What did it mean to her?

She stared up at his kind face. "It means that you were chosen to help me keep Joan safe, forevermore. You must swear to her safety.''

For a knight to extend his protection to a woman was as good as marrying her, and still Bryce did not hesitate. While he did not understand what his ring had to do with Roshelle, or with sweet Joan, for that matter, as a knight of the Suffolk guard, he could do nothing less. As a man who had lost his heart, he could do nothing less. "Aye, milady." He nodded. "The maid Joan hath my protection unto death.''

Roshelle kissed his ring, tears spilling on his hand. "My dear and noble man, I must share with you my burden, one I have carried so very long . . .''

Roshelle's mistake was in possibly imagining a man's protection was as good as hers. A woman protects her loved ones by caring for them and keeping them from harm's way, and for many years Roshelle had vigilantly seen to it. A man follows a different path completely.

"So do you see now?''

"Aye." Bryce saw any number of things, and one of them was that he would leave this very afternoon for Burgundy. "Milady, I will keep Joan safe. This I swear oath to.''

Wilhelm had the task of trying to dissuade Bryce.

Vincent gave his task to Owens and Richard, and knowing Roshelle so well, he explained exactly what she would do. "First you will see her enter the chapel, where she will pray until just before the sun sets. She will return to her rooms to prepare for it. The next hour or so you will follow her about the castle as she dispenses with certain cherished possessions. No doubt she will visit the stables to give her mare an extra bucket or two of grain and fresh water. Then she will retire to her rooms to wait for the night, wait for the hour when all is quiet and everyone sleeps.''

"What then?" Owens, Wilhelm's young squire, asked.

"Just bring me word, that is all. And tell me if she does anything different.''

The two young men ran off.

Much later that evening, Richard burst into the great hall, where the knights had gathered after supper. Sharp blue eyes scanned the hall for his Grace's face, but at last he was not there. "Sir, where is my Grace?"

Wilhelm looked up from the table. "He went to the river for one of his swims.''

'' 'Tis almost dark now!''

"Ah, darkness is pending only. He should be returning. Look for him on the village road.''

For no reason he knew, the great red giant turned toward the stained-glass windows of the hall where he beheld the image of a frail Christ upon the cross. The loud, boisterous talk of the men faded in his mind as he stared, measuring the pending darkness. He felt a tremor of apprehension. The last faint light of day disappeared and the darkness, he saw, was upon them.

Perhaps if he had been able to dissuade Bryce . . .

He thought of the ring, the story Cisely had told him. What if it did protect Bryce and gave him an advantage? What if he did slay the beast of Burgundy?

So he had sent six good knights with Bryce . . .

After a long swim, Vincent had stood on the riverbank watching as twilight painted the world in colors of rose and violet. Shadows lengthened, stretched by the sinking sun, then disappeared altogether in the night. The air was thick and humid and hot. Not a breeze stirred, yet the moisture from his skin dried almost immediately, and as he stood on the river's edge, listening to the race of water, clouds spread quickly across the velvet sky, swallowing the faint shine of emerging stars.

It would be raining tonight . . .

Young Richard spotted his Grace in the distance, emerging from the place where the river road merged with the village. He raced up to him, breathless and flushed. "Milord!"

Vincent swung the cloth over his shoulders before pulling a plain cotton tunic over his bare chest and lifting his hair out from underneath. The race of his squire's footsteps drew his gaze. "Richard—"

"Milord!" The young man stopped in front of Vincent and tried to catch his breath. " 'Twas as you said. Everything, save for one thing."

"Yes?"

"The lady prayed in the rose garden outside the gates." He searched his lord's gaze, dark and impenetrable. " 'Twas a sad thing, too, somehow. Her beauty against the newly blossomed roses, all white and pink and red. Owens had sworn he was going to bawl if he watched any longer."

"And now?"

"She has returned to her rooms."

"Very well, then. Race back and give word that no one is to be in the stables tonight."

"No one but the grooms?"

"Mind my words, boy. No one. And go to that rose garden . . ."

The hour neared midnight and all was quiet. She came quietly out to the steps of the keep. The air felt thick and heavy with the promise of rain. Joan would not be afraid with Bryce; he would keep her safe now. No star or moon lit the night sky; the darkness was complete. Her blue eyes gazed up to her room, where the dim, flickering candles came from within. She closed her eyes, and thought she heard the soft sound of Cisely's tears.

"You cannot come," she had said over and over. "No,

Cisely! I will hear no more protests. Your life is with him now, with Wilhelm. Vincent has promised him some land, so at least he will be a lesser baron, even if it is in England. And you have my blessing, and Charles's . . ." For a long while they had clung together, desperately holding on to their last moments. "I love you, I love you and someday, I promise to return to you!"

She drew a deep breath before stepping swiftly, quietly, down the stone stairway of the castle keep. She did not think. Not now. She couldn't. To think, imagine, feel even a moment of the pain of leaving him would drop her to her knees, and the only thing worse was the idea, the certainty of his death. She had the long rest of her life to remember, and by God's grace, so would he.

For you, my love, for you . . .

As if to spur her speed, she leaned against the cold stone wall and closed her eyes, conjuring a picture of his death. She panicked, leaped up and ran, clutching the sack to her chest as if to slow the race of her heart.

For you, my love, for you . . .

She kept to the shadows of the outer buildings, the kitchens and ovens and armory, and finally came to the stables. She stopped outside the large wood doors, listening for the sounds of the grooms' slumber. It was so quiet. A familiar horse caught her scent and neighed, but otherwise it was so quiet.

She pulled open a door enough to slip inside. Four torches lit the enormous dark space. She stood in the open space of the grooming room. Fresh straw covered the floor, filling the air with its familiar rich scent. Built against the corner was a hill made of bundles of hay. A rope hung from the rafters above, still and unmoving in the quiet night as the children slept. Vincent himself had put it there, then showed the waiting children the fun of dropping from the loft into the pile of fresh-mown hay. How the children had loved this small piece of fun!

"The sound of heaven is the laughter of children," Papillion had once said.

Her blue eyes adjusted to the darkness. Bare feet stepped quietly over the straw-covered floor, heading toward Etoile's stall. But where were the grooms? The stable hands who slept here? Why, how strange—

"Roshelle."

The sack dropped to the floor.

Distant thunder rumbled from far away as he emerged from the shadows and stood an arm's length away from her. An arm's length. The distance stopped her heart and stole her breath, immobilizing her for one second too long, and in the suspension of the moment she took in the changed sight of him with a gasp: a raw, animal-like power emanated from his towering muscled frame. His face was hidden in shadows and she could not see his eyes. He wore only breeches, these belted just above the narrowing of his waist by a thick black belt, a dagger hanging on his hip. She watched the breath rise in his massive chest, the savage strength of each and every well-carved muscle like a pronouncement of her helplessness. Like his scars. The angry red blaze where a would-be assassin's arrow had pierced his flesh and yet had failed to kill him spelled her doom. She had no chance; he'd give her no chance.

Lightning lit the sky, flashing in the window high above and, for a flash, illuminating his eyes. A scream caught in her throat. All tenderness and love banished in the determined depth of those eyes; they were hard and hot with his passion. All she knew was that she would die with him; that she could not live unless she knew that somewhere in the world the sun shone on his face; somewhere in the world his gaze beheld a better world he had shaped. "No . . . oh, no." She started to back away. "Vincent! Do not do this to me—"

"I was to wait until Henry blessed our marriage."

The words riveted her to the spot. "Marriage!" The pain of it brought her blue eyes down and she held herself tight. "Marriage. A faraway dream, one we cannot have in this lifetime. It cannot be! Vincent, Vincent, my fear is the certainty of your death! Imagine if it were me, if I were to die—''

"Hush!" His eyes blazed with sudden fierce emotion. "Words are worthless, I did warn you."

She spun and bolted and then screamed. Screamed as two quick strides brought the iron strength of his arms around her. With a violent wrench, she tried to pull free, but he lifted her off the ground, holding her flailing arms tight against his length as if she were but made of cloth. Terror seized her, and as her legs pounded furiously against his shins with wild desperation, she tried to wrench free, but never had she felt his strength or the merciless-ness of his power—

"Vincent, I beg you—"

He ignored her cries as effortlessly as he ignored her struggle, fierce though it was. For he knew no words would ease the fear of what he would do, what he had to do.

Inviolate power and strength radiated from him, from his desire; she felt the waiting threat of his enormous shaft on her side. She did not know she was crying until the sound abruptly stopped. Lightning cracked in the sky again, flashing light in the upper windows and illuminat-ing the knife now at her throat. She went very still. Fear choked her as his other arm held her backside against his length, the heat of him penetrating through the heavy cloth of her cloak. The blade sliced through the clasp of her cloak. The thick cloth fell from her shoulders. She cried out as the cold, hard steel touched her skin, then ripped effortlessly through the cloth of the traveling tunic and the cotton undergarment beneath. Her small hands desper-ately struggled to keep the cloth to her skin, but another twist of the blade and a rip, and she felt a brush of warm night air against her naked skin.

He tossed the dagger into the darkness.

Thunder rumbled in the faraway distance.

She twisted with a long pained cry as his fingers snaked around her wrist, pulling her arm against her back as he lifted her small weight into his arms and carried her to the soft bed of hay. The long rope of her plait coiled against the straw as he laid her to the ground and stood over her. Like a hunter over a kill. The thrilling rage of his desire kept him blind to her terror and all he knew was he'd have her by force before he'd know her with love.

She sprang up.

Instantly she felt his bare foot against her stomach, knocking her back and stealing her breath. He took a pace back and deftly snapped the buckle from his belt and stepped out of his breeches. Lightning cracked once more against the sky. Her heart pounded and she gulped huge gasps of air, terrified by the enormity of the threat of his magnificently hard staff.

She only knew the terror of it. The image of a grave brought a pained cry as with a desperate surge of strength she flung herself to the side to escape his grasp, but it was too late. It had always been too late. He pulled her effort-lessly beneath his body. Her clenched hands pounded against his rock-hard chest. He caught her hands, pinning them tight to the cushioned, pungent ground and stilled her struggle as he let her feel his threatening weight. Even as she squirmed and struggled, she felt his hot skin against her nipples, the brush of crisp hair and the hard staff of him against her thigh.

A hot slap of fire shot through her.

It terrified her. She threw her head back, as if in pain. Tears filled her eyes. It would not end! By the saints, it would not end until he died, and he would die. He would. This one moment to trade for his death!

"Vincent, I, I be-g-g—"

His mouth stopped her protest. As a last desperate pro-test in the futile hope to make him see, she yielded him no inch. She kept her mouth closed hard and her teeth clenched. He forced her lips apart, his demanding tongue sweeping into the sweet recess of her resisting mouth until she couldn't breathe or think or know anything but the plundering domination of his kiss.

His tongue swept through every height and hollow and

whether it lasted a minute or an hour, she would never know. She didn't know anything but the mounting horror of being forced closer and closer to a waiting gallows. His lips lifted from her swollen ones but briefly, long enough to let her draw a gasping breath that sent a rush of hot chills down her spine and exploding in her loins. She twisted her head to escape his mouth, but only to feel his lips sliding down the arch of her neck and back to her mouth.

She didn't know how hard she struggled to free her hands from his grasp or that he held both with one hand. She knew only the hot and tantalizing pressure of the kiss, that she was sinking into a swirling darkness of pure sensation. A place where death lay waiting.

The moment he released her mouth she emerged with a pained cry of his name. "Vincent! Vincent! No—" Like a wild animal, she fought to escape, but his hard-muscled legs stilled her struggle as his hand wrapped cruelly around her plait, drawing her neck up at an arch. His lips moved downward to her breast.

"Fight me all you want, Roshelle . . ."

Her pained cry stopped in her throat as his mouth covered one rosy pink tip, his tongue circling, then sucked, then circled more until it grew large and taut, forcing the hot, penetrating pleasure into her resistant flesh and mind. Hot chills seized her, rush after rush, her breathing changing from hard and fast to small, quick gasps that barely managed to sound the urgent "No."

The sound of the driving rain against the stable roof drowned out the roar of blood pounding in her ears as his strong-muscled leg parted her thighs and she felt his seeking fingers find the moist avenue of her womanhood. She was shaking her head in terror, but he stroked her. With a cry, she arched her back instinctively, opening herself wider. Relentlessly he stroked her tender flesh, until he felt the gentle swell and sweet wetness of her body welcoming him when she would not.

"Now, Roshelle."

"No . . . no . . ." She tossed her head back and forth, her last denial as he lifted himself partially up, his knees forcing hers helplessly farther apart. And farther. She felt the hard, hot tip of him push against her opening and she screamed. Lightning ripped through the sky and, ending the virgin's curse forevermore, he thrust himself into her.

A hot, searing pain ripped her in two.

He felt the virgin's tear as a hot, tight warmth enveloped him in a pleasure so intense it was painful. For a mercilessly long moment he stopped as the intensity of it rocked through him, and for the same long moment she thought she was dying instead. Then the pain began to recede, resonating into tight, hot contractions deep inside. She heard the husky sound of her name from far away as he slid all the way out before moving in again, forcing her tightness open to accommodate his enormity, again and again, over and over with agonizing slowness, until she felt the hot length of him stab her womb and touch her soul.

"Love, love, sweet mercy, I have died . . ." He desperately sought some measure of control, harder as he kissed her, and she closed her eyes; the warm communion of his mouth with the joining felt like a penetrating sweep of her heart. He broke it only to stare into her lovely eyes, struck to his heart by the sadness there. He fought to offer reassurance. " 'Tis over now, Roshelle, 'tis over."

"Aye, 'tis over . . ."

For fate would make her pay the cruelest of prices for this joining. He knew this, too; she could see it in his eyes. Desperately he tried to deny it as he lifted and thrust, lifting partially up from her to watch the miracle of flesh darken her blue eyes. Red-hot sensation resonated through her and she was calling his name, crying, feeling him everywhere inside and out; and his own pleasure, the mercilessly tight sheath, grew more, and more, carrying him to a place he had never been before—

Suddenly darkness swirled all around, swirled and

swirled, bursting into bright, hot colors, then red. Bright red blood and darkness again. A white rose and a red rose entwined, bursting into flames. A scream in the night. Ecstasy rocking their souls . . .

Chapter 12

Helpmesavemehelpmesavemehelpme . . .
Roshelle was gone, Bryce was gone.

Dying torches lit the dark hall. Joan stepped quiet as a mouse to the lord's chambers. She knew never to wake people. She pressed the lever. The heavy wood door creaked as she gently pushed it open, but the pounding rain drowned out the sound. The lord's servant slept soundly on his pallet, his sleep undisturbed as she stepped through the outer room of the lord's chambers. She paused outside, listening, but she heard only the relentless pounding of the rain.

Savemehelpmesavemehelpme . . .

She pushed open the door and peered inside. Red embers from a dying fire cast the faintest light into the spacious chambers. No one slept in the bed. Roshelle was not there; she was not in her own rooms. Roshelle was gone, Bryce was gone, Roshelle was gone.

Savemehelpmesavemehelpme . . .

"Who goes there?"

The woman clutched the gold coin tightly in her hand, pulling the folds of the cloak about her person as she stepped back from the gates. She tried to look up to the castle wall where the guard called down from, but the driving rain hit her face. So cold and dark. " 'Tis Malissa from Reales! The lady of the castle sent me for her servant Joan.''

"Joan of Orleans? Called out in the middle of the night in this bloody weather?"

She shouted up, " 'Tis a matter of life and death!"

The captain knew, of course, that Lady Roshelle tended the villagers' ills with medicine and potions. After all the trouble she had given him and the duke, the lady turned out to be an angel of mercy; she had given him a miraculous potion that cured him of his homesickness and its melancholia. Yet to call anyone out in this rain, even to save a life—"

"Hurry! Please, all haste!"

"God's teeth, woman," he cursed, then cursed his luck at having drawn the short straw that got him duty on this wretched night. "At least step out of the rain while you wait."

The captain of the guards knocked on the door. "Joan! Joan, are you in there?"

Helpmesavemehelpmesaveme . . .

Joan clutched the blanket about her neck and backed up against the wooden boards of the wall. The guard opened the door. She knew John of Suffolk, the captain and Bryce's friend. Still he stood there swallowing up the space with his great width. "There ye be, Joan—" He noticed the wide fear in her pretty eyes. "Sweet saints, maid, why are ye afraid? Be it the storm?"

She did not answer.

"Ah, lassie." John smiled fondly; they were all fond of the girl, her sweetness like no other. " 'Tis just a passing bit o' weather." The wind howled suddenly, a haunting sound that belied the spoken words.

"Are ye missin' Bryce already?" He had not been the only knight who had attended the afternoon mass at the army chapel today, a mass normally empty of participants. Seemed the whole camp wanted to send prayers with Bryce and the lucky men picked to accompany him. "By God's will, he will return soon."

She shook her head. Bryce was gone . . .

"Well." He looked about the empty room, the premonition of evildoing pricked at his mind and he paused. "Ah." He waved his hand, dismissing the feeling with the rationale of his purpose. "Lady Roshelle be waiting for you in the village."

Joan's relief was immediate and heartfelt. "Mercy, Roshelle! She is awaiting me!"

"Come. Grab a cloak—"

She shook her head, already on her feet and heading out the door and so happy. Roshelle awaited her! "No cloak. Please, Roshelle—"

"Well, ye can borrow mine," he said as he swung his off his shoulders. "Cannot very well send ye out in cotton rags, can I, now?" He imagined Bryce's bountiful lust cooled by the maid's head cold and he chuckled. "Bryce himself would make me answer to that!"

John led Joan down the stairs and out into the courtyard, where two guards, roused by wooden lances, stood in the still dark and rain-washed night. John chided them for their obvious anger. "Do ye imagine your duty will always wait for a sunny morning? Ah, I've a mind to tell his Grace we got some fair-weather loyalty in the ranks. Step alive, men!" The men straightened and he called out the order. "Raise the gates."

From high atop the battlement John watched the two men lead the two women through the darkness that was night. The rain fell unceasingly. He looked up at the dark clouds. Cold rain splashed on his face. He turned east to where the sun should be rising any time now.

Yet he saw only the dark hills beneath a darker sky.

The thought of Roshelle eased Joan's fear. Roshelle awaited her, the thought sang in her mind. She would be safe with Roshelle. Roshelle always saved her in the rain.

The woman suddenly stopped. One of the guards turned to see her kneeling in the dark. " 'Tis me boot. I've a pebble in me boot. Go on ahead. " 'Tis the cottage with the light in the window."

The guard turned back, separated from Joan and the

other guard now. A dark figure, like a demon in the night, moved on him. An aborted cry sounded. The other guard stopped, spinning around. ''What the devil—''

A stampede of horses came at them. Emerging from all sides in the darkness, three mounted men raced toward him. He reached for his sword. Too late. The rush of two swords and a Spanish saber stopped his cry and dropped him where he stood.

''Helpmesavemehelpmesavemehelpme . . .''

Six shadows moved toward her. Sounds of noise and laughter and rain echoed through her head. The shadows surrounded her. Smells of wet and mud and violence. Cold metal blades brushed over her clothes and skin. Neat lines of blood where her clothes fell from her skin.

''Helpmesavemehelpmesaveme . . .''

Cold stings where rain touched her nakedness. A dark gloved hand reached to her long plait. There were words of marvel, a violent rip. A fist slammed into her stomach. She felt herself falling, falling, and then snatching hurting hands . . .

Helpmesavemehelpmesaveme . . .

A blinding burst of light exploded. She felt his hand, gentle now, pulling her away. She was floating and it was a marvel. She started to look back, to see into the darkness and rain where the shadows knelt over a fallen form, but it looked so far, far away . . .

''Again, Roshelle. I will have you again.''

The words pulled her up from a dark sleep. Her blue eyes opened to see his face, so close to hers. So terribly close. Warm, soft fur brushed the length of her skin. He had carried her back to his solar chambers. The gray light of dawn filtered into the room, diffuse and mysterious, shrouding him in a dark but warm light, but she did not smile.

Fate would let her smile no more.

They lay naked and entwined in each other's arms on a bearskin rug beneath a hot fire blazing in the hearth.

Rain still fell outside.

"Aye," she whispered huskily. "Love me again . . ."

He kissed her tenderly and gently, ignoring the hard and hot ache in his loins. Each time he had her, he wanted her more. The violence and passion of the first time had sent him reeling into darkness, returning to feel a pounding ecstasy of no earthly cause. And the moment his senses collected and gathered, he felt the stirring heat in his loins; she was like an unquenchable thirst, and he wanted her again and again and again . . .

Still kissing her, he dropped his hands to the nape of her neck, sliding to caress her shoulders, lingering there. He broke the kiss and pulled away to let his gaze study the upturned face he could not stop kissing: the feminine velvet of her dark brows and lashes, her lips, the lightest flush staining her cheeks.

She held herself perfectly still, listening to the escalating thud of her heart, her quickening breath as his hands finally slid over her shoulders before traveling in a warm caress down her arms.

She flushed beneath the warmth of his gaze.

"Roshelle . . . Roshelle." He said her name as his hands came over hers. Only then did she realize she still clutched the two tiny rosebuds, the white one for her name and the red one for his love that blessed it. He gently pried her fingers from the stems and set them to the side by the firelight as his lips found her neck. Chills rushed to greet the tender play of his lips on her neck and ear and finally her mouth again as he came over her.

She felt the hard length of him, the shocking heat from every place their bodies touched. Yet he broke the kiss to caress her neck gently, the sensitive spot beneath her ear, and tell her he would take his time. She drew a shaky, uneven breath. The tension erupted in warmth, a sweet, pulsating warmth that made her arch her back, timidly seeking his mouth again . . .

As if to reward her, the kiss was hot and tantalizing. She wanted it to last forever. He stopped only to draw a deep breath and say her name over and over as if it were part of the incantation of the spell by which he claimed her. She closed her eyes, gasping as he teased the sensitive spot on her ear again, first with his fingers, then with his tongue.

He watched the rosy hue spread with the touch of his hand. A bright flush shone on her cheeks, her lips were moist and full, slightly swollen from his kisses, while her small, quick breaths tasted like honey when he caught them in his mouth.

"Roshelle," he said as his hand moved over the curve of her waist to lightly brush her breasts. The light touch washed her in sensations so tantalizing, they passed through her in feverish shudders. "Oh, Roshelle," he began again, after the pleasure of seeing this. "I want so badly to be gentle, to lead you softly to love's call . . . but each time . . . Help me, Roshelle—"

Yet she knew there was no help for it.

Her blue eyes filled with emotion as her arms curled around his neck, her fingers combing his dark hair. His words meant nothing to her, the emotions underlying them meant everything, emotions manifesting as he kissed her again. And while her emotions were strained and stretched, her senses heightened with a dramatic intensity. Her head swam with the sweet onslaught of sensations, all of them: the flat of his palms rested on the small of her back, where they lightly grazed back and forth over the curve of her buttocks, the warm, moist lips molding hers, the heady taste of his mouth and the lingering salty taste of her tears.

A tingling warmth followed the caress of his hands, the teasing play of his tongue. Those hands slid from her back to court her hip and, moving whisper-softly, he grazed the satin skin of her side before covering her breasts. Shivers, a thousand tiny sparklike shivers, erupted where he touched her. She gasped with pleasure, the pounding of her heart dropping just below her abdomen as his palms circled the sensitive peaks. Her soft gasps made him caress her in ever-deepening strokes as he watched with wonder and no small amount of pleasure the sensuous color drawn by the erotic pattern of his hands.

No thoughts existed as his seeking mouth found her breasts. His lips moved softly back and forth over her nipples, his tongue stroking the very beat and pulse of the wellspring of her desire. A warm onslaught of voluptuous sensations tumbled through her and she didn't know her fingers curled into his hair as if to keep him to her or that she cried softly until his mouth met hers again and the sound abruptly stopped.

The erotically probing kiss dissolved her will to breathe yet filled her with need; she needed to feel all of him. "Oh, no, my love," he whispered, biting her ear as his hands came over her form. "Let me carry you higher . . . farther . . ."

She didn't know what was happening, only that it was; the way he began touching her, kissing her, brought her to a towering peak, leaving her wrapped in a heightened tension that suddenly burst in tiny ripples of pleasure. A journey he repeated over and over, each time carrying her higher and higher, until he had transformed her. She became a wild supple creature in his arms, and seeing this, watching her, he felt the full force of the potency of their blinding love.

He wanted to hold back a moment more. Slowing his pace, he lightly brushed her cheek with his lips before heating her own, kissing her with an erotic tenderness that felt both satiating and driving until he broke the kiss. His mouth hovered over hers and he gently bit her lips as he studied her.

"Roshelle . . . Roshelle, look at me . . ."

Her blue eyes opened.

"I see in thine eyes my love. I see it." The idea scared him. "A sadness I have seen so many times in my dreams."

She searched his face.

"I have a dream where I see you standing in a tall white

tower. There is this sadness in your eyes. Just as I reach out to you, I fall away. It haunts my dreams, Roshelle . . . Where does it come from?''

"Do you not know?''

He tried to deny it; to the end he would deny it.

Agony changed her eyes. "Your time is but an hour-glass, turned upside down . . .''

With vicious fierceness, he said, "No, no! 'Tis over now. Forever, Roshelle. I will love you forever—''

"I will love you forever.''

Which would not save him. The idea that it was too late, that it had always been too late, made her reach her arms tightly around his neck with the desperateness with which she clung to his life. "Love me, Vincent . . . Love me as if it were the last time you ever shall.''

And he kissed her, fiercely, passionately; he kissed her as he thrust inside her. She didn't know when the fear dissipated or even that it did, until the sensation changed, dreamlike, it changed, as he transformed her into a magnificent winged creature soaring ever higher and higher to a place she had never been, ever closer to the edge of that cliff. Once there, he catapulted off the side, and instead of falling, he carried her soaring through the air, intense waves of pleasure washing her mind, body and soul with him.

Her blue eyes opened again many hours later. She found herself staring off at the two entwined roses near the red embers of the fire, painted black by the darkness that was night.

Vincent read the messages from England near the fire-light. Henry did indeed bless the marriage proposal and, even better, so did Louis Valois. They both assured him they would endeavor to make the negotiations with Rodez go quickly, though of course this would be a problem.

He'd no doubt lose half his fortune in the process.

Bogo wrote that he was investigating the matter of the curse, that he hoped to obtain evidence of Papillion's ruse, evidence that would even convince the lady. He wondered what this could be and, dear Lord, how badly she needed this.

"The fear, 'tis still in her eyes," he whispered with feeling as at last Roshelle slept. "I thought 'twould end when I took her virginity—"

"Aye." Wilhelm nodded, having spent the past two days, during which Vincent kept Roshelle locked away in his chambers, trying to ease Cisely's worry. "Cisely says it does not matter, that 'tis too late now." He shook his head. "I think 'tis a madness they have, after all these long years of their suffering. I suppose only time will soothe their wounds and tell them differently. Though it is strange how this curse has protected the girl all these years—"

"The curse has not protected her all these years," Vincent interrupted as he stirred the logs in the hearth, explaining, " 'Tis the belief in the curse that has protected her. Add in a few coincidences and the world thinks it has witnessed a miracle. What Papillion neglected to teach her was that her will supersedes any and all curses. What is a curse but a dozen words? When she gave me the treasure of her heart, she broke the curse, as if it never was—"

Wilhelm smiled at the happy thought. "Let us hope she comes to see this when you tell her you will make her your wife, that both Henry and Louis have sent their blessing, that Henry is so pleased, he will make the negotiations with Burgundy himself."

Vincent looked over to the bed where she slept. Her long hair spilled off the side to brush the floor. Her beauty caught his breath. "I've half a mind not to wait—"

A knock sounded at the door and Cisely opened it. "Roshelle! Roshelle—" Before Vincent or Wilhelm could stop her, she rushed inside in a blur of dark gray and maroon made from her gown. "Roshelle! She is gone!"

Her blue eyes opened, dazed with sleep. "What? Cisely—"

"Joan is gone!"

Alarm changed Roshelle's face. "She is safe with Bryce—"

"The guards said Bryce left three nights ago." Cisely spun toward Wilhelm and Vincent with her accusation. "You never told us! *Mon Dieu!* You never said—"

Wilhelm started to explain. "We did not want you to worry—"

Cisely put a trembling hand to her forehead. "All this time I thought she was with him—but this morning when the rain stopped, I needed her and I sent Lorette to the guardhouse. The captain, John, said she left two nights ago to attend you in the village, that a woman came and got her in the middle of the night—"

Roshelle's blue eyes closed, as suddenly the cruel world came into sharp focus and the long-ago words echoed dizzily through her mind: "To know love, however briefly, is to never regret it. Someone will come to teach you this. Her name is Joan . . ."

"No." The denial sounded in a whisper, desperate and pain-filled. She said it again. "No . . . please, no . . ." Then she flew out of the bed. Vincent caught her arm, putting a quick brake on her flight.

"Wait, Roshelle. Easy. I will send the men out looking for her—"

With a heartfelt cry she wrenched herself from his grasp and ran from the room. She flew into the hall and down the steps. "Roshelle, wait! God's curse, girl—" Vincent stopped speaking and raced after her. Wilhelm followed and as Cisely watched them disappear, she felt a jolt of sick dread. Her very flesh went clammy with the terror as she realized what Roshelle had. The roses, he would lay her in the roses . . .

Roshelle sped down the castle keep's stone stairway. Her bare feet hit the mud and she sank ankle-deep before falling. Mud covered her thin cotton nightdress. Vincent called from the top of the stairs as he rushed down for her, but she did not hear. She leaped up and ran across the courtyard and through the gates.

In her dreams she imagined the whole castle surrounded by roses of red and white and every color in between in the place where once the moat had been, and in this dream she laughed beneath a bright, shining sun. A small but meaningful concession to this man, the Duke of Suffolk, an English lord, and to the peace over France he promised her. A peace that changed the foul waters of a moat into a glorious rose garden that filled the castle with its heavenly scents. She had started with five small bushes, and carefully, so carefully, she had buried their roots in the moist soil on the western edge beneath the battlement wall where the morning sun would shine on their dark green leaves, and with a sad joy, she had watched the tiny blossoms growing and unfolding with each passing day.

"Behold your fate, Roshelle . . ."

And the roses were set to flames.

Vincent froze as he came upon the scene that would haunt him for the rest of his life. Then he could not move fast enough. He rushed to the spot and stopped, freezing as he bent to lift her up.

Roshelle had fallen over Joan's cold, lifeless form in the mud of a rose garden. Tears streamed down her face as her hands jerked viciously, clawing at something left in Joan's hand. With a gasp, he saw it. Roshelle desperately tried to pry open the fingers of Joan's hand that held a black rose.

The knock sounded louder, more insistent. "My Grace—a word!"

The image of Angelique's blond beauty disappeared, dissipating as the duke gradually became aware of his surroundings. Terese's amber-gold eyes replaced the blue ones in his mind. She smiled at him as he held the jeweled goblet to her lips and she swallowed. A trickle of dark red drew a line down the side of her chin, in the slight crease of a wrinkle. Which he noticed suddenly. She was aging so fast. Why? It ruined everything. She began to look less and less like her. Like one of his tricks, the more he stared—

The knock sounded again.

"Yes?" The duke kept his eyes on Terese's face. "What is it?"

The door opened and two knights entered. They took in the strange intimacy of the sight: the tall, black-robed figure looming over the lady, enveloping her figure in black silk, so that all they could see was the swirl of her loosened blond hair about bare shoulders.

"What disaster made you interrupt me?"

"My Grace, there be a knight outside, a man of the Suffolk guard, accompanied by six others, insisting on a challenge."

The news surprised him, pricked his interest. He had so few challenges these days; he rather missed the entertainment. And a Suffolk guard to boot. "Did he say his name?"

"Bryce de Warren of Suffolk."

"Bryce de Warren . . ." He had never heard the name before; his eyes focused hard.

The two guards exchanged glances, hesitating. "We tried to pay him off with a bag of coins, then two bags, but he would not have it."

A warning chill shot up Rodez's spine. "He wouldn't, would he?"

"Nay, milord."

"And his challenge?"

"The man says he will avenge your threat to the woman who holds his heart, that nothing less than your spilled blood will answer his charge."

"A woman? Her name?"

"Joan of Orleans."

"Joan?" Terese was very interested in this. "Who, milord, is Joan of Orleans?"

The Duke of Burgundy threw his head back and laughed, loud and long he laughed. For at this very moment Joan would be drawn from Roshelle's protective bosom, taken a few miles away to the base of the so-called Archpriest's camp, where rutting pigs would line up until the very breath of her life at last left her body. And into Flanders arrived the equally witless idiot demanding the killing thrill of his blade through his lovesick heart . . .

"She is no one. Absolutely no one."

Pleased, strangely excited, he snapped out orders. "Fetch my servants. Show our noble knight to the east lawn, where I shall join him shortly for a fine dance unto death in a May rain."

With six men behind him, Bryce waited impatiently under the sweeping branches of an old beech, watching the rain fall unceasingly from dark skies. He and the men had ridden through two days and a night of rain, stopping only last night at an inn, where they had bought a pallet to gather their strength in sleep. The tales the good peasants told of the castle and the Duke of Burgundy only reinforced the idea that he had to do this or die in the trying. He ate a hearty breakfast, saddled his horse, cleaned and oiled his weapons, and then it was time.

He rode directly to the castle gates.

At last, when the Burgundy guards saw he and his men were not going away with a bag of coins, they led them through the castle gates, around the massive stone fortress, past gardens and stables and smoking kitchens to the east lawn in back. The rainwater had made the lawn into a lake, enough water to drown in. They said the duke was coming, and as God be merciful, the deed would soon be done.

For you, Joan, and for you, Lady Roshelle.

As the minutes passed, gathering into the hour, the banter among the knights of Suffolk quieted, the men shifting nervously from foot to foot, no one wanting to admit out loud that the only words left to say were to God. For Bryce's safety and their own. If Bryce met his death today, it would be up to each one of them in turn to answer his call for justice. So be it.

Bryce felt the rising heat of his blood chase away the

chill of two long and hard days of riding in the rain. A thick, muscled hand came to his face, wiping away the wetness; his square steel bonnet might stop an arrow, but it did nothing to protect his vision from the rain.

Best to take it off. He removed it, holding it under an arm. His other hand rested on his sword.

At last he saw him.

Flanked by two neat rows of guards, the tall, princely figure emerged from the castle wall to step imperviously into the driving force of the rain, a long black cloak billowing out behind him in the wind. Bryce's heart sank as he watched the Duke of Burgundy move with an unearthly grace. The man looked very slender. It was generally believed that he, a knight of Suffolk, might hold the swordsman title for all of Henry's realm if only he weren't weighted down by the bulk of his muscles. Vince and Wilhelm both believed he was that good, and in a battle, muscles only helped, but not so in a sword fight.

Last night the peasant men at the inn had warned him:

"His speed be like a slash of a whip . . ."

"So fast, thine eyes cannot follow it . . ."

"The just knight hath no chance—"

"For there be dark and devilish doings at that castle . . ."

Bryce was not afraid of dying. A knight could ask for nothing more than a good death for the just cause, and this call was far more than just. This was a Christian call and God was with him, he knew . . .

The Duke of Burgundy swept before him, took a long moment of assessment before he bowed. Bryce offered a slight nod of his bonnetless head, an insult. The duke straightened, a slight smile on his lips and excitement in his eyes. The excitement made the ceaseless ringing in his ears die, become a barely audible din.

"Behold, milord, the knight Bryce de Warren of Suffolk, your challenger."

"Well, noble knight of Suffolk, state your grievance in plain language and be quick about it."

"Ye know it well." Bryce lifted his head and narrowed

his eyes, but said in an even, level tone, somehow frightening because of it, "I've come to answer the threat you made to Lady Roshelle Marie St. Lille of Lyons and Bourges. The threat that promised to take from her the maid Joan of Orleans, to use and abuse her before you promised to bring her death."

The words were said utterly without feeling, and yet the Suffolk knight conveyed his utter disdain and contempt for the man, any man, who would threaten a helpless lady in such a despicable manner. As if the Grand Duke of Burgundy amounted to no more than an offensive worm, to be crushed beneath the man's boot.

Which was how Bryce felt.

The Burgundian guards shifted nervously beneath the gentle pounding of the rain, their silence filling with amazement. Amazement not for the deed the knight challenged, for they each knew the duke was capable of a good deal worse. Rather, it was the very simplicity of the man's honest emotion that struck their silence: the just cause to avenge a distressed and wrongly used lady's honor. It had been so long since any had heard an honest chord at Burgundy, and the men exchanged nervous glances, torn between awe and respect and laughing outright at his foolishness.

A powerful tingling raced up the duke's spine and shot through his nerves, warning and exciting him. Much better than he had anticipated! He would watch this fool unravel nerve by nerve, savoring every moment. "And what if I said the lady led you false, that she hath lied, no doubt to steal you from the bosom of the very person you seek to protect?"

Bryce studied the strange depths of his eyes through the veil of rain, wondering what devilish trick let him know of the brief struggle between Lady Roshelle and himself for Joan. A fiend for sure, and he wanted to get on with it.

A gloved hand wiped the rain from his face as he straightened. " 'Tis a poor trick to shake me faith." His blue eyes narrowed as his gloved hand rested impatiently on his sword's rip guard and pommel. "I need only place Lady Roshelle's tear-filled eyes alongside these false words that spill from your mouth with an ease the devil himself would envy."

The silence filled with the sound of rain.

"Indeed!" A brow lifted, a grin followed. The idiot was literally too stupid to question his own righteousness. "These moments before you die," the duke said, his voice rich and soothing, "tell me, have you no fear at all, Bryce de Warren?"

"I have nothing to fear."

"Nothing?" he questioned, fascinated by the very idea.

"I've done my best and that's all God could ask of me."

As if mocking the idea, the duke tossed back his head and laughed at this.

Bryce ignored the madman as best he could. "On with it. I grow weary of waitin'."

The duke bit his lip to contain his laughter, his eyes alive with excitement as he felt the murderous rage start to fill him, the excitement of a kill. Yet this idiot was so maddeningly righteous, the day of his death bringing him not a moment of care! He wanted to see this knight's fear before he watched his death.

So he said, "As my challenger, you concede me the right to choose the weapons—"

"It be your right," Bryce agreed as if he had been asked.

The duke felt a twinge of irritation, one curiously bordering humor. This was too much! Yet he knew, in the way he had, the man was loath to use the French saber, that it sat uneasily in his hand those few times he had held one. Pleased with the sudden knowledge, he said, "So I choose the Spanish long knife and the French saber."

The French saber was as good as an English sword, and so, the Spanish blade of no consequence except for the end. "Good enough," Bryce said.

Two guards raced away toward the armory to fetch the weapons.

Dark brows arched over darker eyes. Good enough? Was it not the very worst possible choice of weapons for an Englishman? Was the man trying to trick him?

The duke watched as Bryce calmly withdrew his sword, handing it to one of his men. Then he cracked his thick gloved knuckles. Instead of the fearsome anticipation of God's judgment, this knight had the indifferent air of a man waiting for a maying party.

Something was wrong here; the duke's gaze flew about the rain-washed straws, searching for the familiar spirit. This was a trick, one of his tricks. He knew it! He felt it. Yet nothing stirred in the surrounding area and his gaze returned to rest hard on the knight.

Bryce ignored the intensity of the duke's gaze as best he could. Within minutes the guards returned with two sets of weapons. He withdrew his hands from the warmth of his gloves. He slipped his right hand into the pommel of the French saber and whipped it through the air, adjusting to its heaviness. Luckily, since arriving at Reales, he and Vince had started sparring with them. True, he was soaked through his clothes, but then so was the duke. He gripped the Spanish long knife in his left hand and turned to face the duke.

The duke raised his saber and with a vicious edge snapped, "A good day for dying, Bryce de Warren, is it not?"

"Aye." Bryce raised his saber, lightly touching the duke's and putting in his mind that this man would threaten torture and finally death to the sweet, innocent and simple maid Joan. "I go with God."

I go with God—Papillion's dying words . . .

The terrible ringing started in his ears. His dark eyes filled with rage, sudden, fierce rage as he stared into the knight's familiar blue eyes. Before the steward had even called out the on-guard, and completely taking a stunned Bryce by surprise, the duke swung with all his might. The blade ripped through the steely muscle of Bryce's right hand. Bryce cried out with a shocked grunt as his saber dropped to the ground, shocked by the sheer injustice of that swing. The onlookers stared in disbelief at the blood soaking through the wet cloth of his tunic.

Rodez found himself staring at the gold ring.

"Remember, Rodez, the simplest tricks are the best . . ."

He looked up at the blue eyes. The ringing became a frenzied roar in his mind. With his fingers gripped tightly around the saber and long knife, he grabbed his ears. Bryce cried out with a loud war cry, and with the Spanish long knife raised, he lunged. Like a stick frozen in ice, the duke did not move, his mind seized by the roar of beastly laughter.

With his great strength, Bryce thrust the blade deep in his heart.

The ringing stopped abruptly. Rodez looked down at the novelty of the knife through his chest. With one moment left, he looked back at Bryce and, seeing Papillion instead, he uttered with viciousness, "The girl is already a day long dead—"

The blue eyes blazed with the knowledge. The duke contorted with pain. With shaking strength and vicious fury, Bryce withdrew the knife to plunge it again. And again. Bryce then struggled to his feet, lifting his face to the rain-filled heavens. Rain washed his face of blood and tears, and his agonized cry sang loud and long in the stilled and stormy sky.

Time was her enemy, grief her companion.

The grief felt sad and sweet and deep.

Roshelle lay unmoving on the bed, as if her stillness had the awesome power to slow the march of time. Time that led ever closer to her fate.

The trumpet sounded outside.

Roshelle closed her eyes and listened. There was a secret in this grief. As if Joan's spirit hovered nearby, singing its sad song: "To know love, however briefly, is to never regret it . . ."

She knew the truth of the words; she felt them in her grief. She had been given the miracle of Joan's life and love for such a short time. Such a short time. Yet in those five precious years there was not a moment of regret. Not even the weight of her grief could make her regret. A grief so heavy and painful, its terrible longing to see Joan smile one last time, to reach out to touch her one last time and say good-bye.

Yet this was not so with Vincent.

When she peered into the waiting darkness of the future to see the world where he did not exist, she knew regret. A regret so strong and deep and powerful, it would wash away her life. It was a simple and vivid fact in her mind, as hard and cold as any reality: she could not live without knowing he did.

She would die a thousand times to save him . . .

A thousand times . . .

Words echoed through her mind, words of Vincent's disbelief: how can mere words manifest in reality . . . And you think that old man's death owed itself to the curse . . . A coincidence—surely! Was not Edward drunk? I believe I rescued you . . . As I recall, your screams brought me to the door . . . At what point exactly will a man die? Kiss me again, Roshelle, and see if I won't trade my life for another . . .

Words were superficial now; they had always been superficial. For he did not believe in the curse; he had never believed in it—'twas but an amusing farce to him and his.

Yet this amusing farce had kept her safe and alive to at last come to know his love. She did not know how Papillion's desperate measure to keep her safe worked; nor did she know the mechanism that kept a heart beating throughout a lifetime, or how the sun shone throughout the millennia; she did not know how stars were spread across distances so great no mortal imagination could follow, or even how a tiny green bud knew which day to

open its leaves to feel the sun. Life itself was a miracle
she could neither explain nor understand. So, too, the
curse. Vincent had reached into her heart and touched her
soul. He would die, and with his death would come a
regret more powerful than any reason she had for living.

She would die with him.

It was strange, too, that within the pattern and texture
of life she knew she was not meant to die. Not now. She
did not know how she knew this, but she did; her fate—
one so dearly paid for—was to find peace at last, a place
where she could spend her life exercising the gifts Papillion had given her. Compassion and kindness and healing:
she was meant to help women bring their children into the
world and to ease the discomfort of the dying and help the
hundreds of calamities in between: the broken bones and
rotted teeth, the fevers and pneumonias, the aches and pain
and weariness brought by hard labor and headaches and
bleedings. These gifts would vanish, though, vanish as if
they never were, if he was taken from her in death . . .

The door opened. Cisely slipped inside. Like Roshelle's,
her eyes were red from tears. She wore a gown of midnight blue for mourning, a sheer white apron over that.
She held the ends of the apron in each hand.

She came to the bedside. "Look, Roshelle."

Her blue eyes lifted. Inside the apron were three me-
owing kittens, Hanna's litter. Joan's cat, the one she loved
so.

Roshelle reached for one. Gentle hands enclosed the
small furry ball and brought him to the warmth of her
breast. She closed her eyes, rewarded with the vivid image
of Joan's face. Tears slipped down her cheeks.

A sad and sweet and deep grief . . .

Help me, Papillion.

Noises from outside and the thunder of hooves riding
into the courtyard drew Cisely's gaze. Instantly she was
afraid. Like Roshelle. Cisely lifted the other two kittens
onto the bed before rushing to the alcove to look down
into the courtyard. Roshelle slowly came to stand by her.

Papillion, show me . . .

The men of Suffolk crowded into the courtyard, over thirty and more arriving. Arrows were strung into bows, swords were drawn and hands tightened around pommels as if they waited the order to attack. Four mounted men remained seated as they let their horses circle and dance amidst their loud, obscene curses and raucous noise.

"Who are they?" Cisely's brows drew together. "Why do they not dismount or stop? Oh, look! He smashed it to pieces!"

A stallion's hooves crashed over the piggery man's wooden cart as if it were no more than doll-size, and as Roshelle watched, listening to their hoots and calls and curses, she grasped the point to it. A demonstration that they were wild beasts who lived outside the restraints and conventions of the world.

"Like brigands from an outlawed army, they are!"

Roshelle nodded and gasped. "They will be killed!"

"How do they think to come here like this?"

Suddenly Vincent emerged on the steps of the keep.

The Duke of Suffolk's appearance had an immediate effect on the rampaging and stampeding outlaws as they attempted to still and quiet their mounts in order to stare up at him. A formidable presence Vincent was, his unconventional height and steely strength donned in an austere expression of his unparalleled status: he wore a rich dark blue tunic that sported expensive brass breastplates and black leather shoulder pads, all belted, with black breeches and tall black boots. He wore no weapons, but then he did not need any for he might have worn a crown for all the aristocracy expressed in the contempt and displeasure he directed at the wild men.

Wilhelm stepped behind him, just as threatening.

"God's teeth," the boldest man shouted from atop a beige stallion, with a narrowing smile. "If it is not the high-and-mighty duke himself!" He laughed and the others with him, causing the restless horse to leap forward.

"Aye. You stand before the Duke of Suffolk, assaulting

me and mine with your vile presence here at Reales. And yet you must know men die for less.'' His voice thundered down. ''I would know why.''

The man raised his hand to shield the bright sun from his eyes as he boldly met Vincent's gaze. '' 'Tis a simple matter, milord. You must endure my company or Reales will be attacked by the army of the archpriest.''

''The archpriest . . . Oh, thank God.'' Roshelle's relief was intense and heady. The archpriest's army of brigands traveled from castle to castle, demanding money to stave off an attack. They were no threat to Reales. Vincent had plenty of money to pay them off and get them on their way again . . .

''How much do you think they will demand?'' Cisely asked.

''Who knows?'' Roshelle shrugged. ''Vincent is so very rich, they could ask for anything.''

As whispered amusement swept through the waiting men of Suffolk, Vincent conferred with Wilhelm.

''Why are the men laughing?'' Cisely asked.

Roshelle studied the scene below. More and more men of Suffolk rushed into the courtyard. She spotted the good captain John joining a group of his friends. They conferred in whispers that erupted in laughter, shakes of heads.

A warning chill shot up her spine.

The four lawless knights grew restless with the wait, their confidence melting away as Vincent shook his head and said, just loud enough for all to hear, ''No, Wilhelm— too bloody a spectacle. I prefer a good, clean hanging . . . Aye, a painless death, but—''

Suddenly Roshelle was running.

She emerged in a burst of dark blue colors from the open side doors of the keep. The stunning beauty of the girl brought a sudden silence through the crowd as she briefly took in the changed circumstances: a number of Suffolk guards had inched closer to the mounted men, so that at last fear had worked into their faces. They had thought they'd be allowed to return to relate the duke's message back to the archpriest—even the refusal. They were suddenly uncertain.

More uncertain as Roshelle dropped to her knees, her skirts fanning behind her over the stone steps, the length of unbound hair over that as she looked up at Vincent. "Pay the ransom, milord!"

She saw the devil's amusement in his eyes as he stared down at her. "Pay them? I will not! I mean to hang them!"

"No! No! You are so rich!" She held tight to the cloth of his breeches, her heart, mind and soul put into the plea. " 'Tis nothing to you! You can just pay them and they will go away—"

A low, threatening rumble rose louder from the ranks of his men, eager to give these outlaws a measure of English rule and then get on with this battle. For Joan's death had put them in a somber black mood. English civility and pragmatism were at last disgusted with the bloody and murderous result of the French chaos and anarchy. The rumble grew.

Thinking to get her out of the way, Vincent reached a hand around her arms to lift her up but stopped and froze as he heard the outlaw's low, vicious chuckle: "You would do well to picture that beautiful lady backside to the ground with her thighs spread—"

A dagger sliced fast through the air, piercing his flesh before the last words were finished. All gazes flew from Wilhelm—who knew Vincent was unarmed at the moment—to the man as he cried out in a grunt. The man seized the handle of the dagger and tore it from the muscle of his arm. With an animallike fury, Vincent roared, "You fool! You cannot win! You are outnumbered four to one!"

"Please to God," Roshelle cried, tears streaming down her face, and she knew, she knew. "This is how you will be taken from me! I beg you!" She was clinging to his leg, blinded by her tears, when she felt his powerful grip seize her arms, lifting her up and into Wilhelm's arms to take her away.

"Vincent!"

He turned to the urgent cry, seeing first John standing on the well wall to watch. He followed John's gaze to the man's horse to realize the trophies decorating the seat were made by a woman's plaits.

He saw it but too late: for so did Roshelle.

She screamed as John withdrew his sword from its sheath and tossed it through the air. With a well-practiced catch, Vincent caught the pommel in a deadly grip as he came quickly down the stairs. The man watched in mounting alarm as, with violence in his gaze, the Duke of Suffolk approached the man's horse. A hand snaked out to catch the leather straps of the bridle to steady his horse's fear. With sword raised and a slight twist, Vincent caught a plait at the tip of the blade and raised it in the air. So that the last thing the man saw before Vincent plunged the blade through his heart was a blinding streak made of gold, the color of Joan's hair.

Blood spurted over his hands as he withdrew the blade. The horse lifted in fury and fright, neighing as its hooves crashed back to the ground and the lifeless body dropped to the mud. The men were with Vincent, they had always been with him, so he never even gave the order before the other three men were surrounded and slain.

"Prepare for battle!"

A cheer went up, drowning out Roshelle's cry as she felt the sharp sting of the blade pierce her heart.

For it would be her death, too.

Any man with a shovel was offered one ducat apiece to dig the mass graves, along with the unusual order that they might keep any booty found on the dead before they were tossed into the graves. English battle law. Dozens of gray-robed Benedictine priests from the nearby abbey moved somberly over the massive piles of bloodied bodies. The Duke of Suffolk, standing on the uppermost hillside surveying the scene, closed his eyes; above the whispered Latin drone of priests, the scraping of the shovels and the English liege song, he heard the melody of her voice say the parting words in his changed dream from last night, "Your life for mine, my love. I wait for another lifetime . . ."

"Milord?"

Two Suffolk captains waited for the duke's order. Which did not come. The men turned, then followed Vincent's gaze to the valley below, where the battle had been fought and won. Four hundred English soldiers had met and soundly beaten the brigand army. Vincent and Wilhelm themselves had slain the man called the Archpriest. Yet the duke stared unseeing into the scene drawn from the conclaves of hell.

Twilight was settling over the land; the setting sun dipped behind the hills faraway. The count of English dead lay at seventy-two and stayed, the number ablaze in his mind. Like the wretched scent of death.

Wilhelm and Owens, his squire, and a number of his knights, along with their squires, climbed up the hillside to him. Vincent drew a sharp breath, a stab of pain as he thought of his young squire. Dear Richard.

Wilhelm and he had fought back to back as they always did, and in the heat of the battle, as the scent of blood and death filled the air and the ground was saturated with the mangled bodies of the slain men, as the bloodlust pumped furiously through his veins, from the corner of his vision he had caught sight of young Richard, his sword raised. The boy never saw the man with a halbert charging from behind. Vincent's warning sounded too late.

Too late; it had always been too late . . .

Squires were not allowed to fight until their knighthood, but Richard had been only one month away from his vows and spurs. The young man had fallen to his knees begging for the privilege to fight at his duke's side. The thought of the boy's sweet mother, Lady Eugene, the Baroness of Colmar, had made Vincent say an unequivocal "No." The boy would no doubt have plenty of days to fight, and he said no, so he would never have to meet with his mother to tell her the words that make up every mother's worst fear: "Madame, your son . . ."

The boy had known Vincent would forgive him the offense, if only he had lived.

"Milord?"

Vincent turned to the two waiting captains. "Mount two more patrols for the area west of Rouen," he said. "The order stands: all men fleeing are to be slain on sight."

"Aye!"

The men left as Wilhelm came by his side, his arm bandaged but a slight wound considering. Wilhelm placed his good arm on Vincent's shoulder as their eyes met, the unspoken love of a lifelong bond powerful and deeply felt. Vincent closed his eyes for a moment and said, "I am afraid."

Wilhelm knew without words what Vincent feared, and there was good reason. "Owens and Robert are bringing up fresh horses now, but, Vincent—" His eyes blazed with sudden intensity as he gave Vincent the news. "Bryce has returned to Reales. The Duke of Burgundy hath been killed by that good man's just sword. The castle at Flanders was soon swarmed by the peasants, and the word is the mob killed your sister-in-law and her infant son."

A wave of relief nearly made his knees collapse and would have, except for the one thing, the only thing, that mattered to him now. "Roshelle?"

"Roshelle waited for Bryce to return to have the mass sung for Joan. They spent the day consoling each other, but—"

The darkly intelligent eyes were a blaze of emotion as he waited.

"Roshelle has left for Orleans."

A blanket of smooth gray clouds made for a sunless sky over Reales and the forest land around the township where horse and rider flew. Beast and girl appeared as one, like some winged creature desperate for flight, as the rider's fear spurred the horse to ever greater speed. Hooves thundered over the dying carpet of bluebells. The girl's dark gray skirts lifted over the sable-colored horse, while her bare legs clung tightly to the beast's side. She leaned forward, her long unbound hair appearing as part of the horse's mane, inseparable, as she gave Etoile free rein to race to the familiar place of prayers. Tears blinded her; the hot sting in her eyes had nothing to do with the wind of their flight but everything to do with her fear. The fear that it was already too late.

A lone bird circled the gray heavens far above.

Etoile slowed as she reached the familiar glen, stopping in the center. Roshelle slipped off the strong back, falling to the ground where she meant to kneel, but beneath the weight of her fear, she collapsed in a small ball and held herself tight. Etoile pranced in a lively circle, snorting with anticipation before she contented herself to wait by the side, keeping a concerned eye on her fallen mistress.

Greyman came to a nearby branch and neatly folded his wings at his side, watching, too. The forest teemed with life, oblivious of the march and folly of its fellow creatures, and for a long time Roshelle tried to quiet and focus her thoughts on the sounds: the symphony of robins and sparrows, the shrill calls of squirrels, her own mare's labored breathing and shuffle of hooves; but somehow all she heard was the steady pounding of her heart. Like her relentless tears. Like the relentless march of time that she had to stop. Somehow she had to stop it.

For she knew with the certainty of her next breath the simple fact: she could not live knowing he did not.

Papillion, help me . . .

"Forever, Roshelle, forever . . ."

Aye, forever I love you . . .

He would die! For loving her, he would die. The curse which kept her safe and alive—the very force that bought her the time and fortune to at last come to know his love!—would now turn darkly, always utterly unmindful of the consequences, much less the change brought by her love. The curse would lead him to death. As it had killed so many times before, but this time she would die with him.

Papillion, help me . . .

Yet she could not quiet the emotional avalanche brought by the fear. Not at first. She had no idea how long she knelt there crying, unable to transcend the vivid image of her punishment in a dark prison of the world where he did not exist. An hour, maybe longer, when gradually she felt the warmth and light of his grace.

Slowly, bit by bit, the penetrating warmth stilled her heart. She felt her emotions quiet, abating like a receding moonlit tide, and in their place the warm light grew. This warmth reached through her fear to gently envelop and soothe the weariness of her soul by answering her prayer. The light imparted a message, and with it, understanding and salvation.

The white tower . . .

He will be saved, the curse broken at last.

Without the magic and force that made the curse and changed her fate, she would never have lived to know his love. She had been kept safe and alive so that she at last came to know his love. To know love, however briefly, was to never regret. There would be no regrets. For she'd have the gift the rest of her long life to cherish the memory. As would he . . .

She woke as if from a dream. The light was gone and the world came into sharp focus. Greyman swooped down to rest on her shoulder. Etoile nudged her face. Tears still filled her, but a different kind. Tears of gratitude as she turned to face the east.

A place where her peace waited.

A loud and strange bird call sounded in the night.

" 'Tis him! The Duke of Suffolk!''

Instantly three torches were thrust into the wet ground where they smoked and sizzled in the mud. Smoke filled the air, but it would dissipate in time. Two more hoots pierced the air.

"Two knights ride with him!"

"Only two? A bloody piece of cake."

"Arm thy bows and ready thy positions!"

Six men took their places at the crest of the slope. Five men held bows, arrows strung tightly in the strings as they crouched in the surrounding bushes and trees, waiting in the darkness. Only one man held a saber, its blade razor-sharp.

The man smiled, a toothless grin disappearing in the moonlit darkness. He was to take the head, and this prize would earn him the bulk of the reward from the Duke of Burgundy.

His hand tightened around the saber.

The three riders rode at breakneck speed through the night. A galloping stampede over the well-traveled road that led to Reales. Moonlight shining from a crescent moon created fast-moving shapes and shadows, but it was but a blur in the Duke of Suffolk's mind. He felt nothing except the wind of his flight, the urgency that made his heart pound in a relentless rhythm that perfectly matched his galloping steed until—

It was only a second, one second in which the dark blur of the landscape burst into a blinding white light which faded to the image stolen from time: Roshelle knelt at an altar of the cross. Her slim figure donned the crisp white cloth of the order, the magnificent auburn tresses spread all around her on the floor where she knelt. Shorn hair haloed her lovely face as she whispered the vows that would steal her life from him.

And then the image was gone.

His loud cry sounded through the night and instantly Wilhelm and Raymond, another of the duke's knights, drew back on the reins, slowing their mounts in fast, tight circles as they turned to Vincent.

Gustave lifted high in the air as he fought the bit, crashing to the ground again as Vincent pulled hard on the reins, his cry echoing over the darkened landscape; loud and long he cried. The three steeds, half wild from the weariness of the relentless gallop, turned for several long minutes in frantic circles. Alarm seized Wilhelm as he searched for the danger that simply could not be seen. "Vince, what is it?"

"Assassins." Vincent repeated the words he heard so clearly in his mind. "Beware the assassins waiting just ahead!"

For many years after, Wilhelm always claimed both he and Raymond heard Roshelle's voice in their minds as well, the melodic voice of the lady filled with death-defying urgency as she cried out to them across the many miles separating them, "Assassins! Beware the assassins waiting just ahead!"

A warning that saved their lives.

Bryce prayed over Joan's grave in the rose garden.

Cisely knelt at the altar of the castle chapel outside the great hall. Candles lit the altar, above which a plain cross hung. Her pretty amber eyes were red and ringed with dark circles as she stared through a blur up at the cross. She was praying. She was praying with all her heart and soul.

Bryce had returned with the news that he had killed the Duke of Burgundy at last, that his death had brought a peasant revolt sweeping over Flanders as hundreds of common folks ransacked the castle, burning and looting and at last finding his mistress and her bastard child—

No, do not think of their deaths; but still the biblical prophecy echoed in her mind: the children shall inherit the sins of the father . . .

A trumpet sounded in the distance. Alertness broke through her heartfelt prayer and set her on edge. She wiped the tears from her eyes and turned toward the door. Far away from atop the battlement she heard the sudden cry: " 'Tis him! The Duke of Suffolk!"

Cisely leaped up, gathering her gray skirts, and ran.

The gates opened just in time. A loud cheer went up. Vincent, Wilhelm and Raymond rode into the courtyard at a gallop. Vincent swung off Gustave before he had reined him to a stop, his bad leg throbbing. Blood covered his thigh but he did not notice. Most of his wounds had opened, torn apart by the hours of hard riding, and they were noting compared with the mind-numbing weariness threatening to drop him where he stood. He pushed the weariness back and forced himself to stand erect. A vassal—he did not even know the old man's name—rushed to the well to draw him water as he raised his voice above the cheering to ask the only question that mattered. "Where is she?"

Like a sudden shift of a breeze, silence rushed over the waiting people and, one by one, gazes dropped to the ground. In sudden murderous viciousness, he demanded again, "Where is she—"

"Milord, milord!" Cisely appeared from the top steps of the keep. In the haste of her flight she appeared as a gray blur. She was crying, emotionally overwhelmed with joy at the living, breathing sight of them, joy mixed with the sorrow of her loss. She ran to where Vincent stood and dropped to her knees before him. Wilhelm seized her hand, but she would not raise up as she told him, "She saved you! She saved you. The curse is gone, vanished and vanquished, for she shall say the holy vows—"

"No . . . By the saints!" Vincent grabbed Cisely's thin shoulders. "Say it isn't true!"

Tears streamed down Cisely's face and she was nodding, nodding and crying. "She has joined the sisters at Saint Catherine to take the vows that will break the curse and save your life. A small price to know you live and breathe in this world, a very small price."

The dark reality crashed through his mind, body and soul, dropping him where he stood as blackness swirled through his head. He gasped for breath. He grabbed the water cask and poured it over his head and face, and with all his last strength he denied it to the end. "Get me a fresh horse!"

The green-and-gold banner of the Duke of Suffolk's colors flapped madly in the wind of their flight. Women carrying baskets of wares to the Orleans marketplace leaped from their path, staring with awe and wonder at the English lord and his men as they galloped past, a look of determined urgency on their stern faces. They raced up the slight incline and rounded the bend. Seeing the city below, the Duke of Suffolk raised his arm, and the six knights behind him reined in their stallions, stopping to stare down at the city of Orleans spread below them.

Two-story-high stone houses lined up in neat rows leading from the grand castle of Pierrefonds in the center of the city where the Dauphin lived. Nearby, the enormous four towers of the Cathedral of Orleans jutted up into the clear blue summer sky, the bell tower rising in its center. To the right lay the colorful canopied tops of the marketplace, scattered around the guild building. Smaller wooden houses surrounded the outskirts. The duke's darkly intelligent gaze surveyed the scene, doubling back and back again.

Then he saw it.

The Abbey of Saint Catherine. Nestled on the green hillside on the far outskirts of the city lay a rectangular stone building, two stories high. Stables and a pasture stood behind it on the green hillside, and to the right, on the other side, was the small chapel.

The church had a white stone tower.

Chapter 13

"**O**h, but I must speak with her!"

" 'Tis forbidden, you know this." The hard lines of Bishop Bruce de Borne's face looked drawn, as if he feared a sudden blow to his head. "The cardinal has expressly forbidden it."

"Yes, but the cardinal does not know why she is doing this. You see, she thinks—"

"She thinks?" The bishop appeared mildly amused by the idea, glancing toward the heavens as if for help. Mere mortal considerations always irritated him and it seemed to pain him to ask the obvious. "What could it possibly matter what a woman thinks or reasons? The lady is utterly inconsequential."

"No, oh, no," Father Herve hastened to explain. "You see, it all started when I was asked by the Duke of Suffolk's steward, a man by the name of Bogo le Wyse, to investigate this whole matter of the curse, and I—"

"That is quite enough." Bishop Bruce de Borne's jeweled hand went to his forehead as if to hold a headache in place. Papillion had discovered him in a pie shop, of all the ungodly places, and to this day he had trouble believing it. He shook his head; it worried him, this sinking of standards in the priesthood . . .

"But you see, my Grace, she thinks she has to say the holy vows to save—"

"I said, not another word!" Cold, sharp eyes focused hard, the bishop's anger plain. "I will not condescend to hear any more about that girl's evil ideation, this ridiculous curse of hers. She has been prepared. I daresay 'tis a fitting end to her pathetic story anyway. A virgin's curse indeed! Yet another of that man's delusions, I am sure. The next thing I shall hear is that the lady has pretenses of holiness because of this repulsive curse or spell or whatever she has incurred.'' His jeweled hands came from behind his back and motioned furiously in front of his crimson robes as if he were sweeping the whole preposterous story away. "Which reminds me: I must mention to the abbess to strictly watch this girl's humility. I daresay the good abbess will have to nurture and develop that virtue by giving her all the dirty work and whatnot, cleaning out the latrines and stables and so on.''

"Dear me, I do not think the lady—''

"Yes, yes, whatever.'' Bishop Bruce de Borne rarely let his subordinates get a word out before interrupting them. "Do keep in mind the fortune at stake here. Practically enough for a whole tower of the cathedral, if we can increase the land yield in Normandy, that is. And the one thing I am very good at''—he smiled—"is squeezing indolence from the cotters' souls.''

Father Herve watched the bishop's hand squeeze an imaginary cotter's neck and he swallowed. "For which the cotters are sure to be indebted to you, but for now—''

He cast Father Herve a scornful look and interrupted him again. "I doubt seriously the poor sods have either the delicacy of mind or the disposition to appreciate my effort, but in any case, a peasant's gratitude is nothing to me when I have God's own.'' And the bishop pointed upward as if Father Herve might be in doubt of the heavenly direction. "No, indeed. Well, come now, let us get on with it. My supper will be waiting.''

Small beads of perspiration lined Father Herve's forehead as he followed the bishop to the altar. Dear Lord. He needed help. Papillion would not like this at all. Papillion never meant the girl to take the holy vows. Had he intended such a thing, he would have raised her to it from the start. To make it all so much worse, Roshelle Marie's motives were all so unnecessary.

There was no curse. There never was a curse.

He must find a way to speak to her before she said the vows. Dear Lord, dear Lord . . .

"Father Herve . . ."

The good father wiped his brow, staring at the austere altar before him. Everyone waited. The Abbess of Saint Catherine stood nearby. Two neat rows of black-robed priests streamed from either side of the altar. The kneeling sisters of Saint Catherine lined the hardwood pews, their whispered prayers sounding like the hum that clings to a beehive. Yet he stared at the right side of the church, where a neat row of solemn-faced warrior priests stood. A necessary caution, the cardinal had said, surely with the knowledge of who owned the lady's heart and fear of that man's interference. Surely.

God in Heaven, help me . . .

Afternoon sunlight poured ribbons of color through the fine stained-glass windows that told stories of miracles. A warm stream of rose-colored light fell upon Lady Roshelle Marie St. Lille where she knelt before the bishops at the altar, as still and unmoving as a picture on canvas. She wore only the modest white robes of the sisters; this loose-flowing cotton garment was belted at the waist by a thick white rope. A small gold cross hung from her neck. The long braid of her hair made a thick and neat line down her back, coiling at her ankles.

The gold shears—brought from the Cathedral of Orleans for the special purpose—lay upon a crimson velvet pillow on the candlelit altar, the hooded ceremonial vestments at the side.

Bishop Bruce de Borne's patience stretched taut, and his fist tightened dramatically at his side. Cardinal Cecile de Grair would never have permitted Father Herve to say her mass, especially knowing the lady had insisted just to irritate him. That Father Herve sing her mass was the only condition of subjugation to the vows. A condition that probably had nothing to do with the man's gift. She probably imagined she was honoring Papillion—and therefore humiliating the cardinal, for Father Herve had been one of the few priests to defend Papillion when the time had come. As punishment for the fool's misplaced loyalty, the cardinal had sent Father Herve on a long and arduous journey to bless the holy battlefields of the Crusade in Turkey, surprising them all when he managed to return in good health, none the worse for the rigors of an often deadly journey. Beggar's luck, no doubt.

Well, no matter now, he supposed. Within the hour it would be done. The church would inherit the wealth of Lyon and Bourges, and for the price of one new novitiate.

A fortune in a matter of minutes.

He would be late for his supper at this pace.

"Father Herve . . ."

The whispered reprimand visibly jerked Father Herve, and he glanced nervously behind. If only the cardinal had not viewed the prospect of the girl's fortune with such transparent eagerness! Greed was the devil's limb, he knew, and while he did not feel comfortable contemplating his superior's motives, much less the nature of his soul—

A harsh whisper said, "I am warning you!"

Oh, Roshelle Marie, my poor dear child. His gaze swept across the small chapel, as if looking for a source of heavenly intervention. Having no choice, it seemed, he drew a deep breath, released in the full rise of song. He would draw the ceremonial mass out as much as possible, yet would it be long enough?

Long enough for what? What was he expecting? Another of Papillion's miracles? Perhaps the Duke of Suffolk himself? The duke was at war, though, on a battlefield far, far away, and unless the good man could fly over the hundred or so miles between them . . .

Slowly the crescendo built and Father Herve's hauntingly beautiful voice filled the chapel. Bishop Bruce de Borne sighed, listening, almost willing to forgive the father his sins for that voice. A voice from God, the people believed, a voice that had assured Father Herve's place in the church the first time Papillion had presented it to the papal court, and the Pope claimed afterward that he had heard the Gregorian chants sung the way the angels sang them in heaven. Then, too, Father Herve's masses always brought a significant emptying of pockets into the collection box . . .

The deep, rich voice of Father Herve's song in the stilled air of the church stirred his listeners with its beauty as he sang the traditional mass, though all gazes remained fixed on the girl Roshelle Marie. The Latin words would lead Roshelle Marie in humility and love to become Sister Sharon. The rose of Sharon. With that transformation, the curse would end for all time. It would be over. She would step into a new and different life and, God willing, she would be graced with peace. The peace would be the gift for making Vincent safe for all time.

Vincent. The name was her own incantation, one whispering through her heart, stirring her soul with the burden of its love. Her eyes were closed and her mind conjured the image of his face: the thick dark hair that framed the jutting raven-black brows arching over the darkly intelligent eyes, eyes filling with passion and love; the impressive crook of his nose, the mark of his cleft and his mouth, dear Lord, his mouth as he bent to kiss her, turning hell into heaven with the touch of his lips . . .

Vincent, I love you, I love you, forever . . .

For you, my love, for you . . .

Cisely would send her word of his safe homecoming, a message that would bring salvation. For her life depended on receiving that message; she anxiously awaited this, though she knew it would not, could not, come until after the vows were spoken. The whole of these past long and tumultuous years was spent in an arduous journey to reach this point of his safety.

For you, my love, for you . . .

The priests joined Father Herve to sing the next verses

and the chapel filled with the collective sound of this prayer. Roshelle Marie still did not move, not even to wipe the tears sliding down her pale cheeks. The raised voices faded at last. There came a shuffling of feet, more silence, broken only by a distant sound of horses' hooves, a hummingbird in a tree, a fly furiously beating its wings against the glass in its struggle to be free.

Soon. Very soon now.

There was something wrong in the silence, though, so lost in her tragic circle of thoughts, Roshelle did not notice. The clamor of horses drew nearer and nearer still, though no one at first noticed as all gazes lifted to Father Herve, waiting. Yet the priest seemed to have forgotten his place and purpose as his bright dark eyes stared intently at Lady Roshelle kneeling at his feet.

The entire force of Father Herve's consciousness went into a prayer for heavenly intervention. Bruce de Borne's angry, insistent clap of hands jerked him back to the cold reality of the chapel again. The congregation waited patiently for him to begin. The simple lift of his hand felt like the lift of a tabernacle-size boulder. Smiling, unmindful of the father's struggle, the abbess knelt and lifted the shears. These were kissed. The older woman genuflected once and rose. Three steps brought her to Roshelle's back. Roshelle closed her eyes, waiting to feel the lifting of the weight from her back for the last time.

For you, my love, for you . . .

A loud commotion sounded outside, immediately mobilizing an alarmed Bishop Bruce de Borne. He motioned violently to the abbess to cut and she might have, if only she had seen the violent motion. She did not. Because her gaze, like all others, was fixed on the door to the chapel where from outside came the sound of horses neighing angrily as the riders reined the beasts to a fast stop, men flying off mounts with a rancorous clang of metal and curses, English curses greeting the excited French of the two or three sisters outside, warning of sacred rites and holy vows and the mortal sins of men . . .

Doors pushed open with a loud bang. Heads confronted the unconventionally tall figure silhouetted against the afternoon light. A rush of outraged voices greeted the man. Priests issued warnings; some, soft explanations. Still other voices sounded with shaking fists, "how dare thees," and harsh warnings of the consequences of interrupting holy ceremonies. The sisters all seemed to stare with open mouths, all of them genuflecting as if the interruption were an evil that needed warding off. Everyone waited for Father Herve's voice to put an end to this sacrilege and send the man out—but a strange, very pleased grin changed the father's weathered face as he rocked back on his heels and imagined the argument he might have had with Papillion: whether this constituted a true heavenly intervention or not.

He would say yea, Papillion would argue nay. Which was the whole point. Papillion had never believed in magic at all, not even the heavenly inspired kind. The war with Rodez had all been to show that awful man there really was no such thing on earth, or rather, that someday man's knowledge would explain the whole of the great mystery. Papillion would argue that because we witness a "miracle" or do not understand the mechanisms of an event now does not imply the mystery was either magical or divine. "Say a man comes to see a little green dragon on his shoulder," Papillion would explain. "He sees it, feels it, he can even hear it. Does this mean the green dragon is real? Of course not. Our experience, even the knowledge of the senses, is not, cannot be, a criterion for reality, as this very knowledge is often erroneous."

Sometimes, though, the mystery seemed so great . . .

A number of men at arms came up behind the tall man at the church's open doors, filing past him to come inside, and the assembly heard, "Did you see that, Wilhelm? Did you?"

"Aye," he said. "One more minute and you would have lost that hair."

"And I swear I would have used the rope of it as a noose."

No one knew whether he meant a noose for the abbess, holding the shears, or for Roshelle herself, but no one wanted to clarify the point, a moot point now, for the abbess had dropped the shears with a loud clamor on the floor.

Then suddenly came a silence.

The blaze of his coat of arms worn on his padded leather tunic said his name and gave his title: Vincent de la Eresman, the Duke of Suffolk. Harsh lines, deeply etched on his strong face, lent a deadly air about him. Blood mixed with mud on his boots. The now stilled chapel echoed with the clang of his gold spurs as he walked down the center aisle, approaching the kneeling figure. He stopped suddenly, grabbing the back of a pew. After the many furious battles fought and won, the three arduous days and nights without sleep, the long, hard ride to reach this point, only to witness firsthand how very close he had come to losing her, he felt a fierce wave of dizziness wash over him where he stood. Blackness, merciful but deadly now, threatened, and just as he felt the blood vacate the muscles of his legs, Wilhelm's strong hand came to his arm, lending him the necessary support for the crucial next minutes it would take to state his claim and take his stand at her side.

Forever, Roshelle, forever . . .

Upon hearing that voice, Roshelle froze where she knelt, just froze. The sudden hard pounding of her heart brought a slight tremble to her hands, but still she did not, could not, move as his voice echoed through her mind, and with it the knowledge that he was alive.

He was alive!

Tears of gratitude blinded her. She collapsed into a heap on the floor, tears falling onto her hands as she kissed the rosary beads over and over. He was alive. He was alive . . .

The sweet miracle of it seized her. It worked, it worked.

The curse was over. The sacrifice had the awesome power to end the curse and save his life. She had not even said the holy vows yet and he was saved. The mere promise of saying them had saved him. There was no choice now; there never had been a choice. And while she knew she must finish the act that would separate her soul from his for this lifetime, she would feel his arms around her one last time . . .

Blood pumped hard and fast into Roshelle's overworked heart and she could not draw enough air into her lungs as tears streamed over flushed cheeks. Still, somehow, she managed to stand on uncertain legs and move toward him until, stumbling, she felt those strong arms come around her form, and tightly hold her against his body.

For the last time, she clung to him desperately, for the last time. He held her slender form so tight he feared he might hurt her, yet it wasn't enough; it would never be enough. The love pounding through him felt so physical, so alarmingly physical, that it acted as a powerful tonic able to sustain him for a few precious moments more. His lips gently grazed her forehead and closed eyes as he drank in the sweet perfume of her being. He caught a tear as it slid down her cheek, marveling at the surge of emotion and desire. Dear Lord, he wanted her now, in a chapel full of priests and nuns; weak with blood loss and mind-numbing fatigue, on the very edge of collapsing, he wanted her.

"Roshelle, Roshelle," he whispered against her lips. "I love you. Forever, Roshelle, forever . . ."

She was crying, overwhelmed and utterly unable to speak. Had she been able to speak, it would have just been to say what she said with her eyes as she looked up at him, with her lips as she took his large hands in hers and kissed them as if they were more precious than life, and they were, they were.

Bishop Bruce de Borne was weighing the difficult equation: the odds of winning a battle in the chapel and if they won, a huge if, the likelihood of the lady wanting to say the holy vows over the slain body of her lover. Added to that was the greater difficulty: Pope Benedict had Henry's support lately and the English king's support was badly needed, yet what would Henry do if one of his dukes was slain by French priests?

Still, the fortune here was so large, so very large . . .

Vincent had but moments left to him. All consciousness rested on his goal, the only thing that mattered to him: taking his place at Roshelle's side, forevermore. To the neat row of priests he said: "The lady is mine. I claim her." He withdrew the parchments from behind his belt and waved them in the air, ignoring the widening pool of blood at his feet. "I have decrees from Henry, the King of England and Wales, and Louis Valois, the Duke of Orleans, now the young lady's custodian, and the seals of both." He tossed the papers to the altar. "You are commanded by the highest authority—"

"This cannot be tolerated!" Bishop Bruce de Borne shook his finger, unable to release his precarious hold on the girl's fortune. "The highest authority is and always will be the church. She has made her choice—"

"I warn you all," Vincent said to the priests as his free hand gripped the pews, his voice giving no sign of his physical weakness or agony as it thundered loudly through the chapel, "God will lose such a battle and simply"— his voice lowered compellingly to Roshelle—"because I want her so much more."

"Oh, but of course you do!" Father Herve agreed, smiling, as if this were a perfectly happy conclusion to the dilemma, and it was, it was. Yet his eyes remained firmly fixed on the warriors' hands that gripped the pommels of swords, and with this in mind, hoping to ease Bruce de Borne's objection, he added, "And naturally, you would be willing to, ah, offer"—a dark brow rose with the suggestion—"some financial compensation for the honor and privilege of marrying the lady?"

Roshelle started with a shock. "No, no—"

Vincent's hand came unkindly over Roshelle's mouth as

he waved his free hand in acquiescence, willing to ride a banner through Hades to reach that point. "Very well. Is that in agreement with the bishop?"

For anxious minutes Bruce de Borne did not speak, only glared, first at the Duke of Suffolk, then at Father Herve. Better than nothing, he supposed, though no compensation from Suffolk would offset the loss of the lady's wealth. On the other hand, he knew Pope Benedict, and that man would hold him personally responsible if this skirmish resulted in losing King Henry's support. He would lose much. Oh, women, curse them! Thank the good Lord he would never feel such violent, unpleasant emotion for such impossibly silly creatures.

"Agreed, but reluctantly." He found the tear-streaked face and sighed, softening despite his better instincts, though nonetheless he had to ask, "Only with the lady's concurrence. What does the lady say?"

"Oh, no," Vincent said quickly, his hand still over Roshelle's mouth, her hands over his. Her blue eyes were wide with worries and fears and thoughts of death, his death, but he would listen to that no more. "I cannot, will not, listen to what the lady says. I've suffered enough for her madness, this peculiar French madness. Fortunately for her"—his voice lowered—"I want her despite this maddening proclivity for inane beliefs and superstitions." A fierce dark gaze studied the wide frightened one and he said in a whisper, "I want her with every breath I take, and so desperately that I would know a slow and tortuous death each day of my life without her." With feeling, he demanded, "Do you hear me, Roshelle?"

She felt the sweet force of his words, drawing her to him with a promise of the dream that could not be—a dream that would become a nightmare, her nightmare. Papillion had raised her to perceive the mystery of life and its magic, and that magic had laid too many still, lifeless bodies at her feet to doubt its power again. The struggle shone in her tear-washed eyes as she weighed two very different but equally devastating types of death. "Roshelle, Roshelle,'' he whispered to her still, letting his lips drink of the sweet fragrance of her upturned face. The room quieted more reverently than with prayer as the people strained to hear what he would say to her; the drama of this scene would be told for years to come. "I will take you by force if I have to—" The emotion he put to the words brought a sharp stinging pain up his leg and spine, followed by a breathlessness and small but growing pinpoints of gray light swirling about his vision, all of which he tried desperately to ignore to tell her, "If you were to separate your soul from mine in this life—"

Roshelle could not bear it. She tore his hand from her mouth and cried, "I have lived with it, the curse! I have witnessed so many dead and slain bodies laid at my feet because of the curse—"

Vincent shook his head, grimacing with a sharp riveting pain. The room spun. For a brief moment he marveled at the spinning shapes, blurring, then darkening, and from far away he heard her call his name . . .

"Vincent!"

He fell to the floor and she fell on top of him. Wilhelm knelt at his side, too. "I need a cloth to bind this wound," he said. "And some hot water to clean it." Three guards rushed outside to do his bidding. "I daresay the duke left us here more from sleeplessness than from blood loss."

Roshelle's mind filled with the unspeakable agony of the idea that it was too late to save him. She looked up, her tear-filled blue eyes pleading with Papillion's friend, Father Herve. "Please to God, I must save him! The holy vows—"

"Vows will not save him! If indeed he needs saving. You are wrong, wrong, wrong," Father Herve said, and urgently, too, adding, "You think you must say the holy vows to break the curse and save his life, but this is wrong—"

"Mother in Heaven, you do not know what you are talking about—"

"Oh, but I do, my dear, I do. I have wanted to tell you; I thought I would before you said the vows, but, but—"

He stopped, glancing at Bruce de Borne, who had rushed to the fallen man and now, kneeling, removed his vestments. Father Herve was so shocked by the bishop's benevolence, he quite forgot what he was saying. For the bishop bundled the crimson cloth into a pillow and carefully placed the gathered material of his holy vestments under the duke's head. A man returned with a dozen rags and another with a bucket of water. Wilhelm removed a dagger and ripped the cloth from Vincent's wound, which gentle hands washed clean.

Roshelle reached for a cloth to help, first wiping her eyes so she might see, but it was no use. Still she tried. Blinded, she dipped it in the bucket and tried to wring the water out, but her hands trembled too violently. She dropped it with a distressed cry. "Dear Lord, my hands—"

A thought suddenly seized her mind; she went very still. This was meant to happen. Vincent fell so he would be stopped from preventing her from saying the vows. So she could save his life! 'Twas part of the magic, still working—

"Father Herve, please, now—"

"First you must listen to me. Please! Papillion himself would have insisted. And if you still want to say the vows when I am done telling you how I discovered there is no curse, you may—"

"Father Herve!" Bruce de Borne looked up with fury, his own thoughts traveling in much the same circle, except that instead of seeing the duke's fall as magic, he saw it as divine intervention meant to separate the girl from her fortune. For the holy church, of course. Yet now this bumbling fool would try to dissuade her! "You can believe I will give the lady her vows if you will not—"

A dagger put to his throat stopped him cold; Wilhelm was quick. Shocked gasps sounded from the wide-eyed audience. The priests held still, nervously watching the red-haired giant's threat, but all Wilhelm said was, "I want to hear this priest wipe away the lady's madness, even if the lady does not. And I believe I would be willing to shed the blood of a bishop to do so.'' Meanly, he added, ''Truth is, I would not hesitate.''

Bishop Bruce de Borne stared down at the dagger. A slight shove made him nod. The dagger was drawn away.

''All words are superficial now, save for my vows,'' Roshelle cried, her hands clasped in prayer. ''I will listen if I must, but hurry. Hurry, Father!''

Seeing the girl was listening and his superior silenced at last, Father Herve rubbed his hands together in excitement as if he were about to begin a feast. ''Well, then, I suppose I should go on. Roshelle, please, look at me. I need to see your eyes. Yes. Very well. It all began recently when a friend of mine asked me to investigate this matter of your curse, and hopefully, to find the evidence necessary to prove to you its deception. You know of whom I speak.''

Roshelle shook her head in quick negation, her eyes wide with tears and anxiety.

'' 'Twas the duke's steward, Bogo le Wyse.''

''Bogo?'' Confusion changed her face. ''But how can you know that good man?''

''As a matter of fact, I met Monsieur le Wyse many years ago at one of Papillion's lectures at the Sorbonne.''

Roshelle remembered Bogo had mentioned he had heard Papillion lecture there. ''I do not see—''

''Bogo never believed in your curse—''

''Aye, but belief does not alter its power!''

''I am not so sure. You see, when Bogo begged me to investigate, I, too, despaired of finding anything new to tell about it. I daresay more words have been put to explain the curse than any number of biblical passages these days. Yet I did manage to find Sergio's—''

''Sergio? He is long dead, I know he is dead! 'Twas Sergio's deathbed that Papillion was attending when the cardinal's soldiers arrested him, many years ago now. Sergio is dead, my Grace—''

"Yes, yes." Father Herve nodded quickly in acquiescence. "But I spoke with his wife, who is getting on in years but who remembers well the events in question. She remembers Sergio talking about that fateful night Papillion spoke the famous words of your curse. It seems Papillion had the whole thing perfectly planned out from the start. He knew of Rodez's plan to force Louis to give you in marriage to the Duke of Normandy; Papillion always had a number of spies and informants. He knew he had to do something to save you and he began devising his strategy, but now here is the point, my dear: there was no magic in his preparation. You see, Sergio's wife remembers Sergio spending several months training a dove to drop a poisoned pellet into a designated goblet."

There, he had said it. Smiling now, rocking back on his heels, Father Herve waited for her enlightenment.

Roshelle wiped her eyes as if seeing could possibly help her confusion, much less the agony of her desperateness. What was he going on about? What did that matter?

Vincent stirred with a dream and she gasped. Dear Lord, she had but minutes left before he woke and forced her away, and then he would die, like all the others, he would die—

Roshelle looked around, seizing on the nearest help. "Wilhelm! Help me. I must—"

"Listen to him, milady, listen." Strictly, he cautioned, "I do not want to have to exercise this force Vincent spoke of using."

"Do not you see, milady?" Father Herve asked, it seeming so obvious to him. "There was no magic or curse. Papillion knew words never did have the power over life; words are but vessels for ideas, no more, and poor ones at that." With an exasperated sigh at her confusion, he repeated, "Do not you see? Papillion knew better than anyone that the words of your curse were utterly meaningless unless he made it real. So he did. He had that bird drop a poisoned pellet into the Duke of

Normandy's cup.'' With emphasis, he declared, ''There was no magic to it!''

Father Herve did not think to say the rest of what the old woman had said. Apparently, Papillion had many times tried to kill Rodez as well, knowing it was the only way to keep Roshelle Marie safe from that man's revenge—alas, without success. Sergio's widow claimed her own husband's death was the result of Rodez's revenge upon surviving the last failed attempt, that Rodez poisoned Sergio and then alerted the cardinal to the presence of Papillion at his deathbed.

The black vestments blurred in Roshelle's mind as she stared up at Father Herve, so that the beautifully embroidered gold crosses in between the large gold buttons blurred in her mind, becoming a backdrop for her rapidly spinning thoughts. Papillion could have done that; he would no doubt have done anything necessary to save her from the fate of being the Duke of Normandy's wife. She had left just before Papillion had appeared, but she remembered well the story of the four gray doves landing on the goblets on the dais. The Duke of Normandy was famous for the amount of drink he could consume; no doubt he finished the contents of that drink.

What did it mean, though, if Papillion had seen to it that the Duke of Normandy drank a deadly poison to make the curse come true? Did it mean what Father Herve claimed it did, that Papillion had no faith in the power of the curse because, because it was only so many words . . . ?

Oh, Papillion . . .

''But the others? My second husband?''

''Did he not die on his way to battle, some significant amount of time after he spoke the marriage vows to you? And does not the curse specify 'men who attempt to lie with you'? It said nothing about marrying, did it? And I believe much has been made of the fact that he never, ah''—he struggled to find the delicate words to describe the act—''made the attempt, did he? 'Twas a coincidence. As was each death you choose to examine. Should I go through each one, or is it enough to point out you are not a milking maid or a cotter's hussy? Rather, you are a revered lady of the French court, and there are grave consequences to harming or violating your person, are there not? One cannot assault you with impunity, my dear. It stands to reason most if not all"—he emphasized these words—"who dared would meet a violent end.

"Yet the point is, the only point to think of is that Papillion himself did not believe in the power of the curse. He only meant to save you from a particular unpleasant fate as wife to that godless man. And listen to me, my dear! I know Papillion never meant you—of all people!— to say the holy vows. I know he never meant to keep you from a life of love and happiness."

Timidly, afraid of finding a flaw in his logic, she let herself consider the idea that the curse was little more than empty words, Papillion's clever trick to save her from her first marriage only. Her thoughts traveled over each and every death and mishap attributed to the curse, as they had so many times before, except now with the light of a much harsher scrutiny: Edward might have been drunk and fallen; Vincent might have saved her from those five awful brigands for no more rhyme or reason than to provide a knightly, noble answer to a maid's screams sounding through a dark night. She supposed it could just all be a terrible coincidence . . .

Yet the last time Vincent had almost convinced her the curse was nothing but words an assassin's arrow had pierced his head and side, and then just as the man tried to rape her, Wilhelm had killed him. Struck him dead. Would the same thing have happened without the curse?

A difficult question. It was possible, she supposed. Rodez had sent the assassin and Wilhelm had been worried over the sighting of it. Wilhelm might have been out in the forest to rescue her and Vincent. It was possible, she supposed . . .

As she struggled with all her heart and mind to believe

this, she slipped her hand into Vincent's. Even in his unconscious state he clung to it as to a lifeline. She wanted
to believe it was true, that there never was a curse; she
wanted it more than anything in this world.

The people around her held very still, afraid to breathe
as they waited and watched the effect of Father Herve's
words on the lady.

" 'Tis just so hard to believe after witnessing death at
every turn and—"

"And yet your vision has been shaped by your belief in
the curse." When the doubt remained in her eyes, he hastily added, "My dear lady, reflect! Think, my lady, this
was exactly what Papillion hoped to have happened. Until
now."

It was true that Vincent had made love to her. He had
carefully drawn her heart and soul from the physical confinement of the world to send her spinning through heaven.
Heaven. And he was still alive. She had not said the vows
yet and he was alive. Her blue eyes found the still and
sleeping face she loved . . .

In a rich, compelling voice Father Herve said what he
knew was true. "Papillion only meant to keep you safe
until the moment you gave your heart and love to a man,
to this man. Because, Roshelle Marie, love—your love!—
is more powerful and real than any words could ever be.
Is that not true, Roshelle?"

It was true, and she felt it physically. As she knelt on
the sunlit floor of the chapel staring down at him as he
slept, she felt the miracle of her love cascading over her
like a glorious light from heaven, and it was indeed
more powerful and real than anything else on earth. She
took his large warm hand in hers again and she buried
her face there, kissing it again and again, letting the
warm avalanche of emotions wash over her with a sudden burst of a thing she had not felt in a very long time.
Hope.

Forever, Roshelle, forever . . .

Roshelle's hand in his brought a familiar dream spinning

vividly through his mind. The dream of the white tower. Roshelle was calling to him from far away, atop the tower made of white stone. He felt the familiar surge of desperation to take her away in his arms and carry her back to the solid foundation of earth, to hold her slim softness to him and take her lips. He began climbing and climbing, climbing until his muscles ached and perspiration drenched him, until he felt his next breath to be his last, but then, then suddenly he reached the top and saw her there.

She looked more beautiful than words: shrouded in white cloth from head to toe. Yet for a moment he panicked. He could not lose her to this madness. To never taste the sunshine of her mouth or drink in the perfume of her skin again, to never see her blue eyes darkening with passion or hear the sound of love from her lips again. A death indeed, and he felt desperate to stop it . . .

Yet the familiar dream changed. No cloth covered her head. The long rope of her hair dropped over her shoulder and fell on his waist, coiling in a pile of rich russet silk, and while there were tears in the blue pools, there was also joy.

Her hand rested softly in his.

The sweet lyrics of her voice pulled him back to the world and he woke, opening his eyes to see her lovely face. Roshelle's joy was a marvel to him; the emotions it evoked in his heart made him know he was not dreaming. "Roshelle, my love . . ." He reached a tender hand to her face and she closed her eyes, savoring the feel of his smooth fingertips on her skin.

"I have said the vows. The marriage vows. You must say yes now. To make me your wife."

"Yes," he said, "yes. I love you, forever, Roshelle, forever . . ."

The softly spoken vows were blessed and the promise was sealed forever as Roshelle Marie laid trembling lips to his. A promise of forever starting with this moment.

No words could ever express the emotion shimmering in her blue eyes as at last they closed over a curse of a thousand tears and then opened to his promise of forever . . .

Epilogue

"**B**eg me, Roshelle."

"Beg you?" she screamed in protest, squirming for all she was worth, but with his large strong hands under her arms, he held her over the frigid cold waters with a shocking ease. In desperation she socked his forearms as best she could, but she might as well have hit the trunk of an oak tree for all the effect. "Never, never! You can go to Hades with a banner—"

Vincent lowered her. Her bare feet touched the water. She screamed again as a jolt of shivers raced up her spine, but her eyes were bright with excitement. "My dress, my dress!" One of her favorites, yellow-and-cream cotton, for the harvest-day feast tonight. " 'Twill take two hours to get warm. If you do, I will, I will—"

"Yes?" An interested brow rose, and he watched her expression change from outrage to helplessness and back again, making him laugh.

She deserved it, God knew, she deserved it.

Yet Vincent's gaze returned to the low bodice that seemed much too tight, as if her dressmaker had made a mistake of two or three meaningful inches. A maddening tease. He could hardly concentrate on his task, much less on the escalation of her threats . . .

After a long, hard search, he had caught her in the midst of the forest as she searched out roots and herbs for her medicines. Yet she had already dressed for the feast. All the better. A yellow ribbon held her long hair back, while a whimsical array of daisies crowned her head, falling now with her frantic effort to escape. He knew that dress, too; it was one of his favorites, yet it had never looked quite that . . . small. Mason's dishes must finally be having an effect and, dear Lord, what an effect . . .

He felt his loins fill with heat and he chuckled; one way or another, he'd have her pay. His heart might be heavy with the weight and bounty of his love, but it always manifested itself physically. At any given time he had only to draw upon hundreds of memories of the girl to feel it and in force: the time the villagers had solicited his help to remove a gypsy camp from Suffolk, through which he'd learned Roshelle had been there all day, finding her as she danced around the gypsy campfire like a heathen princess; the time he had found Roshelle hiding in the forest, crying so softly that sad day her medicines had failed to save a village child from the ravages of a flux; the night on Michaelmas when, at church, she had sung a song written and sent to her by Father Herve, a hauntingly beautiful song about lost love, a simple girl Joan and Papillion; the joy and pride on her face the day she, with bloodied hands and filthy skirts, had single-handedly saved her horse and pulled the breached colt from its womb.

Forever, Roshelle, forever . . .

He watched as her blue eyes danced with laughter and gaiety yet, as he dipped her feet again, filled with fear and outrage. "I will never forgive you!"

"Not good enough, love. I did warn you, did I not?"

For a brief moment the memory of last night's lovemaking made her breath catch. She had led him on a merry lover's chase through Gregory Castle, then out into the moonlit night, past the dark lawns and pastures to the bank of the lake, where, after she tossed a branch into the lake, she hid in the nearby bushes. He ran to the lake's edge, and spotting the dark moving object in the water, laughing with anticipation, he tore his clothes off and dove in.

Only to discover his mistake at the exact moment he heard her wild peals of laughter as she ran away, heading back to the castle. Wet, cold, in a maelstrom of ire and rage and laughter all mixed together, he seemed to have his revenge as he finally laid her to the bed. Or so she thought. The maddening tease of his lips, the skilled sweep of his hands, were so deceptively sweet and tender and gentle, yet he purposely, maliciously, kept her at the very edge of ecstasy, waiting until she said his name over and over . . .

He dipped her feet again, laughing when she screamed. "Pride goeth before the fall," he said.

He would, he really would. "All right, all right! I beg you . . . I beg you—"

He imagined that bodice wet and he said, "Still not good enough."

"Not good enough?"

"Any last words?"

"Wait! Wait!" she managed breathlessly through her laughter, amazed at the ease of his strength and scared he would, he really would. "Oh, please, my Grace—"

He started counting, or tried to through his laughter.

Desperate, she played her last card. "What if, what if . . ."

"Yes?"

"What if I told you I am . . . Oh, Vincent, I am with your child . . ."

His changed expression would live in her mind forever, and he whispered, "What?"

Her blue eyes grew serious and she nodded.

Quite suddenly everything changed. He pulled her safely to the dock at once, yet he drew her slender shape against his. The long auburn hair slid over the arms that held her, while her hands lay gently against his upper arms as she stared into the eyes that she loved. She felt the tight intake of breath in his chest as he urged in a husky whisper, "Do not tease me about this, Roshelle."

She shook her head, then watched the curious effect of her announcement. His joy burst with laughter as he swung her around and around, her skirts lifting in a pretty circle with the spin. He lowered her feet gently to the ground as he leaned over and kissed her.

"I love you, Roshelle, forever . . ."

She heard her name the instant before his lips claimed her. Not a gentle kiss either. A kiss filled with all the passion and fierceness of his love, the promise he made her for the rest of their lives. A promise she returned. Her hands slid around his neck, her fingers slid over the tousled mass of dark hair as she gave him the warm sweetness of her mouth . . .

Even as Roshelle stared at the changing color of the lake from atop her horse, a hand lifted from the reins to touch her mouth as she remembered that kiss and the fierceness of his passion released in their lovemaking on the water's edge beneath a thousand stars. The day she had told him . . .

Well, that was then and this was now.

This was war!

She stared without seeing the darkening colors of the lake water. The only difference the good people of Suffolk noticed between the early autumn days and the summer days that preceded was the colors, a gradual darkening of the forest green and the lawns surrounding Gregory Castle. During the long, lazy days of summer women met to wash at the lakeside, exchanging pleasantries and gossip, advice and complaints, while their children fished or raced ingeniously carved wooden boats or, on particularly hot days, managed to brave swimming these cold, icy waters, and the lake always appeared like a clear glass bowl, tinted a lovely blue-green by the surrounding forest and blue sky. Then during these first days of the changing season, the deep waters of the lake seemed to exchange, day by day, the blue for the green, as if swallowing up the last of the sunlight to save for the winter months ahead. The sun on the mountains deepened, too, from the yellow-gold of a young maid's hair to the richer burnt gold of an old woman's jewel box. The peasants often said the wind was the last to know of the changing season, for autumn always brought a warm desertlike wind off the lakeshore.

Roshelle turned Etoile into this wind, and kicked her into a gallop. She rode at a breakneck speed around the lake and into the forest woods, as if the speed of her flight could ease the disquiet of her emotions. She felt furious. One day before their son's christening and he was adamant. "I am resolute, Roshelle . . ."

Yet so was she!

Horse and rider emerged from the forest onto southwest lawns, and instantly Roshelle reined Etoile to a quick stop. Not wanting to stop, the horse lifted high in the air, fighting the bit before turning in quick, agitated circles. Roshelle almost lost her seat as the glory of the garden blinded her with a riot of its color in a second summer bloom.

"The second bloom of the rose is always the most magnificent," Papillion had said. "Until the third summer bloom . . ."

"Dear Joan," she whispered in awe, "if you could see it now."

It looked only like a rose garden from where she sat atop her horse. The artistic arrangement had meaning only when viewed from Gregory Castle's solar rooms high above. The duke had ordered dozens of plants from all over England, and roses had arrived in every color and shade imaginable. Henry himself made a gift of dozens. These cuttings had been planted in a loose form of swirls and swirls of breathtaking color that created a giant rose blossom when viewed from atop Gregory Castle in the solar chambers. Then, planted in the very center of the creation, another, smaller blossom bloomed, made of white flowers, and in the very center of this grew a red blossom.

"The white rose for your namesake, the red for your love. Love that blooms in the very center of my heart . . ."

Renewed fury brightened the Duchess of Suffolk's cheeks as she remembered these honeyed words and placed them alongside those just spoken to her husband hours ago. When he had announced easily, as if it had no consequence whatsoever: "The papers are already signed."

"I beg your pardon, milord! I signed nothing."

"Your signature is not necessary, madame."

"But in France—"

"I would remind you that your lovely feet stand on the merry shores of England now."

She had looked at Bogo for confirmation. Bogo was her fiercest adversary in their frequent debates and arguments, but at the same time, she knew whom to count on in a pinch. This was a good deal more than a pinch. Yet that good man had nodded reluctantly. She had turned back to her husband. "So it is true—you do not need my signature! Well, then, you shall have to change it for me."

"Roshelle," he said in that voice, "I am resolute. You will soon grow accustomed to it—"

"Never! Never! I would remind you that I am French—"

"Through no fault of your own, sweetling. I manage not to hold it against you—"

That did it. She spun on her heels and stormed out. Unmindful of her waiting women, or of the continuous stream of guests arriving each hour at Gregory Castle or, indeed, of the rumor that put Henry himself only miles away; unmindful of what all this entailed—the idea that she should be getting dressed, minding the servants and attending to a thousand and one details of the feast tonight—she stormed out.

Tomorrow was the day. The image of her son's tiny face emerged in her mind; she felt a synchronous leap of her heart and she turned toward Gregory Castle, where he slept, Cisely watching over him. Somehow, some way, she must change his father's mind before tomorrow. "For you," she vowed with all the love she felt for the boy, "for you I will not let him win this!"

Roshelle kicked the horse's side. Etoile neighed, as if in complete agreement, which because of the horse's nationality she did not doubt. Feeling the loosened reins, her mistress's weight as she leaned forward for flight, the spirited creature leaped into a lightning gallop toward home.

From Gregory Castle, an interested gaze peered from the alcove window overlooking the lawns on which the horse and rider flew like the wind. A surprised brow lifted. The girl appeared like a blur of blue velvet. The mane of the spirited horse matched perfectly the girl's hair, and as mane and hair were entwined like a banner with the speed of flight, horse and rider looked like one.

A wild creature of enchantment.

His breath caught as the girl reined in the creature hard, and before the horse even stopped, slippered feet slipped to the gravel courtyard. Few men could manage that trick. A groom rushed up to take the reins. Her women waited anxiously at the grand doors to the entrance hall, bursting out in a flurry of pretty colors made by their gowns, greeting the duchess with excited admonishments and how fare thees and the news that "he is still asleep, milady."

"Still! He sleeps still—"

"Come and see . . ."

The girl in blue velvet followed her women through the doors below. Smiling, the man returned to the tall-backed chair before the long, austere desk of the Duke of Suffolk. Plain brown suede boots came to the tabletop. He leaned back, hands holding his head, savoring the precious few moments of privacy.

Within minutes footsteps sounded outside the doors.

"Milady, you will not believe—"

"Please do not bother me with another title or name, there are so many spinning through my head now." Half of England had arrived for her son's christening, it seemed, which was the root of her trouble. "I must be alone to think. Cisely will tell me when he wakes. That is all."

"But, milady—"

"Please, please, leave me be."

"Very well, milady."

With a slight creak, the door opened. There she stood. Unaware of another's presence, she pushed the door shut and lowered the latch. Leaning against the door, she closed her eyes.

Vince, you devil, the stranger thought as he almost laughed out loud, observing the famous girl up close. The duke's steward, Bogo le Wyse, had said Lady Roshelle Marie was indeed a fair and pretty maid, and Louis, of course, had agreed in a flurry of French superlatives, and still he had not expected this. Thick dark lashes brushed against flushed cheeks; thin brows arched with dramatic influence over her closed blue eyes. Delicate lines drew the comely face. Dark red lips made a hard line, as if she were troubled by something. The long russet mass of hair tumbled in chaotic disarray around her slender shoulders and down her back, falling in silken streams over the bodice of her gown. The ample curves of her breasts strained against her gown, and yet that was the only sign she had just a month ago given birth to a healthy, bonny young boy, the young Viscount of Suffolk, heir to Gregory Castle and the Suffolk lands beyond.

Roshelle always came to this room to think and read. While Gregory Castle was every bit as grand as Vincent had told her those sad days back in Reales, more even, and each of the countless rooms was lovely, decorated with sunlight and gay, festive colors, none was as lovely as this room. Large and spacious, in the shape of a rectangle with a huge stone hearth and tall, wide windows looking out on the lawns and the pastures and the lake beyond, this room had the distinction of housing most of Suffolk's hundreds of precious manuscripts. The Duke of Suffolk paid three scribes annually to copy and illustrate manuscripts. Piles of scrolls and leather-bound copies of famous works sat in the dark wood, gold-trimmed and glass cases against one wall; the illuminated manuscripts lined another whole wall. She had only read twenty-nine so far; she had the rest of her life to read the next two hundred. Expensive Persian rugs kept the room warm, and Vincent had his mother's famous tapestries in here, perhaps the most beautiful items of all.

Roshelle's favorite hung on the opposite wall: done in rich blues and greens and grays, it depicted the mythical unicorn standing in a light fog, staring off at its observers with sad, wild eyes. Papillion would have treasured the work of art; he would have claimed its creator had been touched by the great mystery of life. It was Vincent's favorite, too, and as she stared at the haunting sadness in the creature's doleful eyes, she wondered how Vincent could love her so, and yet do this to her.

Her son, her son. She closed her eyes and her mind produced a vivid picture of her son's plump face, rosy cheeks and impressive, hawklike nose—yes, one saw this distinguishing feature already—all in all, a perfect little replica of his father, except for the bright blue eyes, beautiful eyes that were so like Papillion's. The image brought a swell of emotion through her, and with the emotion came her desperation.

She began pacing in front of the cold ashes in the hearth. "He cannot! He cannot," she cried out loud in her distress, stopping, turning again. "Dear Lord, help me . . . help me . . ."

A brow rose, a smile followed. "Madame, pray tell—"

Roshelle jumped visibly and her hands flew to her heart.

"A thousand pardons, milady. I did not mean to startle you!"

"I thought I was alone."

"I fear I could not help but overhear your distress. Pray tell, madame, what is amiss?"

Her blue eyes studied the strange man. She tried to place him at the holy feast last night but could not. "Beg pardon, sir, do I know you?"

"Methinks not."

Her blue eyes stared in turn. A rugged, not unhandsome face stared back. He had piercing black eyes, a fine large nose and wide lips, curving with the suggestion of a smile, all set on a round yet distinguished face. He wore richly made but common clothes, no coat of arms on his plain tunic or spurs on his boots. Despite his boldness in taking the duke's favorite chair, she assumed he must be one of their landed guests' stewards or perhaps just a valet, and with that she dismissed him as inconsequential.

"Perhaps I can help?"

She shook her head, her thoughts returning in force to her dilemma. "I think not. Unless you have a cure for stubbornness?"

"And whose would that be?"

"My husband, that's who!"

"Ah." The man's eyes filled with amusement. "I know it well. He is indeed famous for it."

"Aye," she agreed, supposing all the world was familiar with the fault. "Not only is it the cause of my present despair, but it shall be the cause of my lifelong unhappiness if I do not find a cure for it."

He, too, had felt considerable grief from this very fault of the lady's husband and said with a sympathetic sigh, "I fear I know no cure, milady."

"Aye, I did not think you did."

"Well, but tell me, what has the wretched man done now?"

She waved her hand in agitation, and seemed to be speaking as much to herself as she was to him. "He has threatened to do something to my son that will cause me great pain. And as I said, not just a passing pain," she assured him, shaking her head as she resumed pacing. "But rather a pain and an insult I shall have to endure my whole life long!"

"Yes? And what could this grievous insult be?"

The man appeared sympathetically alarmed, and with feeling, she told him in a high melodic French voice: "He has signed the church's baptismal records and christened our son with the name, the name of his king!" She flushed with a fresh rush of emotion just thinking about it. "Oh, 'tis too awful to contemplate. He has named him Henry, in honor of Henry, the King of England!"

The man blanched upon hearing this apparent horror. "Dear Lord . . ."

Roshelle misunderstood his response. "I suppose you do not see this insult as so bad, since you are obviously English. Like my husband. No doubt you feel, as all Englishmen do, that the only thing better than Henry is God and heaven!" Her impassioned voice rose with anguish and she clenched her fists. "Yet my husband has completely ignored the fact that I am French. French, and not only am I French, but I have lived in that poor country all my life. I have lived through Henry's army's purges and plunderings and wars. I have seen my people fall victim to his ungodly quest for the French throne, and so perhaps you can imagine how I will feel if I have to call my son that name! Dear Lord, I can hardly pronounce 'Henry' without cursing in the same breath—"

The man suddenly tilted back in the chair with a roar of laughter and Roshelle stopped instantly, turning to him with a start. Confusion lifted on her face as he continued to laugh; indeed, for a long minute it seemed he could not stop. Irritation replaced her confusion. "I fail to see anything amusing in my dilemma, sir!"

"No, no, I beg your pardon, madame." He wiped his eyes, his chest bouncing still, though he managed to quiet the roar. "Of course not. There is nothing amusing about a young mother cursing her firstborn son every time she calls his name." Yet the thought made him laugh again and he swore, "Oh, heaven help me here . . ."

"Heaven help you?" She looked confused, then, returning to the problem, added with feeling, "I am the one in need of heavenly intervention."

"Is your husband quite adamant?"

"Aye. He has already signed the papers. Dear Lord, what am I to do? What can I do?"

The question remained unanswered for several long minutes. Perhaps she could change Vincent's mind if she discovered a worthy alternative. 'Twas a small chance, granted, but it seemed the only hope. The name would

have to be English, of course, for Vincent's surname was
French and he felt that was quite enough honor to his
mother's country of origin. So! There was the name Oliver
or Richard or George or John or Calvin or Peter, but, dear
Lord, a distressed hand went to her forehead, she did not
like any of those names.

Yet she would choose any one of them over the dreadful
name Henry!

The man stared off at the tapestry as he turned the dilemma around in his head. He had more than one reason
for helping the lady. Yet how could he? How could he
change her mind about the famous English name Henry?

It came to him all of a sudden. He slammed his fist
against the tabletop, struck as he was by an inspiration.
"I have it! By God, I have it! Milady, being somewhat of
a history buff, I happen to know that one of the first kings
of your beloved country was also named Henry, was he
not?"

Her blue eyes focused on him instantly.

"And was he not a valiant, brave and just king, too?"

"Aye," she said slowly. "Aye, he was." She nodded.
"Many knowledgeable people think he was our best and
greatest king. Papillion did. I have been told the history
of his campaigns many times and, why, why—"

The name echoed in her mind. Henry the First of
France, Henry the First of France! She stopped, her hands
going to her cheeks as she considered the name in this
new light. 'Twas perfect! Her son did not have to be named
after the King of England just because he was christened
Henry; he could easily be called after Henry of France!
And "Henry" was a goodly, strong and noble name for a
boy . . .

"Would it work, madame? Could you not think of
Henry the First of France when you call your son, while
your husband thinks of another namesake?"

Roshelle's smile grew, a happy light filling her eyes.
"Why, I could. Henry of France. Henry." She repeated
the name, clasping her hands together and turning to him

with all her great excitement. "Why did I not think of this? I believe it is a perfect solution. I could even come to like the name Henry if I thought of it that French way. Why, 'Henry' is a goodly, just and strong name for a boy and, and now that I think of it, I believe my boy does look like a little Henry!" She laughed with pleasure and gratitude. *"Merci,* monsieur! *Merci!* I am indebted to you and so grateful!"

The man grinned at having served the duchess so well. Roshelle noticed for the first time the merry sparkle in his gaze: eyes, she saw suddenly, that were shrewd and clever and not so simple, really . . .

She was suddenly curious. "I shall tell your master of my gratitude."

"In heaven, then."

"Pardon?"

"Oh, nothing, nothing."

"Well, what party are you with, good sir?"

"Oh, madame, I do hesitate to say."

"Yes? Why?"

"I fear I am with the king's party, madame."

Her blue eyes widened with alarm but the man hastened to assure her. "Please do not be alarmed, madame, for the secret of your dilemma is quite safe with me."

She trusted him, without knowing why; she felt certain her confidence was safe with this man. "Dear me." She thought of her dress, all the things yet to be done in preparation of meeting Henry at last, of wanting so to make a good impression, despite her animosity. For she wanted to speak with him. If she could just have a moment or two alone, if that were somehow possible, then perhaps she could plead her case for France and convince him, somehow, to give up his foolish quest. A grand notion, but then she would always believe in the magic and miracles of the great mystery of life.

Her thoughts traveled in these circles, and she turned back to the man to ask, "The king's party has arrived already?"

"Well, no. Not yet. My stallion was a bit feisty and so I raced on ahead."

"Your stallion?" She looked doubtfully at his clothes. "You are not, why, you are not one of the king's knights?"

"In a manner of speaking . . ."

"Well, do you know the king?"

"Aye, that I do."

She turned away, musing. "My husband has made me swear not to bother him with my pleas for my country's people, and though I agreed, I had my fingers crossed. For I must speak to him—"

"Oh?" He was interested in this. "And what is it you would say to the man?"

"Nothing to the man, but I fear quite a lot to the king. I would beg him to reconsider his quest for the crown of France, of course, and though it is no doubt a foolish prayer, I would do this by presenting the reasoning that England herself would be so much better off if he would consider signing a treaty with Charles, a peace treaty, one that binds our two countries together and leads to the prosperity of both. You see, once there is peace, there can be trade again. Papillion always said that the measure of a country's well-being is the weight of its merchants' purses, and if he just thought about it in this light, the king might see how much the merchants on both sides of the Channel would benefit, and therefore the populace. France needs English textiles, armaments and foodstuffs, and naturally, such a treaty would open up trade routes for England through Switzerland, the Holy Roman Empire and Italy as well. England, as you might know, would benefit from our mills and wine and timber from our forests, and I have been thinking that such a treaty might be predicated on, well, on his marriage—"

"The king's marriage?"

The man appeared startled by the idea, then amused, and Roshelle quickly added, "Well, but you see, Henry does need to be married, does he not?"

"Indeed. I happen to know he gives the very question much thought."

"I believe it. He is not getting any younger and he still has not chosen. Of course, the King of England can only marry a princess of impeccable royal lineage, and how many are there in our world?"

Roshelle went on to answer the question, describing each living princess before dismissing each for her damning faults: age, vanity, piety, ugliness as well as various inescapable political liabilities. The man had heard the exact list many times before; he was impressed with her judgment.

"So," she concluded, "as anyone might see, that leaves only one princess, and fortunately for the king, she is intelligent and pious, charming and good. If she suffers any fault at all, I am sure I do not know it, and I know her quite well."

"Yes, yes? Who is this virtuous lady you would have as queen?"

"Why, Catherine of Valois, of course. I could not but help think that, as the daughter of the king, Charles the Sixth, and half sister to the Dauphin, Catherine of Valois would be such a fine queen, a queen of England God Himself would surely smile on—"

A light knock sounded at the door. Failing to notice the curious effect of her speech on her audience, Roshelle motioned to a servant to answer the knock before she realized there were no servants here. Not if this man was a knight.

She rushed to the door.

The door opened. Roshelle looked with surprise at the group of men. Dressed in a fine black-and-gold doublet, Vincent stepped in first, staring with some alarm at finding Roshelle in the room. His Majesty's steward, Lord Albert, followed, then his head archer, Sir John, and two lords and chancellors, Richard of Avingdon and William of Wykeham.

"Your Majesty . . ."

Alarmed that she had yet to don a proper dress or even a caul, she searched the group for the man who would be Henry of England. Yet all gazes went to Vincent's table as heads bowed respectfully, including her husband's.

Roshelle suffered a moment's confusion. A very long moment of confusion. Yet there was no escaping the humor on the man's face. It announced both his name and his exalted title. Her blue eyes widened dramatically, and she gasped. Vincent looked from Roshelle to Henry and back gain, alarmed by the look of horror on Roshelle's face.

He started to introduce Roshelle when Henry erupted into laughter again.

Roshelle closed her eyes and begged for divine intervention as she dropped to a deep curtsy. "Your Majesty, I . . . I—'' Her blue eyes lifted briefly, lowering quickly. "I hardly know what to say, how to even begin my apology. Oh, God of mercy, when I think of what I said, of all I said—''

"There's no need to apologize and please, call me my Christian title . . . that is, if you can manage to do so without cursing."

Vincent stared down at Roshelle, not knowing what she had said to the King of England and wishing he would never know. He sighed, then asked, "Why do I have the distinct feeling this is something I am going to hear about for years?"

"Decades." Henry still laughed. "Decades. I must congratulate you, Vincent. I know of only one person in all of England able to be so startlingly frank with me, and believe me, the lady's uncensored speech is as refreshing as a cold dip in frigid waters."

While Vincent glared at Roshelle, the men chuckled nervously, and only because Henry laughed so loudly. "And then adding to the lady's obvious unmatched beauty and charm is a most unexpected wisdom as well as perspicuity of counsel. As a matter of fact, she has just presented me with a most arresting idea.''

The men looked stunned, waiting to hear of it. Roshelle crossed her fingers. Again. Dear Lord, he had listened. The King of England had listened to her speech. He was not angry. Not only had she amused the King of England with her grandiose monologue, but he had heard her concerns.

''Yes.'' Vincent was very interested. ''And just what counsel did my dear wife give you, your Majesty?''

''Lady Roshelle has just recommended none other than Princess Catherine of Valois as a possible candidate for queen. For the life of me, I do not know why my counselors and bishops had not thought of the virtuous lady before!''

The men exchanged glances of disbelief. Lord Albert stepped forward. ''I believe, sire,'' the steward said with the barest hint of sarcasm, ''that the reason you have not heard that woman's name mentioned before has much to do with the war between our two countries.''

King Henry of England had never been interested in the numerous obstacles to his course of action and he dismissed these with a wave of his hand. ''Small objections, all in all. Certainly we should write to the good lady and see her response. She is a princess, and such a match, I believe, would no doubt please not just God but the merchants and—''

''The merchants, sire!''

The King of England smiled at Roshelle. ''As I am sure you all know, the measure of a country's well-being is the weight of its merchants' purses—''

The roomful of men burst into an excited, heated debate of the merits of this plan and Vincent turned to a wide-eyed Roshelle. Another memory to add to hundreds of hundreds of others: Roshelle's historic first meeting with his king. Trying without much success to

control his laughter, he leaned over to kiss her forehead.

"Forever, Roshelle, forever . . ."

A promise she would see that he kept, just as soon
as . . . "I must see to our little Henry . . ."

Now that you've enjoyed
Jennifer Horsman's
AWAKEN MY FIRE,
sample another of Avon Books'
Romantic Treasures—
FIRE AT MIDNIGHT
by Barbara Dawson Smith

*Lord Kit Coleridge is known throughout London
society as a dissolute rake, but a ghastly murder in
his home during a New Year's Eve party quickly so-
bers him up . . . especially when he meets Norah
Rutherford, the murdered man's beautiful widow . . .*

A sound pierced the ice. A distant knocking. Then
voices, coming closer. Footsteps.

He opened his bleary eyes. Reality struck. He was
slouched in the wing chair, his legs extended toward
the dead ashes in the grate. Watery sunlight poured
through the slit in the draperies.

Damn, but he was chilled to the bone. He lifted
his head and felt a beastly crick in his neck. The
mantelpiece clock drew his gaze. Jesus God. Who
would call at six-forty in the morning?

Before he could rise, the library doors opened. A

footman marched in, a black cloak over his arm. Half hidden behind him glided a woman.

"M'lord!" exclaimed Herriot, his cheeks reddening, his brown eyes as round as the gold crested buttons on his livery. "I'm sorry, most awfully sorry. Didn't know you was in here. The lady, she was most insistent on seein' you. I . . . I'll show her elsewhere until your lordship be ready." He started to back out, almost colliding with the caller.

As if she hadn't heard, the veiled woman came into the library, her slender figure clad in unrelieved black.

Standing up, Kit plowed his hand through his hair and stepped into his shoes. He felt cold and rumpled and churlish. "If you'll excuse me," he said to her as he started toward the door, "I'll join you in a few moments."

"No. I will speak to you immediately."

The ragged edge to her voice caught his attention. He stopped. To Herriot, he said, "Send Betsy to light the fire. It's freezing in here."

"Aye, m'lord." The servant bowed and dashed out.

The woman hovered near the doorway. She wore black suede gloves and fingered her only adornment, the brooch pinned at her throat, an exquisite knot of seed pearls set in onyx. The high-collared gown fell to a straight skirt with a modest bustle, and seemed designed to disguise the womanly curves of her hips and waist.

She lifted the veil and drew it back. His chest clenched and his weariness slid away.

The filtered dawn light gave her skin the translucence of a cameo. Her fine cheekbones bore a natural winter-kissed flush more lovely than any color out of a pot. Beneath a black ribboned fedora, her curly red hair was scraped into a topknot, as if she were determined to tame its sensual beauty into ladylike neatness.

Kit gaped like a schoolboy at a sweetshop window. Heat banished the chill from him. He wanted to undress her. He wanted to see her titian waves cascading around her slim white body.

He formed the most charming smile he could manage, given his unshaven state. "I don't believe we've met. I'm Christopher Coleridge. My friends call me Kit."

She raised one auburn eyebrow. Fingers fixed at her sides, she came closer and stopped a few feet from him. Her long-lashed green eyes perused him with relentless intensity. She viewed him with the cool distaste one might afford a poisonous snake.

My name is Norah Rutherford," she said. "I came to see where my husband was murdered."

Clinging to the frayed threads of her composure, Norah tasted the bitter satisfaction of catching the marquis off guard. His smile faded, though the set of his mouth retained its naturally wicked slant. Hands at his hips, he regarded her with a boldness that confirmed his notorious reputation.

She had expected a libertine. He hadn't disappointed her. The image of a self-indulgent aristocrat after a long night of debuachery, he stood coatless, his collar hanging open. Black hairs curled at the unbuttoned top of his shirt. Fine lines of weariness bracketed his mouth and eyes. An unshaven shadow hugged the teak-hard contours of his jaw and cheeks.

Yet even in his unkempt condition, Lord Christopher Coleridge commanded attention. His rugged masculinity and tousled onyx hair oddly reminded her of the promise of perfection in an uncut gem. He had tiger's eyes, dark and direct and dangerous.

She had heard rumors of his wild parties, whispers of his gambling and womanizing. No true lady considered him proper company, especially unchaperoned. But today, shock and disbelief had overpowered her scruples.

"Please sit down, Mrs. Rutherford." Coming closer, he extended a bronzed hand.

Panic constricted her chest. She stepped out of his reach. By custom she should curtsy, but her pride rebelled at paying homage to a man who preyed upon weak women. "Thank you, but I prefer to stand. This is hardly a social call."

"Of course. I sincerely regret the unfortunate circumstance that brings you here."

His sympathy, the very gentleness of his tone fired the icy void in her heart. She disliked platitudes, especially from this philanderer. "My husband's death was more than mere misfortune. According to Inspector Wadding, it was murder."

He paused in the act of donning his formal coat. "Yes. I had intended to call on you today and offer my condolences."

"Never mind that. I would rather you tell me exactly what happened."

"I doubt I can add anything to what the inspector already said to you." His voice lowered. "But please know, Mrs. Rutherford, that I hold myself accountable. If I can atone by helping you and your children in any way . . ."

Untimely tears prickled at the back of her throat. Norah swallowed her secret sorrow and looked at the soiled glassware littering a side table. She felt as used and empty as those vessels. "Maurice and I were never blessed with children."

"I'd be happy to help you make any arrangements," the marquis went on softly. "I'll notify your acquaintances, or do whatever else I can to make this tragedy more bearable for you."

His persistent kindness nearly undid her. She held tightly to her control and reminded herself that his sympathy rang false. He only wanted to unburden himself of guilt. "If you truly wish to be of service, your lordship, you may start by showing me where my husband died."

Frowning, he cocked his head. "There's nothing to see. My servants have tidied up."

"Nevertheless, you'll show me upstairs now."

She pivoted toward the hall. "Or I shall find the way myself."

He stood still, a predator garbed in the finely tailored suit of a gentleman. In a flash of black humor, she guessed this was the most unorthodox reason a woman had ever used to get herself into his bedroom.

Shrugging, he motioned to the door. "Since you insist."

They went out into the lofty hall and up a staircase so grand ten people abreast could ascend its marble glory. A fog of unreality swathed Norah. The tap of her footsteps mingled with the heavier echo of Kit Coleridge's shoes on the marble steps. She glanced sideways at him. Thoughtful absorption firmed his exotic dark features. He exuded an aura of banked energy, his vitality and strength evident in his springing steps. Her own limbs felt as dead and stiff as coral, and so brittle they might shatter with the slightest handling.

He opened the door at the end of the upstairs passage and ushered her inside. Fabrics in the rich hue of Siberian jade lent the bedroom a surprisingly cheery comfort. Silver-framed photographs decorated the tabletops. Her numbed senses registered the warmth of the fire and the faint masculine aromas of shaving soap and earthy musk.

She paused, aware of Lord Blackthorne standing silently behind her. She had expected something murky and foreign and cavelike, the lair of a tiger. From nowhere came the image of him luring a woman here, charming her with the mesmeric music of his voice, enticing her with the hypnotic luster of his eyes, and then pouncing, stroking, overpowering her . . .

Norah forced down a shudder and walked to the foot of the bed. Pale sunbeams trickled through the windows, slid past the silk hangings, and pooled on the plush bower within. The pillows were plumped, the ivory linens smooth with the sheen of satin, the goosedown coverlet thick and inviting. A place to sit and read. A place to cuddle on a cold night.

A place to die.

She groped within herself for grief, but found only a dreamlike void, as if her soul had separated from her body. As if she hovered above the well-appointed room and looked down at the woman standing by the empty bed, her face bleached of color against the jet-black of her gown, her fingers twined together. She fancied herself a painting on display at the Royal Academy: *Young Widow Faces Tragedy*.

Beside a vase of hothouse calla lilies on the nightstand, metal glinted. Her heart took a tumble and brought her crashing back to earth. On stiff legs, she went to examine the object. The fluted gold match case was topped by a lustrous pearl set in a bed of rose diamonds.

"What's the matter?" asked Kit Coleridge, from behind her.

"It's Maurice's matchbox," she whispered. "The one I gave him for Christmas."

Kit picked up the small piece and examined it, the gold bright in his topaz-brown hands. "It must have fallen from his pocket. The maid probably found it when she was tidying up." His gaze lifted to Norah. "May I take it? The police may consider it a clue."

"Of course."

As he went to put it on a side table, she stood immobile by the bed. Against her anesthetized skin came the sensation of warmth on her cheeks, a wetness which seeped from her eyes and slid down, spattering like raindrops on her hands. She gazed at the splotches of moisture on her gloves. The suede would be ruined. Winifred would scold. And Maurice wouldn't be present to temper his cousin's crossness.

He was dead.

The desperate disbelief that had propelled Norah here in the wintry dawn abruptly fled. Oh, Blessed Virgin. He had been consorting with another woman. And Norah hadn't even guessed.

The cruel blow deprived her of breath. She felt as naive as she had been as a young bride who had escaped the confinement of a Belgian convent only to have her romantic dreams strangled by the bonds of marriage. Long ago she had accepted that Maurice kept a part of himself closed to her. Didn't every man? Didn't she hide a part of herself, too?

A virtuous wife refrained from plaguing her husband with questions; she performed her duties with grace and modesty. By force of willpower, Norah had disciplined her baseborn tendency toward disobedience and outspokenness, even when Maurice refused to publicly acknowledge her artistic talents.

Even on the infrequent nights when he exercised his conjugal rights. Even when he was detained evening after evening at his club.

His absences had grown more numerous in the past half year. How foolish she had been not to realize. All those evenings he must have been meeting a scarlet woman in a scarlet cloak.

The faithless blackguard. With the filthy coin of deceit, he had repaid her efforts to be a worthy wife. From a corner of her mind crept a shameful sense of relief and liberation . . .

Her rigid control crumbled. A floodgate of feelings spewed forth. She trembled under the onrush of fury and frustration. Her body ached and burned and hurt. Her heart pounded a terrible, suffocating rhythm.

The bed loomed before her, the site of sinful luxury where Maurice had betrayed his vows and ripped apart the fabric of her life. All for his own manly selfishness. The clamor inside her surged to a storm tide. Rage misted her vision.

She reached blindly for a pillow and hurled it aside. Glass crashed. The sound barely penetrated the roaring in her ears. She threw herself on the bed and tore at the counterpane. Her fingernails raked the sheets. Sobbing breaths burdened her chest.

She hammered the mattress. "How could you do this to me?" she gasped. "How could you do this?" She knew no curse black enough to express the humiliation heaped upon her by a cheating husband.

Arms like steel bars locked around her, caged her frenzy. "Mrs. Rutherford . . . Norah . . . stop. Please stop."

She bucked within the restraint. "Let me go!"

"Calm yourself." The voice slid over her, as low pitched and soothing as the purr of a cat. "Don't fight me. I only want to help you."

Warm breath blew against her cheek. She lay trapped, wriggling uselessly against the coverlet, pinned by the heat and hardness pressed along the length of her.

"Go ahead and weep. I'm here for you. For as long as you wish."

Weakness saturated her limbs. She melted into the satin sheets. Her crying shuddered to a halt. A blessed blanket of deliverance sheltered her from the malestrom of emotion. Like water running from a sieve, the madness swirled away and left her shaken and vulnerable.

Hands turned her, guided her head onto the solid pillow of a shoulder. Her cheek met the smooth linen of a shirt. She kept her mind tightly shut to all but the comfort radiating from the embrace. With each slowing breath, she drew in the fragrance of a man, alien yet agreeable. She felt the pleasing pressure of lips moving against her brow, and the lulling stroke of fingers over her wet cheeks. A whimper of need rippled in her throat. From where the sound arose she could not fathom. She knew only that she needed the strength of his arms, needed the closeness of this man . . .

"There now," he murmured in her ear. "You'll be fine, Norah. I'll take care of you."

Kit Coleridge. It was Lord Christopher Coleridge holding her, kissing her forehead.

Awareness burned a path of color up Norah's cheeks. She thrust her head back. His flagrantly handsome features loomed so near she could discern each individual black lash that shaded his tiger's eyes. The fullness of his lower lip, the soft slant of his

mouth suggested wicked intimacies, profane pleasures.

She was lying beside the most notorious rake in
England. In the bed where her husband had died
mere hours ago . . .

FREE BOOK OFFER!

Avon Books has an outstanding offer for every reader of our Romantic Treasures.
Buy three different Avon Romantic Treasures and get your choice of an Avon romance
favorite—absolutely free.

Fill in your name, address and zip code below, and send it, along with the proof-of-
purchase pages from two other Avon Romantic Treasures to:

AVON ROMANTIC TREASURES
Free Book Offer
P.O. Box 767, Dresden, TN 38255.

Allow 4-6 weeks for delivery.

- -

(Please fill out completely)
AVON ROMANTIC TREASURE FREE BOOK OFFER!

Name_____

Address _____

City_____ State_____ Zip_____

Please send me the following FREE novel:

_____ 76214-5 SPELLBOUND   _____ 75673-0 DEVIL'S DECEPTION
     by Allison Hayes   by Suzannah Davis
_____ 75921-7 DREAMSPINNER   _____ 75742-7 BLACK-EYED SUSAN
     by Barbara Dawson Smith   by Deborah Camp
_____ 75778-8 CAUGHT IN THE ACT   _____ 76020-7 MOONLIGHT AND
     by Betina Krahn   MAGIC
                                           by Rebecca Paisley

I have enclosed three completed proof-of-purchase pages.

Offer good while supplies last. Avon Books reserves the right to make substitutions. Limit
one offer per address.

Offer available in U.S. and Canada only.
Void where prohibited by law.   Offer expires September 30, 1992.

ISBN 0-380-76701-5

Proof
-of-
Purchase

Avon Romances—
the best in exceptional authors and unforgettable novels!

THE EAGLE AND THE DOVE   Jane Feather
76168-8/$4.50 US/$5.50 Can

STORM DANCERS   Allison Hayes
76215-3/$4.50 US/$5.50 Can

LORD OF DESIRE   Nicole Jordan
76621-3/$4.50 US/$5.50 Can

PIRATE IN MY ARMS   Danelle Harmon
76675-2/$4.50 US/$5.50 Can

DEFIANT IMPOSTOR   Miriam Minger
76312-5/$4.50 US/$5.50 Can

MIDNIGHT RAIDER   Shelly Thacker
76293-5/$4.50 US/$5.50 Can

MOON DANCER   Judith E. French
76105-X/$4.50 US/$5.50 Can

PROMISE ME FOREVER   Cara Miles
76451-2/$4.50 US/$5.50 Can

Coming Soon

THE HAWK AND THE HEATHER   Robin Leigh
76319-2/$4.50 US/$5.50 Can

ANGEL OF FIRE   Tanya Anne Crosby
76773-2/$4.50 US/$5.50 Can

America Loves Lindsey!

The Timeless Romances
of #1 Bestselling Author

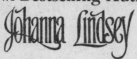

Johanna Lindsey

PRISONER OF MY DESIRE	75627-7/$5.99 US/$6.99 Can
DEFY NOT THE HEART	75299-9/$5.50 US/$6.50 Can
SILVER ANGEL	75294-8/$4.95 US/$5.95 Can
TENDER REBEL	75086-4/$5.99 US/$6.99 Can
SECRET FIRE	75087-2/$5.50 US/$6.50 Can
HEARTS AFLAME	89982-5/$5.99 US/$6.99 Can
A HEART SO WILD	75084-8/$5.50 US/$6.50 Can
WHEN LOVE AWAITS	89739-3/$5.50 US/$6.50 Can
LOVE ONLY ONCE	89953-1/$5.50 US/$6.50 Can
BRAVE THE WILD WIND	89284-7/$5.50 US/$6.50 Can
A GENTLE FEUDING	87155-6/$5.50 US/$6.50 Can
HEART OF THUNDER	85118-0/$4.95 US/$5.95 Can
SO SPEAKS THE HEART	81471-4/$5.50 US/$6.50 Can
GLORIOUS ANGEL	84947-X/$5.50 US/$6.50 Can
PARADISE WILD	77651-0/$5.50 US/$6.50 Can
FIRES OF THE WINTER	75747-8/$4.95 US/$5.95 Can
A PIRATE'S LOVE	40048-0/$4.95 US/$5.95 Can
CAPTIVE BRIDE	01697-4/$4.95 US/$5.95 Can
TENDER IS THE STORM	89693-1/$5.50 US/$6.50 Can
SAVAGE THUNDER	75300-6/$4.95 US/$5.95 Can